Holy Spy

Holy Spy

RORY CLEMENTS

HODDER &
STOUGHTON

First published in Great Britain in 2015 by Hodder & Stoughton
An Hachette UK Company

1

© Rory Clements 2015

Maps drawn by Rodney Paull

A CIP catalogue record for this title is available from the British Library

Hardback ISBN 978 1 848 54849 7
Trade paperback ISBN 978 1 848 54850 3
Ebook ISBN 978 1 848 54851 0

Typeset in 12.5/16 pt Adobe Garamond by Servis Filmsetting Ltd, Stockport, Cheshire

Printed and bound by Clays Ltd, St Ives plc

Hodder & Stoughton policy is to use papers that are natural, renewable and recyclable products
and made from wood grown in sustainable forests. The logging and manufacturing processes are
expected to conform to the environmental regulations of the country of origin.

Hodder & Stoughton Ltd
338 Euston Road
London NW1 3BH

www.hodder.co.uk

For Jack, Max, Imogen and Phoebe
with love

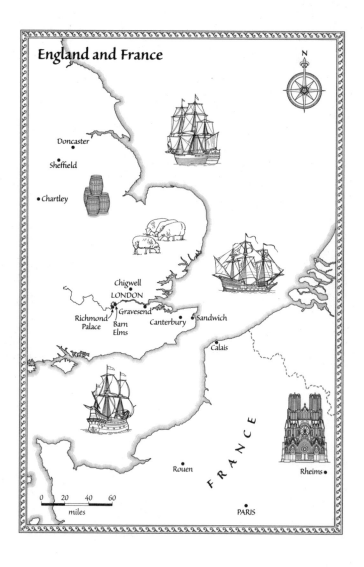

England and France

N

Doncaster

Sheffield

Chartley

Chigwell

LONDON

Gravesend

Richmond
Palace

Barn
Elms

Canterbury

Sandwich

Calais

FRANCE

Rouen

Rheims

PARIS

0   20   40   60
miles

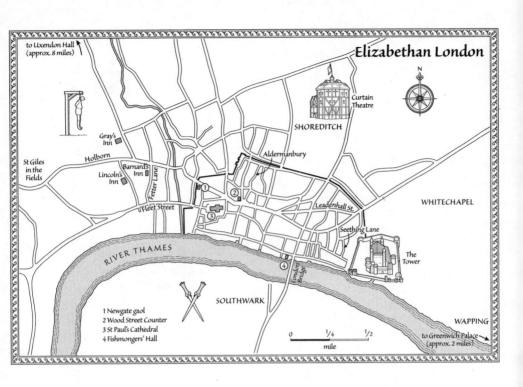

Elizabethan London

to Lixendon Hall
(approx. 8 miles)

Curtain
Theatre

SHOREDITCH

Gray's
Inn

Holborn

Aldermanbury

St Giles
in the
Fields

Barnard's
Inn

Lincoln's
Inn

Fetter Lane

WHITECHAPEL

Leadenhall St.

Fleet Street

Seething Lane

The
Tower

RIVER THAMES

London Bridge

SOUTHWARK

WAPPING

1 Newgate gaol
2 Wood Street Counter
3 St Paul's Cathedral
4 Fishmongers' Hall

0   ¼   ½
mile

to Greenwich Palace
(approx. 2 miles)

Chapter 1

Rheims, France, 1585

G OODFELLOW SAVAGE STOOD before the cross with his head bowed, his long, military beard flat against his chest. Once spoken, these words could never be undone. A vow made before God could not be broken.

The air was heavy with the fragrance of incense. In the north transept of this magnificent cathedral, at the heart of the city, a young priest swung a thurible, his black-robed figure throwing shadows from the flickering glow of a dozen candles that decorated a nearby table.

Goodfellow inhaled the holy smoke deeply through his long, hooked nose. He had been over the matter of the vow a hundred times or more. He had lain long nights without sleep in his narrow seminary cot debating whether assassination – killing in cold blood rather than in the heat of battle – could truly be lawful in the eyes of God. His mind said yes; his heart was not so easily won over. But in the end . . . well, here he was.

One of his companions, a young man with pudgy pink hands, clasped his shoulder. 'Say the words, Goodfellow. Say them.'

Savage nodded, then took a deep breath. 'In the sight of these witnesses, I swear by Almighty God that I shall not rest until I have slain the usurper Elizabeth Tudor, eternal enemy of the Holy Roman Church. I crave the benediction of the Church and the Lord's blessing on this my poor sword and on this my solemn undertaking.'

The words seemed to ring out so that the whole world must have heard them, but in truth they were little more than a whisper. Had he truly made the vow? He leant forward and placed the sword on the flagstones before him.

'And so I give up my soul, wretched sinner that I am, to His mercy, in the certain knowledge that my own life is now forfeit.' Yes, he knew *that* well enough. No man could kill the Queen of England and escape with his life. His own death would follow as sure as the sun follows the rain.

He fell forward, prostrating himself, his arms outstretched so that his fingertips touched the honed blade. Somewhere in the distance, a bell clanged, summoning the young seminary men to their studies. Savage scarcely heard it. He was alone with Christ.

In the pleasant garden of a small auberge, not a furlong from Notre-Dame de Rheims, John Shakespeare lay back and rested against the trunk of a sycamore tree, enjoying its cool shade. The air was hot and still; no one but a fool or an indentured man would venture into the sun on such a day. He heard a whistle and opened his eyes. Across the way, he spotted the boyish figure of Gilbert Gifford in his priestly robes.

Shakespeare raised one finger, then closed his eyes again. Five minutes later he stretched his arms and yawned. He picked up his book and cup of wine, rose lazily to his feet and sauntered back towards his room in the inn, where he went to his chamber and shut the door behind him.

Ten minutes later there were three raps at the door. Shakespeare opened it and admitted Gifford, glancing around to ensure they were not observed.

'Well, Mr Gifford?'

'He has vowed to kill Her Majesty.' His voice was a whisper.

'Do you believe he will truly attempt it?'

'It is a vow made before God, not a promise to man. A vow is immutable. Once made, it must be fulfilled. He knows this and understands it. This is why he took so long to come to his decision. He is a soldier and has a soldier's honour. I believe he would rather slit his own throat than repudiate this vow. He plans to return to England before autumn.'

'And then?'

'That is up to you and Mr Secretary. Seize him on arrival at Rye or Dover if you wish, and I will testify against him. Or you can watch him and wait. I rather thought that was Walsingham's plan.'

Shakespeare did not reply. It was not his place to disclose Sir Francis Walsingham's plans to any man, least of all to Gilbert Gifford. He looked at his angelic, smooth and beardless young face with a curious mixture of admiration and distaste and wondered, not for the first time, whose side he was really on. A man who did not know the truth about him might be taken in by his deacon's robes, but Shakespeare knew better.

'Or if you wish, we could merely put an end to him here. A bullet to the head, a blade to the throat . . .'

Shakespeare ignored the suggestion. 'How does he expect to carry out this mission?'

'That is for you to discover.'

'What do you know about John Savage, Mr Gifford?'

'Lower your voice if you would, Mr Shakespeare. We are not the only spies in Rheims.'

Shakespeare stifled his irritation, smiled and waited.

'I know little more than I have told you,' Gifford said at last. 'Men call him Goodfellow for his sweetness of nature, which you might think sits uneasily with his present intent and his known ferocity on the field of battle. He is tall – so tall that his feet extend a foot beyond his cot. Taller even than you, Mr Shakespeare, and muscled like a fighting dog. He is a soldier and poet who has fought with Parma against the Dutch rebels. And yet he is also full of charm and wit; no man could meet him in a tavern and not wish to buy him a gage of ale. He has no money but much good cheer.'

'And yet here he is at Rheims, training for the priesthood and plotting the death of the Queen of England.'

'He is devout. I think he saw much bloodshed in the wars and was moved towards the spiritual life. But my cousin, the good Dr Gifford, and the priest Hodgson had other plans for him. They have been working on him for three months now, persuading him that his true vocation lies in the qualities God gave him as a man-at-arms. It was explained to him that the Holy Vicar of Rome and Father Persons of the Society of Jesus consider it not only lawful but desirable to kill the Queen. He took much persuading . . .'

Yes, thought Shakespeare, and I am sure that you played the major part in moulding him to your will. Perhaps you were the main instigator, Mr Gifford.

'I want to meet this Mr Savage.'

'Not here. He would become suspicious. We will work out a scheme whereby you encounter him by chance. You will, of course, have to feign fervour in the cause of papism.'

'Then do it. And do not commit any of these things that you have told me to paper, even in cipher. I will carry word to Mr Secretary.' Shakespeare allowed himself a smile. He was aware that this day he had chanced upon the very thing his master had been seeking for many months: the first tentative steps towards the death of a queen.

Chapter 2

London, England, 1586

THREE BODIES COILED and writhed on the large tester bed. They looked to Shakespeare like adders dancing in a springtime frenzy. The man was on his back, his body arching as the two slender whores, sisters, ministered to him and to each other. Shakespeare watched them through a small hole in the wall and felt ashamed. No man should observe his fellow humans in their carnal ecstasy. He pulled back from the spyhole and Thomas Phelippes immediately took his place.

'You see,' he said in a whisper. 'They are remarkable fine specimens of their sex, are they not? Such sisters are surely the desire of every man's loins.'

Yes, they were comely. Shakespeare had been stirred, but he would not admit it to the slimy Phelippes. 'I have seen enough. Let us go.'

Phelippes grinned, his thin, pitted face more repulsive than ever. Behind his grubby spectacles, there was a challenge in his watery eyes. 'I can arrange them for you, if you wish. No silver need change hands. Just say the word.'

'No. Let us repair to the tavern to discuss this.' He pulled Phelippes away by his bony shoulders.

'Very well.' Phelippes slid the cover across the spyhole and ran a hand through his lank yellow hair, raising his eyebrows in mockery at Shakespeare's distaste. Treading softly, they made their way out of the Holborn house and into a taproom in the next street where they ordered pints of ale. Shakespeare drank deeply, as though the draught might cleanse him.

'Mr Shakespeare, it was important you should view Gifford thus. I think Mr Secretary will be more than satisfied with our report.'

'Perhaps. But it was unseemly. And I am certain very costly.'

'I could watch the Smith sisters all day. Have you ever seen such paps and such womanly bellies?'

'They know their trade, I grant you, but I thought you had a new bride to look to, Mr Phelippes.' God preserve her! How could any woman bear to look on his reptilian face each morning?

'And Gifford! He is so small and hairless, so pink-skinned! He looks as though he should still be at his mother's teat, not a whore's.'

'Do not be deceived, Mr Phelippes. Gilbert Gifford is twenty-five years of age and man enough for our needs. It is the very innocence of his appearance that gains him entry into men's trust. Often to their detriment.'

'But do *you* trust him? And what of Mr Secretary; does he trust the pink thing?'

Shakespeare smiled. He knew that his master, Walsingham, trusted Gilbert Gifford as much as he trusted any man, which was not at all. Shakespeare sometimes wondered whether he himself might be spied on by others in the employment of the Principal Secretary. Well if so, then so be it; the watchers would have a dull time of it. No whores, no salacious connections.

As for Gilbert Gifford, a man who went by many names, Walsingham's fear was that he would vanish, his work unfinished. He was like a will-o'-the-wisp, one minute here, the next gone. And that was the point of these two fair sisters of the skin. Their task, for which they were being paid very well from Mr Secretary's purse, was so to bewitch Gifford that he would stay and do his master's bidding. It was a plan with obvious flaws, for there were whorehouses in every city of the world. These two would have to offer something that could not be found elsewhere. So far, they seemed to be doing all that could be hoped for, and more.

'Do they have the pox, Mr Phelippes?'

'Ah, so you *are* interested?'

'Just answer my question.'

'No, they do not have the pox. They save themselves for the best, which is why they are so highly prized – and *priced* – like spice of the Indies.'

'Good. They will only make themselves available to Gifford at *our* behest. I would have them retain their mystery and freshness so that he does not tire of them, for without him we have nothing.'

Chapter 3

THE AFTERNOON SUN fell across his face. He shifted his chair so that he was in shade. Alone in the parlour of his house in Seething Lane, he was sitting at the head of the oak table where he took his meals and did much of his work.

This day John Shakespeare had put aside his labours on intercepts and correspondence from the world's embassies. All he had in front of him was a copy of the Holy Bible, a quill, an inkhorn and a sheet of paper with three names on it. One of them had a few words next to it: *agreeable disposition, respectable family, untried, a little young.*

There was a rap at the door from the anteroom.

'Come in.'

Boltfoot Cooper pushed open the door and limped in. 'The second woman is here, master.'

Shakespeare nodded to his assistant. 'Bring her through, Boltfoot.'

Boltfoot shuffled off and reappeared a few moments later, in company with a woman of middle years, perhaps forty, with greying hair beneath a lawn coif. She had a brisk walk and a competent air. Boltfoot ushered her forward and she approached the head of the table, stopping four feet from Shakespeare.

'Mistress Rymple?'

She gave a quick nod, not quite a bow. 'Indeed, Mr Shakespeare, sir.' She held out a paper with a broken seal. 'This is a letter of commendation from my last employer.'

Shakespeare took it from her, unfolded it and read it. The letter said that Annis Rymple had performed her duties as lady's maid to her employer's satisfaction but that her services were no longer required as her mistress had gone to God. The letter was signed by the widower. Shakespeare handed the paper back to her. 'How long had you worked in your last position?'

'Twelve years, sir.'

'You were a lady's maid. You know there are no ladies in this house.'

'But I would make a suitable housekeeper, I am certain.'

'What were your duties?'

'I dressed my lady and busked her hair. Her chamber was my world and when she went to the country, I was always her travelling companion.'

'What of cooking, baking, brewing, shopping, laundry and sweeping? Those are the duties we must have performed here. We would have hens, too, for eggs, and I want a pig.'

'There were other servants for those duties, but I am sure I will adapt well enough. It was made clear to me by the factor what was required. You are a single gentleman, I believe. It will just be you for whom I must do these things, will it not, sir?'

Shakespeare turned to Boltfoot, who was hovering like a hawk by the door. He did not look happy. 'And Mr Cooper, of course.'

Annis Rymple looked slightly taken aback. 'If that is what you wish of me, then I will obey your orders, Mr Shakespeare. I can cook pies and bake cakes and bread and I am sure a fine house such as this has a spit for roasting.'

'How much did your last employment pay?'

'Five pounds from Lady's Day to Lady's Day, with a week at Easter to visit my mother in Hertfordshire.'

Shakespeare scratched a few words against her name. *Experienced, good reference, most likely capable. A good age. Unlikely to come with child.* He smiled at her and nodded. 'Mr Cooper, if you will take Mistress Rymple back to the anteroom, I believe we have one more candidate to see.'

'She has not arrived, master. The choice is between Mistress Rymple here and young Miss Cawston, whom you have already met.'

'Well, offer them both ale and I will make my decision presently.'

Boltfoot gave a perfunctory bow of the head and retreated with Annis Rymple.

Shakespeare watched them go. It seemed clear to him that the older woman must be the correct choice. The other one had no experience of service and he did not have the time or patience to indulge her fumbling efforts to run this household, modest though it was. He rose and walked across to the latticed window that looked out onto the sun-drenched yard. It was unkempt and unused. There should be chickens clucking there and, yes, a pig or two. He needed a mature, proficient woman. Mistress Rymple would do well enough.

He turned at the creak of the door. Boltfoot had returned.

'Master . . .'

'Tell Annis Rymple the job is hers if she can start without delay. Send the other one, the girl, away with a shilling for her trouble.'

'Yes, master.'

It occurred to Shakespeare that Boltfoot seemed disappointed. Well, that was not his concern. 'Go to it, Boltfoot.'

'Master, you have another visitor. A fine-dressed gentleman, by name of Severin Tort.'

Shakespeare frowned. He knew the name, of course. Severin Tort was a lawyer renowned for his unparalleled knowledge of the laws governing contracts and covenants between merchants. It was said he would have been made a judge by now were it not for his quiet insistence on clinging to the old faith.

'Well, bring him through, fetch brandy – and then deal with the maids.'

Severin Tort was lean and short with a lawyer's clever eyes. Too clever to trust, perhaps. He wore black, broken only by the white lawn ruffs at his throat and cuffs and the silver sheen of his hair. He had a strangely modest and restrained air about him for one accustomed to arguing cases against the most learned men in the realm.

Shakespeare proffered his hand in greeting. 'Mr Tort, it is a pleasure to welcome you to my home. Naturally, I have heard of you.'

'Indeed, and I have heard much of you, Mr Shakespeare. I know you were a Gray's Inn man, which is my own alma mater. I must thank you for receiving me unannounced.'

'Will you sit down? Mr Cooper will bring us brandy presently.'

Tort took a chair halfway down the long table. He sat neatly, his hands loosely clasped on the tabletop. 'You will be wondering why I am here, but before I reveal anything I must tell you that it is a confidential matter. I would ask that you say nothing outside these walls.'

'Mr Tort, that will depend on what you say. I cannot give you such a pledge without knowing more.'

Boltfoot brought in a tray with a flask of brandy and two glass goblets. Shakespeare nodded to him to leave and indicated that he should close the door after him. He poured a brandy for his guest and one for himself.

'What if I were to tell you that it concerns Katherine Giltspur?'

Shakespeare frowned. The name meant nothing to him.

'You probably know her better as Katherine Whetstone.'

The name hung there. It sucked the air from Shakespeare's body. Had he heard correctly?

Tort repeated the name. 'Katherine Whetstone. You do know her, I think?'

Know her? He knew the name as well as his own. Kat Whetstone. He had loved her. They had been lovers for over two years. 'Yes, I know her – *knew* her,' he said.

She had lived with him, in this house, and they were as good as man and wife. Indeed, he had begun to assume that eventually they would be married. And then one day he returned from his work in Walsingham's office and she was no longer here. All she had left was a note. *Do not look for me, John. This life of yours is not for me. We always knew that, which is why we never made vows. God be with you. Your loving Kat.*

'Good. It is as I thought, sir.'

The heat in the room was suddenly overpowering. Shakespeare looked into Tort's shrewd eyes, seeking some clue as to his reason for being here. Did the lawyer know what he was doing, reopening this bloody wound? Even eight months away touring France, the Low Countries and the Italies had not repaired the tear in Shakespeare's soul. He still thought of Kat every day. A glimpse of fair hair, a laugh in the street, any manner of looks and sounds could bring her lovely face to mind, for it had never faded from his imagining. He conjured up a smile for the benefit of his guest.

'Kat Whetstone. Yes, of course I know her – but I have neither seen nor heard of her in two years.' His voice was brisk with affected indifference. 'I was surprised to hear her name.'

'But you know her well?'

Shakespeare did not answer the question, though he could have said: We took some comfort and pleasure in each other's company. Our bodies were as one. For that was what it was – comfort and pleasure and the joys of the flesh, but never love; not to her, surely never love. Why did he still try to convince himself thus? Of course he had loved her, although he had never told her as much. He framed a question of his own for Tort.

'From her new name I take it she is now married?'

'She is widowed, very recently.'

'Married and widowed? This is sad news indeed . . .'

Tort's surprise was clear. 'Have you heard none of this? Her late husband was Mr Nicholas Giltspur, a merchant of great wealth and renown. Surely you have heard of their great riches? They have more gold and silver than any other merchant in London. And the Giltspur Diamond? Everyone must know of that. Mr Giltspur's death is the talk of the city.'

Shakespeare had, of course, heard of the great diamond, but had heard nothing of the death, having travelled back and forth across the narrow sea these past weeks. He shook his head. 'I have heard his name, though I have never met him. And I certainly know nothing of his death. I have been away much . . .' He trailed off. 'You mean, she is Nick Giltspur's widow?' He wanted to laugh at the irony. Kat Whetstone, who had pledged never to marry, had attached herself to one of the wealthiest men in England. But then his humour turned to dust as he began wonder why an esteemed advocate should be bringing such news. When did lawyers ever bear good tidings?

'Have you truly not heard of the court case, Mr Shakespeare?'

'Court case? I know nothing of any death or any court case. I have been deeply involved in my work, Mr Tort.' Trailing Gilbert Gifford from Rheims to Paris and Rouen – then to

England, then back to France and finally, this week, returning once more to London; all the time ensuring that Gifford was content. These were matters that could not be discussed in this company. 'And so the tittle-tattle of the streets has passed me by. But you have worried me. Please, tell me what this is about. Anything pertaining to Kat Whetstone will always be of interest to me.'

'She has been married and widowed within the space of a two-month. Her husband was murdered last week. Stabbed with a long-bladed bollock-dagger near Fishmongers' Hall, on Thames Street. The killer was caught at the scene of the crime and made no attempt to conceal his guilt. I would entreat you to brace yourself, Mr Shakespeare, for indeed I bring shocking news.'

Shakespeare downed his brandy, then poured himself another. Whatever was coming next, he did not want to hear it. 'Continue, Mr Tort.'

'The killer was a wretch named Will Cane. Not only did he confess his own part in the terrible deed but immediately implicated Mistress Giltspur. Under questioning and in open court, he said she had offered him a hundred pounds to kill her husband: ten pounds to be paid before the murder and ninety afterwards. He was quite clear and consistent on this – and he said it all without coercion of any kind.'

'God's blood, no!'

'I am sorry, Mr Shakespeare.'

'Is this true?'

Tort nodded.

'No,' Shakespeare said, as much to himself as to the lawyer. 'I cannot believe such a thing of Kat. It is preposterous. Beyond madness.'

'No, well, neither can I believe it. But we are in the minority. To the rest of the world, she is the basest example of womanhood, a succubus and she-devil, a murdering hell-hag. She is now a fugitive, wanted as an accessory. Meanwhile, the killer is due to be hanged. If she is apprehended, she will doubtless follow him to the scaffold within days or hours – unless the mob gets to her first, for I fear they would tear her apart. And so she must remain hidden.'

Shakespeare was silent for a few moments, still trying to absorb the hideous news. Dozens of questions welled up, but one overrode the others. 'I ask again, Mr Tort. Why are you here? Why have you come to *me*?'

Tort sipped his brandy. 'Mistress Giltspur has asked me to come to you, that is why.'

'Then you know where she is?' Shakespeare demanded.

The lawyer avoided the question. 'She believes you have influence and powers of investigation . . . that you may be able to help her.'

'Help her? How? She cannot believe I have any influence to remove a charge of murder.'

'She has some belief – or hope, at least – that you could discover the truth behind this foul murder and clear her name. *Before* she is arrested.'

'But if she is guilty, as it seems—' He stopped in mid-flow. Kat – a murderess? There was a ruthless, ambitious streak to her – but murder? 'Mr Tort, what is your connection to the case?'

'Though I am not versed in criminal law, she is my client, as was Nick. He would have expected no less of me than to help her. As to her whereabouts, it is possible I might have a way to get word to her. But before I say more, I must repeat my request: that this conversation is confidential and will not be repeated outside these walls.'

'Very well, but speak.'

'I will take that as a pledge. Kat says I can trust you. I pray it is so, for yes, I can take you to her.'

Shakespeare stiffened. Assisting a murderer to evade justice was in itself a capital offence. 'I am a very busy man,' he said. He was Walsingham's man night and day. There would be no respite in the days ahead now that Goodfellow Savage was in the country plotting to fulfil his treacherous vow. But he could not say no to Kat Whetstone. An image of her lying across his bed came to him. The early-morning light slipping in through the shutters and lighting her generous breasts. She was snoring softly, her lips parted to reveal the gap in her teeth. The memory stirred him and haunted him in equal measure.

Tort seemed to take his acquiescence as read. 'But you will go to her?'

'Yes.'

'Let us meet on the morrow. I will come for you and we will ride together. But first you might try to talk to the killer, Cane. He awaits death in Newgate. I believe his execution is to be at Smithfield, and soon. Perhaps you could persuade him to tell the truth. At least you might be able to form some judgement of him and try to discern the reason behind his foul lie.'

'Have you spoken to him?'

'I went to him, but he would not utter a word, nor even raise his eyes to meet mine. He remained slumped in his chains, unmoving. And so I left him to his fate.'

Shakespeare studied Tort, uncertain of him. 'You believe her to be innocent?'

'*Believe* is a strong word. Let us say I *hope* she is not guilty. I confess the evidence stands against her.' He thought about what he had said, then shook his head. 'No, I cannot believe her guilty.'

'I will go to the condemned man directly. As for meeting Kat, how far is she from here?'

'Fifteen minutes' ride, no more.'

'Should we not go this evening?'

'It is impossible. It must be tomorrow.'

'Come to me at midday. I have a meeting in the morning, one that I cannot miss.'

Tort rose from the bench. 'Thank you, sir.'

'You still have not fully explained what she is to you, Mr Tort.'

'As I said, she is my client.'

Shakespeare took his hand again, wondering just how much this attorney-at-law was holding back. He was certainly concealing a great deal more than he revealed.

'And I beg you, be circumspect, Mr Shakespeare, for she is being hunted most strenuously. And Justice Young is leading the pack.'

Chapter 4

THE NEWGATE KEEPER shook his grizzled head. 'You're too late, master. He's gone to Smithfield to dance his jig.'

'How long?'

'Half an hour since.'

Shakespeare uttered a curse and ran to his horse. Within moments he was remounted and kicking the beast into a sharp canter northwards along the narrow confines and low overhangs towards Pie Corner. Within two minutes, he burst into the six-acre plain that made up Smithfield, a dusty expanse where men sometimes came for livestock dealing and flesh trading and at other times for the Bartholomew Fair. Today it served another purpose: a place of execution.

He urged on the animal past the ancient buildings of St Bartholomew's Hospital. Ahead of him a crowd packed the centre of the open land. Traders had set up stalls to sell cakes and ale and hot mead. Some executions brought out the dark humour in onlookers, but this day there was nothing but anger.

All eyes were on the black wooden scaffold, where a figure suspended from a length of rope jerked and struggled in its ugly death throes. The crowd was agitated, shouting and waving their fists, wanting him to suffer. Shakespeare drove his bay stallion onwards, pushing aside men, women and children. People uttered oaths and spat at him as he passed.

He slid from the horse and handed the reins to a bewildered onlooker. Shakespeare was aware that the eyes of the hangman, his assistant, the priest and the law officers were all on him.

The condemned man had ceased his dance. He hung limp, his bound body swaying in the summer breeze, but the noise of the crowd showed no sign of abating. The murderer's death was not enough; they wanted yet more vengeance, more pain. The officers braced their halberds and pikes menacingly to deter the throng from surging forward: the ugly mood had been anticipated. Shakespeare strode up onto the platform.

'Is he dead?' he demanded of the hangman.

'Aye, dead enough, but we'll leave him hanging an hour.'

'It was Will Cane, the murderer?'

'Yes, master. If you have brought a reprieve, you are too late. And I thank the Lord for it, for this lot – ' he nodded towards the crowd – 'would have ripped him apart rather than see him pardoned.'

'No, no reprieve. I wanted to talk with him before he died.'

'Then you have had a wasted journey. Who are you?'

'John Shakespeare. I am an assistant secretary in the office of Sir Francis Walsingham.'

'What would Mr Secretary want of a common felon like Will Cane?'

'Did he say anything – make any confession?'

The hangman laughed. 'He did.' He nodded towards the clergyman, who stood clasping a Bible at the edge of the scaffold. 'Ask his confessor or any member of this crowd.'

'I'll ask *you*, hangman. What did he say?'

'Told it all, about the lewd wife. Couldn't stop him. Spoke so much he had a coughing fit, and so I cured his cough for ever. And you may now call me Good Doctor Hangman, if it please you.' He laughed aloud at his own jest, and his sly assistant grinned like a fox.

Shakespeare turned away, revolted, and directed his attention to the cleric.

The well-fed vicar, who wore a black cassock and a black cap on his head, met Shakespeare's eye.

'Well? What is *your* version, reverend sir?'

'He said he was a poor sinner and commended his soul to God, desiring that he might be forgiven his transgressions, a thing I consider highly unlikely given the monstrous nature of his crime.'

'Is that all?'

'By no means.' The vicar raised his voice and indicated to the assembled onlookers, who roared and brandished fists. 'As these good folk will all testify, he said he wished to go to his death with no lie on his lips and so he repeated the assertions made in court, that he was a hired killer, and that he had been offered a hundred pounds for the murder. Mr Cane was a wicked, wretched man, but at least in his final moments on earth he named the confederate in the heinous crime. Her turn here will come soon enough.'

'Whom did he name?'

'Why, the widow, Katherine Giltspur.'

At the name the crowd howled their loathing. This was a crime that struck at the very heart of all they understood and held dear: a wife murdering a husband. This was a knife to the sanctity of the family and the hearth, God-given things not to be besmirched.

'You see, sir,' the cleric continued. 'The whole of London knows her to be a black-hearted whore, lower than the snakes of the field, more cruel than the scavenger birds of the air. There can be no more unnatural crime before God or man than the killing of a husband by the woman pledged to give him succour.'

Shakespeare looked down at the baying crowd. Half had their eyes fixed on the hanged felon and the other half were watching him, wondering, perhaps, which way to turn their ire. He cursed; a dying man's confession was sacrosanct. No one would doubt it. Innocent or guilty, Kat's cause was hopeless.

He strode over to the hanged man and pulled the hood from his head. A pair of bulging, lifeless eyes stared back at him from a blue, bulbous face incongruous above the thin, hemp-encircled neck. He was a man of about forty years of age, dark-haired with a reddish beard. His face was engorged and yet scrawny, as though he had not eaten in a week. His tongue lolled, red and encrusted. Ugly streams of blood dripped from his nostrils and the corners of his grimacing mouth. Shakespeare doubted that he could have weighed a hundredweight. He was a poor specimen. The world would be none the worse for his passing.

Shakespeare turned back to the cleric. 'Did he say anything else? Did you see him at Newgate before he came here?'

'No. There was nothing else.'

'Then say your prayers for his soul.' *And I will pray for Kat's.*

'No, sir. I will not pray for his soul. I will pray for his eternal damnation, in the fire of pain, for ever, with the she-devil who paid him.'

In the morning, Shakespeare came down from his chamber and discovered a woman with a broom sweeping up the rushes in the parlour. She bowed to him nervously. It was not the maid he had told Boltfoot to hire, but the other, younger woman. He frowned at her, and she scurried away.

'Boltfoot!'

His assistant limped in from the kitchen, dragging his club foot. 'Master?'

'That woman is not Mistress Rymple.'

'No, master. It is the other one, Jane Cawston.'

'And yet I told you to hire the Rymple woman and send Miss Cawston on her way with a shilling.'

'As I recall, Mr Shakespeare, you told me to hire Mistress Rymple if she could start without delay. When I asked her, she told me she would need a week, which I considered to be a delay.'

'And so you told her the job was not hers? You took this decision on yourself?'

Boltfoot did not look at all unnerved. 'What was I to do? You were engaged with the lawyer Mr Tort, master. I thought you would not thank me to disturb you with such a trivial matter. And then you raced out as though pursued by the hounds of hell . . .'

Shakespeare wondered for a few moments whether to sack Boltfoot. At the very least he had to be severely rebuked. 'You have done this deliberately, flouting my authority. You knew very well I wanted the older one. She would know what was required of her and would need no instruction in organising this household.'

'You are right, master. And yet it did seem to me Miss Cawston had great merits too.'

'Merits? You mean she was prettier and younger.'

'But, master, whereas the older one would do things *her* way, I believe that Miss Cawston will learn to do things *our* way. Forgive me if I have erred, sir.'

'You have indeed erred! This is flagrant disobedience. My order was clear . . .'

'Then I offer my heartfelt apologies, master. But I would say that Miss Cawston will work until Lady's Day for two pounds all found, whereas Annis Rymple had hopes of five pounds.'

Other men would take a birch rod to a servant who displayed such insubordination, and yet Shakespeare found himself scarcely able to stifle a laugh. He dared not let Boltfoot see the smile playing treacherously around his lips, so he turned his back. 'Send Miss Cawston to me,' he ordered. 'I suppose I had better welcome her to our household.'

Jane Cawston stood before him nervously clutching the handle of her broom.

'Tell me once more about yourself, Miss Cawston.'

'As I said yesterday, sir, I am the eldest of twelve girls. My family lives in the north of Essex near the town of Sudbury. My father is in service to a yeoman farmer.'

'And what has made you seek work in London?'

'My sisters are all growing. They need the space – and one less mouth to feed. Nor is it easy for my father without any sons. My wages will help, too, master.'

He guessed her age at about eighteen or nineteen. Her face was round and pretty, framed by soft auburn hair. She was strong enough and healthy and had a warmth and serenity that would add cheer to this house. Boltfoot had probably been right in his choice. She would learn quickly enough.

'And you believe you can organise this household in the way we require? Floors cleaned, mattresses turned, food on the table, ale brewed, livestock in the yard, our clothes laundered by and by, the front step swept, lanterns lit at dusk, management of the housekeeping allowance?'

'Yes, master.'

'And you will be expected to take messages if Mr Cooper and I are not here.'

She nodded hurriedly, like a hen pecking.

He thought she seemed a little uncertain. 'Miss Cawston? If you are going to live here with two men, you must be able to do these things. And if you have troubles, you must bring your concerns to us.'

'That is it, sir. Two men. I had expected to find a family with women and girls. I am not used to the ways of menfolk. I have heard stories—'

Shakespeare smiled at her. 'You have nothing to fear, I promise you. There will not be any beatings in this house, or any other unchristian behaviour. That is my word. Now, what are we to call you?'

'Jane, if it please you, master. I like to be called plain Jane.'

'Well, Jane. Perhaps you would make me eggs – two eggs – boiled until hard, with some manchet bread and butter. And some milk, if we have any. I have an important day ahead of me.'

Chapter 5

I N ALL THE eight years that Shakespeare had worked for Sir Francis Walsingham, he had never experienced a meeting such as this. Usually, the Principal Secretary kept his briefings small and intimate with no more than two or three present across a table: the fewer privy to a secret, the less the seepage. But today five men were here in this airless little room at the rear of Walsingham's Seething Lane mansion.

Outside the window, the clouds were as dark as gunpowder. Inside, the atmosphere was brittle. They talked in snatches, watching each other furtively, restive and suspicious.

At last the door opened. Walsingham entered. At his side was a tall man whom Shakespeare recognised as Sir Robert Huckerbee from the Lord Treasurer's office. The room fell silent. The Principal Secretary's face was sombre and gaunt, as always, but his dark eyes were alert, skipping from John Scudamore to Arthur Gregory and Frank Mills, then to Nicholas Henbird. Finally they came to rest on John Shakespeare, and lingered.

Each of these men had his own role in Walsingham's extensive spy network. Each had his own special skill. Each was trusted as much as he trusted any man.

'Gentlemen,' Walsingham said in his grave, insistent voice. 'Be seated.'

There was a scraping of wood on stone. The noise jarred. When all was quiet again Walsingham tapped the table with the hilt of his quill-knife.

'I think you all know Sir Robert Huckerbee. He is here to ensure financial rigour and to report directly on our operations to Lord Burghley. Without his purse, none of what we do would be possible.'

Huckerbee bowed in acknowledgement. Whereas Mr Secretary was dark-browed and zealous, Huckerbee had the light patrician air of one born to a life of public service with great rewards expected in return. He had served Lord Treasurer Burghley as comptroller for many years and was renowned for his loyalty and diligence.

'Now,' Walsingham continued. 'I have called this rare meeting because the time has come. Listen with care, for if you do not know the whole truth, you will trip over each other. If we do not work as one, then our efforts are doomed to failure.'

He paused. The room was silent.

'We have one aim: to save this realm and our beloved sovereign from forces that would destroy us. To do that, we must have the head of the Queen of Scots. She has plotted against us too long.'

He had spoken the thing that all men knew but refrained from saying. This was Walsingham's ambition: the death of Mary Stuart.

The Principal Secretary paused to allow the enormity of the mission to sink in, then resumed his address. 'Every man here must know that the Scots devil has conspired ceaselessly to snatch the throne of England. She would murder our Queen – her own cousin – to achieve her aim. This is fact; there can be no argument.'

Shakespeare felt Walsingham's eyes alighting on him once more.

'John, do you believe this?'

The sweat dripped at Shakespeare's neck. Yes, he knew it well enough. Mary's conspiracies had plagued the country these past decades. Any one of these plots could have cost the Scots Queen her head, deservedly. She had tried to murder Elizabeth Tudor and would do so again given the chance.

And so he nodded. 'Yes, Mr Secretary, I believe this to be true.'

'Then we may proceed. For over a year now, I have been striving to gather the proof that will do for this Scots devil once and for all. Unlike other countries, unlike this Queen of Scots herself, we do not murder our enemies in their beds or in dark alleys, but bring them to trial and punish them when their guilt is proven. And so it will be with her.

'We must do this because only her death will end her plotting. Only her death will protect us. Were she monarch, she would have every man in this room hanged, and she would bring back the Inquisition first introduced here by that other Mary – Mary Tudor – with its burnings and horror. So we must find evidence strong enough to bring the Queen of Scots to justice – evidence that will convince Her Majesty Queen Elizabeth of her cousin's guilt. Evidence that will satisfy every royal court in the known world.'

Four men murmured their assent. Only Shakespeare was silent. Yes, he believed the Scots Queen guilty. And yet . . . and yet he wavered. There was a difference between catching a felon after a crime has been committed and using artifice to provoke a man or woman to commit such a felony. The word was *entrapment*. Could it ever be justified?

Walsingham continued. 'Everything we do in the coming days has but one objective: to bring down Mary Stuart. All other matters are to be subsumed to this one end: the Scots devil's head on the block. Nothing less. There are other guilty players who will also lose their heads, but none of them must take precedence over her.'

Again, the murmuring. The assent.

'Good. Then all is understood. And so, gentlemen, I can now reveal to you that we have a way to secure the proof we need. Mr Thomas Phelippes is this very day at Chartley, organising what may soon lead to the final act of this tragical tale.'

Every man in the room was aware that Mary Stuart had been moved to a new place of confinement, the moated manor house of Chartley in Staffordshire. She had been conveyed there from Tutbury on Christmas Eve and was now utterly cut off from all but her immediate courtiers and secretaries. The days of open correspondence with her supporters in England and abroad were gone. Now not a letter was allowed in or out.

Her keeper, Amyas Paulet, was a Puritan who would not be moved by pleading or tears. When she complained to him, he turned his shoulder and walked away. She, in her turn, was said to be more defiant than ever, openly insisting that she would have back the crown of Scotland and would inherit the throne of England. But such words were a long way from implicating her in conspiracy. How could she conspire when she was held in such isolation?

Walsingham explained. 'Tom Phelippes has devised a secret method of delivering letters to Chartley – yet the Scots Queen has been led to believe it was devised by her friends at the French embassy and among the English exiles in Paris. At the heart of it is Gilbert Gifford, a man believed by Mary to be trustworthy. And so she has confidence in the method, as do her courtiers. She can now receive and send letters certain that they are not read by Mr Paulet or Tom Phelippes.' He laughed, a hissing sound through the teeth.

'This means,' Walsingham added, 'that she now has the means to *incriminate herself*. All she needs is to find a conspiracy and she will assuredly fix herself to it. This is her nature. And it is our good fortune to have discovered a band of conspirators for her; a group of young men who plan to instigate an invasion, an uprising and an assassination. With a little nudge, she will reveal her heart to them. She will condemn herself by her own hand.

'So who *are* these conspirators? Some of the names will be familiar. They cluster around Anthony Babington in the taverns and inns of Fleet Street, Temple Bar and Holborn. They are known as the Pope's White Sons, such is their devotion to papism. They spend their nights talking treachery. Some might think them a brainless, worthless bunch of sluggards with no hope of ever doing harm, but they would be wrong, for they have made a covenant of treachery and death. For all their gentle birth, they deserve no pity, no mercy. Do not forget this.

'Their numbers are swelled by two men whose intent is yet more significant. Their names are John Ballard, a priest who goes by the alias of Captain Fortescue, and John Savage, known as Goodfellow, a soldier turned lawyer who has sworn before the cross to assassinate the Queen. The plot now has purpose and becomes plausible. Ballard is presently in the north, seeking assurances among the Catholic gentry that they will rise up against us. He is under the control of my man Harry Slide. Savage, meanwhile, is at Barnard's Inn, and is controlled by Mr Shakespeare, who has befriended him. As they gather momentum Babington will put their foul plan to the Scots devil and beg her assent. She will then hazard her hand in writing – and we will have her.'

He scanned the room. 'It is your task, gentlemen, to keep control of this conspiracy. Discover men's weaknesses and use them. Make them play their part.' His eyes met Shakespeare's again. 'You, John, have one of the most difficult missions of all

– to so infiltrate the Pope's White Sons that they believe you are one of their number. Can you make them trust you?'

'I hear mass with them. They believe me to be a papist.'

'But they know you work for me.'

'They think me a big catch. They hope to use me to discover your secrets.'

'But I ask again – do they trust you?'

'I think Babington does. Why would he not? All his fellows are well-born gentlemen, all connected to the court and the Queen's Councillors. There is no reason that my link to your office should alarm them. I would say I fit in well. But do they all trust me? I think not. They never discuss their conspiracies openly.' He paused. 'And yet I see and hear enough.'

'Well, play it their way. Keep close to Goodfellow Savage. If at any time you fear he has actually devised a method to kill Her Majesty, do not act with undue haste. Consult me before interceding. Give him rope. Soothe his fears. Nothing must be allowed to divert the plotters from their course. They will be allowed to remain at liberty until Mary Stuart's death warrant is certain. We may never have another chance.

'This means you must keep these people happy. Supply them with wine, weapons and women to suit their weaknesses. You all have your several roles, gentlemen, and money will be no object. Sir Robert Huckerbee here will ensure that whatever funds are necessary will be available from the Treasury coffers.'

Huckerbee stiffened, as though the prospect of laying Burghley's purse wide open were a personal affront. 'All out-goings will be accounted for,' he said. 'Waste and extravagance will not be tolerated.'

Walsingham smiled at his companion. 'Indeed, Sir Robert. Which brings us to the question of Gilbert Gifford. In many ways, he is the one that worries me most. He is the man who brought us word of Savage and he is the man so trusted by the exiles in Paris and by the French embassy in London that they hand Mary's letters to him. Gilbert Gifford is at the core of all our plans and yet I feel that none of us truly knows his heart. And so we must keep him content – whatever the cost.'

Shakespeare nodded. He wondered how content the austere Walsingham would be if he knew that Treasury gold was going to pay the extortionate fees of a pair of whores. As the Smith sisters' soft, unblemished bodies amid the tangle of white linen sheets came to mind, they dissolved into another bedroom, long ago. He saw before him a candlelit chamber and the soft curves of Kat Whetstone. Would he really meet her again this day? The prospect was at once intoxicating and too painful to bear.

From somewhere in the distance, outside this small, stuffy room, he heard the rumble of thunder.

Chapter 6

Severin Tort arrived with the tolling of the noonday bells. The sky was dark and the rain was starting. As Shakespeare pulled open the solid oak door lightning dispersed the gloom, followed almost immediately by a rolling cannon-roar of thunder.

'Good day, Mr Tort. I would invite you in to wait out the storm, but I fear I do not have time for such a delay. How far is our journey?'

'Shoreditch, close to the Curtain playhouse. No more than two miles from here.'

'Then let us ride and pray the lightning strikes elsewhere. Follow me to the stables.'

Both men were dressed for the impending downpour: heavy topcoats – too warm for the sultry weather – wide-brimmed hats and riding boots. They rode without talking through the grimy streets northwards to Aldgate, then west along Houndsditch on the outer side of the city wall. At Bishopsgate they turned right, past Bethlehem Hospital along the busy, well-worn street to Shoreditch. The rain was coming hard now and they kicked their horses into a canter, weaving in and out of the wagons and carts that crowded the mud-churned high-way in both directions.

Shoreditch, just a mile from London, was very different

from its greater neighbour. This, as the austere city aldermen saw it, was a place of sin and debauchery, of drunken vagrants, bare-breasted whores in the street, of filth and bowling alleys and criminals. Worst of all, it housed the twin Gomorrahs of England – the playhouses known as the Theatre and the Curtain. Had it been within their power, the aldermen would have closed them down as dens of iniquity, lairs of drinking and whoredom and every other vice, but the playhouses were outside the city walls and beyond their jurisdiction.

Severin Tort reined in outside a surprisingly fine building in a street of alehouses and tenements near Curtain Close. After the two men had dismounted and tethered their horses, Tort hammered at the door of the main house; two knocks, a pause, then three knocks.

The door opened slowly and a man in a leather jerkin stood before them, a pair of iron scissors in his hand. He looked at the drenched figure of Severin Tort and seemed to recognise him, then studied Shakespeare. He said nothing but took a step to one side to let them in.

Shaking the rain from his hat, Shakespeare entered a work-room. It reminded him of his father's glovemaking and whittawing shop. The walls were limewashed and there were windows at two sides for light. A table was adorned with the tools of the seamster's trade: needles, more scissors, threads, candles to work by. In front of it stood a high three-legged stool. Two dresses hung against a wall.

'Oswald Redd here is a sharer at the Curtain. He has charge of the costumes. Mr Redd, this is John Shakespeare.'

The two men shook hands with a perfunctory nod of the head. Redd was a good-looking man of a similar age to Shakespeare, mid to late twenties, but four or five inches shorter than Shakespeare's six foot. He was well named, for his hair was copper-coloured, and his skin was tinted by freckles that seemed more joined up than separate. He was clearly anxious.

'Mr Redd works with Mr Lanman of the Curtain. He is seamster, writer, player and carpenter.'

'Does he know—'

'Yes. He is giving her refuge.' Tort turned to Redd. 'You have my word, we can trust Mr Shakespeare.'

Redd held up his scissors with the blades parted. 'Good,' he said, 'because I'll spill his blood with these if he does anything to harm her.' He turned to Shakespeare. 'She has told me of you.'

'I know her of old. Four years ago I met her in Sheffield where her father had the Cutler's Rest inn.'

'What was she to you?'

Shakespeare saw the jealousy in the man's eyes. Bloodshot eyes which were as red as his hair. 'A friend,' Shakespeare said. 'She saved my life.' He looked more closely at Oswald Redd; was he her lover or one that wished it so?

'Come up,' Redd said. 'It's not safe down here with these windows unshuttered.'

They climbed up a ladder through a hatchway to the first floor. Redd went first, followed by Shakespeare, then Tort. The floor was divided into two rooms. One was a bedchamber with a narrow bed, brightened by a harvest-yellow coverlet, the other a small parlour with a table and two chairs and a dark-wood coffer with candlesticks. The house had fireplaces at both ends. It was obviously quite recently built; part of the burgeoning construction in the villages surrounding London as increasing numbers of the dispossessed converged on the capital.

Another ladder led up to a second storey. Redd called up quietly through this hatch. 'Katherine. It is safe.'

Even before he saw her, Shakespeare felt a stab to his heart. He wanted to turn away and take horse back to Seething Lane.

But it was not possible; his feet were fixed to the floor as surely as nails driven into oak.

He heard footfalls on the boards above, then the softer sound of her steps descending the ladder. He saw her small, unshod feet and then her skirts of plainly styled fine linen. Finally she reached the bottom and turned to face him. She was smiling nervously.

'Kat, I thought I would never see you again.'

'Had you forgotten me, John?'

'Are you insane? No one has ever forgotten you.' He tried to match her smile. 'This is a strange and difficult reason to meet.'

Kat turned to Tort and Oswald Redd. 'I would speak with John alone. Perhaps you would take Mr Tort to the alehouse, Oswald.'

Redd seemed reluctant to leave, but Tort took his arm. 'Come, sir, I will stand you a cup of ale.'

After their footfalls had receded and the front door had banged shut, Kat moved forward into Shakespeare's arms. It was a tentative move, but once there, she did not draw back from him. He smelt her hair, that fresh scent he knew so well. At last, with a long sigh, she pulled away. Her eyes were uncertain, as though she had lost the confidence that once so marked her. 'You are wet through, Mr Shakespeare.'

'Aye, and sweltering. The rain might fall, but the air still has its summer heat.'

'Let me remove your coat.'

Shakespeare slid out of his dripping topcoat and watched as she hung it on a hook behind a door. 'That feels a great deal easier,' he said.

'What have you heard about me?'

'Nothing save this hideous news of murder. I have been in France and elsewhere in recent months. I did not even know you were wed.'

'Come, take a seat with me in the parlour. I will tell you everything.'

Sitting at the dark-stained table, he could not take his eyes from her. Each time she spoke, he saw the beguiling gap in her front teeth. Little about her had changed except her weight. She had put on half a stone, so that her face had filled out and her breasts were heavier. She still frowned when listening or concentrating and her hair was still long and untidy, as though it had been blown in the wind. She still enchanted him. And yet there was a fear in her blue eyes he had never expected to see.

Shakespeare spoke first. 'You married Nicholas Giltspur. And now he is dead, murdered by one Will Cane, who is himself now dead. I saw him die.'

'Hanged already?' She seemed shocked.

'His dying words were that you had offered him a hundred pounds to kill your husband. That is compelling evidence for any jury or judge. I am sure you will not be surprised to hear that the crowd did not appear to wish you well.'

'You do not need to tell me that. Do you think I sleep at night, knowing what is said of me? I believe myself as reviled as a Salome or Jezebel.'

'Then what do you say to *me*, Kat? Did Will Cane speak true?'

'Do you need to ask me that, John?'

'Yes.'

'No, the man did not speak true. Nor do I know why he should lie. I have never met him. I loved my husband and never wished him harm. You know you can believe me.'

Shakespeare shook his head. 'No, Kat, I know nothing of the sort. I know that you are posssessed by great ambition, which is like the devil's talons to the human soul. I know that

Nicholas Giltspur was among the wealthiest of men and that his death must have left you heiress to a fortune beyond most men's dreams. So what I want from you now – with nothing held back – is your story, from the moment you walked out on me until this day. If you dissemble or omit detail, I will know and I will walk away without a backward glance.'

Kat leant forward and put her hands to her head. He spotted the small mole on the underside of her wrist. Another of her perfect imperfections. He had kissed it often enough. He believed he knew every inch of her body: her breasts like exotic fruit, her welcoming thighs of smoothest, softest silk, her lips . . . he had kissed all these portions and more. Many times.

'Kat?'

'I will tell you everything. I left you because . . . John, surely you *know* why I left you. My letter explained it. Surely we need not go over this again. It is long gone.'

'If it is so long gone, why did you think to call on me?'

Shakespeare had never truly understood why she left him, but the truth was he did not really want to hear it. 'Just tell me what happened next. Where did you go? How did it lead to the marriage bed of Nicholas Giltspur?'

Kat clasped his hands. 'You are a good man, John – I am certain there is none better in this world – but your goodness was not enough. I should never have lived with you. Those nights in Stratford and on the road north, we should have left it at that. Somewhere in your mind there was always a future marriage, but it could never have been me. I could not fit your plan, never be the goodwife to give you children and keep your house.'

'Perhaps.' His voice was a little sharp. 'Now tell your story.'

She paused, weighing up her words. Her eyes did not stray from his. 'The truth, then. There was another man.'

'Oswald Redd?'

She nodded. 'Yes.' Her voice was quiet but clear. 'I met him one day when I came with you to the Curtain. I cannot recall the play, but there was a time while we were waiting when you went to find some ale. I think you met someone. Oswald saw his chance and approached me. He had already caught my eye. There was some spark and it grew from there . . . I am sorry.'

'Don't apologise. I did not come here for that.' Shakespeare did not believe she was sorry, or that she had regrets. He knew that she felt no shame; but nor would she have wanted to hurt him.

He looked around the room. It was pleasant enough, but plain, with no sign of the affluence of which she had always dreamt. 'Did you live here with him?'

She nodded again.

'Like man and wife, as we had lived?'

'John . . .'

'No, I should not have said that. I never had any right to expect anything of you.' He took a deep breath and forced a smile. 'And then you left him for Nicholas Giltspur.'

She nodded again.

'It seems it is becoming a custom with you.' He did not wait for her to protest, but pressed on. 'How did you meet Mr Giltspur?'

'I will come to that.'

'No. Tell me now. Go straight to the heart of the matter.'

'Very well. I met my husband through Henry Lanman, the chief sharer of the Curtain. Nicholas was entertaining a great party of merchants from France and the Low Countries and he brought them to see a play. I was at the playhouse helping Oswald with the wardrobe.

'After the play, when the audience had mostly departed, the whole company of players joined Nicholas and his party in drinking and feasting on the stage. Lanman introduced me to him. Much wine and spirit was taken. Men will call me what they will, but I confess I left Oswald that night and went to Nick's city house in Aldermanbury. I was in love.'

He snorted with derision. 'The Curtain has much to answer for. Perhaps the playhouses are indeed the sinks of iniquity that the city fathers and the Puritans would have us believe.' He immediately regretted his words, spoken only to torment her. He was glad when she ignored him and continued her tale.

'Within six weeks, we were wed. And though you will scoff, it is true that I loved him.'

'Not his money.'

She managed a small laugh. 'Your suspicions are correct: I would not have married him had he been poor and lame.'

'You have always been honest in that.' Her avarice had been a source of amusement to him; she had spoken with innocent candour of her desire to be the wealthiest woman in the land, richer even than the Countess of Shrewsbury and the Queen of England.

'He attired me in fine dresses with pearls and emeralds. Our house had thirty servants and I had my own lady's maid. Nicholas was besotted with me and I believe I did well by him in return, treating him with a wife's tender caresses and holding court for him when he so wished. I would have remained his loving and faithful wife. But . . .'

'But he was murdered.'

'Six days ago, his steward Sorbus came home, stricken with horror, and said that his master had been struck down in the street, stabbed in an unprovoked attack. He told me the killer had been apprehended.'

'Did you then hasten to the scene of the crime?'

She shook her head. 'I had fears . . .'

'Any wife would have rushed to her husband's side. Surely this is so?'

'Mr Sorbus told me that the killer was implicating me. He told me Justice Young was at the scene of the murder and would be along presently with guards to take me into custody. I told Mr Sorbus that I had best dress suitably and went to my chamber. My mind was in a whirl of sorrow, horror and bewilderment. I could not understand what had been said or why, but I have an instinct for survival as strong as any animal's, and so I slipped from the back of the house.'

'What then?'

'I took horse and came here to Shoreditch directly and have not moved from the care of Oswald since. Without him I fear I would now be dead. They are searching high and low for me. The justice, Richard Young, is leading the chase and I am told he will not relent until I am hanged.'

Yes, Shakespeare knew Richard Young. He was a hard man, a defender of the new Church and the rule of law.

'You surely knew that in fleeing you immediately made yourself appear guilty.'

'I had no choice. The rabble would have torn me apart. Even if I had got to court, the testimony of Mr Cane would have hanged me.'

Shakespeare listened to her voice. The soft northern burr had an edge to it that he had never noted before. She was clearly under strain, but that did not mean anything. She could be lying; she could be telling the truth. There was no way of knowing.

'And now Mr Redd is helping you to stay hidden, putting his own life in peril for the harbouring of a fugitive. And you wish *me* to work for you, too.' He snorted with laughter. 'You could forgive a man for thinking he is but one of a collection, kept concealed in a closet until his services are required by Kat Whetstone.'

'I did not know who else to turn to. Without Oswald's help I would be dead.'

'Why do you not go home to Sheffield? Your father would keep you safe.'

For the first time, tears filled her eyes. 'My father died last year. The inn has been sold. Anyway, I could not go to Sheffield. I am sure that word has already been sent there. And so, it is true, I *do* need Oswald – and I need you, too. Who else but you could inquire into this matter?'

'What of Severin Tort? Is he also part of your collection?'

'He was attorney to my husband in his commercial dealings. That is how I met him.'

'And?'

'And that is all. Severin is a good man, a widower. God knows he has problems enough with an ungrateful son who causes him endless misery. He needs no entanglement with me. John, I know I do not deserve the help of any of you, but what am I to do? I have no one else to turn to.'

Shakespeare stood up and paced over to the window. Outside in the rain-swept street horsemen and carters passed by, huddled against the weather. A pair of women hastened along westward. Were they wives or whores? What did such judgements matter? Kat was a creation of God as much as any saint. If He had made her thus, then it ill behoved mortal man to disparage her. It was only the one matter that should concern him; the question of murder. Did she or did she not pay for the death of Nicholas Giltspur?

'Tell me what you know of the killler, Will Cane.' As he spoke, he kept his gaze fixed on the street below.

'I never even heard his name until I learnt from Mr Sorbus that he had been arrested for Nicholas's murder and was claiming he had been hired by me.'

'What have you heard of him since?'

'No more than Oswald has heard from tittle-tattle in the playhouses. That and the broadsheet he brought me.'

He felt her arms snake about his waist, but still he did not turn away from the window. She nestled her head into his shoulder. Lightning flashed and lit the distinctive roundel of the Curtain playhouse. Shakespeare shivered.

'Do you recall the night we huddled together against the storm in your bed at Seething Lane?' she whispered.

How could he forget such a night? He said nothing. For a few moments he imbibed her warmth and scent, but then the thunder rumbled and he turned and moved away from her.

'John?' Her eyes showed hurt.

'You do not need to do this. You *have* my attention. Do you have the broadsheet still? I would like to see it.'

'I will fetch it for you.' She disappeared.

What in God's name was he doing here? He had a vital role in the biggest and most important enterprise that Walsingham's intelligence service had ever undertaken and here he was expending energy on behalf of a former lover who should have been long forgotten. Not only that, but he was involved with two other men in actively concealing a murder suspect's whereabouts from the sheriff and justice of the peace. They were all accomplices after the fact of murder: Shakespeare, Tort and Redd. They would all hang if their crime became known. He began walking towards the door just as she reappeared.

'Kat, I must go. I cannot help you. I should never have come.'

She held out a single sheet of paper. 'This is what is said about me.'

He took the broadsheet. It was a scrap, badly printed on poor quality paper, the sort of rough publication that was sold in the streets around St Paul's whenever there was a big trial or execution or news of foreign battles. He read it quickly, guessing the words where a letter hadn't been inked properly or was too worn to print.

Lamentable tragedy of Mr Nicholas Giltspur, Esquire, most wickedly murdered by his disloyal and wanton wife.

With the malice, deceit and unnatural lewdness of a hag, Katherine Giltspur, newly married to the most honourable and Christian gentleman Mr Giltspur, stands accused of bribing the known felon Wm. Cane to murder her husband most foully and cruelly, to satisfy her filthy avarice for gold and to leave her free to indulge her unbridled desire for carnal pleasures with other men.

The Recorder of London Mr William Fleetwood has sentenced the abhorrent Cane to be hanged by the neck until dead at Smithfield. A hue and cry for his accomplice continues, though it is feared she has travelled north to Yorkshire, whence she came. It is as though she has vanished into the air like a sprite. Any man or woman with knowledge of her whereabouts must reveal it or be themselves damned as accomplices to murder.

He put the paper aside. 'Kat. You have no idea what manner of undertaking I am now involved in – a work that will involve me night and day for as long as I can plan. Give me one good reason to think I should divert myself, even for an hour, from my own endeavours.'

She tried to smile, but it didn't work. She shook her head instead.

'I can't, John,' she said. 'I can't give you any reason why you should believe me or help me.'

Chapter 7

SHAKESPEARE RODE BACK to London with Severin Tort. The storm had passed, leaving a bright, breezy afternoon with white clouds and a new freshness in the air. The two men talked of Oswald Redd.

'He seems to me a man capable of anything,' Shakespeare said. 'He is at the edge of some precipice, unsure whether to cling on or plummet. Could Redd have been involved in the killing?'

'I could imagine him wishing Giltspur dead and even compassing the act in a jealous rage, but what could he have had to gain from the blame being laid at Kat's door? All his actions prove that he is desperate to keep her safe, yet now she faces arrest and execution.'

The two men fell silent. At Bishopsgate, Tort spoke again.

'Can you do nothing for her?'

'I wish I could, Mr Tort. I would dearly love to believe that she was innocent.'

'I believe her, Mr Shakespeare. For what it's worth.'

'Yes, I know you do.' She could make any man *want* to believe her. He knew her too well to doubt that, and yet not well enough to be sure of her guilt or innocence.

As Tort disappeared into the throng of tradesmen and carters, Shakespeare pulled on his reins and headed up between the fine houses of Foster Lane until he reached the junction with Noble Street. He brought his mount to a halt in front of a magnificent building. It was largely new-built and stood four storeys high, of brick and wood with a tiled roof topped by a dozen ornate chimney stacks.

The Recorder of London, William Fleetwood, welcomed Shakespeare into his comfortable withdrawing room. Despite the difference in social standing and ages – Shakespeare was twenty-seven while Fleetwood was grey and well into creaking old age – they had forged a friendship based on a shared desire for justice, a disliking for flummery and a loathing of treason. More than anything, they enjoyed each other's company.

'Look at this, Mr Shakespeare,' Fleetwood said, removing his spectacles and laying a paper before him. He signalled to one of his many servants who brought over a selection of sweetmeats, while another poured two glasses of fine Burgundian wine 'You must excuse my poor copy.'

Shakespeare read the words.

'*No free man shall be taken or imprisoned or denied what is rightfully his, or made outlaw or sent to exile, nor will he be proceeded against with force except by the lawful judgement of his peers or by the law of the land.*'

'Well?'

'It's Magna Carta, Your Honour.'

'Of course it is, chapter thirty-nine – and I will not be subjected to *your honours* in my own home.'

Shakespeare laughed. It was an old jest between them. 'Then it will be my *honour* to address you as plain mister.'

'And so the thirty-ninth clause – what does it say to you?

'It says, Mr Fleetwood, that no man may be punished without due process of law.'

'A fine summation. You were a loss to the law when Mr Secretary snatched you away.'

'What is your interest in the clause, Mr Fleetwood?'

'Bridewell. It was given its charter as a house of work and refuge for the poor, but has become a prison by another name. As you know, Mr Shakespeare, I am not squeamish when it comes to administering the law of the land and will hang a dozen rogues and murderers in a day if necessary. But I will not execute or lash a man without evidence of guilt.'

Shakespeare drank some of the wine. In court, the judge was considered a hard man who believed himself fair and just; yet Shakespeare thought him unnecessarily harsh at times. Justice needed to be tempered with mercy. It was a point on which they were unlikely ever to agree, and he did not pursue it now: Fleetwood was in full flow.

'The burghers order their squadrons of ruffians to lift men, women and children from the streets and take them to Bridewell for the mere fact of vagrancy without evidence of felony or misdemeanour, simply to clear London of its human night soil. No trial, not even an appearance before court. And once there, Mr Shakespeare, they are punished further by severe floggings at the whim of the keeper. If Magna Carta is to mean anything, then it must mean that Bridewell is unlawful in its present form. It is an abomination for English men, women or children to be punished without first being found guilty of some infringement of the law.'

Shakespeare nodded. 'I agree entirely.'

'It is the likes of Justice Richard Young and Mr Richard Topcliffe, MP, who feed this wickedness. They are such men as I would expect to find with forked prods in the deepest circles of hell.'

'What can be done about the matter?'

'I am composing a treatise, which I intend to lay before Her Majesty. I doubt it will be acted upon; the merchants of London will not allow it, for they are at their happiest when vagabonds and masterless men are gathered up and disposed of like rats. And who is strong enough to deny them when they feed the exchequer with gold and plate? Yet I must have my say, for if injustice is unseen it can never be corrected.'

Fleetwood took a piece of cake and thrust it into his well-fed mouth. His cheeks were red from the warmth of the room and the fervour of his argument. 'Eat, Mr Shakespeare, eat. The cake is good!'

Fleetwood would not let him leave without sampling the delicacies of his kitchens, so Shakespeare took a sweetmeat. 'Thank you, I will.'

'You know, Mr Shakespeare, you are not only a great loss to the law but I truly believe you would have made a fine judge. A little too soft, sometimes, but rigorous and fair . . . like me. Sometimes I think I am but a voice lost in the wind against the likes of Young and Topcliffe.'

'Without your voice, England would be a poorer place.'

The judge brushed the compliment away with a sweep of his hand, sending cake crumbs flying. 'I do not need flattery. You are here for a purpose are you not? You have not called at my humble home to taste apricot cake, I assume.'

Shakespeare smiled. 'Indeed. I wanted to ask you about a case you recently tried at Justice Hall. The matter of Will Cane for the murder of Mr Nicholas Giltspur.'

'May I ask your interest?'

'I used to know Giltspur's widow. I have seen in the broadsheets that she is implicated, which surprised me, I confess. It does not sound like the Katherine I knew.'

'Really?' Fleetwood sat forward, his sharp little eyes alive with interest. 'Describe her to me if you would. In court, she was painted by Cane and the prosecution as a devil whore.'

'Well, she was never a saint, that is true. But devil? Whore? Neither of those words would have suited Katherine Whetstone, the name by which I knew her. In the days of our acquaintance, I would have called her an adventurer – an adventuress if there is such a word. She had a great desire for wealth and position and a remarkable beauty with which to acquire it. But I could not imagine her stooping to murder.'

Fleetwood took more cake, grinned and patted his ample belly. 'I must work hard to fill this cavern,' he said with a light laugh. 'It seems forever empty!' He paused, then nodded. 'Very well, what do you want to know?'

'What evidence was given against her? Was it conclusive, in your judgement?'

'I don't suppose you know where she is, Mr Shakespeare?'

'If I knew where she was, it would surely be a felony not to reveal it.'

'That does not answer my question, but we will let it pass for the moment. Was the evidence conclusive? Indeed it was.'

'Perhaps you would describe the course of events as they were outlined to you.'

'The facts were straightforward. Mr Giltspur was dining at Fishmongers' Hall. It was a great feast, I am told. When he emerged at about midnight, his steward Sorbus and others of his retinue were waiting to convey him home by his carriage. As he stepped towards the coach, his killer moved out of the shadows and thrust him a single deadly blow to the throat. The weapon was a bollock-dagger with a nine-inch blade. So violent was the thrust that the blade pierced poor Mr Giltspur's throat from beneath the left crook of the jaw to the right. The killer removed his weapon and dropped it in the street. Mr Giltspur died within a minute in a floodtide of his own blood. This was all confirmed in a report from the searcher.'

'And the killer?'

'He managed no more than twenty paces as he tried to escape up New Fish Street. He was brought down and apprehended by Mr Giltspur's servants. At no time did he bother to deny his guilt and he immediately revealed that the dead man's widow had contracted him to do the evil deed. "Hundred pounds she said I'd have. Ten before and the rest on proof of death," were the words he used, as I recall. The servants all confirmed this. And Cane said the same to me himself, from the dock.'

'Did he name the woman who had hired him?'

'Yes, he did so at the scene. Then later at Newgate and also in my courtroom. There can be no question of her identity. He said it plain and described her in detail, down to the gap between her teeth and the mole on her wrist, all of which were agreed upon as distinguishing marks by those who knew her.'

'And did he say how she came to meet him?'

'No, he refused to say more, only that he had been to Giltspur House, in Aldermanbury, and that she had admitted him to her bedchamber, where the transaction had been settled.'

'And that is it?'

'That is it. He swore all this on the Holy Book and asked mercy of God. I sent him down and he was dispatched yesterday at Smithfield. I fear the punishment was not adequate to the crime, which I consider to have been among the most heinous I have tried. For a wife to kill a husband must always be considered petit treason.' He leant forward and touched his guest's hand. 'Mr Shakespeare – John – I fear that if you are looking for some hope that your friend is innocent, then you are to be sore disappointed. The case against her is simple and clear. When she is caught, she will hang.'

'So it seems.' The old judge could have no concept of how heavy-hearted he felt. This was raw, gut-churning news. He had one last question. 'Was anything known about the killer, Cane?'

'The constable told me he was an associate of Cutting Ball and his crew. Certainly the use of the bollock-dagger as a weapon would bear this out, for they all carry them, as though it were their livery. I imagine that if you wished to find a hired assassin, Cutting Ball or his villainous friends would be a good place to start.'

Cutting Ball. Shakespeare winced. A name to be feared. It was said he took a share of all the crime proceeds north of the river from Whitechapel to the Isle of Dogs – and that he handed down his own brand of outlaw justice to any man or woman who dared defy him. A justice that involved more pain than even the Tower torturer could manage to inflict. He stood up. 'Thank you, though I fear you have brought me no joy.'

Fleetwood heaved himself to his feet. 'Cutting Ball,' he said. 'Now there is a man I would dearly love to have before me in the dock. God willing, the egregious Mr Ball will be apprehended and brought to my sessions house in Old Bailey, where I may send him to his doom.' He rubbed his plump hands together. 'And I hope and trust this will occur one sunny day soon.'

Chapter 8

'BOLTFOOT, HAVE YOU heard of a man named Cutting
Ball?'

'Yes, master. I do believe every man and woman in London
town knows of him.'

'What have you heard?'

'I know that he is reputed to be an infamous villain, much
given to violent persuasion in the getting of coin. I know, too,
that he is held in dread, especially in the wharfs and quays east
of the bridge. It is said he demands one part in a hundred of all
cargoes unladen from the Indies carracks and has some hold
over the wharfingers and lightermen. Some say his true name is
Ball and that he is called Cutting for his custom of cleaving
men's balls from their bodies, very slowly, before he kills
them.'

Shakespeare was surprised to detect an edge of awe, even
fear, in Boltfoot's description. Had he perhaps encountered
some of Cutting Ball's men during his time as a ship's cooper?
There must surely have been times when he was docked in the
reaches of the Thames where the outlaw held sway. But
Boltfoot afraid? No, that could not be so; Boltfoot was
frightened of nothing under heaven.

They were in the kitchen, which already seemed a lot less
dusty and more polished in the few hours since the arrival of

Jane Cawston. She opened the door, looked in and saw the two men at the table, bowed quickly, then scuttled away like a startled rabbit.

Shakespeare followed Boltfoot's gaze. 'A comely girl that, Boltfoot, would you not say?'

'Comely enough, master,' Boltfoot growled as though the words were torn from him with a hot iron. He raised his eyes with mild defiance. 'But take a look in the larder for that's where you'll find her true worth. She's been to market and brought home food.'

Shakespeare held up his tankard of ale. 'And a fresh keg, too. Perhaps you were right after all.'

Boltfoot grunted and took a quick draught of his own ale.

'I have a task for you, Boltfoot. I want you to go to the taprooms and hovels where Cutting Ball rules and find out what you can about a felon named Will Cane, who was hanged yesterday.'

'The one who killed the merchant? It's the talk of London. The wife paid Cane to kill her husband so she could inherit all his wealth.'

'So it is said. And do you know the wife's name?'

'No, master.'

'Katherine Giltspur, born Katherine Whetstone.'

Boltfoot had known Kat as long as had Shakespeare, and he had been here during the years she shared Shakespeare's bed in this house. The blood seemed to drain from his weather-worn cheeks and his brow furrowed in bewilderment and disbelief. 'Kat . . .'

'Yes, Kat Whetstone. *Our* Kat.'

'But how . . .'

Shakespeare shook his head. 'It is all as much a mystery to me as it must be to you. She married him two months ago and is now a widow, in hiding, wanted for his murder.'

'Not Kat!'

Shakespeare shrugged. 'I want to agree with you, and so I would like to discover more – especially about Will Cane, who was a known associate of Cutting Ball. Find his haunts and talk to those who knew him or knew of him. What sort of man was he? Had he killed before? Who were his friends? Was he married? Listen to tittle-tattle; sometimes there is a semblance of truth there. But bear in mind the hard possibility that the truth may be as simple as everyone believes: that Kat paid Will Cane to murder her husband.'

'No, Mr Shakespeare,' Boltfoot said stoutly. 'No, I will not believe that.'

'Then find me a better explanation. For if we do not, our Kat will surely die with a noose about her pretty neck.'

Anthony Babington gazed through the clouds of tobacco smoke at his assembled friends and felt a surge of pride. They were here, at this feast in an upper room at the Plough Inn on the south side of Fleet Street, near Temple Bar, because of *his* presence. He was their leader and their inspiration.

He rose from his chair, hammered his tankard down for silence, sending up a spray of strong beer, and called the gathering of young men to order. As their hubbub subsided to a murmur, he raised his tankard.

'Raise your cups! The death of usurpers!'

The sixteen other men around the table all stood up, held their own tankards aloft, roaring their approval. 'Death to usurpers! Death to usurpers!' They threw the contents of their drinking vessels down their gullets then brought the empty tankards onto the tabletop with an explosion of banging.

'Now charge your goblets and tankards and let us drink to the Pope's White Sons!' Once more they shouted and drank. Babington sat down and the other men followed his lead. He looked about once more. At his right hand sat John Shakespeare, one of the newer young gentlemen, recommended by Goodfellow Savage as a fellow of influence and secret knowledge; just the sort of man they needed. Was he to be trusted, though? He knew the mass well enough, but any spy worth his salt could learn that. On the other hand he was too valuable to be dismissed. He had already brought information about the inner workings of Sir Francis Walsingham's intelligence network and promised more. Well, they would watch him carefully. And use him ruthlessly. Walsingham might think himself cunning, but Babington knew that he was a great deal cleverer. If Shakespeare was a spy, he would find out soon enough.

Shakespeare was becoming more than a little drunk, yet even through the fog of smoke and alcohol he could not rid himself of the tautness in his neck that came with playing a part. An hour earlier he had betrayed his religion to hear mass with these men at a house nearby. Now he was seated at Babington's right hand, drinking to the death of the Queen he had sworn to serve loyally.

Through the haze of his inebriation, he studied Anthony Babington: the doublet of gold and silver threads shining in the candlelight; the long, carefully tied hair, so soft and clean; the small gold earring; his puffed-up pride. The word *popinjay* might have been coined for him.

A sudden hubbub of hail and welcome made Shakespeare look towards the door. Two late arrivals were entering – Edward Abingdon and Charles Tilney. Shakespeare knew them well and a sudden chill crept over him. Abingdon and Tilney were courtiers with access to the Queen, honoured members of the Queen's Guard. And here they were among a group of malcontents and putative traitors with insurrection and assassination in mind.

He put his fears aside for another day. For the present, nothing must be said or done to raise alarm in the minds of those gathered here. Instead Shakespeare raised his tankard to the two men. Tilney came and clapped him on the back and pushed his way onto the bench on his right side.

'Well, well, Mr Shakespeare, I had not expected to meet *you* here.' His voice boomed.

'Nor I you, Mr Tilney. It seems we both have a taste for interesting company.' He moved a little way further from his new companion, who was known as 'Roarer' Tilney with good reason.

'Does Mr Secretary know you are out?' Tilney shouted.

Shakespeare grimaced. 'Mr Secretary may own my body, but he does not own my soul. And what of you, Mr Tilney? Does Her Majesty know that you are here? I had thought you to be a Gentleman Pensioner with care for her safety. Should you not be guarding her royal body with your life?'

'Why, she does not need *me*! She has God on her side!' Tilney bellowed with laughter at the preposterous notion that a Protestant God could protect anything or anyone. Eyes turned his way and then, seeing who it was, turned away again.

'You speak so loud, I suspect you are heard at Greenwich, Mr Tilney. Watch your roaring lest you ruin us all.'

'They are looking for men who huddle and whisper, Mr Shakespeare. When I roar, the spies know I can have nothing to hide. And what of you? You talk in hushed tones here, but are you not heard at Seething Lane?'

'What are you suggesting?' Shakespeare's senses sharpened, despite the ale he had drunk.

Tilney shrugged. 'It was but a jest. I have come for ale and good roasts with fine company, no more.'

'It was no jest. I do not like your insinuation.'

'Insinuation?'

'You know why I work for Walsingham. I will not be defamed by you or anyone else.'

Tilney shrugged. 'I meant nothing by my remark. If you inferred anything, examine your own conscience.'

'Damn you, Tilney, I will not listen to this.' Shakespeare turned away, as though nursing hurt pride.

Anthony Babington had evidently been listening to the exchange. 'Pay him no heed, Mr Shakespeare. The likes of Tilney are a mischief that must be endured. We need such men.'

'Forgive me. I am too sensitive.' Shakespeare changed the subject. 'Is there word from Captain Fortescue and Mr Maude? We must hope they return soon.'

'Indeed, Mr Shakespeare. They are much missed, but they are doing God's work.'

'In the north?'

Babington raised a finger, like a schoolmaster. 'We do not ask such questions. It is enough that they are God's soldiers, which is a noble calling. Are you a soldier of God, Mr Shakespeare? Will you take up your sword and pistol and follow me?'

Shakespeare was momentarily nonplussed, surprised by the openness of the invitation. At last he found a light way to reply. 'My weapon is my mind. I fear I would make a better target than a shooter. But I will do all that is required of me. I am yours to command.'

'What then, Mr Shakespeare? What will you do when God calls you?' Babington gazed around the room at his drinking companions with a measure of scorn. 'Will you crawl back into your hole and tell yourself that it was nothing but a brandy-fuelled game, more to do with feasting than carrying out His holy work?' His voice lowered. 'Or will your blade taste blood for Him?'

'Do you doubt me? Perhaps you doubt the other fellows here?'

'They will do well enough. But I am intrigued by you. Mr Savage says you are to be trusted, but I do not know you as well as he does. And you answer my question with questions.'

'Let my actions speak while others boast.'

'Then I will trust you.' Babington's smile did not extend to his eyes.

Although all those present looked up to Babington as their leader, for he was their senior in wealth and swagger, Shakespeare thought of him as a boy leading boys. The test would come when they were required to be men.

'And if you are as true as I must believe, then you are indeed of the first importance to us,' Babington continued.

Shakespeare gave a little bow of his head. 'Indeed, Mr Babington, I do not know whether to be flattered or afraid.'

'I do not flatter. If you are afraid, you must conquer it. As for these others . . .' Babington gazed once more around the noisy room, 'their comfortable life cannot endure much longer. The real work must begin. You, Mr Shakespeare, are the dog in the yard to warn us of impending harm. You will be the one to bring word to us if the satanic Walsingham begins to take an unhealthy interest in those gathered here.'

Shakespeare bowed again. 'Mr Babington, I must tell you that he already takes an interest in you. He takes an interest in *everyone*, both in England and across the great capitals of Europe. It is said he even has agents in Peru and the Indies.'

'But us in particular?'

'I have told you about the information he receives from street spies.' Half-truths, Shakespeare thought wryly; he would not mention the spies who watched from the inside, men like Slide and Gifford and Shakespeare himself. 'Mr Secretary knows the Pope's White Sons as recusants of noble and gentle birth. But there are many such in London and further afield. In some counties of the Midlands and the north, there are many more Catholics among the gentry than there are Protestants. Walsingham does not like them, but nor does he take most of them seriously.'

'But we are not in the shires.'

'It means nothing. Why, the court itself has its share of men and women who stand firm to the true faith. Walsingham knows all their names. He watches them all, but will only move against them if they are too open in harbouring priests or engaging in sedition. And so he will keep a watchful eye on you and your friends, but no more than he does with any other young men he suspects of being unsound in religion, as he sees it.'

'And does he never suspect you?'

Shakespeare laughed, although to his own ears it sounded somewhat forced. 'He suspects me every day. But I would say he suspects all those he employs and every man he works with. I would not be surprised to learn that he even suspects old Lord Burghley. The Queen herself, perhaps!'

'Then be a good watchdog for us. Bark loud when you sense danger.' Babington's own voice lowered to a whisper. 'Protect us well and we will have a new world shortly. Before this summer's end a fatal blow will be struck against the usurpers. I have had this promise from Captain Fortescue, who has the ear of Mendoza himself.'

Bernardino de Mendoza, Spain's ambassador to Paris. Here, between the twin cities of Westminster and London, the beating heart of England, this man Babington was speaking with reverence of his country's most lethal enemy. At times these young men, these Pope's White Sons – the Bishop of Rome's *innocent children* as they would have it – seemed almost harmless, but Shakespeare knew that there was a great deal more danger here than a casual observer might ever imagine.

Babington patted Shakespeare's arm, then stood up and signalled for quiet. His tone was serious and solemn. 'Tonight we drink to absent friends and pray that they are with us before too long. A health to Captain Fortescue and Mr Maude and their faithful servant Mr Gage as they return from their great good work in the service of God. We wish them God speed to our bosom and promise that we will do all we can to emulate them by carrying out our own work. Each man must find his own path to salvation, but I believe in my heart that all here are resolved to work for the true faith. I would wish for a peaceful transition, but wishes sometimes need a little poke.'

The young men all rose again. Shakespeare drank with them, but could not conquer the churning in his stomach; all those present knew that Captain Fortescue was, in truth, the priest John Ballard, a conspirator who would wash this land with English blood in the cause of his faith. But only Shakespeare knew the real identity of his constant companion, Bernard Maude. In truth, Maude was Harry Slide, the slipperiest of the earth's creatures, an intelligencer for Shakespeare and Walsingham.

Shakespeare was alone when he left the Plough soon after midnight. He was unsteady on his feet but that could not be avoided. As a relatively new recruit to Babington's circle of drinkers and debaters, he had to gain their trust by drinking as heavily as they did. Now, however, he had no alternative but to ride, for he had no intention of walking all the way across London at this time of night.

He took a deep breath of the cool air. Above him the sky was clear, purified by the rain. It promised fine weather come morning. He tried to shake himself sober, but his head was swimming. All he wanted was his bed and a blanket.

At the west side of the inn there was an arched entrance through to the mews where carriages were parked and a bank of stalls was set aside for customers' horses. Shakespeare stumbled into the archway, unable to see his way, for the wall lantern had gone out. He looked around, bleary-eyed, hoping to find the night ostler; *he*'d find the nag and help him up. But first he needed a piss. He faced the wall, splayed his legs, and fished in his hose for his prick.

He failed to hear the sound of footsteps behind him.

The first blow was a kick to the back of his legs, just behind the knee. The strike crumpled him instantly and was followed, as he went down, by a hard push in the small of his back. The surprise of the attack gave him no chance. He fell helplessly towards the cobbles, only putting out his hands instinctively at the last moment to prevent his chin and face smacking into the stone. Sprawling on the ground, he tried to climb back to his feet, but a rough-edged boot caught his ribs, then a hobnailed toe smacked into the side of his head.

'Papist vermin. Pope's dirty son!'

He cried out, more in bewilderment than pain, and scrabbled backwards. There were three of them; spotty youths in apprentices' blue tunics and aprons. He reached towards his belt for his poniard, but one of them kicked it out of his hand, and then brought his own dagger close to Shakespeare's face.

'Let's carve something pretty on you.'

Shakespeare smelt his fetid breath through the fug of his own alcohol-laden senses.

'A cross? A picture of the scarlet whore? What'll it be, vermin? What shall I carve?'

Shakespeare grasped the knife-hand and twisted hard at the wrist. The attacker yelped, but his friends moved forward, their eyes angry beneath their flat caps. One of them wrenched

Shakespeare's hand away; the other put his boot on Shakespeare's chest and thrust him backwards, so that he fell against the wall.

'Let's do the filthy boy-priest!'

'Slit the verminous rat's throat! See the blood all scarlet like the Pope's rotten robes!'

One of them grasped Shakespeare's throat in a shovel-sized hand and squeezed. 'Give us the dagger,' he growled at one of his fellows. 'I want to burst his eyes.'

'Here.' The blade was handed over. 'And then you can stick it up his arse. That's what these foul boy-priests like. That's what they do with each other in their rancid beds a-night. Christ's fellows every one.'

Had he been sober, Shakespeare would probably have fought them off, for they were not strong, but he was floundering and couldn't focus clearly enough to fight or reason with them. The point of the dagger was coming closer to his right eye. 'I have money,' he rasped, the grip tightening on his throat. 'My purse . . . take my purse.' He tried to fish for the purse at his belt.

'We'll have your glazers *and* your purse.' An unpleasant sniggering, breath like a dunghill dog's.

And then the hand was no longer gripping him and the dagger fell away. For one terrifying moment he thought it was being pulled back for the final plunge into the watery heart of his eyes. He closed his lids tight, but immediately opened them again and saw three other shapes behind his attackers, pulling the youths away. He heard a groan as a punch connected with a stomach, then an oath followed by an anguished groan and the sound of running footsteps.

Shakespeare put his hand to his throat and gasped for breath. He rested his head back against the wall, desperate to dredge up some strength.

'Mr Shakespeare?'

It was Anthony Babington, holding a lantern and peering down at him.

'I drank too much . . . they set on me . . .'

'Have they hurt you? Let me see.' He gave the lantern to one of his comrades, then knelt down beside Shakespeare's trunk and began to examine his head, holding it this way and that with soft, gentle hands. Satisfied with what he saw, he turned his attention to Shakespeare's body and limbs, moving them to test for fractures.

'I'm not hurt. I must ride home.'

'Your head has taken a blow.'

'It's nothing. A kick by a boy. Please, help me up and I will trouble you no more. Thank you for assisting me, Mr Babington.'

Babington and one of his companions took Shakespeare under the arms and lifted him slowly to his feet. 'No bones broken?'

'Maybe a bruise or cut, that's all. I thank you again.'

'It was nothing. We are brothers in Christ, are we not? Who were they?'

'Apprentices, curpurses, I don't know. They called me papist vermin, so they clearly had an idea who I was.'

'Ah.' Babington shook his head. 'Maybe someone in the Plough alerted them to our presence. It would not be the first time something like this has happened. A group of them beat poor Chidiock here outside the Three Tuns last month.'

Shakespeare studied Babington's two companions: Chidiock Tichbourne and Thomas Salisbury. They had both been at the feast, his closest friends.

'Can you walk unaided?'

'Yes. Please, I entreat you, pay me no more heed.'

They released his arms and he took a couple of paces, but

caught the side of his foot on a cobble and stumbled into the archway wall.

'Come on, you're coming with us.'

'No . . .'

'We will brook no argument. Thomas lodges near here. We will help you there and put you to bed until you have regained your balance.'

Shakespeare no longer had the strength to argue. And somewhere in the deep recesses of his befuddled mind, he realised that he would rather like to see inside the quarters of the treacherous Thomas Salisbury.

Chapter 9

B OLTFOOT SPENT ALL evening limping around the taprooms and bawdy houses of Billingsgate and eastward
until he was outside the city walls at Whitechapel, and from
there to the river, listening to the talk where he could and striking up conversations when possible, which was not often. Most
men and women shunned him.

He wondered whether his method of introducing the subject of Kat and the murder was a little too blunt, but he had no
idea what else to do. His master had asked him to listen in to
conversations before, but this was different; he wasn't merely
gathering tittle-tattle but trying to steer the subject of the conversation – and looking for certain people.

'That's a fine old tale about the merchant getting himself
murdered by order of his strumpet wife,' he said to one
whore in the Burning Prow, down by the wharfs at St
Katharine's.

'Aye, and what's it to you?' she replied, looking at him with
a cunning, rheumy eye.

Boltfoot was uncertain whether she was measuring him up
for her stinking bed or a coffin. *At least you wouldn't catch the
pox in a coffin.* 'Just saying it's a fine old tale,' he continued.
'Like a story from the Old Testament. It's poor Will Cane I
feel for, getting caught up in the middle. Got his neck stretched

✠ 64 ✠

and she's escaped like a sprite. Or a witch. Sounds like a witch, I'd say.'

'Do you want to stick it in or don't you? If you do, it'll cost a shilling. If you want frigging, it's sixpence, coin upfront. And if you don't, then stow you, for I'm not here to discuss the weather and the tides.' She was busy picking a scab from her face as she spoke and exuded an unwholesome smell. A man would have to be desperate or drunk.

'All I want's some friendly chatter to pass the night,' protested Boltfoot. 'I'll get you a gage of cider for your company.'

'I don't want your cider and I don't want your company. You're an ugly brute and if you're not a buyer, you can take your mangy foot and get out of my sight before I cripple the other one.' She signalled to the bawd at the door, a younger woman with a pretty smile and businesslike eyes. 'Here, Em, get the lads to throw this sheepshit out. Shove him in a pile of nightsoil to sweeten him up.'

The woman at the door strolled over. She was a lot more appetising than the trug he had been trying to engage in conversation. She gazed at Boltfoot, then nodded to the whore. 'No need for trouble, Aggy. He'll go peaceful, won't you?' She put her hand on his upper arm and began guiding him towards the door. Boltfoot tried to shake off her hand, but her grip tightened. 'Be friendly, then no one'll get hurt.'

'I only wanted to buy her a drink and talk a while.'

'You look like a mariner. Go up the street to the Topsail Arms. You'll get talk a-plenty there. The Burning Prow is for them as wants a little spice with their beer.' With her free hand she opened the door and pushed him out. 'Go kindly and you'll be doing yourself a favour, Mr Mariner.' She moved her red lips close to his ear. 'Come back with half a crown when you want to jostle and jumble and I'll find you a better dish than Aggy there. One that washes and won't fart in your face.'

'Wait. Can I talk with *you*, mistress? Five minutes of your time and you'll have a shilling. That's all I want.'

'Who are you?' Suddenly suspicious.

'That don't matter. I want a little bit of information, that's all. About Will Cane.'

'You a friend of Will's? You're no law man.'

'No, I weren't his friend. Just want to know the truth, that's all.'

'And what might your name be?'

'Cooper. By name and by trade.'

'You'd better tell me your interest then, Mr Cooper. Elsewise, how will I know whether I can help you?'

'Then you knew him?'

'I didn't say that. But I'll tell you this: folks in these parts don't like those that come around with questions.'

'He's dead, though. No harm can come to him now. Folks say he was a confederate of Cutting Ball.'

'Cutting Ball, eh? Now there's a tiger of a man.'

Boltfoot looked at the woman's eyes. Was she making merry of him? 'You know something of him, mistress?'

'Cutting Ball? No, no, Mr Cooper. That's too dangerous for a maiden like me.'

This woman was no more a maiden than Boltfoot was a bishop. He grunted his scepticism. 'Anyway, it's the woman I really want to know about . . . Mistress Giltspur.'

'Who do you work for, Mr Cooper?'

'That's my business.'

'Not good enough. Try again.'

'And I say again, it's my business. But if you've got information, I've got silver for you.'

'Mr Cooper, you look a fair fellow, so let me give you a little warning. Go home and keep your mouth sewn as tight as a seafarer's shroud, else you'll wake up with your throat cut one fine morning. Do you hear me?'

'Aye, but—'

'No buts. Take heed. I could have you taken from here right now, sliced open and dropped in the river. And when your body was washed up, no one would care a groat. So go. If you want a gage of ale, go to the Topsail, but don't ask no questions there either, for you are delving into matters that are of no concern to you, nor any other common man with an interest in being alive.'

And then she was gone, and Boltfoot found himself alone, standing beneath a lantern outside the alehouse. The scents of the river mingled with the stench of the dung-clogged street. Old memories came rushing back like the tide: the smell of pitch and brine, the feel of the rolling sea beneath scrubbed oak decking, the sawdust and shavings of the barrels he'd built for Drake and the crew of the *Golden Hind* as they laboured against hunger and exhaustion to cross the great Pacific and get home. Memories of a time he never wished to experience again in this life.

He stood there for a minute, then began dragging his club foot down towards the Topsail Arms. What in God's name did Mr Shakespeare expect of him? He must know that no one around these parts would open their mouth to a stranger. Once again he tried to make conversation, but the other drinkers looked at him as though he were an unpleasant piece of jetsam, then turned away.

He tried the same method at the Old Wharf and at an alehouse that had no sign but which he knew of as the Bishop's Prick. He moved on northwards, but even after a score of taverns he had still got nowhere. Tired and despondent, he decided there was no more to be done this night and set off to traipse along the path back towards the city.

The way was ill lit and almost deserted. Boltfoot kept his hand on the hilt of his cutlass as he walked slowly, trying to avoid potholes and piles of waste. He had not brought his caliver; a gun would not have been welcome in the drinking holes he'd been visiting.

He planned to enter the city by way of Postern Gate, the old entrance just north of the Tower, once a great arched building and now fallen into ruin, but he was stopped by a broad-chested watchman. The man approached him from behind, swinging his lantern and pushing the shaft of his halberd aggressively into the ground in front of Boltfoot.

'Where you going?'

'Get your pole out of the way. You trying to trip me?'

'I'm Potken, the watch for this ward, and I'll put my halberd where I like. Down your gullet if I so desire. Now where you going, maggot?'

'Home. Seething Lane.'

'You don't look like no denizen of Seething Lane. If you want entry to the city, come by day with the carters and wagoners.'

'I'm a serving man. My master's house is there.'

'And who would your master be?'

'John Shakespeare.'

'Shakespeare? Never heard of him.'

'He's a Queen's Man. Assistant secretary to Sir Francis Walsingham. Argue with *him*, if you will.'

The watchman was not tall, but he puffed up his heavy chest like a cockbird and pushed out his ragged-bearded chin. 'Is that so?'

The tactic had no effect on Boltfoot. 'Aye, and I've been on an errand for my master, which is not for your ears, nor anyone else's. And by now he'll be wondering where I am, so if you'll let me pass, I'll be on my way.'

'Hold fast. What's your name?'

'Cooper. Mr Cooper to you.'

'Well, Mr Cooper, I don't trust a word you say. Seething Lane, eh? That's close enough – second on the right – so I do believe. Perhaps I should accompany you home, maybe have a word or two with your master. And if you're lying to me, then it'll be straight to Bridewell and the treadmill with you – and I'll have your name down for the Friday floggings.'

'A turd in your throat, watchman.' Boltfoot limped on. He was almost at Mr Shakespeare's house when he felt a hand clamping his shoulder and swung round, his cutlass out.

'Touch me again and I'll cut you open like a Spaniard.'

Potken backed off. 'Put up your strange sword, Cooper. I've got a message for you.'

'What do you mean?'

'Em from the Burning Prow wants to see you tomorrow. Says she's got word for you. Come again through the Postern Gate and I'll take you to her.'

'Why didn't she tell me this herself?'

'What sort of muttonhead are you, Cooper? Do you think she'd talk with you among witnesses? Come at your leisure and she'll make it worth your while.' He laughed and his barrel chest heaved. 'I'm sure of that well enough.'

Boltfoot stared at the man, furious with himself. Now Potken knew he worked for Shakespeare – and so, as day followed night, would the woman known as Em. He cursed his loose tongue. He would have to warn Mr Shakespeare.

The watchman turned away, his laughter ringing in the cool night air. Boltfoot rapped at the door. It was opened by Jane in nightgown and cap, bleary-eyed and ready for bed. Boltfoot nodded to her and turned back again. He had spotted a movement in the shadow of a doorway a little way down the street. The watchman was still watching.

*

Shakespeare awoke on a narrow truckle bed. He opened his eyes but at first he could see nothing. He turned over on his side and groaned at the pain in his head. He could just hear low murmurings – little more than whispers – coming from the other side of the door.

Delicately, he pulled himself up to a sitting position, took several deep breaths, and forced himself to stand. The events of the night came back bit by bit. The drinking, the attack, and then the short walk here to this modest lodging in a street behind Temple Bar where he had promptly fallen asleep. But perhaps there was still something to be gained. His head might be pounding, but the effects of the alcohol had mostly worn off. He was thinking more clearly.

He put his ear to the door. He could hear Anthony Babington and Thomas Salisbury, but their words were muffled and indecipherable. Then they went silent. Shakespeare heard soft footfalls and quickly he pushed open the door, scratching his head groggily as he did so.

Salisbury was standing in front of him. His strawlike hair and the knife in his hand made him look quite mad: a malign scarecrow.

Shakespeare's gaze dropped from Salisbury's unsmiling face to the knife.

'This?' Salisbury said, holding up the blade. 'I was cutting a piece of bread. We wondered whether you might be awake. Perhaps you'd like a slice, Mr Shakespeare?'

Shakespeare yawned. 'Bread, Mr Salisbury? Why, yes, that would suit me well. And a little milk if you have it. To settle my gut.'

'Then bread and milk you shall have.'

'Thank you.' Shakespeare stepped forward into the room. It was large and light, with many books. Some of them, he noted, were stacked high and had similar covers, as though newly printed and ready for distribution. Catholic tracts from the seminaries, perhaps?

'How are you feeling, Mr Shakespeare?' Babington asked solicitously. He was stretched out on the settle, feet up and hands behind his head. 'I must confess you look rather ragged and not a little shabby.'

'I *feel* yet worse than I look.'

'Almost as tattered as Thomas Salisbury here. You, however, will tidy yourself up and go bravely, whereas Mr Salisbury will always look like a wild man of the moors. Even Mr Mane's ministrations can do nothing for his hair and his tailor has quite given up on him.' Babington laughed and swung round to make space beside him. 'Come, sit with me while Mr Salisbury fetches you sustenance.'

Shakespeare took the offer of the seat with gratitude. Not for the first time he was struck by Babington's easy elegance and good looks. It was not surprising that he had caught the Queen of Scots' eye when he delivered letters to her in the years she was held in Sheffield Castle. How different might his life have been had he chosen instead to fawn over Elizabeth, for she would undoubtedly have been won over. He could have cheered her days with jests and scandalous tittle-tattle.

'Where is Mr Tichbourne?' Shakespeare asked. 'I recall he was with you when you saved me from those young dogs.'

'He has returned to his own lodgings near St Bart's. Chidiock needs his sleep, poor wretch. He has the constitution of a young maid and we have drunk him into oblivion. Likewise you, it seems.'

Shakespeare affected to bridle. 'I seem to remember it was a fine, merry feast and that my cup was filled as fast as any man's.'

'I noticed that you conversed with Mr Tilney. What did you talk about?'

Salisbury returned with a cup of milk and Shakespeare drank it down. It was rich and thick with cream, the way he liked it. He nodded his appreciation to Salisbury, handed back the cup and picked up the hunk of bread from the platter that had been placed at his side. He took a bite and chewed. The two men were waiting for him to speak, but he did not hurry in his eating. He needed to consider his response carefully. When he had swallowed the morsel and patted his mouth with his sleeve, he met his host's eye. 'He said I should follow you in all things, Mr Babington.'

'What else?'

'He expressed surprise that Walsingham let me out.'

Babington smiled. 'That is indeed a matter of interest, and has been ever since Mr Savage introduced you to our little band of brothers.'

'I have been completely open with you, Mr Babington. Ask me questions and I will answer them.'

Babington put up a palm. 'Mr Shakespeare, I beg you, do not feel insulted. Be assured that I was most happy that you joined our cheery group of diners and drinkers, for I know you come of good Warwickshire stock, wedded to the true faith. You are familiar with the mass and you are confessed. But I must tell you that there are those among us . . .' His gaze strayed to Salisbury, then back to Shakespeare '. . . who have their doubts about you. Can a man work for both Walsingham and the Pope? Some men wonder whose cause you truly serve.'

Shakespeare frowned, then spread his hands. 'They could ask the same question of every man at the Plough. What of Tilney or Abingdon? They are sworn guards of the Queen's body. Who do they serve? Even Mr Salisbury here, who can say what is in *his* heart? Was he not brought up as ward to the demon Leicester?'

'You are right, of course. We must all have faith and trust in each other, otherwise Walsingham and Burghley will have won the battle before the trumpet is even sounded. But I am obliged to mention it, for it is a matter that comes up time and again. One of our number whispered to me last night that you were known to be a deal too close to Mr Secretary and that you should be shunned.'

Shakespeare raised both his hands. 'Mr Babington, Mr Salisbury, if you do not trust me, then I will bid you good fortune and withdraw from your company this moment, for I can well understand your fears and I have no wish to cause you sleepless nights, let alone difficulties with your fellows.'

'Can you not say anything in your defence? A single word to prove where your loyalties truly lie? For whether you are with us or against us, you must know that there is a great deal more to our band than a gathering of friends enjoying good food and speaking our minds. Any man of wit must see that.'

Shakespeare shook his head. 'You must take me or leave me. And I will not hold it against you if you cast me out. Now, if it please you, I must depart, for Mr Secretary will require my presence soon after dawn so that he may set me on the trail of papists and traitors . . .'

This elicited the faintest of smiles from Babington and a scowl from Salisbury.

'Forgive me. It was in poor taste.' Shakespeare stood up, as did Babington. After the briefest of hesitations, they shook hands.

'Good morrow to you, Mr Shakespeare.'

'I would speak with you more when my head is clear. Perhaps I can calm your fears.'

'Come to me in the early afternoon and have a trim. We will be at Mane's of Bishopsgate. Come see how he struggles with Mr Salisbury's thatch! And rest assured, sir, I have no desire to cast you out. I think you can be of more value on the inside of our band than ever you could be on the outside. But we must proceed cautiously.'

'I understand.' Shakespeare bowed. 'And I thank you once again for intervening on my behalf. And you, Mr Salisbury, for the use of your bed these past hours.' He held out his hand in farewell, but Salisbury declined to take it.

A strange image flashed into Shakespeare's mind: the schoolroom at the King's New School in Stratford, where the master, Mr Hunt, was telling the boys of the lives of the Romans and of the plot against Julius Caesar. 'Brutus was the leader of the assassins, but it was Gaius Cassius who drove him to his cruel act – and Cassius who struck the first blow.' A picture now came to him: the face of Babington attached to Brutus's body, and Salisbury's atop the humourless Cassius's.

Chapter 10

WALSINGHAM GAZED AT Shakespeare's bruised head and winced. 'I think Mr Mills rather overdid it.'

'Sir Francis?' Shakespeare could not conceal his irritation. Did he detect a dark smile lurking around the corners of his master's usually dour mouth?

'Forgive me. It was my idea. I felt it would not work if I told you beforehand, but I thought it would help.'

'I am still unsure—'

'I asked Mr Mills to organise a mild attack on you, in the sight of your fellow diners at the Plough Inn. He found three young apprentices and gave them a shilling each for their night's work. They were supposed to knock you to the ground, throw insults at you and threaten you with a dagger. They were not supposed to damage you, but it had to be believable.'

'They could have killed me!'

'No, no. If it had got out of hand, Mr Mills would have called off his hounds. He was watching and directing them from the shadows. The idea was to show the others in your band of traitors and drinkers that you were truly one of them, suffering for the cause as they do. It worked, did it not?'

Not for the first time, Shakespeare tried to peer deep into Walsingham's dark eyes and discern his true character, but it was a wasted effort. Perhaps his wife or children knew him well, but no one else was allowed into the secret corners of Mr Secretary's devious soul. 'Yes,' he said. 'It worked. A little too well. Babington had to rescue me.'

'Well there you are. Safe and sound and a little closer to your prey.'

They were in Walsingham's austere private room at his Seething Lane mansion. Having arrived home two hours before dawn, Shakespeare had managed no more than an hour and a half of sleep. Then he washed himself thoroughly and hastily ate a breakfast of eggs and ham, prepared for him by the new housemaid, while he caught up with the news from Boltfoot about his vain quest for those who knew Will Cane. Shakespeare heard the tale with interest.

'Go to the watchman. Find this woman again,' he ordered Boltfoot. 'She must know something. But be wary. I fear you are more likely to be robbed than assisted.'

Boltfoot nodded. 'I don't think they liked me asking questions.'

'Then employ subtlety, Boltfoot.'

'Yes, master.'

Boltfoot grunted but Shakespeare could tell he was unhappy; perhaps he did not understand the word *subtlety*. Well, he didn't have the time or inclination to explain it. He wanted answers and Boltfoot might now be well placed to find them.

'And master, I must tell you that the watch and the whore now know that I work for you and where you live.'

'That is of no consequence. I have nothing to hide. Keep up your good work. Someone must know the truth about Will Cane and this murder.'

He dismissed Boltfoot, finished his eating and strode down the street to his appointed meeting with his own master. Now here he was, learning that the attack on him outside the Plough had been ordered by Sir Francis himself.

There was a knock on the door and a messenger entered with a paper, which he placed on the table before Walsingham, then bowed and left.

Walsingham broke the seal and began reading. 'Was Savage there last night?' he inquired, not looking up from his letter.

'At the Plough? No. I had expected him but he did not arrive. I will seek him out later today.'

'He is losing his nerve.'

'Do you have some information?'

Walsingham held up the letter. 'Gifford said as much to Tom Phelippes. He told him that Savage is altogether too comfortable at Barnard's Inn and makes no effort towards fulfilling his vow.'

'Are Mr Phelippes and Gifford still at Chartley?'

'Yes. Hopefully there will be movement there soon. But it is Savage that concerns me here and now. We cannot let him slip away. Keep his courage strong. Keep him zealous.'

Indeed, he had had such worries about Savage himself. Why would a man about to martyr himself for his faith be so diligent in his law studies? However, he did not voice his fears. 'He is not a man to break his vow. Babington calls him "the Instrument". Like a cat, he watches and waits his moment.'

Walsingham folded the paper and put it to one side. 'The *Instrument*? Meaning what I imagine it to mean?'

'That he is the instrument by which Her Majesty is to be assassinated. That is what one must assume, though no one has spoken openly of it, and certainly not Savage himself.'

'They do not trust you well enough yet. Do you think they might turn on you?'

'Thomas Salisbury might. He is certainly one of those with a desperate air. He intends to see this thing through. And last night there were two newcomers – two members of the Queen's Guard. I fear their purpose.'

'Ah, Tilney and Abingdon. Fear not, they will never again get within a furlong of Her Majesty. How many are there now in these Pope's White Sons?'

'At least twenty, perhaps twice that number. They come and go. Babington tries to recruit more members and, to that end, he takes inordinate risks. He is becoming increasingly careless, hence my own acceptance. But what else can he do? All the men he wants are members of the gentry or are at court or are associated with the inns of court. Every one of them could be a spy sent to watch him, but it is a risk he is willing to take. Perhaps he is too vain and foolish to believe he could be duped. As for me, he thinks it a great coup to have someone from inside your office. I am to be their dog, barking when you get too close.'

Walsingham said nothing for a few moments. There was utter silence in the room. He was thinking. At last he sighed. 'There are so many strands, John. Am I overreaching? The costs rise daily. I have never seen Sir Robert Huckerbee in such a sweat as he hands me Treasury gold and silver.'

Shakespeare knew that Walsingham did not expect a reply. Anyway, his own thoughts were elsewhere, specifically a loft room in Shoreditch.

'Are you with me, John?'

'Mr Secretary?'

'For a moment, I rather imagined your thoughts to be drifting.'

'Forgive me.'

'Tell me more about Babington. He is married I believe.'

'He has a wife but he has left her at the family home, Dethick Manor in Derbyshire, with their small daughter. As you know, he has spent most of the time since their marriage either in London or France, making mischief with the Scots Queen's people. The fact of his marriage does not necessarily mean a great deal to a man such as Babington.'

'And his closest friends are Tichbourne and Salisbury.'

'Yes, he met Tichbourne in France. What we know of Tichbourne is that he comes of recusant stock in Hampshire. The whole family has been questioned about their popish practices. As I said, the one that worries me more is Thomas Salisbury. I thought for a moment last night that he meant to kill me.'

Walsingham shrugged. He did not expect his intelligencers to worry about a small matter such as their own lives. He carried on with his train of questioning. 'Is there more than common friendship between Babington and these two men?'

Shakespeare understood the slant of Walsingham's question. 'Possibly. He now lives at Hern's Rents in Holborn, but it is only a few months since he lodged with Salisbury near Temple. Whether they were bedfellows, I know not, if that is what you mean.'

'That is precisely what I mean. Are they Christ's fellows? Which brings me to my next question: do you think Babington would fall for Robin Poley's charms? I want someone with him twenty-four hours in the day. *You* cannot be with him and keep a close watch on Goodfellow Savage, but Robin surely could.'

Robin Poley. It was a name that had come up before in recent weeks. Poley was a retainer of Walsingham's daughter Frances and her husband Philip Sidney, and lived with the household at Mr Secretary's country property, Barn Elms, a few miles upstream from London. What was it about this young man that made Walsingham believe he could be employed as an intelligencer? The only time Shakespeare had met him, he had seemed obsequious and ungenuine. However, he clearly had wit, charm and a handsome face. Most importantly, he was a Catholic – and known to be so among the papists of London. In short, Shakespeare realised, he was precisely the sort of shallow, garish man that Babington liked.

'It is a possibility,' Shakespeare said.

'Let us see how we might introduce them. Think on it, John. If his inclinations are as I suspect, I doubt he will be able to resist young Robin.'

Shakespeare looked up at the house on Aldermanbury that had belonged to Nicholas Giltspur. Aldermanbury was perhaps the loveliest of London streets and this building only added to its lustre. It was a goodly sized, well-maintained mansion with an arched stone gateway that was carved with the effigies of saints; evidence of its clerical past.

Until half a century ago it had been part of a great abbey; now it had been renovated and beautified and was a rich man's dwelling. But that man was dead and his widow was in hiding.

Shakespeare handed the reins of his horse to a groom and strode up the flagged path to the great double doors. They were fronted by two guards, each with drawn sword held aloft so that the blades made lines to the sky in front of their noses. As he approached, they clicked their heels.

'I would speak with the chief steward,' he said to one of the guards.

'Wait here. I'll fetch Mr Sorbus.'

The guard went inside, leaving Shakespeare outside with the other sentry, then returned two minutes later in company with a small man, as slender as a maiden. He wore the plain black coat, hose and falling band of a senior steward.

'Yes?' The word was curt and unhelpful.

'Are you Mr Sorbus? I am inquiring into the death of Mr Giltspur.'

'Yes, I am Sorbus. Who are you? What is your interest?'

'My name is John Shakespeare. I was once a friend of Mr Giltspur's widow.'

'You will have to tell me rather more than that, Mr Shakespeare.'

'I am a Queen's officer, assistant secretary to Sir Francis Walsingham.'

'And he is interested in Mr Giltspur's murder, is he? I had not thought a common murder the territory of so great a personage.'

'No, this is nothing to do with Mr Secretary. It is personal. But nor would I call it a common murder. Indeed, it is most uncommon – and inexplicable. As I said, Katherine Giltspur was a friend. I wish to know what happened and why, for I find it hard to believe that she hired someone to kill any man, let alone her husband.'

Sorbus breathed a dismissive sigh. 'The facts are plain. Every man has heard them from the killer's own mouth, and the absence of Mrs Giltspur must speak for itself. She ran away like a thief in the night on hearing of the death of her husband. What grieving widow would do that?'

'I would come in a while and speak with you, Mr Sorbus. I would also speak with other members of your staff.'

'That is not possible.'

'Why? Do you have something to hide?'

'Good day, sir.' He jerked his chin towards the sentries. 'Escort this man from the premises.'

Shakespeare felt deep frustration and helplessness as he rode away. The steward, Sorbus, had been uncooperative, but perhaps his own rejoinder had been a little too sharp.

The problem was that without Walsingham's authority, he had no power of interrogation, nor warrant to enter Giltspur House; and Walsingham would hardly wish one of his principal intelligencers to be taking an interest in a domestic crime, however sensational and unusual it might be.

The rainstorm was now a distant memory and the day was fine. London looked its most beautiful and one could almost ignore the summer stench of the middens and sewage kennels as he rode the short distance along flower-lined streets. He tethered his horse beneath a spreading plane tree in the church-yard of St Paul's, then went towards the cool crypt where the Searcher of the Dead did his work.

He had first met Joshua Peace in Warwickshire almost four years earlier. Joshua was the son of Mother Peace, who had been searcher in the county for longer than anyone could recall. Many had shunned her, fearing her as a witch or necro-mancer. It was a slur that also stuck to her son among the more ignorant of the rural peasantry, but the truth – as Shakespeare knew – was very different, for Joshua had travelled widely in the Italian lands and cities and had learnt much from the great artists and anatomists. That was why Shakespeare, with Walsingham's agreement, had arranged for him to come away from Warwickshire and place himself instead at the service of the City of London.

Peace was pulling strands of tangled hair from the dead eyes of a woman's corpse. He turned and smiled. 'John, this is a pleasant surprise.'

'Thank you, Joshua. I have not heard many welcoming words this morning.' His eyes strayed to the mouldering body of the woman laid out on the slab. He quickly looked away, nausea welling up. 'And if you have any potions for a cup-shotten head then do not keep them from me.'

'We could take some wine, if you wish. The Three Tuns serves a goodly vintage.'

'Perhaps a cup of small ale.'

Peace removed his bloody apron and hung it from a hook

embedded in the damp stone wall. 'Come then – and tell me what has brought you here.'

At the tavern, they sat together in a small booth where they would not be overheard. 'It is about my old friend Kat Whetstone.'

Peace's eyes brightened. 'Well, well, Kat. Yes, how is she? I have not seen her in an age.' And then his smile faded. 'I thought I heard that you and she—'

'You are right. We are no longer together. In truth, Joshua, she left me. But that was many months ago and she has since been married and widowed – and has landed herself in great peril. I believe you examined the body of her late husband, Mr Nicholas Giltspur.'

Peace looked aghast. 'Is she the widow? God's blood, John, I had no notion.'

'No, nor did I. But do you know the tale told of her?'

'If she is Giltspur's widow, then I fear I do. She has an appointment with the hangman, that much is certain.'

'You have met her more than once. Do you believe her capable of so heinous a crime?'

Peace spread his hands helplessly. 'I – I have no opinion on the subject. You are the one who knew her best, so I must be guided by you. *Is* she innocent, John?'

Shakespeare clenched his lips tight, then shook his head. 'I suppose not, for why else would the murderer, Cane, say such things?'

'And yet your face tells me that you do not believe her guilty, which is why you are here. You are hoping that I found something when I examined Giltspur's corpse.'

'I know you didn't, for I have spoken to Recorder Fleetwood. Giltspur was slain by a single stab to the throat with a bollock-dagger. That is the testimony you gave, is it not? And it accords with everything said by the witnesses and the killer himself.'

'Indeed, and I still have the weapon. It was thrust from the left, beneath the extremity of the jaw, piercing both the great arteries. He knew exactly what he was doing and there is no doubt that it caused Mr Giltspur's death. The blood drained from him as quickly as from a beast at the slaughter.'

'Can I see the body?'

'It has already gone for burial at St Mary, Aldermanbury.'

Shakespeare supped his weak ale and felt more refreshed than he had all morning, but no happier. 'Then I fear there is nothing more I can do for her.'

'And yet . . .'

'Joshua?'

'Finish your ale, John. I have something to show you.'

Chapter 11

THE ROTTING CORPSE of the woman on the slab was still uncovered. Shakespeare tried to avert his gaze. Joshua caught his eye and laughed without malice, then placed a sheet over the dead woman.

'Does the look of death and the stench never unsettle you, Joshua?'

'I was born to it. My mother took me with her whenever she went into a house to examine a body, and I helped her. I feel no more uncomfortable with the dead than with the living.'

'Few have your stomach, I think. Now tell me, what did you wish to show me?'

'I have another corpse here, one that I think you should see.'

'Not this woman?'

'No.'

'Then who is it?'

Peace hesitated as though unsure how far to trust his visitor.

Shakespeare soothed his worries. 'Joshua, you well know that you can entrust me with anything – just as I once placed dangerous information into your safe keeping.'

'Yes, of course. It was mere caution on my part. Wariness has become a habit with me over the years.' He took a deep breath, then nodded quickly. 'Very well, I bought the corpse from the Smithfield hangman.'

Shakespeare was yet more intrigued. 'The body of Will Cane?'

'Yes. I paid five shillings for it. I am sure you are as aware as I am that revealing this to anyone else could lead to a great amount of trouble, both for myself and for the executioner.'

'Why? Why did you buy it?'

'I wished to examine it.'

'You will have to explain further. Surely, the cause of his death was self-evident – to wit, hanging by the neck until his breathing and heart stopped. I saw it myself. What could you have hoped to learn?'

Peace pushed open the door to the adjoining room, where he kept the tools of his trade and corpses awaiting examination. 'Come through.'

Will Cane's body was on a narrow wooden table. He had been sliced open from the throat, all down the chest and through his abdomen to his privy parts. His ribs had been pulled apart and fixed back with iron appliances, thus exposing his internal organs.

Shakespeare held back, disinclined to look too closely. 'What have you been doing to him? He reminds me of a beast after the butcher has been at work.'

'I dissect the cadavers of hanged felons to further my knowledge of anatomy. It seems to me that they may as well serve some useful purpose in death, for few have done much for the world in their short and wretched lives. The great anatomists of Bologna and Padua believe that once the inner workings of the body are understood, we will know how to cure its defects. And I agree with them.'

Shakespeare had no argument with Peace's thinking, but he was concerned by the risk the searcher was taking. 'Clearly, I will say nothing, Joshua. But you must be careful in this work. Have you thought of trying to join the Company of Barber-Surgeons? I do believe they have licence to dissect four criminals a year. Otherwise you are in peril, not least from the surgeons. There are already those who believe you to be a necromancer and there are many jealous of your position here. Be circumspect, I beg you. Like me, you have enemies to contend with in this town.'

'Fear not, I take precautions.'

'Then, Joshua, why are you showing me this body? What relevance can it have?'

'Look more closely, John.'

He moved forward and gazed into the cavity of the dead man. He was repulsed by what he saw, for it did not look at all natural. Nothing was as he had expected. Attached to the organs, there were shapes and growths that no body should contain. He turned back to Joshua with a questioning frown. 'Explain. What am I looking at?'

'A body riddled with impostumes and cankers. His bowels, his liver, his lungs. The tumours are everywhere and are malignant. He must have been exceedingly weak. And look at his face. The blood from his mouth has come straight from the lungs.' Peace ran a hand across the thin rim of hair that circled his own pate. 'Do you understand now?'

Shakespeare nodded. He had seen the point Peace was making even as he spoke the words. 'You are saying that he was dying anyway?'

'There is no doubt about it. His appointment with the hangman merely hastened his death by a day or two – and saved him a great deal of pain.'

'And he would have *known* that he was dying?'

'He could not have thought otherwise. There was nothing any physician or apothecary could have done to save him. He would have been certain that his end was close and must have raised a great effort of will to carry out his mission to kill Mr Giltspur. To tell the truth, I am astonished he had the strength to make his way to Fishmongers' Hall, let alone wield a knife. The trial itself, standing before the judge in Justice Hall, must have been torture. At the end, hanging would have been a blessing to him.'

Shakespeare looked more closely at the body. Wretched and emaciated, it was more bone and skin than flesh.

Peace stepped towards a shelf attached to the wall and picked up a weapon. Shakespeare took it from him and turned it over in his hands. It was an evil-looking thing that had done for Nicholas Giltspur. A narrow, slaughterman-sharp nine-inch blade protruded from a hilt-guard in the shape of a man's balls and a hilt in the manner of an erect prick.

'Can I take this?'

'You are welcome to it, John.'

Shakespeare began to think aloud. 'His mortal sickness would explain why he was unable to escape his pursuers. He only managed a few paces before they pulled him down. And the state of his lungs would explain his coughing fit at the scaffold. But how will this help Kat? Indeed, can we now deduce that she is innocent, or not?'

'That is for you to work out. I merely deal in facts. All I can tell you is that this man died of strangulation by the noose, but that he would have died soon enough anyway. These are facts that would be of no interest to a court of law, even if I was in a position to present them. If you have had any dealings with Recorder Fleetwood, you will know that nothing will override a dying man's testimony. To him such things are sacred. Why would a man who knows he must meet his maker in a few minutes go to his death with the mortal sin of a lie on his lips? As to Cane's motives, that is for you to consider.'

Shakespeare did not need Peace's help on the question of motive, for there was an obvious one: knowing he was dying anyway, Will Cane had agreed to commit murder fully intending to be apprehended and executed. Which meant he could not have been committing the crime for money, as he had claimed, but to destroy both Nicholas Giltspur and his wife. But why? Shakespeare rubbed his brow and felt the bruise where he had been kicked. Perhaps he wasn't thinking clearly. Perhaps there was another possibility that *did* involve money. What if Cane had been hired to commit the crime on the understanding that the money was to be paid to someone else after his death? Someone close to him like a wife, or child who would otherwise be left destitute once he was gone.

The question then was this: who else apart from Kat would have stood to gain from the death of Nicholas Giltspur? Only one person could answer that.

He rode to Shoreditch at a strong canter, weaving his horse in and out of the wagons and livestock with reckless haste. When he arrived at the house by the Curtain, he pushed open the door without knocking. Oswald Redd was at his workbench and turned in shock, evidently not pleased to see him.

'Mr Redd, forgive my sudden intrusion. I have urgent business with Kat.'

'How dare you walk in like this? You have interrupted my work. I must mend this gown by the next performance. Please leave immediately, Mr Shakespeare.'

'It is not you I wish to see, Mr Redd, but Kat.' His voice was low but pressing.

'She is not here. Now go!'

'Mr Redd, I have no intention of leaving until I have seen her. Is she in the loft?'

'No, she is not here. No one is here. Now please be gone, sir.'

'Then where is she?'

Redd looked as though he would explode. He was shorter than Shakespeare and armed only with tailoring tools, but his furious eyes suggested he would happily take on an army in his present mood.

'Mr Redd, I do not wish to hurt you, but I will have my way.'

'God damn you, Shakespeare, we have a safer place. She came here only to meet you. Do you think she would entrust the knowledge of her whereabouts to a Walsingham man?'

Had she really said that? Had she really not trusted him? Why, after all this time, did Kat still have the power to make him feel betrayed? He fought to contain his feelings, instead concentrating on Oswald Redd's raw emotions. Rivalry would do neither of them any good – and would certainly not help Kat. He forced a little smile, intended to mollify his host. 'Mr Redd, I am here to help.'

'I do not need your help.'

'If you do not cooperate with me, then you will be harming what little chance Kat has of escaping the noose.'

'Why do you want her?'

'As I said, I have urgent business with her – information that may be to her benefit. Questions to ask . . .'

'Then tell me – and I will pass it to her. Or if you prefer, write a letter for me to deliver.'

'No. I want to see her.'

Redd shrugged, immovable.

'Mr Redd, you have to trust me.'

'No, Mr Shakespeare, I do not.'

Shakespeare was finding it increasingly difficult to stifle his fury. This was going nowhere. Perhaps Redd was lying; perhaps she was still here, hidden. He drew his sword and held it loosely at his side, not threatening but as a warning should

Redd decide to attack with scissors or some other utensil. 'I am going up through the house. I believe she is here.'

Redd turned away, realising perhaps that his poor choice of implements could not compete against an unsheathed sword.

Shakespeare climbed the ladder to the first floor and searched. He looked about the rooms, calling her name softly. Unless there was some prepared hiding place, she could not be concealed here; and, anyway, why would she not come out on hearing his voice?

He ascended the ladder to the loft, which was almost dark, lit only by the light from the hatchway. He had no candle, but as his eyes grew accustomed to the gloom he saw that there was nowhere she could be hidden. Nor had she been living here. The space smelt dank and musty. Cobweb curtains had been knitted across the rafters and purlin. As he looked about in the dim light it became obvious that the room had never been inhabited and was used merely as storage for stage properties and costumes. Angrily, he descended the ladders to the ground floor where Redd was cutting a strip of woollen cloth with his iron scissors.

'God's blood, Mr Redd, I need information if I am to help. I have reason to believe now that Kat may be telling the truth, that Will Cane's accusation was false. And if this is so, as I hope and pray, then it means someone else was behind the murder. What I need from Kat is this: who else might have had a motive? Who stood to gain from Nicholas Giltspur's death and Kat's execution?'

Redd put down the scissors and crossed his arms across his chest. 'If that is all you wish to know, then the answer is simple. Giltspur's nephew, Arthur, will inherit all his wealth if Kat is disqualified. Arthur Giltspur, that is the man you want.'

'Do you know him? Where will I find him?'

'With some slut, most like. Try the stews of Southwark. Or else go to Giltspur's mansion in Aldermanbury, for Arthur was part of the household.'

'Does Kat believe he is behind the murder?'

'All she knows is that it was not her. Nicholas Giltspur was a man of immense wealth. Any such man will amass enemies as fast he he gains pearls.'

'And you, Mr Redd . . . you must have had cause to wish him harm, for did Kat not leave your bed for his? Perhaps you wanted vengeance on Nicholas Giltspur. Perhaps, too, you wished to bring Kat to her doom for betraying you so callously.'

Redd looked at Shakespeare as though he were mad. 'Hurt Katherine? How little you understand the human heart. Can you not tell that I love her? I would do anything for her . . . including killing you. Now go, sir, go.'

Chapter 12

As Shakespeare walked along Camomile Street, he spotted the red and white spiralling on the pole outside a newly painted frontage in the centre of a wood-frame building.

Mane's of Bishopsgate was the prime barber shop for the modish young men of London, a place to be seen and to converse over a goblet of brandy during the daylight hours. A place, too, of notoriety for the talk here was careless and subversive.

Babington was already there, along with many of those from the Plough Inn feast. There was a hubbub in the large front room where the barber and his assistants did their work amid high excitement and much laughter. Shakespeare estimated there were at least thirty young men present, including some who had not been at the dinner but whose names he noted mentally. He spotted half a dozen women among the menfolk and wondered who they were; sisters, most likely.

One thing was certain: they were all defiantly Catholic.

Many of the assembled members of Babington's band of friends drank their spirits and gossiped loudly. Others lounged in the barber's chairs, having their beards and hair dressed. Chidiock Tichbourne stood up from one of the chairs and admired his new-cut beard in a small mirror. He spotted Shakespeare and hailed him with a wave of the looking glass.

'Take this chair, Mr Shakespeare, take a chair and allow Mr Mane to trim you. A shorter cut is this year's mode. There is no finer barber in all of London. He will curl you or poll you, to suit your humour.' Tichbourne stroked his own newly shaved beard, which was trimmed to a point, and gazed at it once more in the looking glass. 'What say you to my *pique-devant*? Is it not the finest of fashions? Do I not look a little like the satanic Ralegh?'

'Very fine, Mr Tichbourne. And yet more devilish than Sir Walter. But please, you must allow me to thank you for your assistance last night. You were gone before I awoke from my drunken slumber.'

'It was nothing, sir, an adventure.'

Babington approached Shakespeare trailing young men in his wake. 'I am glad you have come. There is a purpose to our meeting here today. Some of us are to be painted for posterity and I would like you to be one with us.'

Shakespeare was shocked. 'A portrait? Is this wise?'

'What has wisdom to do with anything? If I were a wise man, I would be in Derbyshire tending my estates and dying a slow death of idle boredom.'

'But a portrait will serve to draw yet more attention our way . . .'

'Which is the point, precisely. My friends do not avert their eyes from the great wrongs inflicted on us by the odious men who would supplant the true faith. Our children and grand-children will look upon this picture and stand in awe. You will doubtless find fault with the inscription I have demanded: *Hi mihi sunt comites quos ipsa pericula ducunt.*'

'*These are my companions in danger.* This is madness.' Shakespeare looked around him at the barber and his apprentices. Who could know where *their* loyalties lay?

'I had believed you brave, Mr Shakespeare.'

'This is not about courage but staying alive long enough to bring about change.' Shakespeare sighed and affected a reassuring smile. 'I also wonder whether it would not be more shrewd to meet in private. You must know that any large gathering – such as this one – will be reported back to Walsingham. I know this because I see his reports day by day. London is full of scurvy villains who will scurry to Seething Lane with such tittle-tattle for the price of a gage of ale.'

Babington laughed and clapped Shakespeare about the shoulders. 'Sir, you will be afeared of shadows next. Walsingham can do nothing against us, for nothing is said that could be seen as sedition. We always speak with great circumspection, and couch our oratory in terms with which no man could find fault.'

Shakespeare knew this to be untrue. 'A few moments ago you spoke of odious men. Last night you drank to the death of usurpers . . .'

'I put no name to any odious men. Nor did I name any usurper. What man of loyalty would *not* think a usurper worthy of death? Would not Principal Secretary Walsingham and Lord Treasurer Burghley drink to such a thing?'

'This is sophistry. It will not save you if Richard Topcliffe or Justice Young get you on the rack. You must know that by the law of Henry the Eighth it is treason to call the sovereign a usurper.'

'Yes, I have heard that you spent some time studying law. Very well, you have made your point and I accept it in good grace, Mr Shakespeare. This is why we like you – for you do not fear to show us our faults and you reveal the workings of Mr Secretary's mind. But that is all for another time. Today our task is to be painted, and we will be, in the name of the Holy Mother – for our work is momentous and must be marked.'

'Valour alone is not enough, Mr Babington. You need sound judgement and caution, too.'

For a moment the charm slid from Babington's handsome face and a darkness crossed his brow. 'Perhaps if I had sound judgement I would allow Mr Salisbury to kill you.' And then he smiled. 'But I happen to believe you are of more value alive than dead.'

'And what would Mr Salisbury have me do to prove my loyalty to you and the Pope? Kill Walsingham, perhaps . . .'

'It would be a start.' From Babington's cheery expression and open, guileless eyes, a man might be forgiven for thinking that he was merely an eager young puppy, very pleased with himself but no threat to the commonwealth. 'Forget I said that, Mr Shakespeare. It was, indeed, unworthy. Now sit down in Mr Mane's chair and ask for his Marquess Otto cut. It will do wonders for your lean and straight face. You must look your best, for the painter is setting up his easel and mixing his paints in the back room and would have us all in line within the half-hour.'

Shakespeare was about to stand his ground when the door to the shop opened and two men walked in.

'Why, it is the Instrument himself,' Babington said with delight. 'Welcome, Goodfellow. And you have brought young Mr de Warre. The picture is almost complete. I think the painter will have to ink in a space and add Mr Salisbury at a later date.'

Shakespeare was relieved to have Babington's attentions turned elsewhere. He had found their exchange uncomfortable. Now he hung back while Babington greeted Goodfellow Savage and his companion, but Savage did not linger. He blinked in the gloom of the shop, squinted, then raised a hand in greeting to Shakespeare. He strode through the mass of young men, his powerful hand – so used to wielding weapons of war – outstretched in greeting. His grip was firm and strong and there was warmth in it.

'Well met, John Shakespeare.'

'Good day, Mr Savage. I had hoped to see you last night at the Plough.'

'My purse is empty. Having once captained a company of soldiers, I am now reduced to the lowest of the low at Barnard's Inn and so I must live on commons in the hall with my fellows.'

'Well, next time we dine, I shall be happy to stand your expense.'

Despite himself, Shakespeare always enjoyed the company of Goodfellow Savage. He recalled their first meeting the previous August, at an auberge in Calais as they both awaited the morning packet-boat home. Shakespeare was with Gilbert Gifford, who was heading in the other direction, towards Paris. Gifford and Shakespeare had known Savage would be there, for his movements had been tracked by Walsingham's man Henbird, and so it was easy to arrange an encounter.

At first Savage had been discomfited by the seemingly unplanned meeting with Gilbert Gifford. But Gifford's own feigned surprise and innocent manner had soon won him over. His looks were so boyish that men could not believe that one who seemed so young could have learnt to deceive. Men did not doubt Gilbert Gifford, to their cost.

Shakespeare and Savage had taken an instant liking to each other. With Gifford, they had spent a pleasant evening in the Calais inn, drinking wine and discussing the hoped-for end to the persecution of Catholics in England. It seemed they were all agreed that the sooner Mary Stuart ascended the throne and brought about the downfall of Walsingham, Leicester and Burghley, the better it would be for England and for Catholicism. The matter of Savage's vow to assassinate Queen

Elizabeth to facilitate this transfer of power was never mentioned. Nor, at that first meeting, was Shakespeare's association with Walsingham. That would come later and needed to be subtly introduced.

The chance came aboard the packet-boat to Dover. Gifford had stayed in France, so Shakespeare and Savage travelled together. The sky was blue but the crossing took many hours; the seas were pond-still and the sails barely filled so light was the wind.

'I must tell you, Mr Savage,' he had said, 'that I am employed in the service of Sir Francis Walsingham.'

The words cut the air like lightning. At first it seemed Savage had not heard them; then his hand stiffened as though it might reach for his dagger. 'Walsingham?'

'Yes.'

'Then you are my enemy.'

'No, sir, that is not so. I would be your friend, for we share religion. Nor am I alone in that regard among Mr Secretary's men. We work against the regime from within. He likes to keep us close, thinking to control us. In truth it enables us to keep *him* close. I know much of what he knows and I know his thoughts.'

Savage had pondered a few moments. Suddenly a breeze came up and caught his hat so that he had to clamp it to his head with his soldierly hand. 'Then that is enough,' he said at last. 'In battle, I have to make decisions in an instant and I will do so now, to trust you. My gut tells me you are a good man, and so I would value your friendship.'

'And I yours, Mr Savage.'

They had been hard words to utter, for he liked Goodfellow Savage and he knew that one day, perhaps very soon, he would most certainly be responsible for his death.

Now, in this crowded and noisy barber's shop, he felt that

same stab of betrayal once more. But it had to be done; Savage had sworn himself to his own doom.

'And who is this?' Shakespeare demanded as Savage's young companion joined them.

'This is Dominic de Warre, who has recently joined me in my lodgings at Barnard's.' He lowered his voice and spoke close to Shakespeare's ear. 'He is of the faith, a Pope's White Son.'

'Then he, too, is well met.' Shakespeare shook the young man's hand and studied his face. He looked no more than seventeen – certainly a fair deal younger than Babington's usual cronies, who were mostly in their twenties or a little older.

'You are Mr Shakespeare, are you not? I saw you once at Barnard's Inn.' The youth bowed respectfully as though Shakespeare were his tutor, a thing which might have been possible had Shakespeare not been taken from the law into the employment of Sir Francis Walsingham.

'I studied there a year before going up to Gray's. It is always a pleasure to return to Barnard's of an evening and help relieve Mr Savage's tedious hours of scholarship by forcing him to take wine with me. In truth, he does not usually take much persuading. Now tell me, Mr de Warre, do *you* consider following the law as a profession?'

'No, my stepfather says it is a precarious existence and that I would do better to return to our Lincolnshire estates, when they pass to me from my grandfather. He says I will need the law when I am raised to the magistracy and that such studies will sharpen any young man's mind and help with the drawing of contracts regarding my lands. Normally I would not listen to a word my stepfather says, for he is a cringing piece of work, but he does know the law.'

'Indeed.' And what, Shakespeare wondered, is one as young

as you doing here among these knaves and mischief-makers? Why in God's name has Savage brought you here? You are like a lamb in the company of wolves.

'And are you here because you wish to kill the so-called Queen of England, Mr Shakespeare? The *tyrant* of England as I should call her.'

Had he truly just said that? Openly in front of a man he had just met? Shakespeare began to reconsider his initial impression. Perhaps the lamb had wolf's teeth . . .

Savage seemed as appalled as Shakespeare and put a hand over the youth's mouth. 'Hush, Dominic, or we will wake up one morning and see your head decorating London Bridge.' He turned to Shakespeare. 'Forgive the boy, he is but a babe.'

Dominic de Warre broke free of the restraining hand, looked at Savage curiously, then walked away.

Savage managed an awkward smile. 'Well, I need my beard trimmed and I need brandy. Feel free to buy me one, John Shakespeare, for Walsingham's silver is much like another man's.'

Had it not been for his height and military bearing, Savage could almost have passed for an ill-nourished vagrant; his clothes were plain, old and ragged and his body was lean. Not for the first time, Shakespeare wondered how such a man, seemingly so good of cheer and kind of heart, could be a sworn assassin.

Babington was standing on one of the barber's chairs. He hammered the haft of his dagger on an upturned copper basin. 'Gentlemen, gentlemen,' he called as the hubbub died down and eyes turned his way, 'our painter awaits us. Let us make a fine show for God, the Pope and England.'

'God! The Pope! Freedom!' The words came from the tender mouth of Dominic de Warre.

Shakespeare shuddered. Surely this cry must have been heard in the street. He grasped Goodfellow Savage by his arms. 'Come away, Mr Savage. Do not partake in this madness. I have warned Mr Babington that this notion of a portrait is poison.'

Savage hovered, then nodded brusquely. 'Yes, you are right. Let us find refreshment elsewhere.' He looked around for his young companion, but he had disappeared into the crowd. 'No, I must stay. I cannot go without young Dominic.'

'He is the main reason we need to go. He is a danger to all who congregate near him.'

'He is young. I have a responsibility . . .'

'Stay then. But I implore you, do not have your likeness painted. Walsingham will not need to hear from *my* lips what has occurred here this day; every maggot and kennel rat in Bishopsgate will be scurrying to him with tales of sedition . . . and if he finds the painting, he will have evidence a plenty with names and faces to match.'

Chapter 13

SHAKESPEARE PUSHED OPEN the front door and was met by the new maidservant, who appeared to be flustered and a little fearful.

'What is it, Jane?'

'You have a visitor, master. He is in your solar.'

'Jane, you must put visitors in the anteroom. My solar is my own room. I keep private papers there.'

She nodded hurriedly, like a fowl at its feed. 'Sir, I know that, but I could not stop him. He pushed past me and climbed up through the house. Mr Cooper was not here to help me, so I knew not what to do.'

'Well, who is this man?'

'He said he had many names, but that I might call him Mr Gifford or Gilbert if I preferred.'

Many names. Yes, Gilbert Gifford liked to go by a host of different names: in written correspondence, Walsingham and his men referred to him as Number Four or the Secret Party. When abroad in France or the Low Countries, he liked to use the names Pietro or Cornelys. To the French embassy, he was simply Colderin. It was enough to confuse friends, let alone enemies. So he was back from Chartley; surely that could mean but one thing. 'Very well, I will go to him presently, but first tell me: has there been word from Boltfoot?'

'No, master.'

'When he arrives home, tell him not to venture out without first consulting me. I have new information for him. Oh, and Jane, bring small ale to the solar.'

'Yes, master.'

Gilbert Gifford was lounging on the settle by the window. He had a book on his lap and looked for all the world like a boy at his studies. He did not raise his eyes as Shakespeare entered the room.

'Mr Gifford, what in the name of God are you doing here?'

Gifford dragged his smooth face away from the printed page. 'Why, reading this volume while I waited for you to appear, Mr Shakespeare.'

'You are insane to have come. What if my house is being watched? Are you utterly without wit? You could blow all our plans to dust.'

Gifford laughed, totally unconcerned by the onslaught. 'I took great care, Mr Shakespeare. No one is watching your house. Perhaps you are not as important to them as you think you are. I believe you are quite safe.'

'I wish I shared your confidence. You will never come here again. You know how to contact me: send messages via Mr Mills's office and we will meet at an appointed place.'

Gifford waved a hand in the air. 'I do not have time for such stuff. I dared to hope my appearance here would be a most pleasant surprise, for I come as the bearer of good news. The fish has taken the bait. It seemed to me that you should be among the first to know.'

'Indeed?' His voice retained its sharpness, but he could not fail to be interested.

'Yes, indeed. Letters from the Scots Queen came out of Chartley in the beer keg two days ago and were then handed to me by the Honest Man. I gave them to Mr Paulet and he passed them to Mr Phelippes who is presently deciphering them. Tomorrow they will be brought up here to London where they will be returned to me, resealed by Mr Gregory, and when Mr Secretary gives the word I will convey them to the French embassy intact.'

'That is most excellent news. Do we know anything about the letters?'

'We know that one is addressed to Anthony Babington.'

Shakespeare did not smile but his heart lurched. So the bait was not only taken, but the fish was on the hook. It was exactly as Walsingham had hoped and planned. Perhaps things were moving at last.

'And so, Mr Shakespeare, I have a night in London with nothing to do . . .'

'Then we shall dine together here at my expense. I will have food sent in. Fine roasts and good wine.'

Gifford sucked in air through his small white teeth. 'I had rather hoped to reacquaint myself with the Smith sisters, whose company I find most pleasurable. If you would just tell me where I may find them.'

'You know I can't do that.'

'But you can bring them to me?'

'It is possible.'

'Then do it, I entreat you, Mr Shakespeare. It is only the pleasure of their company that keeps me in England at all. Without them, I shall feel compelled to take myself away from these dangerous tasks that I perform on Mr Secretary's behalf. I know from experience that the young ladies of Paris have much to commend them.'

What was it Walsingham had said? *I do not care what Gifford needs or wants, he will have it. For without him, our carefully constructed house collapses.* And so he must have the Smith sisters. Thus far, their trysts with Gifford had been arranged by Tom Phelippes, but now it was Shakespeare's task.

'Then I shall do my best on your behalf. Allow me a little time, if you would, and I shall secure their services before dark. Will that suffice?'

'Indeed it will, Mr Shakespeare. Indeed it will. And in the meantime, I should like to become better acquainted with your maidservant, who is a most comely wench.'

Shakespeare shook his head decisively. 'No, Mr Gifford, that will *not* do. If I hear that you have interfered with my maid in any way, or even attempted to molest her, then I promise that you will never see the Smith sisters again. I will also see that you are pilloried for lewd dealings – and that your ears are left nailed to the crossbar.'

'Sir, you drive a very hard bargain. Very well, I shall sit here, as quiet as a mole, and read your Montaigne which, I must say, contains most cunning and forthright guidance on the ways of the world. Here, listen to this if you will.' He opened the book and quickly found the spot, then marked the passage with his index finger. '*Quand je joue avec mon chat, qui sait s'il ne s'amuse pas plus de moi que je le fais de lui.*' He spoke with the fluency of a Frenchman, then translated unnecessarily for Shakespeare's benefit. 'When I play with my cat, who knows whether the cat is in truth playing with me.' He smiled. 'That is a rough translation, but do you not think it sums up our own Mr Secretary and his devices? Always be wary of your master, Mr Shakespeare, for he plays with us all. Even as he lauds my services and dispenses gold and gratitude, I know very well that he is planning my execution.'

'Your imagination knows no bounds, Gifford.'

'We shall see. Now go and find the sisters for I have a hunger that must be sated.'

'I will send for you when I have them at the house in

Holborn. Wear your hood and cape. I want none to see your face as you leave this house.'

The ward watch was waiting for Boltfoot at the Postern Gate to the north of the Tower.

'Mr Cooper . . .'

He stopped and nodded by way of reply.

'If you will just follow me, you may learn something about Will Cane.'

'Where is the woman . . . the whore named Em?'

'All will be revealed. There is someone else who wishes to see you.'

'Who? Speak.'

'I cannot say.'

Boltfoot noticed that the man, whose name he recalled as Potken, seemed timid. But afraid of what – or whom?

'If you cannot say who I am to see, then why should I come with you? For all I know you have a gang of cutpurses waiting for me. But if that is your plan, it is ill founded for I have brought no money and nothing of value. Any attempt to rob me will bear no fruit.'

'There is no trap, Mr Cooper. But I warn you now that you will be required to wear a blindfold about your eyes for the last part of our journey.'

The Smith sisters lived in a small stone-built house by the river, not far south of Westminster Hall. The door was answered by a manservant who bowed low and showed Shakespeare through to a comfortable parlour, which was deliciously cool. He was offered refreshment by the brightly accoutred lackey, but declined.

'Then if it please you to wait, sir, I shall see if the misses Smith are able to receive you.'

The room was rich but not gaudy, nothing to suggest that this was the home of the two most celebrated whores in the proximity of London. It could as well have been the town abode of a sober merchant. The two young women arrived within a few minutes. They were dressed in fine clothes as though they were about to venture forth to the concerts with the goodwives of the guilds. Neither of them would be taken for a harlot, for their attire was neither garish nor unduly revealing. Both of them smiled airily at Shakespeare and curtsied with the merest hint of mockery.

'Mr Shakespeare, what a pleasure, sir.'

It was the elder of the two who spoke, the one called Eliza. She was about the same height as her younger sister, Beth, and a little fuller of figure, but there really was very little to distinguish them, for they were both slender, smooth-skinned and with eyes that invited men in. They were fair of face and light of manner, both remarkable specimens. He estimated their ages as early to mid twenties, but it was difficult to be sure. Perhaps their tender-seeming age was mere artifice and the lack of physical work beyond the bedroom. That and the absence of child-bearing, the event that wore so many women into old age and early death.

'Forgive me for coming to you at such short notice, but I have urgent need of your services this night. Mr Gifford has returned and I fear we will lose him if you do not go to him.'

'Ah, the little pink pigling,' Beth said, laughing. 'He is magnificent, is he not, sir?'

'We love our little Gilbert pigling, Mr Shakespeare.'

Shakespeare almost sighed with relief. He had been ready to do battle with them, preparing his arguments both wheedling and threatening. 'Then you will come?'

'Is this at Mr Secretary's behest?'

'Yes.'

'Then if we have any appointments we shall most certainly cancel them. Mr Secretary is our most valued client. Not that he uses our special services for his *own* gratification, you understand. I believe him to be a man of great austerity and delicacy in matters of the flesh and I know he employs us only for the good of England and Her Majesty. Yes, I believe we shall most certainly accommodate you. Are we agreed on this, Beth?'

'We are, sister dear.'

Shakespeare looked from one to the other and was pleased to see that they were in earnest. 'That is exceeding good news. You will be handsomely rewarded, as always.'

'Mr Shakespeare, it is monstrous vulgar to talk of such things before the service is provided. Time enough, sir, time enough. You do not need to concern yourself about such matters.'

'Then how long do you need to prepare yourselves? I would have you at the Holborn house as soon as possible, for I am fearful that our pigling will fly without your company.'

'We will come at once, though it would be a fine thing to see a pigling fly.'

'Never be careless of your pigling, Mr Shakespeare. Foxes like piglings for dinner and crows do love to pluck out their eyes.'

'And when their mother sows try to protect them they do oft-times crush them to death beneath their great weight.'

'Take care of our little pigling, Mr Shakespeare.'

They had curious sing-song voices, tinkling like water over rocks. It occurred to Shakespeare that it was probably an affectation, as, indeed, was their affectionate talk of the pink pigling. They might be costly, but they were whores. Nothing more. That was no concern of his, however, so he played their game. 'That is what I am trying to do. Now then, let us be moving. Will you change your attire?'

'Does our appearance displease you?'

'Indeed not, but—'

'But you thought we would travel in undergarments of silk with silver ties. No, we shall carry our bag of toys with us and come as we are. Beth, perhaps you would order the carriage prepared.'

'I shall, sister dear.' She gave another little curtsy and left the room.

Eliza touched Shakespeare's arm as though to reassure him. It was only the lightest of touches, but it sent a burning surge of lust straight to his loins so that he gasped. She smiled at him knowingly. Oh, she understood well enough the desire she could inflict with a movement of the lips or eyes or the tiniest butterfly fluttering of her fingers.

'Will it be the whole night through?'

'Yes. And I beg you, keep him hungry. Keep him so hungry that he will needs come to you again and again the whole summer long.'

'No man has wearied of us yet, Mr Shakespeare.'

Shakespeare rode behind their carriage. All he knew about the Smith sisters was that their mother had been in the same line of work as her daughters and that she had been favoured by men of high rank and privilege. Phelippes had told him that Eliza was the daughter of an earl and that Beth's father had been a baron, but he had said it with a sly grin that meant it could as well be invention as truth.

Within a quarter of an hour, the carriage stopped outside a wood-frame of shops, alehouses and tenements, a little way south and east of Gray's Inn.

The front of the house had exposed timbers of lightly coloured oak. The housekeeper, a woman of middle years who never asked any questions and provided food and clean laundry for anyone using the house, answered the door and admitted Shakespeare and the two young women with a generous smile.

Inside, the house was pleasantly appointed without being sumptuous. It was a house of many secrets but within the office of Sir Francis Walsingham it was known simply as the Holborn house. The building was rented by Phelippes on behalf of his master and over the years had been used for all manner of purposes: confidential meetings, the concealment of exiles from foreign lands whose lives were threatened, the covert delivery of letters and, from time to time, the night work of the Smith sisters.

Shakespeare accompanied them up to the first floor where they had their chamber, decked in gold and red like an Ottoman's seraglio, with a large four-poster that Phelippes insisted was as big and grand as the Queen's own bed. Shakespeare's eye could not but stray to the small hole in the wall through which he had spied on Eliza and Beth when they were last here with Gifford. The sisters caught his gaze and smiled. Hurriedly, he looked away, but it was clear to him that they must have known they were being watched.

'I shall leave you now. The pigling will be here within the hour. Will that be time enough?'

'Enough, indeed. The housekeeper will lay us a fire and bring sweet wine.'

'You may wish to stay and watch our preparations . . .'

Shakespeare ignored the offer. He was about to take his leave, but then stopped. 'I hope I am not intruding, but I must ask you a question which has troubled me since I met you. I would say that you both have wit and great beauty. From the appearance of your attire and your fine house, I would venture that you have wealth enough. You could marry well and have families. Why then do you choose to remain . . .' His voice trailed off.

'Why do we remain whores?' Eliza laughed. 'Because it is what we are good at. Why do you do what *you* do?'

'It needs to be done.' And God knew, there were times when it was foul, discomfiting work.

'And this needs to be done, too, Mr Shakespeare. We have a heaven-sent talent and work that pleases us. Why should we be at one man's beck and call with all the swaddling clothes and dull nights, when we can do this?'

'We have met such men, sir,' Beth put in. 'French envoys, Dutch merchants, even a Portingall prince of the blood. Many of them have fine manners and good conversation and know how best to please a lady. What goodwife with a dozen brats at her feet can say the same of her life, all drudgery and routine? And when we are not at work, we can choose fine fabrics, eat fine food and idle away the hours in our house by the river.'

'But the risks . . .'

Beth smoothed her hands down her bosom and purred. 'We know all about the risks. We know how to avoid the pox and how not to come with child. When necessary, we have the strength and wit to calm the ferocious beast that resides in some men's hearts. And above all, we have the secret of giving pleasures unknown, learnt at our mother's knee. We choose our clients with great care. You, sir, would most certainly fit our requirements and as a Walsingham man, we would wink at the reckoning.'

'It is a most gracious offer, but one that I must decline.' If, for one single moment he was tempted, he did not wish to let them know. But they knew.

Chapter 14

N O ONE COULD have told what was inside the building. From the outside it looked exactly what it once must have been – a tithe barn. He and the watchman, Potken, had walked along farm tracks into the countryside north of Whitechapel. For the last half-hour Boltfoot had walked blindfold.

He had been reluctant to do so, for no man likes to be so vulnerable and at the mercy of a stranger. But he had finally conceded when Potken told him that without it they could proceed no further.

The going was slow, each step tentative and reliant on Potken's assurance that the ground was flat and nothing was in their way. Boltfoot tried to count the steps and remember the turns and the sensation of the sun on his head and brow; anything to discern their direction.

Now Potken removed the scarf from his eyes and Boltfoot blinked up at the enormous brick and oak construction that confronted him. He looked around. There was no sign of the highway, nor any sound of life save for birdsong and the lowing of cattle. With woodlands on three sides, there was no recognisable landmark for him to gauge his position. This place was well hidden despite its immense size.

Livestock grazed in the fields. In the air, crows and gulls

savoured the warm summer breeze. Then, from inside the barn, they heard the deep ringing of men laughing. Potken waited, seemingly afraid to go in. He whispered in Boltfoot's ear.

'Ask no questions.'

Almost immediately two men in working clothes – guards who looked like farmhands – emerged from the great double doorway. Without a word, they nodded their acknowledgement to Potken and allowed the two newcomers to go in. Boltfoot followed in the wake of the watchman. He expected to see hay and sacks and farm equipment. But his assumption was immediately proved false. This building might once have been a barn, but its purpose had been changed. It was now a great hall with tables that would seat a hundred people if so required. There were no more than a dozen here now, which only served to emphasise its great size.

As he stepped onto the stone floor, complete with rush matting like a comfortable house, he tried to take in what he could see by the light from the door and the dozen or so candles that burned on the tables. His eyes quickly adjusted to the echoing gloom. The only people apart from themselves and the two guards were a group of men and women, who did not look up from whatever it was they were doing at the head of the main table. He heard a man curse and throw down a playing card. Another man laughed. Then one of the women pointed at Boltfoot and he was suddenly aware that she was Em, the bawd from the Burning Prow, the woman who had sent Potken after him. The eyes of the other players followed her finger and stared at Boltfoot.

'Walk forward, Mr Cooper, walk forward,' the watchman said, his voice low and his manner even more brittle than before as he urged Boltfoot on with a push in the small of the back. 'Mr Ball wishes to see you. Be sure to answer his questions directly and fully for he will most certainly know if you dissemble.'

'Ball? You mean—'

'Yes, but do not call him by that name.' His voice even quieter now, yet somehow too loud in this vast space. 'Mr Ball will suffice. And do not meet his eye, Mr Cooper. Do not challenge him in any way, nor seek to interrogate him.'

Boltfoot grunted but said nothing. His shoulders were taut. He wondered about his cutlass, surprised that it had not been removed by the men at the door. But it was surely a hopeless implement here, among such lawless men as these were reputed to be.

One of the group stood up and beckoned Boltfoot and the watchman to approach.

'That's Mr Ball,' the watchman whispered, barely moving his mouth. 'He will kill you without flinching if you displease him.'

Boltfoot had no intention of displeasing Cutting Ball. It was clear to him that there was no way out of here alive if he did not comply absolutely with the wishes of these people. He approached the table.

'What is this, Potken?'

'This is Mr Cooper. You said you would like to talk with him.'

'The man asking about Will Cane? Is this the man, Em?' He turned to the woman.

'That's the worm. Lame in foot and head.'

Boltfoot tried not to meet Cutting Ball's eye. He was man of the world enough to know that such men often took eye contact amiss, as though it showed a lack of respect. Boltfoot had no fear of the man, but nor did it make sense to sacrifice his life without purpose; Mr Shakespeare would not thank him for that.

Ball stood with his broad shoulders rigid and straight. His gaze was both merciless and amused. In his hands he played with a bollock-dagger, turning it this way and that, running the blade along his palm. He thrust out his chin, and his long, forked beard pointed at Boltfoot like the tongue of a viper.

There was something about the man that almost made Boltfoot think he knew him. No, he had never seen him before, he was sure of that; but he had seen a man very like him. Someone with an air of command, born of natural authority and intimidation. The sort of man that others respected and feared, automatically, without quite knowing why.

And then Boltfoot realised where he had seen such a man before: Cutting Ball had the demeanour of a sea captain. But not just *any* sea captain – Drake himself. He could have been Drake upon the quarterdeck, ordering men about on matters of life or death with no discernible alteration of facial expression or tone of voice. Always loud, always full of bluster, but no true emotion. Extra brandy for the men at Christmas, a whipping for a cabin boy, three hurrahs when they passed into the wide Pacific ocean, the lopping of a dissenter's head. All as one and always puffed up like a southern squall. Harsh orders or favours for the crew; never flinching from dispensing whatever measures he considered necessary to maintain order and obedience.

'Why are you lame, Mr Cooper?'

'I have a club foot, Mr Ball. With me since birth, I am told.'

Ball's eye descended to Boltfoot's left foot. 'Yes, I see that now. Sit down, Mr Cooper, take your weight off it. Have you had a long walk here?'

Francis Drake, Cutting Ball. In men's eyes, one was a hero and the other was a villain. To Boltfoot, they were cut from the same cloth; two men who thought themselves beyond the ordinary boundaries of civilised life and society and did what they damned well pleased, irrespective of the destruction they wrought.

Boltfoot sat on the bench, as bidden. He noted the others around the table; there were nine of them, including the woman from the Burning Prow, most of them villainous and staring at him. One of them, eyeing him with amusement, had the soft skin of a gentleman though he wore the rough attire of a working man. Boltfoot ignored them and returned his gaze to Cutting Ball. 'Mr Potken asked me to come,' he said. 'I was seeking some assistance.'

'You were looking for someone to tell you about my friend Will Cane, I believe.'

'Yes, Mr Ball.'

'Why? What do you want to know? He is dead and gone to dust, as we all must go. What could you hope to discover of a man who is naught but blanching bones and rotting flesh?'

'My master John Shakespeare wishes to know more about him. Whether he had family or friends.'

Ball was a man of at least fifty, with the powerful physique of a man half that age. He said nothing for a few moments as though expecting Boltfoot to continue. He wore a sleeveless leather jerkin and no shirt so that the bulging and tanned muscles of his arms were clearly visible. Boltfoot could not help noting the intricate scar running down one arm, a mass of short and long cuts formed to make a curling serpent. Had he had it carved into his flesh deliberately – or had it been inflicted on him by an enemy? Boltfoot suspected the first option.

'Carry on, Mr Cooper. Tell me your story. Leave nothing out.'

Boltfoot nodded. 'Very well. Mr Shakespeare is a friend of Mr Giltspur's widow. This murder has come as a great horror and surprise to him. He had not thought that Kat – Mistress Giltspur – was the sort of person to do such a thing. And so I believe he hoped that there might be some clue to be had from those who knew Mr Cane.'

'And Mistress Giltspur. Where is she?'

'I am told she has fled and is in hiding. That is the story as I know it. I am merely doing my master's bidding.'

'Your name is Cooper. Are you then a cooper by trade?'

'I was, yes. A ship's cooper with Drake. But no more. I have had enough of the sea for one lifetime.'

Ball turned to the woman from the Burning Prow. 'What say you, Em?'

'He is probably honest enough. Hasn't the wit to lie. But I would like to know more. When he says his master is a friend of Mistress Giltspur, that could mean many things.'

'Well, Mr Cooper?'

'They lived together as man and wife, but unwed.' He knew there was no point in trying to lie or evade the question; enough people knew the truth.

Cutting Ball laughed. 'Then your Mr Shakespeare is a fortunate man, for she is a fine-favoured wench.'

'Do you then know her, Mr Ball?'

Ball's eyes clouded like the sky before a storm. 'Mr Cooper, do you think to ask me questions? Would you like to know what happened to the last person who asked me a question?'

Boltfoot shook his head. 'Forgive me. I meant nothing by it.'

'Good.' He moved forward and touched the point of his bollock-dagger into Boltfoot's hose where his prick and balls nestled.

Another man might have recoiled but Boltfoot did not pull back.

'Drake, you say? He is a dog. The one sea captain who ever tried to defy me. I think I will sell you, Mr Cooper. I am sure you will fetch a few shillings, perhaps a mark or two, and then I will make up some of what I am owed.'

Boltfoot could have said that he shared Cutting Ball's low opinion of Sir Francis Drake but wiser counsel told him the subject was best avoided, and so he said nothing.

'You are silent now, Mr Cooper. I repeat my question: do you know where the Giltspur wench is hiding?' He still did not withdraw the tip of his blade from his guest's manhood. Boltfoot had no doubt that if he was given the slightest provocation, he would strike it home . . . and add a sharp twist at the end.

'No, sir.'

'Think again.'

Boltfoot shook his head decisively. 'No, sir, I am certain I do not know. It is possible my master has seen her, but if he did, I was not with him and I have no idea of her whereabouts. He does not tell me such things.' Which was his first lie, for he knew that Mr Shakespeare had gone to Shoreditch.

'Why do I not believe you?'

'I know not, Mr Ball. I can but speak the truth. My master would never tell me more than he considered necessary. I am not privy to his secrets.'

'What does he hope to know about Will Cane?' It was one of the other players that spoke, the one with the rough clothes but the appearance of a gentleman.

'I think he hopes that those who knew him would have some notion as to the truth behind the story he told in court. Perhaps there might have been some unknown reason for the accusation laid against Mistress Giltspur. Some falling-out . . .'

'I think we should fetch your Mr Shakespeare,' Ball said. 'Let him answer my questions directly.'

'He has powerful friends, Mr Ball, for he is a Queen's man and in the close employ of Mr Secretary.'

'That almost sounds like a threat. Have you perhaps heard what I like to do with my fine blade? With one cut, I could unman you and then, as a mercy, I might stake you out on the riverbank and watch the tide come in over your miserable head. And you would find your last breath a blessed release.'

'It was not meant as a threat, Mr Ball. I thought you wished to know who I was and why I was asking questions; Mr Shakespeare is the reason and so I believed you would want to know more about him.'

Ball removed the point of his dagger from the vicinity of Boltfoot's nether parts and placed it back in his belt. He took an ivory dice from his pocket and handed it to Boltfoot. 'Throw a six and you may go unmolested; five and you'll have a beating; four, you lose your balls; three, your eyes; two, a quick death; one, a slow death. Throw it, Mr Cooper.'

Boltfoot held the dice and turned it in his hand. Was it loaded?

'An even thousand he throws three or less.' It was the gentleman player who spoke.

Boltfoot turned to him and saw the light of excitement in his eyes. Was this man really staking a thousand pounds on his life or death?

Ball nodded. 'I accept the bet. Now throw, Mr Cooper. Throw – or I will presume a one.'

He knew he had no option. This man meant every word he said. Boltfoot shook the ivory cube in both hands. He had never been a gambling man, had never seen the point in it. But this was no gamble; this was a straight choice between death or the chance of life. He threw the dice and it rattled across the table in front of him, at last coming to a stop. Two dots showed. A two. That meant a quick death, didn't it?

'Aha, I win!' The gentleman said with delight.

'And Mr Cooper loses,' Ball said.

The woman from the Burning Prow, the one called Em, touched Cutting Ball's bare arm. She wore a low chemise and her large, hanging breasts were scarcely concealed. What was she? Did she run his whores? 'Don't do it. Don't take a stand against Walsingham.'

Ball pushed her hand away with explosive ferocity. 'I'll take a stand against whom I like, including you. Get out, Em. Go.'

She seemed about to say something to him, but then merely nodded her fair head and walked away towards the double doors. It seemed to Boltfoot that she was the only person in this great hall of a barn who did not fear Cutting Ball.

Ball did not watch her. Instead he picked up the dice, turned it and slammed it down so that a five showed. He then grabbed Boltfoot by the front of his jerkin and dragged him to his feet.

'You, get out now. I will not kill you this day for you are a cripple. But if ever I hear that you have come east of the city wall again, I will shove your bollocks down your throat and your eyeballs up your arse. And then the pain will start.' He threw Boltfoot across the flagged floor, then tossed a coin to the watchman. 'Get the lads and give him a good beating, Potken, then deliver him to his master.'

Chapter 15

SHAKESPEARE LEFT GIFFORD to the exquisite ministrations of the Smith sisters, certain that the *pink pigling* would be grunting and squealing with pleasure for many hours to come. Vitally, he would not be taking his leave of them before the new day. It was a prospect that made Shakespeare's own bedchamber seem a desolate place.

The sisters were under instructions to stay with Gifford in the chamber until nine o'clock in the morning. The house-keeper would provide breakfast for them and, while they were eating, Shakespeare would return. The Smith sisters would say a tender farewell and tell their satisfied client how boldly he had performed, and travel in their carriage back home to Westminster.

The plan then was for Shakespeare to take Gilbert Gifford to the Walsingham mansion in Seething Lane. If all had gone as hoped, the letter from the Scottish Queen to Babington would have been deciphered and resealed and would now be there, waiting. If it was as damning as Walsingham hoped, then the way ahead should at last become clear, the months of scheming brought to fruition. The question for Mr Secretary to answer was when and how to deliver the letter onward to Anthony Babington. Timing and method of delivery were all-important.

✠ 121 ✠

For the moment, Shakespeare had an evening stretching ahead of him and he planned to make use of it. First, however, he rode home, intending to take supper.

He tried the door, but it would not open. He pushed again. It must be bolted on the inside, for it would not budge an inch. Exasperated, he rapped his knuckles against the solid wood. From inside, he heard scurrying feet, then a small voice.

'Who is it?'

'God's blood, Jane, it is John Shakespeare. Let me in!'

He heard the bolt sliding back, then the door opened. Jane stood before him, shaking and distressed.

'Mr Shakespeare, sir . . .'

'Jane, what is it? Why was the door bolted?'

'Oh, master, I was afraid. A terrible thing has happened to poor Mr Cooper. He has been attacked.'

'Where is he?'

'He is in the parlour, sir. He has suffered sorely. I have just begun tending to his injuries as best I can.'

'Come, let us go to him.'

'Should I put the bolt back on the door, sir?'

'No.'

Boltfoot was sitting on the settle, leaning forward, head in hands. He was naked from the waist up and his wiry mariner's body was streaked with blood. His hair hung lank and sticky about his face. At his feet there was a basin of bloody water and blood-soaked linen towels.

'Boltfoot?'

He looked up. 'I'm sorry, master.' His cheek was bruised and his left eye was puffed up. The blood was seeping from a gash above his left eyebrow.

Shakespeare sat on the settle beside his assistant and combed the hair from his face with his fingers. 'What happened?'

'I found Cutting Ball. He ordered me beaten and threatened worse.'

'You found Cutting Ball? So he is real. I had almost thought him a mythical being.'

'He's real enough. A dangerous man.'

'So I see. Are any bones broken?'

Boltfoot shook his head, then groaned. 'No.'

'I can send Jane for a physician.'

'No thank you, master. She has been doing well enough cleaning me up. I have suffered worse in my life and I will survive this with an aching head.'

'Where did you find Cutting Ball?'

Boltfoot groaned and put a hand to his shoulder. Shakespeare saw that it was bruised almost black. Boltfoot tried to laugh. 'They beat me with sticks, like a dog.'

'Take whatever time you need.'

'Forgive me, master, but I cannot be sure where he was, save that it was north-east of London. I was led there, blindfold. All I can say is that Ball was in an old barn, well away from the highway, on farmland surrounded by woods. From the outside no man would have given the barn a second glance but inside it was like the hall of a manor. It seemed to me that he ran his empire of felony from there.'

'A palatial barn?'

'In the countryside north of Whitechapel. He was playing cards with some men and a couple of women. After my beating, I was blindfolded again and brought on a cart to Aldgate, where I was dumped and told not to go east of the city walls on pain of death.'

'Are you certain you would not be able to find this barn?'

Boltfoot thought for a few moments. 'It is not impossible. I tried to count my steps and note the changes of direction, but

I was without sight for at least twenty minutes, so it is far from certain.'

'Well, I won't ask you to go back there for the moment. What did you learn?'

'I learnt that he is a tyrant feared and respected in equal measure. I learnt, too, that he considered the assassin Will Cane his friend. One thing that is certain is that he is interested in the matter of the murder, for that was why he had me brought to him.'

'Do you believe he was involved in the killing?'

'He gave nothing away. But there was something that worried me . . .'

'Yes?'

'When I mentioned Kat, he called her a fine-favoured wench, from which I inferred that he knew her – or at least that he had seen her. I put this to him, and that was when his mood darkened. No man is allowed to put questions to Mr Ball, nor are they to refer to him by the name Cutting.'

Kat had mentioned nothing about knowing Cutting Ball, but then perhaps she had no knowledge of his link to Will Cane. *Or perhaps she did.* It was not inconceivable that they had met, and if they had, Shakespeare needed to know the circumstances.

'There was one other thing, master. The whore's bawd named Em was there among the band of felons surrounding Ball in his great hall.'

'Tell me about her.'

'She did not seem afeared by him and risked his ire by warning him to be wary of crossing you or Mr Secretary. He was displeased by the way she spoke and told her to get out, but still she was not scared. It seemed to me there was something between them.'

'Man and wife?'

'It is possible. Or brother and sister.' He groaned again and slumped forward, breathing heavily.

'That is enough for now, Boltfoot. We will speak more later.'

Shakespeare glanced over towards the door where Jane was hanging back. 'Continue your nursing, please, Jane. Then give him broth and put him to bed.'

'Yes, master.'

'And Jane . . .'

'Yes, master?'

'I know this has been a trial for you. You have done well. Thank you.'

Boltfoot put up his hand. 'There was one other thing, master.'

'Yes?'

'I was made to throw a dice for my life. I lost, but Ball spared me anyway.'

'So he has the quality of mercy . . .'

'I think not. He saved me because I am connected to you – and you are connected to Mr Secretary.'

Ninety minutes later, Shakespeare was at Severin Tort's house in Fetter Lane, just west of the city wall. Tort was as neat and well kempt as ever, his silver hair parted and combed to perfection; but the tension in his eyes was evident.

'Is something amiss, Mr Tort?'

'No, nothing, sir.'

'You look out of sorts.'

'It is my boy. It is nothing. He finds fault with the world and speaks his mind too freely. He is not yet sixteen, but I fear for him. These are harsh days, as you must know as well as any man. But he is not your problem.' Tort shook his head, too quickly. The movement betrayed his strung nerves. 'Why are you here, Mr Shakespeare? Do you bring news?'

There was a brittle edge to the voice. Was Tort displeased by his arrival here unannounced? Shakespeare put the question to the back of his mind, to be revisited later. 'Indeed, I do bring news,' he said. 'Much has happened but I fear I have no resolution.' He took in his surroundings. Never had he seen a more well-ordered room. At the desk where Tort studied and wrote, his quills were neatly cut and laid out and his ink-bottle was placed precisely with no black drops staining the wood around it. Each item of furniture – his coffer and chair and settle – seemed to have been lined up like a disciplined army, likewise his books, of which there were many.

'I do not have a great deal of time to talk, Mr Shakespeare.'

'Mr Tort, I have no time at all, and yet you have brought this matter to my attention and so at your instigation I am making inquiries.'

Tort hung his head, chastened. 'Forgive me. It is just . . .'

'Yes? Speak, man.'

Tort looked up and emitted a heavy sigh. 'I had another visitor less than an hour since. The magistrate Richard Young, who is leading the search for Katherine. He came here with a band of pursuivants.'

'Why?'

'He believes I know where she is. He interrogated me and made dire threats against me. He said my faith would be held against me, that I would be accused of harbouring priests and face the scaffold for treason. No London jury would believe me for I was a papist and therefore untrustworthy, he said. He threatened my stepson, too.'

'Why do you think he came to you? He must know something. Have you been speaking to anyone?'

'Only you, sir.'

The unspoken accusation was not lost on Shakespeare, but

he let it pass without rebuttal. 'Could someone at the Curtain know something, someone other than Oswald Redd?'

'Only if Redd has told them. But I cannot see why he would do such a thing.'

'No, Mr Tort, that will not do. Kat lived with Redd. Everyone at the playhouse must have known that they were living together. It would not be beyond the wit of the most doltish player to consider that his house would be an obvious place for her to hide. This tale of murder must be as much a sensation in Shoreditch as it is in London. Perhaps a player went to Young with his suspicions, hoping for a coin in his hand.'

Tort tapped his fingertips together so that his hands formed a half-globe. It was a habit Shakespeare had noted among other lawyers during his days at Gray's Inn; they seemed to do it while thinking through a complex matter. 'I don't think so,' Tort said, his face a blank. 'If a player had told Justice Young about Oswald Redd, then his house would surely have been raided.'

He was right, of course. But it could only be a matter of time before Young discovered this part of Kat's past for himself. Which meant that Redd had done the right thing to hide her elsewhere. But where was she?

'I went to her again,' he told Tort. 'But she was gone. Do you know where she is now hidden, for I would very much like to talk with her again? There are matters to which I must have clear answers if I am to investigate further.'

The lawyer's eyes widened and he shook his head as though surprised by the revelation that she was not at Redd's abode. Was his surprise feigned, Shakespeare wondered, or was he somehow in league with Oswald Redd, keeping vital information from Shakespeare?

'How did you know that she would be at Redd's house when

you took me there? What is your connection to Redd and how did Kat first ask you for assistance? Be straight with me.'

'Why, it is simple enough. Redd approached me and I went with him to her; then again with you. Those are the only times I have seen Katherine and he is the only line of contact I have had with her.'

'And did you know Redd before this tragical sequence of events?'

'No, I had neither met him nor heard of him. Kat sent him to me.'

Shakespeare was thinking hard. If Young's men suspected Severin Tort, then they would undoubtedly be watching him and his house – and they would have followed him to Shoreditch, in which case Kat would by now be under arrest. But that hadn't happened, so Young's interest in the lawyer must be more recent. Why?

'Mr Tort, I have two more pieces of information that I would like to bring to your attention. Let us sit down.' He was irritated to see the lawyer shifting uneasily as though desperate for him to leave. 'God's death, Mr Tort, hear me out. Whatever matters of importance you have to deal with, they will wait.'

Shakespeare slumped down on the settle and stretched out his booted legs; he felt an urge to sprawl himself as an antidote to Tort's impatience and the cloying tidiness of this room.

Reluctantly, Tort took the chair at his desk, his knees clenched primly, as though he wore skirts. He listened in silence as Shakespeare regaled him with the revelation that the assassin, Will Cane, had been close to death when he murdered Nicholas Giltspur. If he was shocked or surprised, it did not show on his impassive lawyerly face. Nor did he speak as he heard of Boltfoot Cooper's experiences to the east of the city. The only visible reaction was a slight tensing of the shoulder and neck at the name of Cutting Ball.

'And so you see, nothing is as it seems. The reason I am here this evening, Mr Tort, is to ask you to help me make the acquaintance of Arthur Giltspur, the dead man's nephew. For if Kat did not do it, then we must find someone else who would have benefited from Nick Giltspur's death and the execution of his widow. So far the only name I have is Arthur's, which I heard from Oswald Redd.'

'I cannot believe Arthur would do such a thing. He is a fine young man.'

'Then you know him?'

'Well, yes, for he was often at Aldermanbury when I had dealings with his uncle.'

'Then arrange a meeting for me as soon as possible. The steward of the house has been most obstructive.'

'Sorbus? Yes, he can be a little too protective of his domain. I will do what I can. And Mr Shakespeare, there is one other thing I should tell you.'

'Yes?'

'When Justice Young was questioning me, he mentioned your name.'

Somehow Shakespeare was not surprised, and yet he was angry. 'Indeed? You think to tell me this now? Why did you not say aught when I arrived?'

'I was unsure how you would react.'

'What did he say?'

'He asked me if I knew you. I could not think what to reply, so I confessed that I did.'

'*Confessed*? As yet, it is not a crime to know me. What more did Young say? Did he mention why he was interested in me?'

'He said that you and Katherine had . . . lived together. He did not express it in quite such decorous terms. He said that you must know where the *murderous trug* – his words – was hiding.'

Shakespeare snorted. Of course, it had been common knowledge among his neighbours and those he worked with in Walsingham's employment that he had lived with Kat as man and wife for two years or more. But how had that information come to Richard Young's attention? Shakespeare went through all those with whom he worked and wondered whether any of them might have informed Young. Mills? Gregory? Scudamore? Would any of them have gone out of their way to proffer such information? And if so, why?

What was certain was that he must now assume he was being followed wherever he went. He had probably been trailed here to Fetter Lane. In which case, if he could arrange a further meeting with Kat he would have to go to great lengths to ensure he lost his pursuers.

He stood up and strode towards the door. 'As soon as possible, Mr Tort. I rather think Mr Arthur Giltspur might offer some insights to this wretched tale.'

'I doubt it, but I will do what I can.'

He pushed open the front door and was about to step out into the night but stopped. He was face to face with Dominic de Warre . . .

Chapter 16

D E WARRE TOOK a step backwards and, without thinking, affected an insincere smile, the sort men and women
produce as a courtesy when confronted close up with a stranger. But then he must have realised that he recognised the face
of the man opening the door, for his brow furrowed in surprise
and puzzlement. Shakespeare rather imagined that his own
expressions must be going through the same rapid alterations.

Why would Dominic de Warre, the young companion of
Goodfellow Savage, be here at the home of Severin Tort?

'Mr de Warre, what an extraordinary surprise.'

'Likewise, Mr Shakespeare. Well met, sir. But why, pray, are
you here?'

'I might ask the same question of you. I was visiting my
friend Mr Tort. He is helping me with a legal difficulty.'

'Indeed? I had no idea you were acquainted. Severin Tort is
the man I must call my stepfather, though it pains me so to
do.'

Shakespeare was gathering his recollections of this young
man from their meeting at Mane's; fervent, indiscreet, dangerous were the three words that first came to mind. But he
merely spoke a platitude. 'Ah, so he is the man who advised
you against a career in the law.' *And the man so concerned by
your wild and untamed mouth.*

'The very same. And I shrug my shoulder and obey him like a dutiful stepson. Tell me, are you leaving or staying? Perhaps you are off to acquire a pistol to shoot one of the tyrants. Oh, I had quite forgot – you work for them, don't you.'

Was he speaking in jest or deadly seriousness? Dominic de Warre's young face was all innocence, but the rashness with which he spoke was terrifying. Such indiscretion in these dark days could cost any man his life, even one this young.

'Your tongue will cost us all our heads.'

De Warre laughed. 'Are you afraid, sir?'

'I have no particular wish to die before my time, Mr de Warre.'

'Then I will bid you farewell – and safekeeping.' The young man touched his cap, smiled knowingly, and entered the house.

Shakespeare let him go. Questions buzzed around his head like bees about thyme, but they would have to wait. He looked along the street. It was about eight o'clock and still daylight. The street was not busy; in the warmth of the summer's evening a group of children played with wooden swords and bows; a few gossips standing with their arms crossed about their motherly breasts talked of the day's news; workmen strode home.

Among them, he could detect nobody that looked like a watcher. And yet he was certain that somewhere there was one.

He rode west along Fleet Street, past Temple Bar and into the Strand. After two hundred yards, he turned northwards into Little Drury Lane, where he reined in. The narrow street was deserted and he had a good view in both directions. He waited a few minutes until he was as certain as he could be that he was not followed, then carried on northwards until he joined Drury Lane itself.

Tugging on the reins, he arrowed north through a farm gate and rode along a bridle path across Lincoln's Inn Fields, constantly looking over his shoulder. A few cows looked back at him and a cowherd sitting on a tree stump eating his bread watched him with disinterest. At Holborn, he took another farm track past Gray's Inn and then on towards Clerkenwell. Every so often he stopped, to be sure that he was not pursued. North of Finsbury Court, he joined the thoroughfare of Hog Lane and rode slowly towards its junction with Curtain Close.

It was a perfect summer's evening and it would be light for at least another hour. The breeze was so slight that the sails of the Finsbury windmills scarcely had breath to turn. Despite the worries crowding in, he could not but think how glorious this English countryside looked on such a day. The prospect that men could conspire to break this peace and tranquillity, to slay the Queen and invite in a foreign power, was an abomination.

His horse snorted and pawed at the dusty earth. Shakespeare dismounted and allowed it to drink from a small pond, then tethered it to a tree and continued the last fifty yards on foot. He pulled his cap down low over his forehead as he walked past Oswald Redd's house and gazed in through the ground-floor window, as any passer-by might do. He could see that Redd was at his workbench. There was no sign of Kat.

Twenty yards further on, in the lee of the Curtain playhouse, Shakespeare took a place against the wall of the tavern. The whole dusty street was alive with men enjoying a beer or cider in the evening sunshine at the end of their day's labours. He ordered a tankard of small ale from a potboy, then drank thirstily, all the time keeping his eyes fixed on the entrance to Oswald Redd's house.

He realised this could be a wasted effort, that Redd might simply close his shutters when the light went and retire to his bed for the night. But he didn't think so. If Redd knew where

Kat was, he was certain to go to her; there was a compulsion in him that would oblige him to see her whatever the risks, and to assist her. It was the same impulse that made Severin Tort put himself in harm's way, and John Shakespeare too – though it pained him to admit it to himself. She had that effect on men, and she used it.

Redd emerged from his house just as dusk settled across the rooftops of Shoreditch. He turned left and walked at a steady pace in the direction of the playhouse. Shakespeare shrank back behind a group of drinkers and observed. Redd continued on past the tavern, going northwards, seemingly oblivious of danger, unaware that he might be stalked, for he did not look around.

Shakespeare waited a few moments, then followed at a distance of thirty or forty yards. Halfway along the lane, he slowed down. He was not alone. Another man, in vagabond rags, was ahead of him, on the other side of the narrow street, also following Redd.

The lane was crowded with playgoers, players, drinkers, outlaws and whores, all looking for amusement to stretch the balmy evening as far as they could, and that made it easier to follow Redd and the other pursuer, a small, bent man with a shining pate, stepping cautiously beneath the jettied overhangs to make himself less noticeable.

This man presented a major problem. If Redd was on his way to see Kat, then her whereabouts would be discovered by the pursuer, who would either arrest her there and then at the point of his sword, or report back to Justice Young. Shakespeare could not allow either eventuality to happen. He had to act, and fast.

The pursuer might be wearing rough clothes, but he was good at his job, for no man untrained in such matters would note him – and certainly not Oswald Redd, who clearly had no notion that he was being tailed.

Shakespeare's hand went to his belt to grip the hilt of his poniard. No, he also had the bollock-dagger that had been used to murder Nicholas Giltspur. With its nine-inch blade, it was a great deal more menacing than the poniard. He drew the sharp-honed weapon, concealing its long blade alongside his sleeve, and quickened his pace.

Ahead of them, Redd was turning right on a track past the Curtain and the Theatre, which Shakespeare knew would lead him into the depths of Shoreditch with its hovels and stews.

Before the turning, there was some sort of cut-through, a narrow alley scarce wide enough to accommodate a horse and certainly not a wagon or cart. This was the moment to move. Shakespeare was at the stalker's heel. He tapped his shoulder, causing him to swivel in alarm. But before the man's hand could reach his dagger, Shakespeare's blade was at his throat.

'Draw your dagger and you will die.' He rasped the words as he grappled with the pursuer. His left arm went around the shoulders of the man – who was almost a foot shorter than Shakespeare – and he wrenched hard, pulling him away from the thoroughfare into the passageway.

The man did not scream out, but he was struggling, fighting hard. Though he was a strong man for his size, Shakespeare was too powerful and forced him to the ground, the tip of the dagger still at his exposed throat. He held him down with a knee on his chest, then relieved him of his short-sword and knife.

'Get off me!'

Shakespeare clamped his hand over the man's mouth and put his own lips very close to his ear. 'Do as I command,' he ordered, 'and you may yet live.' He removed his hand from the man's mouth, ready to clamp it again instantly if he shouted out or screamed.

'I have no coin. Who are you?'

Shakespeare put a finger to his lips. 'Say nothing. Just listen when I speak.'

The man had a length of cord about his waist in place of a belt. Transferring his knife to his left hand, Shakespeare used his right hand to unknot the thin rope and tug it free of his waist. He then ordered the man to turn onto his belly.

'No.'

Shakespeare withdrew his knee from the man's chest, stabbed the bollock-dagger into the ground then flipped the man over. It was as easy as turning a sick sheep. He pulled back the hands and arms and with a few deft movements tied them together hard, then bound his hands to his feet.

'I do not have much time, so tell me now: who are you working for?'

'I tell you this, he'll do for you.'

'Who? Young?'

The man said no more, merely grunted with pain as Shakespeare wrenched the knots tighter. There was no time for interrogation; he had to get away after Oswald Redd. He rose to his feet.

'Don't go anywhere,' he said.

An old man opened his front door and looked on the scene. 'What's this?' he said, pushing out his chest as though remembering bouts from his youth.

'Cutpurse,' Shakespeare said. He picked up the bound man's knife and short-sword and handed them to the house-holder. 'Keep him at your mercy with those while I seek the constable. Do not listen to his stories for I know this felon to be a liar.' He then nodded to the bewildered old man and began to run, trying to follow the route that he believed Redd must have taken.

Reaching the Theatre, the second of Shoreditch's two great playhouses, he stopped and looked along the street. Panting heavily, he emitted a curse. Too late; he had lost his quarry.

But then he saw him, his progress seemingly held up by a stream of playgoers leaving the Theatre. Shakespeare stepped onward at a fast walk. In a few moments he had caught Redd, gripping him by the arm. Everything had changed; he could no longer simply follow him unseen.

'Come with me.'

Redd recoiled, but Shakespeare held his grip.

'Trust me. We must move away from here with great haste.' Glancing around, he saw an alehouse into which many of the playgoers were pouring themselves. 'Over there. I'll buy you a cup of ale.'

'What is this, Shakespeare?'

'Come, sir. Come.' His voice more urgent now, he was dragging Redd across the dusty street.

All the booths, benches and stools were taken, so Shakespeare pushed Redd through the throng and found a space to stand beside a couple of casks. The taproom was dark and rich with the scent of ale and tobacco smoke, a thing that never failed to surprise Shakespeare, even when his man Boltfoot sat with his pipe of an evening. He released his grip on his captive's arm.

Redd rubbed his arm, wincing at the pain. 'Pig's arses, Shakespeare. Was that necessary?'

'It was nothing compared to what you face if you do not listen to me and heed my advice. You are in grave danger of having your neck stretched. You were being followed, Mr Redd.'

'Yes, by you.'

'By me and by another man. Fortunately for both of us, I spotted him before he saw me. In all likelihood he was one of Justice Young's men. It must be obvious, even to the most feeble-witted, that he has been keeping watch, waiting for you to lead him to Kat.'

'What happened to him?'

'I left him trussed up in an alley. I had no choice, but he will be freed soon enough and then he will look about to find us.'

'And why, God damn you, Shakespeare, were *you* watching me?'

'Because I too wanted to find Kat. But for very different reasons. You are an innocent in the ways of men, Mr Redd. All the wickedness you see is but the playwright's imagination. This is real – and you have no notion of the danger she is in. Nor yet the danger to your own life, for *you* will be hanged for harbouring a criminal.'

'Is that so?' Redd's voice was thick with doubt. He shook his head in disbelief. 'And so once you had attacked this other man, why did you not continue to follow me instead of dragging me in here? I might well have led you to her, might I not?'

Shakespeare sighed, exasperated by the naivety of this love-smitten fool. 'Because, Mr Redd, I could not be sure that the man I attacked was alone. There might, even now, be another pursuer on your tail, here in this taproom. If I had allowed you to continue along your merry way, we might both now be arraigned as accessories after the fact. Now tell me, quietly, where she is . . .'

Redd turned his head away. 'No,' he said. 'No, I will not.'

At a wayside inn on the northern highway, just south of the Yorkshire town of Doncaster, Harry Slide was trying to lift the spirits of his two travelling companions. 'Captain, have you heard of the time I did expose the Archbishop of York for the lewd vermin that he is?'

'More times than I care to remember, Mr Maude. But tell it again if you must.'

'No, no, I will not weary you.'

Father Ballard and young Robert Gage looked at each other with knowing smiles. It was, indeed, a story that they had heard before during their travels together through France and England. Bernard Maude was renowned for having extorted a great deal of money from Archbishop Edwin Sandys, having contrived to 'discover' him in bed with an innkeeper's wife. But the crime had rebounded on Mr Maude, costing him a three-year gaol term for demanding money with menaces.

'It does not weary us, Mr Maude for you brought low a great persecutor of the Catholic religion. But we have heard the story at least a half-dozen times.'

Harry Slide feigned hurt feelings. He would always be Bernard Maude to these men. Perhaps it was the fact that both Ballard and Gage – *Captain Fortescue and his faithful serving lad* as they would have it – both went under assumed identities that neither of them suspected Maude himself might not be quite the man he purported to be.

'I fear it is a tale I never tire of telling. And it all came to pass in an inn of good cheer, very like this one and not ten miles from here. But I will spare you the story this night.'

'Thank you, sir,' Ballard said. 'I confess I am a little tired. The day did not go as well as I had hoped.'

They were to stay the night at this inn. In the morning, they would ride south into Nottinghamshire, to the great houses and manors of the Catholic nobility, to ascertain their willingness to rise up against the usurper Elizabeth and her government of heretics. How many men would they be able to muster to support the Spanish invasion? Which were the best ports to give entry to Philip of Spain's galleons? These were the questions that the ambassador Don Bernardino de Mendoza had demanded of Ballard during their recent trip to Paris.

Ballard had assured Mendoza that sixty thousand good Catholic Englishmen would take arms for the Pope – the same number that Spain was promising as an invasion army. But the Spanish ambassador wanted more evidence before a fleet powerful enough for the task could be commissioned. So far, the response had been unfavourable. The Catholics all the way north and into Scotland had spoken reassuring words, but had balked at giving promises. Today had been no more encouraging than any other. They simply did not have the stomach for a fight. Even Ballard was beginning to have doubts.

'Those who should be most forward are most slow; and the older the colder,' he had complained to Slide and Gage as they rode to the inn. But Ballard was not a man to remain downcast long. He was certain things would improve in the region of Nottingham; Mendoza would have his sixty thousand Englishmen.

Harry Slide drank deep of his beer, then wiped his expensive sleeve across his mouth.

As though to put the disappointment of the day to one side, Ballard returned to the subject of the archbishop. 'These Protestants! They are too weak for chastity. They would have wives and whores. Their feebleness will be their downfall, for they will never know the pure love of God.'

'That is true enough. To see the archbishop sweating and grunting like a dog above the young woman's naked flesh was a marvel to behold.'

'It is what we fight against every day of our lives.'

'I had him, Captain, a dirty dog on a leash.'

'But you yourself were made to suffer, Mr Maude . . .'

'I was, Captain, for I could not keep the cleric's humiliation to myself. I wanted the world to know what he had done. An acquaintance with a wagonback press did print me a broadsheet to proclaim the news in London. That was my undoing, for it reached the ears of the archbishop's fellow privy councillors and he realised the secret could not be kept. He confessed all to Lord Burghley. I was sentenced to a term in the Fleet and was fortunate to keep my ears. And though I served two years in my cell, I would have done twenty or more – and lost my ears – just to know that Edwin Sandys is scorned and mocked in every tavern and playhouse in York and London and, I am certain, far beyond these shores.'

'Mr Maude, you are indeed a wonder. I do dare believe you could charm the bees from their hives and the eels from the reeds.'

He took another little bow. 'At your service, Captain.' *And what is more, I shall charm you to the scaffold.* Harry Slide drank the last of his beer. It was time for bed. The sooner they were done with this northern excursion and back in London, the better.

Chapter 17

SHAKESPEARE'S HEAD TOLD him that Kat probably was her husband's killer; only his foolish heart and the evidence of the Searcher of the Dead suggested that she might be innocent – evidence that might yet prove irrelevant.

As for his examination of Oswald Redd, that had achieved nothing. Threats proved as worthless as entreaties. He had cursed the man for the sheep's-head that he was and gripped his hand about his miserable throat. 'You will not help me – which means you will not help Kat. And so I leave you to survive as you may, Redd. I care not a dog's fart for *your* neck, but if you do not heed my warnings, you will be the cause of Kat's death too.' Releasing his grip on the man's throat, he had pushed him in the chest so that he fell back against the huge puncheon cask, then turned away and stalked out into the night. There was no more to be done.

Now, in the pre-dawn gloom, he went downstairs to take his breakfast at the long table. At least there was good food to be had in this house since the arrival of Jane. She was already up, so he asked for bread and eggs, then demanded after Boltfoot.

'He is already up, master.'

'Fetch him to me if you would, Jane.'

Shakespeare took his place at the head of the table and nodded in greeting to Boltfoot as he hobbled into the room. It seemed to Shakespeare that his limp was more pronounced than usual, and he was certainly slower. His face was bruised and one eye was blacking over.

'Good day to you, Boltfoot. How are your wounds?'

'Healing, master. They are as nothing.'

He looked closely at Boltfoot's injured face. 'You look close to death, Boltfoot. Rest up for the day. Jane will care for you with hot broth. I will send her to the apothecary for lotions and herbs.'

'Please, master, no. I have unfinished business.'

'It will wait; remember, this felon Ball has threatened your life if you go east of the city. From all that we know of him, his threat must be taken seriously.'

Boltfoot's face was set hard. 'I cannot let this pass.'

'What do you think you can do? Are you hoping to find Cutting Ball again? You were blindfolded, Boltfoot.'

'I can find the whore Em. I am certain of that. If she is his sister, as I suspect, then she will surely lead me to him.'

'And then what would you do?'

'I will extract the truth from him.'

'Boltfoot, there is a line where courage becomes foolhardiness. You will not be helping our cause if you cross it.'

'But this is not about you and me, is it, master? It is about Kat . . . Mistress Whetstone. Who will save her if we do not?'

Ah yes, that was it. Boltfoot had been almost as distraught as Shakespeare when she left. He had always held a candle for her while knowing she was beyond his reach. Shakespeare managed a smile which he hoped evoked his sympathy, a shared anxiety. 'At least wait until you are whole again. Then we will discuss our next step, calmly, when the heat has gone from your temper.'

Boltfoot said nothing, merely cast the same look at his master as he had done when defying him over the matter of hiring a new maidservant. Shakespeare saw it and knew the battle was lost. The only way Boltfoot would stay in this house today was if he were fixed to the wall by fetters. Shakespeare shook his head with a light laugh. 'Take care, Boltfoot. You are worth nothing dead.'

Shakespeare sighed with relief as he arrived at the Holborn house at nine o'clock and ascertained that Gilbert Gifford was indeed still there. He and the Smith sisters were eating heartily, so Shakespeare joined them, for his breakfast had not assuaged his appetite.

'Thank you, ladies,' he said as he rose to go.

'It was our pleasure, sir.' Eliza gazed at Gifford. *Her little pink pigling.*

'Mr Gifford, if you would accompany me, we have an appointment with Mr Secretary.'

'I want them again tonight. Will you bring them here?'

'First let us talk to Mr Secretary. He may have other plans. Come, sir.'

On their way to Walsingham's Seething Lane mansion, Shakespeare called in at home briefly. Boltfoot immediately approached him. 'A messenger came, master, not ten minutes since.' He held out a sealed letter. 'It is from Mr Tort.'

With his poniard, Shakespeare sliced open the red wax seal, unfolded the paper and read the short missive. *Go to Aldermanbury at noon. Mr Arthur Giltspur has agreed to see you.* Well, that was something, but it might be no more than the last turn of a card in a hand that was already doomed.

Taken alone, a conversation with the dead man's nephew was unlikely to help. Shakespeare had to talk further with Kat. Now that it was clear her husband's killer might have had a way to implicate her, he needed to hear from her own lips the names of *all* those who might have stood to benefit from his death and her downfall.

To one unversed in the labyrinthine twists and turns of his humours, Walsingham's mood might have seemed unremarkable, for he did not shout or curse or hammer his fist. But Shakespeare knew him better than that; Mr Secretary was in an unholy rage, like the churning current beneath a placid sea.

'This is falling apart, John. This infernal trinity – Babington, Ballard and Savage – where are they? Why are they not bringing the strands of their demonic plot together? If they were captains-general, their army would have turned tail or been slaughtered by now. Can none of them hold to the sticking-place? I am told Savage has become a model scholar at Barnard's Inn and is devoted to his studies. Is he to be assassin or lawyer?'

Shakespeare soaked up the onslaught. Only when Walsingham had stopped talking and was silent for a few seconds did he reply. 'They lack leadership.'

'Then *you* provide it!'

'I am not trusted enough.'

'What of Babington? Has he not been placed in the lead role by Ballard? I had thought the others of these Pope's White Sons followed him like sheep.'

'Yes, but Babington is idle and with Ballard gone north, he drifts. As for Ballard himself, he wastes his energies in the futile cause of raising a Pope's army. His head is full of bees. He promises the Spanish he can raise a force of sixty thousand English, when we know he is unlikely to rouse one Englishman from his slumbers.'

'And Goodfellow Savage?'

'Like an obedient, well-disciplined soldier, he is waiting for others to give him the order to strike. All I can say is this: he may procrastinate, but he will never betray his vow. He still means to do it; he merely awaits the time and the method.' He paused. 'But you have the letter from Mary to Babington now, Sir Francis. That surely will spur these men to action.'

'You have Gilbert Gifford with you?'

'He is in the anteroom. Would you have him take it to Babington this day?'

Walsingham gave a brisk shake of the head. 'I will wait until Ballard is back. I want him to boast to Babington about legions of Englishmen rising in the north and foreign armies sweeping in to support them. Only then will he have the confidence to write back to Mary with a detailed plan. A plan she will seize on. A plan that will provoke her into writing to him yet again – and this time giving her backing to treason. That will be the letter that will give us her wicked head.'

'I am anxious about Gifford. The longer we wait, the more likely he is to run; if we do not use him soon, I fear he will be gone.'

'Then tell him straight. If he leaves now, then he is England's enemy and will pay the price.'

'Very well. And I am still giving thought to the idea of using Robin Poley. He would prod Babington on.'

Walsingham nodded gravely. 'There is something of the snake about Poley. Can you introduce him to the plotters?'

'I said I would find a way, and I will.'

Walsingham gripped the edge of the table and stood up. He pushed his dark, glowering face forward and glared at Shakespeare with eyes as cold as moonbeams. 'Indeed? And do you have time for such inconsequential matters? I had thought your energies were all directed elsewhere . . .'

Shakespeare felt the prickles of hair rising on his neck.

'You know what I am talking about, John Shakespeare. Do you think you can go about your private business in this town without my knowledge? How little you know of me after eight years in my service.'

'I protest that I am not neglecting my duties. I cannot spend every minute of the day in the company of Goodfellow Savage. But I watch him nonetheless.'

'How do you watch him from Shoreditch?'

There was no point in dissembling; Walsingham already knew far too much for that. 'May I ask who told you I was there, Sir Francis?'

'Frank Mills told me! You attacked and bound Jonas Shoe, who is one Mills's men. He was working on behalf of Justice Young, trying to snare this monstrous widow, this Jezebel who has got the whole of London talking. Her Majesty is appalled that so wanton a murderess is still at large. Nicholas Giltspur was a good friend to her government and the murderess must pay the full and dreadful price. She committed a crime that is an offence to God and man and she will hang for it. So will anyone who assists her, before or after the fact! Do you now understand what you are playing with, John?'

'And if she is innocent?'

'Pah! The man who wielded the knife implicated her with his dying confession. There is no doubt. None at all.'

'What if he was paid to do so? What if he was dying already?'

'It would have no bearing on the case. His confession is all.'

'A man who was dying – and knew it – might wish to leave his loved ones well provided for. For a sum of gold, he might be persuaded to kill a man and incriminate the man's own wife. In such a case, I believe the second-in-line to the dead's man's inheritance might become the beneficiary.'

'This is preposterous supposition. The squirmings of a desperate felon.'

'No, Sir Francis. This is *not* mere supposition.'

Walsingham was silent. Whatever else he was, Shakespeare

knew his master to be just; he could not work for him otherwise. At last he spoke, his voice a little less insistent. 'If you have something to tell me, then say it.'

'Will Cane's body was riddled with cankers. He must have known with absolute certainty that he was within days of death. More than that, it is clear that he deliberately allowed himself to be arrested. He needed his day in court and his hour on the scaffold so that he could implicate Mistress Giltspur in the most public of ways.'

'How do you know of these diseases in Cane's body?'

Shakespeare had already said too much. Joshua Peace had enough trouble from those who called him necromancer without having the buying of corpses laid at his door.

'Speak, John. You know something.'

'Sir Francis, if I tell you certain matters, I would entreat you not to use them against the man they concern, nor tell them beyond these walls.'

'I can give no such promise, but nor would I ever wish to see an innocent woman hanged. Speak honestly and I will listen.'

Shakespeare nodded. 'Very well.' In a few short sentences, he told his master all that he had learnt from Joshua Peace.

'This certainly provokes thought. But there is more, is there not?'

'Sir Francis?'

'Come, come, John. If you wish my assistance, you must reveal the truth. What is this woman to you?'

'I knew her as Kat Whetstone.'

Walsingham snorted. He knew the name well. 'Now I understand. And you have seen the woman, I take it.'

A man could conceal nothing in Mr Secretary's presence. 'Yes,' Shakespeare said simply. 'Yes, I have seen her. She denies any involvement in the killing.'

'Well, that is no surprise. Where is she now?'

'I no longer know. I was in Shoreditch trying to find her. I need to hear more of her story. She must know who might have benefited from her husband's death.'

'Yes, I see that. How are you hoping to proceed with your inquiries? What would you have *me* do?'

'Give me time to find the true killer. I swear I will not let Savage free of his obligation. I *will* find a way to bring Poley to Babington. And Gilbert Gifford will not flee.'

'You realise you are already an accessory to murder. Your duty under the law is to arrest her and bring her to court.'

'When I saw her I knew nothing of the murder nor the case against her.'

'Who took you to her?'

'I cannot say.'

'Cannot . . . or will not?'

'Will not. Anyway, if I had allowed her to be arrested she would have been hanged before I had any chance to discover the truth. It may still be so. For all I know, Justice Young might already have her.'

'Is she innocent?'

Shakespeare's mouth turned down. 'I don't know.'

'Good. I would be more concerned for your welfare if you had swallowed her story untried.'

'I will not be gulled. I have been well trained by you – well enough to know that the heart of every man and woman conceals dark corners. It may be that she *is* guilty of the crime, in which case I will testify against her myself.'

Walsingham closed his eyes and placed his elbows on the table. His fingers were at his forehead, tapping. The chilly, severe room – a perfect reflection of its owner's character in plaster and wood – was silent except for their breathing and the soft tap-tap of the fingers. A minute passed. Walsingham took a deep breath then opened his eyes.

'I met this woman once, if you recall. I strode up to your house one morning.'

Shakespeare could not forget it. He had come down from his solar to find Mr Secretary in the parlour, sitting at the table, talking with Kat about the weather. And she was not showing him the kind of deference to which he was accustomed. Shocked and flustered, Shakespeare had not known what to say. But then Walsingham had spoken: 'Mistress Whetstone has introduced herself to me and invited me in. I trust I am not intruding.' 'Indeed not, Sir Francis.' 'A small goblet of brandy would suit me well.' And so Shakespeare had fetched the flask and poured three goblets, as though he were a servant. For the half-hour Walsingham was there, Shakespeare had been as taut as an anchor cable in a high wind. And yet her charm had won over the Principal Secretary and his sojourn seemed to please him. Finally he had stood up from the table and said, 'John, I have quite forgotten why I came here. But I thank you for your hospitality – and yours, Mistress Whetstone.' And then he had taken his leave.

Shakespeare had not been fooled. Walsingham had not forgotten the purpose of his visit that day; he forgot nothing. The reason had been simple: word had reached him that his young intelligencer had a woman about the house and he wished to meet her. Nothing more. Clearly she had passed muster.

'She meant a lot to you, I believe. For all that you were living in a sinful union, I liked her – and I was sorry to hear she had left.'

'Thank you, Sir Francis.'

'Forty-eight hours, John. You have forty-eight hours, but I will not call off Justice Young. If you are caught and arraigned as an accessory to murder, *your* neck will be in the noose – and I will not be able to save you.'

*

Sorbus the steward was already at the door of Giltspur House. He nodded to the guards to put up their swords and let Shakespeare through. 'Follow me,' he said tersely, leading the way with small, feminine steps into the depths of the mansion.

From the main part of the house, they crossed an inner courtyard which still had the feel of a monastic cloister, which it had been until the dissolution. Apart from the outside gateway, with its effigies of saints, it was the only part of the property that had retained traces of the house's clerical history. Shakespeare guessed that the ornate central fountain and the fragrant flowerbeds that surrounded it were not the work of the monks.

What most struck him was the heavy security employed within the high walls of this house. There were guards on duty at every turn. Was this the way rich men had to live, in a fortress?

A long building sheltered the far edge of the quad. A dull clackety noise emanated from inside the building and Shakespeare immediately recognised it as the sound of a tennis match in progress. Sorbus opened a door and bade him enter the long penthouse gallery ranged alongside the court, then retreated without a word.

Shakespeare watched the game and listened to the reassuring sound; an echoing clatter as the hard little ball flew from strings and bounced off wood. At each end there was a man in a linen open-neck shirt. Their feet were soft-slippered and they both carried a racket of wood, strung tight with gut. One player's shoulders were rounded and slumping as though the world would fall about him. He was at the server's end and seemed older. The other man, to Shakespeare's left, in the hazard court, looked calm and relaxed. Somehow Shakespeare imagined him to be young Arthur Giltspur.

The server struck the ball carefully, as though his life depended on it. The ball rose and fell in a gentle arc onto the penthouse roof, bounced three times then fell into the receiving court, only to be returned like a gunshot. The server, slow to react, managed to get the frame of his racket to the ball, but only with enough force to send it straight into the net. Shakespeare frowned; the server suddenly seemed very familiar. He found himself laughing – it was Huckerbee, the comptroller from the Treasury. It looked very much as if the self-satisfied patrician were being brought low.

'Fifteen thirty,' the receiver called, then spotted the newcomer. He held up his racket to stay his opponent from serving and walked towards the gallery and Shakespeare while the server, seemingly relieved to have some respite, set about collecting the balls that littered the bottom of the net.

'Mr Shakespeare?'

'Indeed. I take it you are Arthur Giltspur.'

'A pleasure to meet you. Severin Tort told me of you. You are an assistant secretary to Walsingham, are you not?'

'Yes, that is so.'

They shook hands. Giltspur had his racket in his left hand, sloping over his shoulder like a very short halberd. It was an old, well-used implement. The beads of sweat across his brow and exposed throat spoke of a hard-battled game.

'Do you play, sir?' Giltspur asked. 'I am always looking for new opponents.'

'It is my misfortune that I have never had the opportunity. From that last shot it would seem you have a great skill.'

Giltspur grinned. 'At risk of being immodest, I would say that no man in England can best me. But I have yet to play young Robert Devereux, of whom I hear good things, so it may be my pride will come before a fall. Anyway, Mr Shakespeare, you are a young man. There is time enough to learn. I shall give you some words of advice when we are done. But first to business. I believe you have an interest in the tragic case of Uncle Nick.'

Shakespeare took in Arthur Giltspur's appearance. He was an inch or two off six foot and had the lean, hard body of a sportsman. He wore his billowing linen shirt with the throat stays undone, so that his tanned and muscled chest was clearly visible. His face, beneath ribbon-tied fair hair, was friendly and open – the face of a young man with few cares in the world. Shakespeare guessed his age at twenty-four or so.

'Come, Mr Shakespeare, let us go to my solar. This match has given me a raging thirst.'

'Do you not wish to finish your tennis? I see your opponent is Sir Robert Huckerbee.'

'Do you know him?'

'Vaguely.'

'He is an old friend of the family. Do you wish to pay your respects?'

Shakespeare looked across at Huckerbee and their eyes met. The comptroller looked back blankly. It occurred to Shakespeare that he did not enjoy being watched in his moment of humiliation. He turned away. 'No, leave him be. Our acquaintance is merely professional.'

'Well, he was very close to Uncle Nick.' Giltspur laughed, then cupped his hand and whispered in Shakespeare's ear. 'I'm afraid his tennis is not what it was. Let us slip away. I think he will be pleased to retain his twenty-pound stake. He hasn't had a game off me yet and we're into the second set. I will just make my apologies and take my leave of him.'

Chapter 18

THE GILTSPUR HOUSE solar was an exquisite room. High, noonday sunlight flooded in from two large casement windows, both of which were glazed. Giltspur opened the latches to let in some much-needed fresh air.

A servant arrived with a pitcher of cordial and placed it on a table near the window, then poured two cups, bowed and departed.

Arthur Giltspur sat on a cushion-covered settle and swatted at a fast-moving and very noisy bluefly with his racket. 'Got it!' He gazed down at the inert body of the insect and trod it down to ensure it was dead. 'Did you note how I watched it before I hit it? It is the same with tennis. You must watch the ball at all times. You watch it when it is in the server's hand and when he tosses it up. You follow its arc to the penthouse. You watch it as a cat watches its prey. You watch it as Mr Secretary watches England's enemies . . .'

'What do you know of Mr Secretary?'

'No more than any man. I have seen him at court and I met him briefly at a guild banquet, but mostly I know him by repute. I give thanks that Her Majesty has his services. He labours in the dark sewer of political intrigue so that Elizabeth and her subjects may sleep sound abed at night. If you are one of his chosen, then I must respect you, too. But you are not here to listen to my musings. You are come about the death of my uncle. You believe Katherine to be innocent, do you not?'

'You seem well informed.'

Giltspur sipped his cordial. 'Severin Tort has briefed me. He came to me late last night. I know all about you and Kat, as you call her. He told me you had some evidence that all might not be as the murderer claimed in court.'

Shakespeare nodded. Without mentioning Joshua Peace or his own meeting with Kat, he rehearsed what he knew and his own feelings about Kat's character.

'Then I think we have similar thoughts. I cannot believe Katherine commissioned Uncle Nick's murder. She brought only joy and life to this rather cold and empty house.'

'But she had cause to kill him, did she not, Mr Giltspur? Had she not been implicated by Cane, she would now be an exceedingly rich widow.' He met his host's eye, with meaning.

'Say it, Mr Shakespeare. Say what you are thinking.'

'I am thinking that you, too, would become very wealthy were your aunt disqualified from inheritance by reason of her crime.'

Giltspur smiled. 'You believe the prospect of inheriting his wealth gives me a motive for the murder of Uncle Nick and the condemning of Katherine?'

'Some might think so.'

'What if I were to tell you that I am already very wealthy?'

Shakespeare said nothing, waited for him to continue.

Giltspur sighed. His eyes were amused, as though he were making merry at a schoolfellow's expense. 'Very well. Let me complete the picture for you. Of course, Severin Tort could have told you all this, but he is probably so long versed in the ways of lawyers that he is reluctant to say more than he has to, lest he be thought a betrayer of confidences. But this is the way it is. My father, Philip Giltspur, was Uncle Nick's elder brother. They worked together and traded together and built up their remarkably profitable concern: the greatest fishing fleet in the realm. And when my father died ten years ago, I inherited his half. This house, too, is half mine, Mr Shakespeare. I have never wanted for anything nor could I possibly have need of more treasure. And before you ask, I loved Uncle Nick as well as I loved my own father. His death has hit me like the blow of a hammer – and I very much want anyone involved brought to justice.'

Shakespeare still held his eye. Was there more there, inside him, unspoken? Surely a man brought low with grief would deny himself the pleasure of the tennis court. Would he not, too, adopt a more sombre aspect?

'Again, I know what you are thinking. But I will not spend my days in black weeds. We live with death, and so it is my duty to live my life to the full. If you think the worse for me because of that, then so be it; but I refuse to play the hypocrite.'

'I wish only to get to the truth, Mr Giltspur.'

Giltspur raised his palm. 'Indeed, and it is your job to have suspicions. Mr Secretary pays you for your jealous mind. Think nothing of it. I desire every bit as much as you to find the truth of this matter. If Katherine is behind it, then she must pay the penalty. But if she is not, then we must clear her name and look further afield. *You* must look further afield, sir. But you are not alone. I will give you what little assistance I can.'

'You could begin by telling me what you know of your uncle and his business dealings – and then I would like to be taken around this house. I would like to know more about the way he lived. Who makes up this household? I see you have many sentries, all armed, even within the house itself.'

'The walls are ten feet high and yes, we do have guards, to

keep out unwanted intruders.' He raised an eyebrow in Shakespeare's direction with meaning. 'I think you can imagine why this is necessary.'

'I believe the Queen herself does not have such security.'

'Perhaps she does not have so much gold.'

Shakespeare pushed on with his questioning. How many servants did he keep? Were there other kinfolk here? 'And I would like to know more about your uncle himself. Was he married before? Did he have enemies? Most wealthy men do, Mr Giltspur. And if so, who might have wished him harm?'

'Well, I can answer two of those questions straightway. Yes, Uncle Nick was married before, twenty-five years since. But his wife died in childbirth at seventeen years of age; the babe died, too, so he has no issue. I am told he loved his wife very much and that he could never bring himself to find a new wife – until he met Katherine and fell under her spell. She charmed him and he was beguiled. I am sure you know all about that, sir. At the time of his death, Uncle Nick was fifty-six, but he was no December fool falling for a May schemer. He knew what he was about.'

'What other kinfolk did he have, apart from you?'

'There is only one other relative here: my grandame.'

'I would like to meet her.'

'That may not be possible. While she has the constitution of a ploughhorse, she has taken the death of Uncle Nick very badly. I think she has aged ten years in a week. She scarcely stirs from her apartments. But as you are here, I shall send messages to her. She must wish this matter concluded satisfactorily, as much as you and I do. And she can only say no.'

'Thank you, Mr Giltspur.' He hesitated a moment, then forged on. 'And what of your uncle's enemies?'

'I am sure there were people he loathed and others who disliked him. Which of us can honestly say otherwise? But in my uncle's case, I could not name them. He was a genuinely like-able man. His handshake was his bond and to my knowledge he never reneged on it. I did not play a great role in the fishing fleet, but I never heard him speak ill of anyone with whom he had dealings.'

'I have one more question for the present: what manner of man is Mr Sorbus?'

'He had been with Uncle Nick for as long as I can recall. To tell true, I have no idea whether he even has a Christian name or not. We always called him Sorbus, nothing more.'

'He seemed very reluctant to grant me access to you.'

Giltspur laughed loud. 'That is Sorbus! He is the gatekeeper. He believes his main purpose in life is to keep the common rabble away from his master and his master's family. I am afraid he has airs more haughty than a Hatton or Leicester. As far as he is concerned, *you* are the common rabble, Mr Shakespeare.'

'How did he take to his master's new bride? Was she, too, part of the common rabble?'

'Oh, the commonest of common rabble. I saw the way he looked at her and how he affected not to hear her when she gave him commands or made requests of him. No, no, Katherine would not have been at all to Sorbus's taste. The mere sound of her northern vowels must have given him an apoplexy.'

The house was not as big as Shakespeare had imagined from its wide frontage, tennis court and elaborate courtyard. Yet he considered it to be all the finer for its relative compactness; every room had been renovated or built anew with the wealth accrued by the Giltspur brothers. Even the extensive kitchens had a modern character. What was most surprising, however, was the number of servants. Shakespeare lost track of them, but estimated that there were twenty or more, which seemed a great number for a household that until recently had consisted of only Nicholas Giltspur, his new wife Kat, his mother and his nephew Arthur.

'Has there been any trouble with any of the serving staff, Mr Giltspur? Has anyone been dismissed recently – someone who might perhaps bear a grudge?'

'I think that most unlikely, but you would have to speak to Sorbus.' They were walking through the hall. Giltspur raised his racket to point ahead. 'And speak of the devil, there he is. Sorbus!'

Sorbus acknowledged the summons with a stiff little bow and walked with his precise, measured steps towards Arthur Giltspur, where he bowed again and said, 'May I be of assistance, master?'

Of course, thought Shakespeare, this young man is now the steward's master. How was the surly old retainer taking this change of circumstance? No, the word *old* was wrong. He might have been with Giltspur as long as his nephew could recall, but Sorbus was not old. Shakespeare put his age at about thirty-five. He was a stiff-shouldered little man with a nose as sharp as a sundial's gnomon and a costly suit of clothes in unseasonal black broken only by the crisp white ruffs at his cuffs and collar.

'Master?'

'Mr Shakespeare here would like to ask you some questions. Do him the courtesy of telling him everything he wishes to know.'

'Yes, master.'

The lack of conviction in Sorbus's voice was deafening.

'Did anyone among the servants bear a grudge against your former master?'

'A grudge, sir?'

'You know what a grudge is, do you not, Sorbus? It is a desire for retribution for some perceived hurt.'

'Forgive me, Mr Shakespeare. Of course, I know what the word means, but I wondered why you should use it in respect of the servants. I run a well-ordered household. If a man or woman did not measure up to my exacting standards, they would be dismissed instantly.'

'And such a one might have cause to feel vengeful towards this house and all in it.'

'If you say so, sir.'

Shakespeare looked from Sorbus to Giltspur, who shook his head and laughed.

'Really, Sorbus, I think you could be a little more helpful. Mr Shakespeare wishes to discover the truth about Mr Giltspur's murder.'

'So I am told, master.'

'Who acted as Mr Giltspur's valet?'

'That was Thomas. He has now left, for he is no longer required.'

'Do you know where he has gone?'

'To Norwich, I believe, whence he came as a boy. Mr Giltspur here was most generous and agreed to a pension of five pounds a year.'

'It was the least I could do,' Giltspur said. 'He loved my uncle as though he were his father. He was broken by the murder.'

'What are your feelings towards Mistress Giltspur?' Shakespeare turned back to Sorbus. 'Might she be innocent?' He watched Sorbus's face closely but could detect nothing from his expression.

'It is not my place to have an opinion, sir.' The steward's tone verged on insolence.

Shakespeare had had enough. 'You may go.' Sorbus bowed

to Giltspur, but not his guest, then walked back in the direction from which he had come. Shakespeare watched him go, then spread his palms hopelessly.

'I am sorry, Mr Shakespeare,' Giltspur said. 'Sorbus is a lost soul. He is trying to hold himself and this house together and he doesn't really know how.' He lowered his voice. 'I am going to have to pension him off, and I think he realises it.'

'Perhaps.'

'Come, let me show you my uncle's rooms – and I shall see if Grandame will grant you a hearing.'

'Thank you.'

Kat and her husband had slept in separate chambers, connected by a double door, each of which could only be opened or locked from its own side.

'Were the rooms always like this or was it an innovation created for the new bride?'

'I have no notion. Never did I have cause to come to these rooms either before or after the wedding. I have only been up here once and that was since the murder, to see if Uncle Nick kept any vital papers secreted here.'

'Did you find anything?'

'Nothing. Look around the place while I go to see if Grandame will receive you.'

Shakespeare watched him go and wondered how he spent his time; he could surely not fill *all* his days with tennis. Was there a woman in his life? He had said that he realised he must now learn the trade of his father and uncle, but so far he did not seem overly concerned by such matters. Perhaps he had other interests to occupy him. Shakespeare made a mental note to question Severin Tort further, for he was clearly involved in the Giltspur corporation to a great degree.

Nicholas Giltspur's chamber was large but not palatial,

perhaps twenty-two foot square. The bed was big, however, with wonderfully carved posts and a silk canopy of rich reds and golds. The furnishings included a coffer and a small chest. Shakespeare tried them and discovered they were both unlocked and empty. He looked beneath the feather mattress, but there was nothing to be seen. At the side of the window there was a shelf with a few books, mostly either devotional or containing poetry. The only other one was *A Discourse on the Variation of The Compass.* As taught by Walsingham, Shakespeare flicked through the pages of the books to see if any papers were hidden there. Again, nothing. Either Mr Giltspur had lived a very austere and frugal life, or this chamber had been stripped since his death.

The very absence of evidence of Nick Giltspur's life seemed somehow to signify that there were other secrets to be uncovered, somewhere. Surely even the bleak cells of anchorites contained indications of the life lived? All Giltspur's chamber revealed was that he had had money enough for costly fabrics and that he used occasionally to dip into books.

Shakespeare walked through the double doors to Kat's chamber. This was very different, a much more feminine room. Yes, this would have been a bower fit for the ambitious Kat Whetstone. The bed was smaller and less ornate, but there was evidence at least of human occupation here: combs and potions, a wig, an adjoining wardrobe stuffed with expensive gowns and shoes. Beyond that, there were no clues. He was looking out of the window, down onto the central quad, when Arthur Giltspur reappeared at his side.

'Well, we have good fortune, Mr Shakespeare. Grandame has consented to see you briefly.'

'Thank you. Tell me, sir, where is Katherine's lady's maid? I assume she had one. Has she, too, been dismissed?'

'Indeed not. Katherine remains unconvicted by a court. I

will hold any man or woman innocent until proven guilty. And so Abigail remains with us. She has taken over the duties of Grandame's own maid, who is presently in her sickbed. In confidence, I would tell you that she is not expected to survive. As for Abigail, you will see her, too, in Grandame's apartment.'

'Good.'

'Then follow me.'

Shakespeare hesitated. Something was troubling him. It was the book in Nick Giltspur's chamber, *A Discourse on the Variation of the Compass*. The sea. Why had he not made the connection before?

'Mr Shakespeare?'

'Another question: have you heard of a man named Cutting Ball, a known villain?'

'Yes, indeed. I believe it was said in court that the murderer, Cane, was his associate.'

'And do you know anything of the way Mr Ball works?'

Giltspur's brow creased. 'What do you mean?'

For the first time Shakespeare thought he saw a fleeting crack in his engaging facade. 'I mean the character of his criminal activities.'

Giltspur shook his head, the frown gone. Perhaps Shakespeare had imagined it. 'Why, I suppose he cuts purses. Is that not what these people do?'

'Oh, I fear he does rather more than cut purses. He likes to cut faces, too, and he cuts away the privy parts of men who displease him. Also eyeballs, I am told. But more than that is his interest in the fleets of the realm. It is said he demands one part in a hundred of all cargoes landed at the wharfs downriver from the bridge, and that his men burn out the vessels of any who refuse him. What I find myself wondering is whether the cargoes he targets would include the shiploads of fish your family lands. What do you think? Did he ever make demands of your Uncle Nick?'

Giltspur looked perplexed. 'What a strange question, Mr Shakespeare. And one you would have to ask Uncle Nick himself, which, of course, is impossible.'

Chapter 19

'GRANDAME, ALLOW ME to introduce you to Mr John Shakespeare. Sir, this is my grandmother, Mistress Joan Giltspur.'

Shakespeare bowed low with the courtesy due to great age. Mistress Giltspur was in her bed, reclining against a bank of downy pillows. Shakespeare took her to be eighty, perhaps more – perhaps as old as the century itself. 'It is my honour, ma'am.'

She waved him up with a brisk, bony hand. 'Please stand up properly, Mr Shakespeare. I am not the Queen of England and nor am I feeble-minded.'

'Forgive me.'

'There is nothing to forgive. It is I who must apologise for allowing you to see me like this. My mind is still there but my bones are brittle and afflicted by great pain. Now then, what do you want? Arthur tells me that you are an assistant to Sir Francis Walsingham and that you are investigating the death of my beloved Nicholas.'

'That is so.'

'He says you do not believe that Katherine was behind it?'

'Indeed, I have my doubts.'

'And she was once your paramour. Do I have it thus far?'

'It seems you know everything about me.'

'I doubt that very much. Sir Francis's men tend to come with a great many secrets attached. So tell me, what is it you hope to discover?'

'I want to know whether Katherine is innocent or guilty. And if she is innocent, who truly ordered the killing of your son. Nothing more.'

'An admirable ambition. How can I help?' Her voice was quiet but firm.

'Perhaps you cannot. But as I said to your grandson, rich and successful men tend to have enemies. I would know the identities of your son's enemies, for if Katherine is innocent, then the true killer must surely lurk among them.'

'If you are seeking to find Nicholas's enemies, then you are indeed on a hopeless mission. He was known for his charity, honesty and kindness, a faithful Christian of the reformed Church but with no animosity towards the old faith in which I was raised. A man of old-fashioned virtues, not often seen these days when men will crawl over each other for a few shillings. He treated those who worked for him with decency and allowed them their dignity. He would accept no cruelty aboard his vessels, and when a ship was lost he paid generous recompense to the fishers' wives and children.'

'Did you know much about the trade he pursued?'

'How should I know about such things' The old lady laughed, and then began to cough. Her grandson went to her side, but she brushed him away. 'Water, Arthur. A sip of water. Don't fuss so.'

He stood up from the bed. 'Abigail!'

The maid, a plump and pretty young woman, came scurrying in. 'Yes, Mr Giltspur?'

'Bring a cup of water,' Giltspur said.

'And laudanum. I would have laudanum.'

The maid curtsied quickly. 'Yes, Mistress Giltspur.'

When she had hastened away to fulfil her mistress's demands, Shakespeare turned again to Giltspur. 'Is that the Abigail who was Katherine's lady's maid?'

'Yes. Grandame's own maid is in a wretched way and will most likely go to God within a day or two. Abigail has taken on her duties.'

The old widow raised her hand. 'It is my curse, Mr Shakespeare. I am doomed to outlive everyone I love, even my maid.' Her cough was easing, but her voice still rasped a little. 'I sometimes wonder whether God has forgotten about me. Do you know how old I am?'

'I would not care to hazard a guess for fear of offending.'

'Eighty-one, Mr Shakespeare. I am eighty-one. Sixty years ago I danced with the Queen's father. He was charming to me and I knew he was trying to win me to his bed with pretty words, but I would have none of it, for though he had not then become the great killer that we now know him to have been, yet I saw the darkness in him and knew him for a cruel and capricious man.'

Abigail returned with water and a tincture of opium in a small silver goblet, which she handed to her mistress with great care.

The old woman sipped some water, swallowed the opium, then let out a great sigh of contentment. 'Nicholas always told me I should refrain from laudanum, that it would be hazardous to my health. But to me, it is a blessing that relieves all pain. And you know, Mr Shakespeare, there really is very little danger of me dying young.' She attempted to laugh again, but this time it was more a soft tinkle than the cackle of before. 'Now, you asked me about enemies . . .'

'One man in particular interests me, though there may be others. A man known as Cutting Ball.'

'Oh yes, we have heard of him, haven't we, Arthur? Abigail? Is he not a Robin Hood or Jack Cade?'

Shakespeare studied the lady's maid. She was a remarkably well-favoured woman with milkmaid skin and large breasts. How would she have got on with Kat? Shakespeare tried to imagine the two of them together; mistress and maid. Somehow it didn't work.

'There are exciting tales told of his exploits, mistress,' Abigail said. 'I have heard that men often admire him.'

How had Cutting Ball become a folk hero? 'There is nothing valiant about Mr Ball. He does not steal from the rich to help the poor; nor does he seek to improve the lot of the labouring man. He steals from everyone to enrich himself and he murders and maims those who stand in his way.'

There was silence in the room and Shakespeare realised he had revealed himself a little too clearly. He looked at the woman in the bed. She was becoming drowsy, but there was something in her eye that told him she was playing with him. She knew very well who Cutting Ball was and what he did.

And then it struck him: she was not simply the doddering matriarch of this family. She was the very heart of its trading empire. If the Giltspurs had ever paid money to Cutting Ball to protect their ships from his malicious attentions, then she knew all about it. She knew everything. Arthur's father and uncle had not built the clan's great riches; they had merely worked for their mother, done her bidding, been the public face. Mistress Giltspur – *Grandame* – was the power in this household.

'Ma'am,' he said. 'I would value your opinion. Do you believe your daughter-in-law paid Will Cane to murder your son?'

Her breathing was more pronounced, almost a snore. A few words seemed to escape her lips, but Shakespeare could hardly discern them.

'She will be asleep any moment,' Giltspur said. 'I think your questioning is at an end, Mr Shakespeare.'

'Did she say something? I could not catch the words.'

Arthur Giltspur smiled. 'You will get nothing more from her now. When she is awake she is usually lucid. But then the laudanum plays games with her . . .' He paused. 'She wants the diamond. Sometimes she sleeps with it. She says it brings her comfort.'

'The Giltspur Diamond?'

'It is famous, I think. A rare piece. A diamond of one hundred carats, brought from the Africas. It hangs as the centrepiece of a necklet.'

'Is it here with her now?'

Giltspur affected a puzzled expression. 'Your questions go in remarkable odd directions, sir. She either has it with her or it is locked away in the strongroom. It is hers, so I know not.'

For a few seconds more, Shakespeare gazed upon the ancient, lined face and thought he saw the beautiful young woman whom Great Henry had held in his deadly arms. He imagined her wearing her great diamond about her neck, its brilliance catching the light and dazzling all eyes. He saw something else, too: Kat Whetstone, now Katherine Giltspur, fugitive and widow. Though separated by two generations, Kat and the old grandmother shared beauty, immense ambition and unstoppable willpower. When Nicholas Giltspur fell for Kat, he had found a replica of his mother.

'Are you done with us, sir?'

'I am, Mr Giltspur.'

Arthur Giltspur touched Shakespeare's arm. 'Grandame had hoped that Katherine would give her another grandson, to carry on the family enterprise. She despairs of me. The truth is, I have no interest in ships and the sea. Nor fish.'

*

'You have never explained how you were freed from the Fleet gaol so early, Mr Maude. I was told that you were sentenced to three years for extorting money from the archbishop, yet it seems you served little more than half that time.'

Harry Slide was taken aback by the sudden turn of Ballard's questioning. They had been consoling themselves with a well-earned meal after another fruitless day trying to extract pledges of support from Catholic gentry. No one in Nottinghamshire was interested. The lords and knights and burghers had land to be farmed, mines to be dug and, anyway, they all had seminary priests in residence to attend to their spiritual needs. The last thing they wanted was insurrection and civil war. Memories of the 1569 Northern Rebellion and the 1536 Pilgrimage of Grace were all too fresh. Each had ended in ferocious reprisals.

'What a curious question, Captain.' Slide's knife, with a fine slice of beef attached to it, hung in the smoky air, halfway to his mouth.

'I had a dream last night, Mr Maude. It seemed to me that something was not quite right about you.'

Slide shrugged, pushed the beef into his mouth and chewed. He had a mighty hunger from the day's wasted efforts.

'Do you hear me?'

He put down his knife, pointedly. 'Yes, I hear you. A dream, you say? Are you a sorcerer that you take note of such things?'

'It was most vivid. I saw you cloaked in treachery, come to us with a knife behind your back. A winged angel swept you away and dropped you into the pit.'

Slide picked up his knife again and held it towards Ballard. A red drop of beef juice dribbled down its sharp edge. 'This knife, Captain Fortescue? Was this the knife that I held behind my back? Take it. It's yours if it worries you.'

'I don't want your knife.'

'Dreams! Perhaps you will converse with your winged angels next – like Dr Dee. I am surprised and not a little disturbed that you should ask me such things. Do you think I am some sort of spy? Or perhaps you think me a fugitive from justice and would have me returned to the Fleet.'

'I know not, but I would like an answer nonetheless.' He looked to his other companion, Robert Gage. '*We* would like an answer. Why did you serve but half your sentence?'

'And all for a dream.' Slide shook his head as though this conversation was altogether too tedious 'Very well. If you must. I was released early at the archbishop's own request. I am told he felt my continued presence in gaol only served to pro-long the mockery and derision aimed at his person. He wished the whole thing forgotten as quickly as possible.' Slide snorted with laughter. 'A vain hope! Men will make merry at the expense of the dirty Archbishop of York and the landlord's bawdy wife for many generations to come. Does that satisfy you, Captain Fortescue? May I return to my beef while it yet has some warmth to it?'

He met Ballard's eye. It was a dark, scowling thing. He was in his late thirties, mad-eyed and dark-bearded, wearing an extravagant cape laced with gold, and a satin doublet with slashes; attire most uncommon here in the east Midlands. At his side, on the bench, was a hat adorned with silver buttons. He wore the guise of a rich and generous captain-of-war with assurance, as though born to the role; the very image of a sol-dier of fortune. Why, Slide wondered, had such a man – with a taste for assassination and insurrection – not joined a real army rather than the priesthood? Would he not have preferred the blood and thunder of a true man-at-arms to the sneaking and slithering of the underground clergy?

Slide looked away, but was still aware of Ballard's eyes boring in to him. He ignored them, ate his beef greedily and tossed back his strong beer. What a pleasure it would be to observe this priest's blood washing into the Tyburn soil.

'Is that true?' Ballard pressed.

Slide sighed. 'Yes, for pity's sake. Otherwise I would not be here, but manacled in my cold cell.'

Ballard attempted a smile, but it was more like a grimace. 'Forgive me. These checks and disappointments . . . I begin to see enemies in the shadows.'

'Well I am *not* your enemy. Now eat your beef and allow me the same courtesy.' Harry Slide had no more time for this. He had spotted a face across the taproom floor, studying him closely. Was it someone from the past when he lived and operated in these parts? Slide always remembered a face, but in this case he was uncertain. Only one thing for it: find out.

Shakespeare rode to meet Goodfellow Savage at Barnard's Inn. The street here at Holborn Bars was a scene of chaos, with building work proceeding on Staple Inn next door to Barnard's. The new inn was designed as an extension to Gray's and the work was disrupting the movement of livestock and wagons. A delivery of timber had just been unloaded and was strewn across the highway. Shakespeare had to pick his way over piles of oak.

Savage was at his studies, his head bent so low that his eyes were scarce three inches from the paper he read. He had his hands over his ears to blank out the sounds of hammering and shouting from the nearby building site.

Shakespeare clapped his hands. 'Come, Goodfellow,' he shouted. 'Let us remove ourselves from this din.'

Putting down his quill, Savage rubbed his tired eyes and blinked. 'They do their damnable work from dawn until dusk. There is as much noise here as on the field of battle.'

'Let us dine together. I will pay the reckoning.'

Savage stood up from his table and stretched his arms so that he touched the ceiling. 'Free food and ale? You are most persuasive, John Shakespeare.'

'Good.'

Shakespeare looked about the cheerless room where Savage lived, slept and worked with his three fellow lodgers, including Dominic de Warre. Apart from the table there was a basin and four poor beds of straw, but today Savage was alone, red-eyed from his long hours of study.

Together, they walked out into the warm evening air and headed east, away from Holborn Bars towards the Silver Grayling. As they passed Hern's Rents, Savage stopped and looked up at the six-storey tenement. 'Shall we call out Anthony Babington?'

He wanted Savage to himself. 'Another time. Let us talk of women, wine and the hunt. There are days when a man needs nothing more serious than the fellowship of a good friend and a jug of good beer.'

'I hoped you would say that. He pushes me incessantly.'

'Pushes you? In what way?'

For a moment it seemed to Shakespeare that Savage was about to reveal his murderous vow, but he merely smiled. 'You know – the way he pushes us all. Do you think it will ever happen, this rising?'

'One must hope. There is much to plan, many preparations to be made. God will surely show us the way, but we must do our part, too. He gave us free will so that we might choose to follow his path or take the other way. The brave man's path – or the coward's way—' Shakespeare stopped short.

Savage stood rigid, his head held high, his long soldier's beard thrust forward, like a statue, frozen in stone, eyes wide open and staring.

'Goodfellow – is all well with you?'

He shook himself and gasped for air. 'I . . . forgive me, John.'

'What is it?'

'I saw the cross before my eyes. I saw Christ's blood, flowing like molten gold from his wounds. His mouth did not move but I heard his words. He was talking to me.' Another deep gulp of air. Savage closed his eyes.

'Goodfellow?'

'I think it was a sign.'

Shakespeare placed a comforting hand on his companion's arm.

'John, I am sore troubled. What do you believe the Church's teaching to be on the matter of taking one life to save a nation's soul?'

'You mean *assassination*?' Shakespeare barely whispered the word. His heart was pounding. He did not wish to be told this secret. The fact that he had learnt of Savage's vow from Gifford rather than from his own lips somehow made it distant and he had always secretly hoped to find some way to save him. But if he were to have this man's confidence, it would be altogether different. How could he keep such a secret when it flew against all that he believed in? *Oh that my ears should fill up with mortar and that deafness should suddenly take me.*

And yet this was his work: the defence of Queen and realm. His country before his friends. He chose his reply with care. 'I have heard it said that if such an act is carried out for God, and not for man, then there will be rejoicing in heaven.'

'*Regnans in Excelsis* seemed to make it clear, but since its suspension . . . How can a man know where he stands?'

Shakespeare nodded his head gravely. *Regnans in Excelsis.* This proclamation of Pope Pius V in 1570 excommunicating Elizabeth had, in essence, ordered her subjects to rise up against her or risk excommunication themselves. It had supposedly been suspended in 1580, but all that had happened was that the people of England were given freedom to obey her orders to save their skins – all the while waiting, hoping, praying and scheming for her death and the destruction of her regime.

'Do you think it still gives a man freedom to—'

'I think you have said too much, Goodfellow.'

Savage was not to be stopped. 'You are the only man in England whose opinion I trust and respect, John Shakespeare. If I cannot talk with you, then I am alone.'

Shakespeare put his finger to his lips. 'Say nothing.' The street was busy, as always, but they were cocooned in their own private world. Their voices were low. It was safer here than in the tavern. The Silver Grayling could wait.

And then it came out, unstoppable like a flood. 'I have made a vow to kill her. I made it in church, on my knees, before the cross, before God himself. It is a vow I cannot escape – and yet I cannot bring myself . . .' Savage seemed to struggle for breath again. Then he pulled out his sword and held it by the hilt in his huge hands. 'See how my hands shake? Never in the heat of battle did they quiver so. This thought, this unbreakable pledge, turns me to jelly.'

By now bystanders were starting to look. Shakespeare's hand tightened on Savage's arm and he pulled him into a narrow alleyway. 'You will get us both hanged if you speak so publicly!' he hissed.

'I had to tell you, John.'

'Why are you sacrificing your life? What made you promise this?'

'We are all risking our lives – you included, John Shakespeare.'

'But your death is *certain*.'

Savage's smile was the saddest thing Shakespeare had ever seen. 'My life is already done,' he said quietly. 'I surrendered it to God on the fields of Flanders. It was only His will that I should survive when others died in battle. He spared me for this greater purpose.'

Who had told him that? Was it Gilbert Gifford, or others at the seminary in Rheims? There were many men of God who were happy to tell others that the Lord wished them to sacrifice their lives, without once hazarding their own.

'Who else knows of this?'

'Babington, Gilbert Gifford, two fathers in Rheims, Ballard – Captain Fortescue, that is.'

'God's blood, Goodfellow! How do you know you can trust these men? You are in so deep.' Shakespeare groaned. 'I would rather your lips had been sealed and your tongue cut out than that you should have spoken these words to me, for now when I see you, you are in your winding sheet.'

'I will never utter your name. You will never be named accessory.'

'It is your life I am thinking of, not mine.'

'My day is almost done. But you will live.'

'Will I? Do you think any man living can keep his mouth closed on the rack?'

'You are safe. I swear to you, John Shakespeare.'

'So what will you do now?'

'My vow is made. I await only word from Rome. They told me at Rheims that it was lawful if done for God's glory, just as you said. But I must have confirmation from the Holy Father.'

'And who will bring this word to you?'

'I await letters from Morgan in Paris. Gifford says he will bring them, elsewise I must go there myself.'

'And the vision?'

'It has made me unsure . . . bewildered. What do you think it meant?'

Shakespeare shook his head. What was to be done? Savage

was on a course of self-destruction that no one could prevent. For a few moments they stood looking at each other, then Shakespeare took a grip of himself. 'I think I had better get you roaring drunk, Goodfellow. Come, let us drink the Silver Grayling dry.'

'And you are paying?'

'My purse is full. But I must ask you one more thing. The young fellow you brought to Mane's . . .'

'Dominic?'

'That's it. Dominic de Warre. You said he was one of us. But what more do you know of him?'

'He is pleasant enough, but hotheaded. Why, what is your interest?'

'I know his stepfather, Severin Tort. I had not realised the link between them until I saw him at home. It gave me pause for thought. He is only a boy. You and I are men, Goodfellow. If we risk death, that is our choice. But young Dominic . . .'

Chapter 20

JUST BEFORE THE tide turned, when the race through the stanchions of London Bridge was at its tamest, Boltfoot took a boat downriver from the Custom House water stairs. He had his caliver slung over his back and his cutlass at his belt. He was not going unarmed again. Disembarking at St Katharine's Dock, a mile downstream from the bridge, he made his way slowly and carefully along the narrow lanes to the Burning Prow. At the end of the street, not fifty yards from the bawdy house, he found a spot in the shade of a tree where he sat down and lit his pipe of tobacco. The smoke was rich and heady and went some way to ease the aches of his beating.

He had a good view of the entrance to the whorehouse, but the evening was still early and business was quiet. A few men came and either stayed to carouse or left with a woman to one of the rooms they used for their work. He was hoping the one called Em would turn up, but by nine o'clock there was no sign of her.

The other whore – Aggy, the scabby, ill-favoured one he had tried to engage in conversation – came out from the alehouse on the arm of a grizzled mariner. They sauntered northwards. Boltfoot put away his pipe, rose slowly from his place by the tree and followed them. Every few steps the couple stopped to kiss and fumble. The man's eager hands lifted her skirts and stroked her inner thigh, while her hands went into his hose, accompanied by a great deal of grunting and slurping.

The next street was an alley of poor tenements and crumbling hovels where children in rags played in the dust and toothless gossips stood with their arms folded passing the time of day. Many of the houses were nothing but a tangled skeleton of blackened timbers, a commonplace hazard in this part of the city where half a dozen families might squeeze into a house and one accident with a knocked-over rushlight could lead to disaster. Aggy led her client into a leaning house that was isolated between two such burnt-out ruins.

Boltfoot found a spot where he could watch the doorway. The residents of the alley took one glance at his caliver and cutlass and decided not to interfere with business that did not concern them.

Half an hour later the mariner emerged, reeling as though he still had the rolling deck of a ship beneath his feet. Boltfoot smiled as the man strode away. He'd have no money left in his purse by night's end. Boltfoot had seen it a thousand times. He unslung his caliver, loaded it and stepped through the doorway with the muzzle pointing ahead of him. He halted and listened, allowing his eyes to grow accustomed to the gloom. He heard a sigh and a scuffing of feet. She was in the room at the back of the house, behind the half-open door.

He pushed through, his gun at his chest. She screamed. The room was bare save a filthy mattress of straw. She was squatting over a tin basin, her skirts pulled up to her chest so that her bare legs and nether parts were obscenely visible.

Boltfoot ranged the caliver at her and tilted his chin. 'I want to ask you a few questions, Aggy.'

She scrabbled backwards, grabbing the pisspot from beneath her as she did so, flinging it in Boltfoot's direction. He ducked sideways, but the pot hit his left arm and sprayed him with her pungent urine, soaking his sleeve and splashing his cheek.

She cackled. 'Ah yes, the dirty cripple. Come to play, have you?'

'Back against the wall.'

She emitted another foul laugh. 'Is that how you want me? Front or back?'

Boltfoot limped forward and pushed the muzzle of his weapon into her belly. 'Move.'

She stayed where she was, pushing out her chest, defiance in her eyes. 'How much you got, cripple? Shilling for a fuck, sixpence for a frigging. Told you before, didn't I.' She opened her mouth in a roundel. 'Or this for nine pence. That's a favourite with my sailor friends. Reminds them of the cabin boys, so they do say.'

'Comely as you are, Aggy, I want nothing like that from you. What I want is information and I'll pay you more than a shilling for it. Be straight and helpful and I'll make it more than worth your while.'

'Put up your evil-looking weapon and I'll think about it.'

Boltfoot lowered the stock of his caliver to the rubble-strewn floor, dried his face with his unsoaked sleeve, and fished a handful of coins from his purse. 'What's there to think about?' He proffered a few shillings to her. 'That's all you're after.'

'I've got to think about my lovely throat, which I don't want slit.'

'Who'd do that to you, Aggy?'

'Em. Who else.'

'So that's why you wouldn't talk to me back at the Burning Prow.'

She nodded, brushing down her stained skirts and pushing them between her legs to dry herself.

'What's she to Cutting Ball? She's kin, isn't she?'

'Em Ball? She's his sister. Everyone knows that. Where you been living all these years? Now hand over your purse if you want anything out of me.'

'You'll have half-a-crown if you tell me where – and with whom – Will Cane lived. And you'll have another if you can tell me who paid him to kill Nicholas Giltspur. And don't say his wife, because I won't believe you.'

'How do I know you won't tell Em?'

'She's no friend of mine. See this?' He pointed out the bruises on his face. 'Her brother's men did that to me. All I want to know is who killed Giltspur.'

'Well, if it weren't the widow, I don't know who done it. But I'll tell you where Will Cane lived for a sovereign.'

'No. A crown. That's my limit.'

She thrust out her grubby hand. 'Give it to me, then.'

'First tell me where he lived.'

'I'll do better than that. I'll lead you there and you can pay your respects to Will Cane's widow.'

Boltfoot followed Aggy through the grim streets. This burgeoning city of dirt and squalor almost made Boltfoot wish he was at sea again. On second thoughts, anything but that.

She turned southwards towards the Thames and the wharfs. Finally she stopped outside a small house at the end of a wood-frame, in a street a little way back from the riverside. She nodded her head to indicate the place, then walked on, turning westward to retrace her steps back to the Burning Prow. Boltfoot had already paid her five shillings under the threat that he would return and shoot her dead if he discovered that she had betrayed him. She hadn't looked as though she believed him.

Will Cane's house was a surprise. It was not the house of a rich man, but nor was it the sort of hovel occupied by the very lowest. Perhaps he had been a man of some importance to

Cutting Ball, a lieutenant who took a good share of their ill-gotten spoils and had set himself up. For a few minutes Boltfoot watched the front door. Then he walked down the small alley at the eastern end of the wood-frame, hoping to be able to see into the house from the rear. He cursed silently; the backyards were all walled and he had no view into the house. He was just pondering his next move when a water-bearer walked past and stopped, setting down his three-gallon cone-shaped barrel to stretch his aching back. Boltfoot noted the fine carving of the staves and the neatness of the hoops. He leant forward and ran a hand down the smooth surface appreciatively. Perfectly dry.

'Fine cooperage. Not a leak on it.'

'You a cooper then?'

'Aye. Ship's cooper.'

'What's the hagbut for then?' The man thrust his sparsely bearded chin towards Boltfoot's caliver. 'Won't be making casks with that.'

'It's for the shooting of Spaniards and Frenchies. I served my time aboard ships-of-war.'

The water-bearer laughed. 'You're a pirate then.' He was a small man – too small to be carrying such a heavy load.

'Some have called me that. Others call me a true son of England.' He touched the water butt again. 'Got far to go with that?'

'No, just round the corner. The Cane widow.'

'Will Cane's widow?'

The water-bearer's expression suddenly changed from open and cheery to nervous and guarded. 'Why would you be interested, Mister Cooper? A man could die for inquiring into Will Cane hereabouts.'

'So I believe.' He picked up the water butt. 'What say I deliver this to the widow Cane for you?'

'No.'

'You see, Mr Water-bearer, I want a few words with her – but I have no wish to scare her. You can care for my caliver while I'm inside. And there will be a silver sixpence for you when I come out. I will merely tell her that you are abed with the sweat and that I am your cousin standing in for you. Now is that not fair dealing?'

'What is this? What will you do to her?'

'No harm will come to Mistress Cane, I pledge it. This is a matter it were best you knew nothing about.'

'No. I won't have it. You'll get me killed.'

Boltfoot smiled. 'I think you don't understand. The choice isn't yours, Mr Water-bearer. I am borrowing your load whether you wish it or not. He reached into his soft leather purse and removed a sixpence. 'Here, take it. There will be another when I come out.'

The threat in Boltfoot's voice was obvious. The water-bearer was clearly not a man of robust courage. His hand shook as he reached out and accepted the coin.

'Good. Now what's your name?'

'Pearson. Tom Pearson.'

'Well, Mr Pearson, I shall do all in my power to keep you alive.' Boltfoot unslung his caliver and cutlass and placed them in the water-bearer's arms. 'Take those, go to the water stairs and wait for me.'

The door was answered by a plump woman of no more than twenty years of age. Her clothes were plain but clean and well kept. Three small children, all under the age of five, clustered around her skirts.

'Water, mistress.'

'Where's Tom today?'

'Took ill. A slight summer sweat. I'm his cousin.'

✠ 183 ✠

'What's your name?'

'Cooper. I never knew how hard Tom worked until this day. Thirsty work all this fetching and carrying.' Boltfoot feigned exhaustion as he hefted the butt of water inside the front room of the house, watched closely by the large, inquisitive eyes of the children.

'Put it in the corner near the empty, Mr Cooper, and sit yourself at the table. I'll fetch you some ale.' She disappeared out the back with the children in her wake.

Boltfoot sat down and took in his surroundings. It was a comfortable, modest room with a settle and a table and a dresser displaying a variety of pewter pots and earthenware. It was not the sort of home he had expected of a lieutenant to the infamous Cutting Ball.

'Here you are.' Mistress Cane returned with a beaker of ale and handed it to Boltfoot. The three small children trailed behind her like ducklings.

'Thank you, mistress, thank you. You have saved my life.'

'I will *tell* you your life if you wish. Give me your hand.'

He shook his head vigorously. 'No, I'll not have superstition.'

She smiled, then reached out and took his hand. He did not resist. She studied it for a minute, then looked up and met his eyes. 'You will suffer great pain, Mr Cooper. But I say you will find much love.'

He snatched his hand away. 'You think me a fool.'

She continued to smile, but said no more. He drank his ale, his head buzzing. He could not recall when a woman had last touched him. He took a deep breath.

'I am sorry to hear about your husband . . .'

She looked puzzled. 'Are you? Why?'

'Well, I heard—'

'That he got himself hanged for murder?'

Boltfoot nodded.

'Mr Cooper, I must tell you that dying was the best thing Will Cane ever did for this family.'

'I don't understand.'

'Tell me you are not one of Cutting Ball's men come to spy on me.'

'Do I look so villainous? No, mistress, my trade was always cask-making and repairing.'

'You look villainous enough with your bruised face. But I have lived among thieves and killers long enough to know that appearances can deceive. Perhaps you are an honest man.'

She sat down opposite him, looked into his eyes and sighed. 'Will Cane was not a good man. No, that does not tell it well. He was a vicious brute and I fear he may have killed before. More than once, and most cruelly.'

'And yet you married him.'

'This is beginning to sound like an interrogation, Mr Cooper.'

'Forgive me. I—'

'It is no matter. I care not whether you are a Cutting Ball man or from the justice. I am beyond pain and fear. I married Will because he was handsome and dangerous. And because my father wished it.'

'Why would your father have wished you to marry Mr Cane if he was as murderous as you say?'

'Mr Cooper, you really are most inquisitive.'

'It is the talk of Wapping and Whitechapel, is it not? They say a rich young woman paid Mr Cane to murder her husband. The whole world wants to know the truth.'

'So it seems. And if you are wondering whether any of the blood money came into this house, then I can tell you that it did not. And I tell you this, too, Mr Cooper – I would not have accepted a penny of such ill-gotten silver even if it had been offered to me. I would be pleased if you would tell everyone you know this simple truth, for I do not like the stares and whisperings that I have noted at the market since Will was hanged.'

The youngest child began to cry. The widow rose from her chair and scooped her up into her arms.

'I will tell them. But Mistress Cane, how will you survive without a husband? This house is small, but it is well appointed. Surely it will cost you dearly to rent?'

'The house was my father's and now it is mine. You asked me why he required me to wed Mr Cane. The truth is, he was a gambling man and fell foul of Cutting Ball. My father told me that if I did not marry Will Cane, who had taken a great fancy to me, then he would be killed. I was both scared and excited. Before the sickness wasted him, Will had the body of a god. What young girl would not wish to have such a fellow? My opinion changed rapidly when first he beat me. In the past year I have scarce seen Will, which was some relief. He had other women, one in particular, as he was pleased to tell me.'

'When did you last see him?'

'Two weeks since. He came to see the children.' She seemed to stiffen. 'Told them to be good little thieves and to let no man gainsay them. It is their good fortune that they were too young to understand a word he said to them. He told me he was dying and that we would not see him again. In truth I doubted he would last the week. Then he kissed the children and was gone.'

It was clear to Boltfoot that this woman knew nothing of the murder of Nicholas Giltspur, nor of Kat's supposed role in it. 'I am sorry. I had not meant to intrude on you at this difficult time.'

'Oh, think nothing of it, Mr Cooper. It has been some

welcome release to talk of these matters. I am all alone now, you see.' She smiled at him again.

There was silence for a moment and then he nodded. 'Thank you,' he said. Standing from his chair, he made a move towards the door.

'Do not go without the empty water butt, sir.'

'No, no indeed.' He stopped, hesitated. 'Before I go, Mistress Cane . . .'

'Yes?'

'I'm not a water-carrier.'

She smiled. 'I didn't think so.'

Stumbling over his words, not certain how much to reveal, Boltfoot told her that he was investigating the death of Nicholas Giltspur on behalf of his master. 'If as you say he was already dying then he had nothing to gain for himself by killing for money. In which case, you must understand why a man might wonder whether he wished to leave his widow or children provided for.'

'But I have already told you that is not the case, Mr Cooper. And I have also told you I would not accept such money.'

'Then who has the hundred pounds?'

'His whore, of course. And she is welcome to it.'

'Do you have her name?'

'Indeed I do, Mr Cooper, and perhaps you and your master might be the means by which some justice will be meted out. Her name is Abigail and she is a lady's maid in the house of the Giltspur family.'

Chapter 21

Harry Slide was struggling to recall a name. The face across the taproom had looked away too quickly. Why had the man been watching him? Now he was moving towards the door. Slide downed the last of his strong beer.

'With your permission, Captain, I'm going out for a piss,' he told Ballard, clapping the priest on the shoulder. 'Then one more brandy and bed. Let us have an early night for we have a long ride tomorrow.'

As he strolled towards the door, Slide was keenly aware of Ballard's eyes following him. Clearly, he had not allayed his concerns – or Gage's. Were they jittery because their mission had been so unsuccessful, or had he said something out of place? Well, they were stuck with him; and he would smile and reassure them as best he could.

The stranger who had been staring at him reached the door just ahead of him. Slide gave him a slight push until they were both outside and closed the door behind them. 'Do I know you?'

The man met his eye in the light of the lantern. 'I think not. But I know *you*, Mr Slide.'

'Then you are mistaken, for my name is Bernard Maude. You are confusing me with someone else.'

'Not so, Mr Slide. I would spot your reptilian face among a

million in the fiery depths of Hades, so ingrained is it on my memory.'

'Who are you?'

'I was in service to the Earl of Shrewsbury.'

'Sheffield Castle? What did you do there?'

'That is no concern of yours. Suffice it to say that there was much talk about you after you left.'

Slide remembered the Earl of Shrewsbury very well. In those days his lordship had been charged with keeping Mary Queen of Scots prisoner at Sheffield Castle. Yet he could still not identify this man. 'What is your name, stranger?'

'You don't need to know that either. All you need to know is that I remember you well, though you went under another name for a while. And you need to know that I require money from you. Twenty pounds will shut my mouth. Or I shall tell your travelling companions what I know of you, which I doubt you want.'

Slide considered taking out his dagger there and then and slitting the man's throat, but they could be disturbed at any moment. He smiled instead. 'Twenty pounds, you say?'

'Twenty pounds, and I will not be haggled down.'

'I might manage two pounds to make you leave me alone, but no more.'

'Twenty. And if you refuse again, the price will go yet higher.'

Slide was silent a few moments, then nodded. 'Very well, but I do not have such money here in my purse.'

'Then bring it to me in an hour, down at the stone foot-bridge. No one will see us there.'

'Two hours. If you try to betray me I will make it very bad for you.'

'Bring the money and I pledge you will never see or hear from me again.'

*

Harry Slide slipped from the truckle bed in the chamber he shared with Ballard and Gage. From their snoring in the large bed, he was certain they were both asleep. The strong ale and rounds of brandy had done their work. Without a sound, he made his way to the door, raising the latch carefully.

Slide, on bare feet and wearing only his nightshirt, went out and pushed the door back so that he could slip back in as quietly as he had left. From downstairs he saw a light and heard muted voices; the last of the drinkers in the taproom.

He descended step by slow step. If anyone crossed his path, he would sway as though intoxicated, say he needed fresh air. But no one came his way. Quietly he made his way to the back of the inn, through the kitchens, and exited the building into the stableyard, which was bathed in dull yellow light from a pair of wall lanterns. Somewhere from behind a stable door, a horse whinnied and stamped in its stall.

Taking one of the lanterns, he crossed the flagstoned yard to the tack room, where he immediately found what he wanted. Then, more quickly now, he made his way out onto the expanse of lawn that led down to the little stone footbridge over the stream.

Looking around to be sure he was not observed or followed, he pulled his linen nightshirt over his head and hid it behind a stone on the bone-dry grass. He estimated the two hours must be almost up. Stark naked, Slide edged down the grassy bank, then stepped into the chilly water and carefully placed the lantern beneath the arch of the bridge. He slid further into the water, and crept to his left, sinking his body like an eel into the reeds.

And then he once more tested the strength of the harness chain he had borrowed from the tack room, wrenching it taut between his fists. It was more than strong enough for his purpose.

*

Edward Manning had no intention of staying at the inn a moment longer than necessary. It was pure chance that he had been there, for he was riding post from York to Greenwich and had merely stopped for a change of horses and food. By trade he was a courier, riding all day every day and often by night. He knew these highways as well as any man in England.

He also knew a great deal about the missives and documents sent by his masters in the north and at court. He was sworn to secrecy, of course, but vows were made to be broken. This meeting with Harry Slide was too good a chance to miss.

Four years earlier, in 1582, there had been a flurry of traffic between Sheffield Castle and Oatlands Palace. In carrying the letters, Manning had discovered more than perhaps he should have done about the activities and methods of a certain Mr Harry Slide. Now was the time to put that knowledge to good use.

Twenty pounds would set him up well. He already had money put away and this extra would allow him to go into business on his own account; establish his own staging post, with stabling and provender. No more night rides for him, no more aching balls and arse from fourteen hours in the saddle each day. Let others do the hard work.

He led his horse down to the little stone bridge and waited. He didn't trust Harry Slide and had no intention of dismounting.

Slide heard the horse's hoofs; then its snorting as it was reined in. He could just see it in the gloom; it was no more than seven or eight feet from him, at the side of the bridge. He waited a minute. There was no movement, nothing but the animal snuffling of the horse and the pat of a hand on a flank. 'Come down.' The words were little more than a whisper, but loud enough to carry at this time of night. 'Come down. I have your twenty pounds.'

'Slide?'

'Yes. Come down here.'

'Bring the purse up to me.'

'No, I can't be seen with you.'

'I'm not moving. If you're not up here in half a minute I'm riding away and your trickery will be exposed to your companions. What say you, Slide?'

'Are you armed, stranger?'

'Aye, I've got a sword and pistol and I know how to use them.' No highwaymen had ever had any luck against him, nor would they.

'Then bring your weapons down here and you'll know you're safe. I'll give you what you want. But I won't be seen with you. The choice is yours.' Silence. At last, Slide heard the click of a powderhorn lid and the soft sound of powder being poured, and relaxed. All would be well.

The man stopped at the cusp of the bank, then took his first tentative step down the grassy slope to the water's edge. It was steeper than it looked. A man could lose his balance here. The stranger stopped, surprised by the glow of a lantern from beneath the bridge. For the merest second or two, his eyes and weapons were all aligned, pointing at the gaping arch of the bridge and the light. The very place where Harry Slide was not.

It was all the time Slide needed. In one snakelike move, he lunged forward, thrusting his naked torso and arms out of the reeds. His strong hands grasped the stranger's ankles and clamped them tight, like a vice. In the same movement, he tugged like a plough-ox, dragging the man's feet away so that he fell backwards.

The man gasped. Instinctively he released his grip on the weapons, flinging them aside as his hands went down to break his fall. But he fell awkwardly, his spine and shoulder blades hitting the hard earth with a boneshaking crunch that took the breath from his lungs. He let out a low scream and tried to scrabble backwards, but Slide had him fast and pulled him into the river like a predatory sea creature dragging its shorebound prey into its own domain.

Slide did not give the man time to gather his thoughts or find his weapons. They were both in the water now and the thin harness chain was twisted around the stranger's neck, tightening. Slide had his legs around the man and wrenched his head down, down, beneath the surface of the water.

The stranger was strong, but Slide was a trained killer. Using the chain, he held the man's struggling head beneath the water, choking the life from him. He held him there until the struggling subsided, and the body went limp. Another minute passed. Slide's own breathing became less laboured. At last he uncurled the chain from the dead stranger's neck and placed it on the riverbank. He dragged the corpse into the reeds and covered it as well as he could before gathering up the man's weapons and throwing them into the reeds alongside him. Then he waded three steps to the bridge and retrieved the lantern. If he could send the man's horse galloping away into the woods, the chances were that the body would not be discovered for a day or two, by which time he would be long gone. Satisfied with his work, he looked down at his prick and noted with amusement that it was standing to attention.

And then he looked up, and came face to face with Robert Gage.

Chapter 22

'Pass me my nightshirt if you would, Master Gage. I am cold and soaked here. And more than a little exposed.' Harry Slide gave a wolfish grin.

'What in God's name have you done, Mr Maude?' The terror and disbelief was evident in Robert Gage's wide eyes.

'Why, I have killed a man, Master Gage – and have saved the lives of all three of us in the process.'

'I saw you drown him. Why? Who was it?'

'I cannot stand here like this. Give me my nightshirt and then help me up this bank.'

Gage looked about wildly, found the folded nightshirt, and handed it to Slide, who pulled the garment over his head and smoothed it down so that it clung to his wet body. 'That's better.' He stretched out his right hand and Gage helped him up.

'Please, Mr Maude, you must tell me what you have done here, for surely you will hang for this.'

'Now listen. No one will hang if you keep your mouth shut.' Slide tilted his chin towards the reeds where the corpse lay. 'That man was named Slide. Harry Slide. He was a most foul and wicked spy, an intelligencer in the employment of Walsingham. I have no idea how he found us here, but he meant us harm. My action saved us.'

'You cannot just kill men!'

'Indeed, can I not? Are you then not prepared to kill for God's greater glory?'

'No. It is a sin.'

'And yet you are engaged with Captain Fortescue and myself in attempting to raise an army to kill fellow Englishmen and restore the true faith to this land? Is that not what you are signed up to, Master Gage? That and the assassination of Elizabeth Tudor? I had thought you a man of action, not a squeamish child.'

'This is different,' Gage mumbled at last.

'Different? No, it is not different. Slide was our enemy. He would have led us to the scaffold for treason. Now, if it please you, I have work to do. This horse must be made to disappear and the lantern must be replaced. And then, Mr Gage, I require my bed, for killing men is exhausting work, as you will soon find out, God willing.'

John Shakespeare's mind turned with images of men all coated in blood: Savage, Babington, young de Warre, Tichbourne, Salisbury and all their comrades in the Pope's White Sons. But his more immediate concern was Boltfoot's absence.

According to Jane, he had left the house in the early evening, complete with his weapons. Shakespeare paced the solar. A single candle burned in the room, casting strange shadows as he walked across the wooden boards. The house was silent, but soon Jane would be up with the light of day and then there would be eggs, bread and fresh-churned butter on the kitchen table. And Boltfoot would walk through the door . . .

From downstairs, he heard a light knocking at the front door. Why would Boltfoot knock? Puzzled but relieved, Shakespeare hastened down to the front door and pulled it open. A cowled figure stood before him. It wasn't Boltfoot.

'Come in, Mr Redd.'

Once inside and with the door closed behind him, Oswald Redd removed his cloak and cowl.

'Mr Shakespeare, I am sorry for disturbing you this early, but Kat has disappeared. I am frantic with fear.'

'Has she been arrested?'

'I don't know.'

'Where was she hiding?'

Redd shifted awkwardly, clearly reluctant to divulge the place of concealment.

'Come, let us go to the kitchens. We will sit and talk and you will tell me all you know. And this time you will hold nothing back, Mr Redd.'

Harry Slide awoke and emitted a yawn, stretching his arms luxuriantly above his head. Light slanted in through the edges of the shutters. He would stay here another ten minutes; there was no hurry. But then he remembered the body in the reeds. Perhaps it was better to leave this place sooner rather than later.

Rising from the bed, he glanced at the four-poster and was surprised to see that Ballard and Gage were not there. Dressing at a leisurely pace, Slide fixed a ready smile to his lips and went down to the taproom. 'Mister innkeeper, where are my companions?'

The innkeeper was a man of stout belly, grizzled beard and thick legs. His brow knotted in confusion. 'Master?'

'Captain Fortescue and his young serving man. They have left the chamber so I thought they would be taking breakfast here.'

'They declined to eat, sir. They ordered their horses brought to them in great haste, then paid the reckoning and departed.'

'When was this? How long have they been gone?'

'An hour and a half, I would say, perhaps a little more.'

And you say they have paid the reckoning?'

Indeed, master – for all three of you. They said you had more business in the region and would be following them in your own time.'

Of course . . . of course.' He smiled at the innkeeper. 'But I had expected to see them before they left. I overslept, which is entirely my own fault.'

'Will you then have some breakfast, sir?'

Yes, he would. There was no point in chasing Ballard and Gage. He would eat a fine breakfast of sirloin, manchet bread and two pints of ale, and then he would ride at speed for Greenwich.

They stopped at the edge of a meadow grazed by sheep. 'That's the house,' Oswald Redd said, pointing to a thatched cottage half a mile away.

'Who tends the sheep?'

'My brother, Osric. It was my mother's house and farm, but he lives here alone now. I thought it the perfect place for Kat to hide.'

'But surely anyone who was acquainted with you at the playhouse would know of this place?'

'No. I never had cause to speak of it with them. Likewise, these people in the village know nothing of my life in Shoreditch and London. Nor would news of events such as Giltspur's murder reach this far.'

Shakespeare was not so sure. Plenty of travellers on their way to Suffolk or Norfolk must pass this place.

They were near a village named Chigwell, ten miles northeast of Shoreditch. It was open countryside, dotted with sheep pasture and small market gardens. Two hours ago, at the kitchen table in Seething Lane, Redd had finally admitted to Shakespeare where he had hidden Kat.

'And when exactly did she disappear?'

'Yesterday.'

'Did your brother not notice her leaving.'

'He was out tending the flock and mending walls. It could have been at any time between dawn and five o'clock.'

'And what did Osric do when he found her gone?'

'He checked her chamber and saw that her belongings had gone, too. Then he sat and waited until I arrived.'

'Was there any message left to tell you she was going? That she was sorry, perhaps?'

He shook his head vigorously. 'Nothing.'

'And nothing to suggest that officers of the law came and took her away?'

'No. The house was not disturbed in any way.'

'Did she ride or go by foot?'

'Our mare is still in her stable. So unless someone brought her a mount, then she must have walked.'

'Well, let us ride on. I wish to see where she was lodged.'

They trotted across the meadow, scattering sheep as they went. The life of a farmer with little acreage could be hard, but this looked a comfortable place and Shakespeare wondered why Oswald Redd had ever considered leaving.

Redd pushed open the front door and called out. 'Osric?' There was no response.

'We will seek him out later if need be. First, show me her room.'

They ascended a ladder to the first floor. The bedchamber was on the left, through a low doorway with no door. The bed was plain and old. It might, thought Shakespeare, have been here since the Black Death. How many people had been conceived, born and died in it? Kat would not have felt comfortable here.

'What were you planning to do, Mr Redd?'

He looked puzzled. 'I do not understand the question, sir.'

'Well, let me put it this way. Where would she have gone from here?'

'She would have stayed here. It is safe enough, and a comfortable life.'

'This is a sheep farm!'

'I was planning to leave the playhouse and come here to run the farm once the hue and cry had died away. We would have married in time. It will still happen if we can find her.'

'Are you seriously saying that you believe Kat Whetstone might have become a shepherd's wife? Do you know nothing of her?'

Redd bridled. 'I know her better than any man, Mr Shakespeare. She is the love of my life and it was a cruel day when Nicholas Giltspur chanced upon her with his great wealth. Any young woman's head might have been turned by such riches.'

Shakespeare could see the anguish in Oswald's eyes; she had forsaken him not once but twice. Perhaps none of them knew her. He himself had clearly not known her as well as he had thought, for he failed to see what might have made her desert his bed for the doubtful charms of Oswald Redd's. Was there some hidden frailty that made her betray every person who trusted her?

In the corner of the room, there was an old coffer. Shakespeare lifted the lid. The comforting smell of wool rose to his nostrils. The coffer was packed with folded clothes and bed linen. Idly, he picked up the topmost sheet. Beneath it, he noticed a dress. Though plain, it was made of fine linen; it did not look like the attire of a farm wife and certainly not that of an old woman. He pulled it out and held it up.

A chill ran down his spine. 'This is Kat's. She was wearing this when I saw her at your house in Shoreditch.'

Redd nodded. 'It was indeed the dress she wore when she was with me. She brought no other when she fled her home.'

'Then what is she wearing now?' *Or what has been done to her . . .*

They heard a sound downstairs.

'That will be Osric,' said Redd. 'Come down when you are ready.'

Just as he had done at Giltspur House, Shakespeare searched Kat's bedchamber in the thorough manner he had learnt from Sir Francis Walsingham. He removed all the blankets, sheets and old clothes from the coffer but discovered nothing more of interest. He looked beneath the mattress, in the gaps between floorboards, in any nook or hole in the wall, however small. He tapped at walls for hollowness and closed and opened the shutters to see whether any hidden message or object should fall out. Then he lifted the old, scratched washbasin to peer underneath and did likewise with the ancient vials of herbs and potions that seemed more likely to have belonged to Redd's mother rather than Kat. All the time, he felt a gnawing fear: who had hidden the dress – and why?

He went downstairs to question Osric Redd. You could not mistake the two men as anything but brothers: both had complexions the colour of a Thames salmon, but Osric was nowhere near as well favoured as his brother.

'When did you last see Kat?'

'Yesterday morning. Dawn. She made the breakfast, then I went out and she weren't here when I came back.'

'What was she wearing?'

He shrugged. 'Didn't notice.'

'And what was her humour?'

'Don't know. She were making breakfast. Mutton broth with beans. Same as I always have.' He shrugged again and looked at his brother for guidance.

Oswald put an arm around his brother's shoulder. 'Osric is not like others, Mr Shakespeare. He's happier in the company of sheep than people. He'll spot the staggers, scab or scrapie sooner than he'll note a broken leg in a man. He understands them and will note their temper when the same will go unnoticed in a human. Isn't that so, Osric?'

'I like sheep.'

'Mr Redd, a word in private with you, if I may.'

Redd nodded to his brother. 'Off you go then, Osric. Time to feed the pigs.'

'I don't like pigs.'

'I know you don't, but you like bacon, don't you. And without pigs, there'll be none. Now off you go.'

He grunted. 'She took my jerkin, you know. Why'd she do that?' Without another word, Osric walked out.

His brother watched him go, then smiled grimly at Shakespeare. 'Before you ask, the answer is no. Oscric could not have harmed Kat; he has never harmed any creature. Wouldn't even slaughter a hen, let alone one of his beloved sheep. Slaughterman has to do it for us.'

'Her dress was abandoned and hidden.'

'I know nothing about that – nor does he. I doubt he ever spoke more than half a dozen words to her.'

'Mr Redd. We have two possibilities here. Either Kat has taken Osric's jerkin and other articles of clothing from this house and run off wearing them, or something has happened to her and she has never left.'

'Osric's done nothing to her. If he says she took his jerkin, then that's what happened.'

Shakespeare sighed. 'Come, Mr Redd. Show me around the rest of the house and any outbuildings you have here. And set a fire for we must burn Kat's dress. It would do you or your brother no good at all for it to be found here.'

Chapter 23

BOLTFOOT COOPER WAS finding it hard to think clearly; he was almost overwhelmed by the intense stink of pig manure. That and his raging thirst. His hands and feet were bound and he had been thrown here, into this enclosed place, like an unwanted sack of rotting turnips.

At least it was daylight now. They had brought him here many hours ago and seemed to have forgotten about him.

He had been caught close to the Thames, within sight of the river stairs where the water-bearer was waiting for him nervously. There had been three men – brutish individuals with bare arms and bulging muscles – and two women: the whore named Aggy who had led him to the home of Will Cane, and Em Ball.

'That's him. That's the dirty little turd,' Aggy had said, pointing at him.

Boltfoot had nowhere to go and no way to defend himself. His caliver and cutlass were still with the water-bearer, a matter of yards away but as good as a mile for all the use they were to him.

There were plenty of people about, but none that would try their luck against three of Cutting Ball's crew. Everyone knew who the men were by the sleeveless leather jerkins they wore and the curling serpents carved into their arms.

'Well, Mr Cooper, you can come with us easy or with broken bones.'

Boltfoot had looked towards the stairs and the timid Tom Pearson. The terror in the water-bearer's eyes suggested that he had had no part in this. Pearson backed away into the crowd, and why should he not, thought Boltfoot? No reason for a decent working man to sacrifice his life for a stranger. Boltfoot met the cool stares of his would-be captors; they hadn't even bothered to draw their weapons. He shrugged. 'Let's make it easy.'

They marched him down to the water stairs, where they hauled him into a rowing boat and cast off into midstream. A hood was placed over his head. Apart from the lapping of the water and the cawing of the gulls, the only thing he heard was the macabre wit of his abductors. 'We could always drop him in here.'

'It would save him much pain.'

'No,' Em Ball replied – he knew her voice – 'Mr Ball will have other plans for him.'

Within a few minutes the boat had come to another mooring, away from the crowds, and he was dragged out, then thrown over the back of a horse and tied in place. His wrists were attached to his ankles beneath the horse's belly. An uncomfortable ride of about three-quarters of an hour ensued.

Only at the last minute, when he was untied from the horse, was the hood removed from his eyes. Then he was bound tight again and flung here in this pigsty. Apart from the remarks on the river, his captors had said nothing and given him no clue as to what was to happen to him. He guessed that he was probably back by the barn where he had met Cutting Ball, and that his fate was likely to be an unpleasant death.

All his attempts to free himself from his bindings had been in vain. He had stayed awake until it was dark, then he tried to sleep. It was uncomfortable but no more so than some of the berths he had had in his time; ships were not constructed for those who valued soft feather beds. He used a trick he had often employed to make sleep come: summon up the face of a beautiful woman. This time, it was easy; the face and shape of Will Cane's widow came to him, blotting out his pain and the stench of his surroundings.

But now he was awake. From outside he heard footsteps, then a scuffling at the entrance and the bearded face of one of his captors peered in.

'Good morning, Mr Cooper. A pleasant night's sleep in our hostelry, I trust.'

'Never slept better.'

'Good, then you will have strength for the ordeal that awaits you.'

Anthony Babington was not impressed by the painting.

'I believe I have captured the likenesses most precisely,' the artist said with no hint of irony.

'Indeed, do you, sir?' Babington said. 'And which one am I?'

'Why, you are the *chief* gentleman, Mr Babington.' He stabbed his slender finger towards the centre of the painting, without quite touching it. 'Here, in the king's position, in all your dignity and magnifience, sir.'

Babington turned away from the easel. He did not have the energy to argue. The very sight of the picture made him despondent, for it was just one more sign that everything was falling apart.

Thomas Salisbury grinned and patted him on the arm. 'It is not so bad, Anthony.'

'It is *worse* than bad,' Babington said in a muted voice, but loud enough for the painter to hear. 'It is yet shabbier than *you*, Thomas! That is how rough it is. Come, let us away from here before I take a taper to the wretched thing.'

Ignoring the painter's yelps of protest, they walked from Mane's barber shop out into the street. Chidiock Tichbourne was leaning against a tree, smoking his pipe in the welcome shade, and he hailed them over, pointing along the street. Two horsemen were approaching.

'Captain Fortescue and Mr Gage!' Salisbury said.

The two horsemen reined in. Their mounts were flecked with foam and dust; the riders clearly exhausted.

'Thank God you are here, Captain Fortescue,' Babington said.

'Indeed, welcome, sir,' Salisbury said. He cupped his hands to make a stirrup, but Ballard did not move from the saddle.

'A word, Mr Babington.'

Babington approached. He had expected Ballard to return in triumph but instead he and his companion seemed disturbed. Babington's blood began to run cold. 'Where, pray, is Mr Maude?'

Ballard beckoned Babington yet closer, then leant forward across his horse's neck. 'I fear we have been betrayed,' he whispered.

If John Shakespeare was surprised to find Anthony Babington and Thomas Salisbury at his front door, he did not show it.

'Why, gentlemen, how delightful to see you – please come in.'

'We need your help, Mr Shakespeare.'

'Then I am, as always, pleased to be at your service. What is it you desire?'

'We want passports for France.'

Both men were clearly agitated; Salisbury in particular looked even more wild and unkempt than usual. Shakespeare tried to conceal his dismay. The last thing Walsingham would want was these men fleeing the country. He maintained an even tone. 'Do you have business there?'

'We do – and we may be some little while. We fear our estates will be compromised without passports.'

It was an offence for anyone to leave the country without permission for more than six months, on pain of having all their property confiscated. This had been enacted to deter Roman Catholics fleeing abroad to the seminaries, and to punish them if they did so. Anthony Babington was a very wealthy young man; the prospect of losing his Derbyshire estates would be a heavy blow to both him and his heirs.

'And how do you hope I will obtain the papers for you?'

'From Walsingham,' Salisbury said.

The change in Salisbury was remarkable. He seemed drained and timid, a blank stare of panic in his eyes that usually burned with uncontainable fervour.

'You enjoy the Principal Secretary's trust, Mr Shakespeare. Your word will be enough.'

'Gentlemen, this is most difficult. I must think the matter through carefully.' Perhaps this might not be the disaster that he had initially feared. Indeed, it might be just the opportunity he had been waiting for. Yes, he was beginning to see possibilities here. His face remained grave. 'Given the febrile nature of our relations with France, Mr Secretary would be unlikely to grant such documents without first interviewing you himself.'

Babington's expression turned to one of disbelief. 'You truly think he would want to *see* us?'

'It is likely. Do you wish me to inquire on your behalf? He would need a full and convincing account of your reason for wishing to travel.'

Babington and Salisbury looked at each other. Go to Walsingham? It was like being asked to walk into the lion's den.

'Advise us, Mr Shakespeare. Is this really a possibility?'

'Well, yes, a possibility . . . I would put it no stronger than that. My first thought is that it would be best if only one of you applied. If you apply together, he is more likely to become suspicious. I would suggest *you*, Mr Babington.'

'Why me?'

'You are already known at court. You have charm and wit. By which I mean no disrespect to you, Mr Salisbury.'

Babington hesitated, then nodded cautiously. 'And what would you have me say?'

'Well, what exactly is this business on which you are engaged? What is the purpose of your journey? He will insist on knowing the details, so you would do well to tell me here and now.'

Babington shuffled his feet. 'The summer is suddenly become too hot.'

'I fear such an explanation will not serve your purpose.'

'Then what?'

'Well, you might say that you wish to tour the Italies, perhaps, that you have a great desire to collect books and works of art. I am sure he would look favourably on such a request, though he would ask favours in return.'

'Favours?'

Shakespeare laughed. 'Come, come, Mr Babington, you know what I mean. Mr Secretary requires information of anyone who travels. You would be required to spy for him. He would want word of developments at the Jesuit college and he would have you send word of any great men and women you meet.'

'But he would never know if I wrote him the truth or not.'

'Indeed, he would never know.'

'When can you arrange this meeting, Mr Shakespeare?'

'He is a busy man. If you are fortunate, he may issue a passport without summoning you. If you are unfortunate, he will merely turn you down flat, with no meeting and no explanation. We can but hope for the best.'

Babington clasped Shakespeare by the hand. 'Thank you, sir. Thank you.'

After they had gone, Shakespeare called Jane and ordered food and ale, then climbed to the top of the house. He pushed open the door to his solar.

'Good news, Mr Shakespeare?'

He glared at his visitor. 'Not exactly, Harry.'

Chapter 24

Harry Slide had arrived a mere quarter-hour earlier. But before Shakespeare had had time to make sense of his garbled tale, he had been called to the front door by Jane. He had shuffled Harry Slide off to the solar and ordered him to remain silent while he dealt with Babington and Salisbury.

Now he wanted answers.

'Tell me again what happened, Harry – and this time make it convincing.'

'Might I not beg a little food and drink? My ride south has been long and hard, Mr Shakespeare.'

'My maidservant will bring bread and ale. In the meantime, talk.'

Slide spread wide his hands. 'I had thought we were getting on well. If anything, I was more fervent than they. The trip north was going badly for Ballard: there is no interest at all from the northern gentry. In truth, they could not wait to get him out of their houses. But I tried to keep him cheered with bawdy tales and good brandy. I had thought he was retaining his spirits well. And young Gage was always humble and obedient.'

'Get on with it, Harry.'

'We shared a chamber. They had the tester, I had the truckle. When I woke up, they were gone. They had not even paid their share of the reckoning, which I had to fund from my own purse and for which I would hope for recompense.'

'Why did they leave so suddenly?'

He shrugged. 'I fear they suspect me, but I know not why. As far as I know, I did not say a word out of place.'

'This is not good enough, Harry.' Shakespeare knew his man. 'Something must have happened.'

Slide sighed. 'The only thing I can think of is that someone spoke against me. There was a man at the inn who seemed to watch me, but I paid him no note – perhaps I should have approached him?' He turned beseeching eyes to Shakespeare.

Shakespeare knew Slide was concealing something. He knew, too, that it would be very hard to prise it from him. Slide might have the charm of a Ralegh, but he was twice as hard. And deadly, too.

'Never mind that now. We must consider what this means to our mission. How much start did Ballard and Gage have on you?'

'Two hours. Maybe three.'

'And so they are probably in London already.' It explained everything – Babington and Salisbury's panic; their wish to leave England as soon as possible. 'If Ballard believes you have betrayed them, he will immediately spread alarm among the Pope's White Sons.'

'Perhaps not, Mr Shakespeare. Ballard will wish to hold the line. He is not a man to fear for his own life and it is his nature to shun inconvenient truths. Yes, he will say that I am no longer to be trusted, but he will also do his utmost to lighten my importance to the cause and he will do all he can to strengthen their resolve. I know his type.'

Jane appeared at the door with ale and a plate of meats and bread. When she had placed them on the coffer, he nodded at her to leave. 'Eat your fill, Harry. You look as though you need it.'

He could not be angry with Slide. He had placed himself in great peril travelling with Ballard and Gage and his earlier reports had done more than any to reveal the nature of the conspirators. The question was what was to be done now.

'And you are certain that there will be no uprising in the north?'

'I am certain. Not one man, be they the most zealous Catholic ever made, will raise himself from between the legs of his wife or mistress to assist the Pope's White Sons. None will countenance a Spanish invasion or assassination of the Queen.'

'Then you have done well. Your mission has been successful.'

Shakespeare fetched a sheet of paper from the far side of the room, then put it down at his desk beside the quills and ink.

'Write a report for Mr Secretary,' he said. 'Then leave London tonight. All I require of you is word of where you will be and a pledge that you will not return here until this matter is concluded and I have sent for you. Simply disappear. Ballard and Babington must never see you again. Is that understood?'

Slide smiled. 'Indeed, Mr Shakespeare. I thank you for your forbearance, as always.'

'And Harry, I still want to know how Ballard discovered you.'

'So do I, sir.' Slide's face was as open and innocent as any babe's. 'So do I.'

Shakespeare did not bother to reply. Harry was a liar, but he deserved to be kept safe. What of his trustworthy Boltfoot, though? And Kat, too? Where in the name of all that was holy had they got to?

Boltfoot was dragged from the pigsty, then hauled into the great tithe barn. His leg bindings were cut, but his arms remained bound.

Without a word, his captors pushed him down onto a wooden stool and waited.

'A little ale or clean water would ease my throat,' Boltfoot said. He would not mention it before these men, but it was the ache in his club foot that troubled him more than his thirst. He could live without drinking well enough; long days without fresh water in the Pacific Ocean had taught him how to still his thirst through force of will.

'A knife to your jugular would ease it just as well,' one of the men growled.

'Even a dying dog is allowed water.'

A fist hit the side of his head and almost knocked him from the stool. 'Just wait and keep your mouth shut.'

He did not have to wait long. Cutting Ball arrived with his sister at his side.

Ball stood in front of his captive, his bare arms protruding from his leather jerkin, muscles rippling like a prize bull. He gripped Boltfoot's jaw in his powerful hand, and looked into his eyes from a distance of no more than six inches.

'And so you came back . . .'

'I am your guest, Mr Ball, and I have a mighty thirst.'

Ball nodded to one of his men. 'Get him beer.' He turned back to Boltfoot and shook his head like a father forced to punish a recalcitrant child. 'You disobeyed me, Mr Cooper.'

'You are not my master.'

'No, indeed, that would be John Shakespeare, Walsingham's man. Well, he's not here to save you now, and so you must pay the price. Do you know what is to become of you?'

'I am sure you will tell me again if I have forgot it.'

Cutting Ball snorted. 'You do not show fear. Either you are a brave man or a foolish one.'

'Merely resigned to my fate. You have me bound, you have your friends and you have your dagger.'

'This?' Ball withdrew his hand from Boltfoot's jaw and pulled his bollock-dagger from his belt. 'I am a very craftsman with this blade, Mr Cooper. When I play the barber-surgeon I can open up or remove any portion of a living body within half a minute.'

Boltfoot said nothing.

'A mere thirty seconds,' Ball continued, 'but it will seem longer than a lifetime to you. Nothing makes a man squirm more than sharp steel applied to the bollocks.'

One of Ball's henchmen reappeared with a cup of beer and held it to Boltfoot's lips. He drank greedily. It was good, strong beer; if it was to be his last sup ever then let it be a long, deep draught.

'You were a mariner, were you not? A cooper by trade.'

The cup was taken away from Boltfoot's mouth; he had almost managed to empty it.

'Aye. I told you as much.'

'And so you like the sea?'

'There was a time I liked it.'

Cutting Ball turned to his sister. 'What say you, Em? Is this one for the fishes?'

She laughed. 'Indeed, I think him one for the fishes, brother. A fine notion. A fine notion, indeed.'

Walsingham rubbed his hands together. A smile crept over his sombre face. 'This is a clever scheme, John. Well done, sir. Bring Mr Babington to me here on the morrow. In the morning, about eleven o'clock, before Privy Council. I will promise him the earth and all its pleasures.'

'And Mr Poley?'

'I shall send for him now. He will be here, fear not.'

They were in Walsingham's offices at Greenwich Palace. The Principal Secretary had listened intently to the report of Harry

Slide's unmasking by Ballard and the desire of Babington and Salisbury to flee the country and had understood Shakespeare's plan immediately.

Shakespeare took a breath. Now was the time to press an advantage. 'In the matter of Mistress Giltspur, Sir Francis . . . might I beg more time? I have not uncovered the truth and I can feel it close to me. There are matters yet to be understood.'

'Nick Giltspur was a good man – a helpful man. He was much admired by both Her Majesty and Lord Burghley.'

'In what way was he helpful?'

'He was rich and powerful. He offered assistance when required.'

'Can you tell me more?'

'It would not be diplomatic to say more. Suffice it to say that I would be most pleased if his assassin were brought to the scaffold. And if that is his wife, then so be it. But I want to know the truth.'

'Then I have more time?'

'Very little. But yes, if the Babington matter goes as planned, then you have a little more time.'

Shakespeare took his leave of Walsingham and walked through the halls of Greenwich Palace down to the river moorings. He was stepping into a tilt-boat for the journey back to London when he was stopped by an out-of-breath servant.

'Are you Mr Shakespeare, sir?'

'Yes.'

'Forgive me, but Sir Robert Huckerbee sent me after you, for he desires the pleasure of your company. He is in his office adjoining Lord Burghley's apartments.'

Huckerbee? Shakespeare had barely met the man and had scarce passed half a dozen words with him at the meeting with

Walsingham and the other intelligencers. As he followed the servant back into the palace, Shakespeare struggled to think what Huckerbee might want that could not have been communicated to him by Walsingham. As far as he knew, Huckerbee's only purpose in life was collecting, auditing and dispensing money on behalf of the Treasury.

The office was a world away from the austere chambers of Sir Francis Walsingham; walls hung with rich tapestries from Turkey and the eastern Indies, and cut flowers everywhere, their sweet scent cloying. Huckerbee had settles laden with cushions and a leaded window, thrown open to afford a view of the river. Was that how he had seen Shakespeare? Had he been watching for him, or had it been mere chance that he was spotted?

Huckerbee was sitting behind a large desk. He looked a great deal cooler than he had last time Shakespeare saw him, on the tennis court at Giltspur House. Not something to be mentioned, perhaps. He curled his smooth fingers to beckon Shakespeare forward into the room. Yet again, Shakespeare found himself irritated by the man's haughty bearing. Was it his knighthood that made him assume superiority over his visitor, or something in his upbringing? To a man of modest birth, such entitlement was like a stray eyelash caught in the eye.

'Take a seat, Mr Shakespeare. I hope you will allow me to pour you a goblet of Aquitaine brandy.' Huckerbee reached for an ornate flagon.

'No thank you, Sir Robert.' Shakespeare remained standing.

Huckerbee smiled and poured himself one. 'I won't keep you, for I know you are a busy man, but I wished to talk with you about this.' He put down the flagon and picked up a sheet of paper. 'This is a bill of account from the misses Smith, known to you and employed by you as night-workers, I believe.'

'They are whores, Sir Robert. Uncommon whores, but whores all the same.'

'Quite, but it is not a word Her Majesty likes to be used about her palaces. I take it you have seen the invoice?'

'I have seen no bills of account from the Smith sisters. I had believed they would be sending their reckonings directly to Mr Phelippes.'

'No, that is not so in this case. As you know, he is back and forth between London and Chartley conjuring sense out of the Scots Queen's ciphers. I am told that you are now the man in charge of these matters and therefore it follows that you take responsibility for authorising the payment, which I am required to counter-sign.' He handed the paper across to Shakespeare. 'Have I been misled, sir?'

Shakespeare took the paper. *To Beth and Eliza Smith, for services rendered, twenty sovereigns, gold. As requisitioned and agreed by Mr John Shakespeare, gent.* It was written in a fine sloping hand on good quality paper, dated and signed by both sisters. Twenty sovereigns was a vast amount; more than a skilled artisan could earn in two years.

'I had no notion, Sir Robert.' He looked up at Huckerbee and met his condescending gaze. 'I knew they were costly, but they assured me that they always dealt with Thomas Phelippes and Mr Secretary, and that the price was always happily agreed by them.' He placed the paper back on Huckerbee's desk.

'And you believed them, sir? You took the word of two notorious night-workers . . . *whores*? I cannot believe Mr Secretary has ever agreed such a sum. It cannot be justified.' Huckerbee's languorous front had been dropped.

Shakespeare stood his ground. 'We needed their services. Mr Secretary told me to do what was necessary to keep Gilbert

Gifford from taking flight. If the costs are excessive, then I shall answer to my master and if necessary I will order the sisters to re-submit their invoice. But that will be a matter for Sir Francis. Is that all? I have work to do.' He turned to go.

'Wait, damn you, I will not be brushed off.'

All pretence of cool urbanity was gone like a blast of wind on a still day. Shakespeare turned back. 'Do you think to talk to me so? You are not my master.'

'Indeed, I *am* your master in this, Shakespeare, for I control the purse that is paying for this ambitious scheme of the Principal Secretary. The Queen herself has me before her almost every day demanding closer control of Treasury funds – so *you* will hear me.'

Shakespeare said nothing, but waited.

'Mr Shakespeare, am I not making myself clear?'

'If you have something to say, say it, for I have no time for such trifling matters.'

'Trifling, you say? No time? I thought you had all the time in the world, pursuing your own interests around town, and all at the expense of the Treasury. I have heard it said, too, that you have been making use of the whores' services yourself. Perhaps that is why their price is so outrageous. Would Mr Secretary like to hear that you are plundering Her Majesty's coffers to pay for your peccadilloes?'

'What exactly are you saying?'

'You are misusing Treasury funds. There is an ugly word for it: embezzlement.'

'That is slander, Huckerbee. You rave like a Bedlam fool.' Shakespeare was angry now, but his ire was underlaid by anxiety. What exactly did Huckerbee think he knew – and who had been talking to him? Was the Queen herself really involved in this? He sniffed the air. Huckerbee kept his sumptuous display of roses in large urns about the room, but they could not conceal the stink of overflowing middens that was beginning to make this palace uninhabitable; the sooner the court moved on to the fresh air of Richmond, the better. But there was more than the stench of human waste in this room, there was the stink of double dealing, too.

'I will be sending a report to Mr Secretary. You have not heard the last of this, Shakespeare.'

He should have walked out then, but he had to defend himself, even though he had nothing to hide. 'Someone has been putting lies about. Who have you been talking to?'

'My information is sound enough. You spend my money on your own pursuits.'

'*Your* money?'

'The money I dispense. Do not quibble with me, sir. I suggest you restrict yourself to government work or you will pay a heavy price.'

'Mr Secretary will not be gulled by you. He knows my honesty. And if I am engaged in any other matters, he knows all about them, for I keep no secrets from him.' Even as he spoke the words, he wished he had kept his counsel; he was defending himself like a schoolboy in front of an overbearing master. He had handed the advantage to Huckerbee.

The comptroller sat back in his chair. 'Then all will be well for you, won't it, Shakespeare?' His voice had regained its composure. 'If Mr Secretary is happy that you have been going about your own business in his time, then who am I to gainsay him? And if he is content that you use official funds for the swiving of a pair of costly whores, then so be it. But I will not be party to it.'

There was a knock at his door.

'Come in,' he said.

A bluecoat entered and bowed low. 'My lord Burghley requests your presence, Sir Robert.'

'Tell him I will be with him presently. A minute, no more.' He waved an elegant hand at Shakespeare. 'Go, sir. Take your boat.' He screwed up the Smith sisters' invoice and flung it at Shakespeare. 'And take that with you, for I will not sign it off.'

Chapter 25

Richard Young, magistrate of London, circled the red-headed man on the stool. All the while he looked at his captive with a steady gaze. Had he been a cat and his prey a mouse, he would surely have batted it with a paw, claws extended.

Osric Redd was bound tight. His legs were secured at the ankles and his hands were tied behind his back. He was in the centre of the parlour in the farm that had always been his home and he had no idea what was going on, who these men were or what they might want from him. They kept asking the same question.

'Where is she, Mr Redd?'

'I told you. I don't know. Why would I know?'

'Because she was here.'

'Aye, she was here. You asked me and I told you. But I told you, too, that she was gone, and so she is. I need to go to my sheep.'

Young approached Osric and stooped even more than usual so that he might meet his prisoner eye to eye. 'I will break you asunder if you say the word *sheep* one more time, Mr Redd.' Young was a poor-looking creature, his lips dry and downcast from a life lived without humour. He was not strong, but he did not need to be when he had a band of six men with him to do the brutish work of taking and holding men for questioning.

Without warning, Young pushed the bound man full on the chest. The stool toppled backwards and Osric fell with it, his head cracking on the dirt floor with a hideous thud. His chin smacked forward into his chest. Blood began to pour from his mouth.

'Pull him up,' Young ordered. 'Wipe the dog's dirty mouth.'

Two men bent forward and pulled the injured man and his stool back upright. His head lolled to the side and his eyes were closed. Blood dripped from his mouth and nose onto his shepherd's smock. He immediately fell to the floor again, unable to keep his balance.

'I think he's dead, Mr Young.'

'He's not dead. I only gave him a push to jog his memory and loosen his peasant tongue. Give him water and a clip around the head, that'll wake him.'

The man shrugged and and wandered off. Justice Young reached into his pocket and pulled out a kerchief, then thought better of it and put it back. Instead, he pulled out his dagger and cut a large strip of cloth from Osric's woollen smock. He scraped the cloth across the injured man's blood-soaked face. The blood smeared, but kept dripping.

'Dirty dog. Look at him.'

One of his men returned carrying a wooden pail. 'I found this outside, Mr Young. I wouldn't drink it, though. They do say the plague is spread in water, so I won't drink it for no man.'

'It's not for drinking, you dolt.' Young snatched the pail and upended it over Osric's head.

As the water washed down over him, Osric grunted and then opened his mouth and gasped.

'There you are. Told you there was nothing wrong with the dirty dog, God damn him to hell.'

'What do we do with him now? I don't think he knows anything. He don't look too well.'

'Since when did I ask you to think? He has acknowledged that he harboured a notorious fugitive here – and I intend to discover where she is and have her hanged.'

'There was the other man,' Osric said, blood spraying with each word.

'Other man?'

'Aye. The other one. Shake . . . Shake . . .'

'Shakespeare?'

Justice Young knelt on the sawdust and mud floor and raised Osric's head so that he might speak a little easier.

'You say Shakespeare was here?'

'He found the dress, then burnt it.'

'Tell me more.'

'That's all I know.'

'Did he take the woman away?'

'There was a fire set and he did burn the dress.'

'Why did he do that?'

'Can I go to my sheep now?'

'Where is she? Where is your brother?'

Osric opened his mouth, but nothing more came out.

Young rose to his feet and turned to his minions. There was nothing more to be had from this imbecile at the present. 'Convey this man to Bridewell, where I shall resume my questioning in due course.'

'My sheep will worry where I am.'

Young shook his head. This man was a waste of God's good air. 'On second thoughts, leave him. If he's too stupid to conceal the fact that she was here, then he's too stupid to conceal anything else.'

In the meantime, thought Young, I shall resume my search for this sheep-witted man's brother for he, most assuredly, must know the whereabouts of the murdering bitch Katherine Giltspur. He brightened. Maybe he could catch them both and let them dance their last jigs together. Shakespeare, too. Now that would make a fine spectacle for the good folk of London town.

In the pigsty, Boltfoot had been assailed by the stench of dung. Now all he could smell was fish; fish more putrid and loathsome than anything he had ever smelt in all his years at sea.

He was on a ship of some kind and that was all he knew, for they had brought him by night, hooded. When the hood was removed, he had caught a glimpse of masts and rigging, stark against the moon, before they lowered him into the hold and closed the hatch.

It was pitch dark down here. He moved around at will, for he was not bound, but the hatchway was bolted from above. Even with the passing of the hours the gloom did not lighten, but he quickly discovered that his only companions in the stinking cell were barrels, some full of salted fish and meat, but many more empty.

The lapping of the waves and the stench of the fish told him everything and nothing. And then he heard the familiar shouts of a ship's master ordering the mooring lines cast away and the sails unfurled, and he felt the changing motion of the vessel as it turned from landward to seaward with the rising breeze and ebbing tide, and his heart sank.

He guessed he must be in the tidal reaches of the Thames, heading downriver towards the estuary, and then the sea.

It was becoming horribly clear; from the stench of the fish and the wallowing and the creaking of heavy timbers, he was obviously aboard a fishing vessel large enough to head for the deep seas of the north. All ships carried salted fish, but the overpowering smell in this hold told him that fish was not only carried but salted here. Such a vessel could be headed anywhere – the narrow seas, the German Bight, the far north and Iceland. Would that be where they dropped him, as food for the fishes? The sailor's worst nightmare.

And now he would not be able to tell his master that Will Cane, the man who killed Nicholas Giltspur, had been conducting an amorous liaison with a woman named Abigail, maidservant to Giltspur's widow, Kat Whetstone. Was this the intelligence that could save Kat's life? Or might it just condemn her? Either way, it was information that Mr Shakespeare needed, and in a hurry. But he wouldn't get it while Boltfoot was aboard this putrid floating fish stall of a ship.

The sea became rougher and the ship lurched. Boltfoot curled himself up on a coil of rope and tried to sleep. An hour or so out, the hatch opened and Boltfoot blinked open his eyes. Above him, in the square of dark blue, he saw the yellow light of a lantern.

A gruff voice boomed into the echoing hollow of the hold. 'How's it going down there?'

'Like a stroll by Paris Garden.'

'You want some aqua vitae?'

Boltfoot laughed. 'I'll take the aqua vitae, but what I really want is setting down on dry land.'

'Tell you what, I'll bring you a tot of spirit and some tobacco. How does that sound?'

'Good enough.'

'And some food, too. Don't want to starve our new carver of casks, do we? You wait there, Mr Cooper, and I shall return with a fine spread for you in no time.'

So that was it: he had been pressed into service, sold by Cutting Ball for a pound or two. Skilled coopers were valuable men aboard ship. Boltfoot cursed. He had met enough pressed men in his time to know that there was little or nothing that could be done. Once at sea, you were as much a prisoner as you would be if incarcerated in the Tower. And you worked or felt the lash.

The face at the hatch reappeared and a rope ladder was dropped down. The man descended, carrying a rough canvas bag tied to his belt, and the lantern in one hand.

'Here we are then, Mr Cooper.' He put down the lantern, then untied his bag from his waist. He was a squat man like Boltfoot, with an honest, weatherbeaten face. The sort of face Boltfoot had encountered many times aboard ships where men had to trust in each other and in God.

'What's your name, sailor?'

'Turnmill.' From the bag he pulled out a tin mug. 'That'll be yours. Lose it and you'll have to pay for another from your share of the take. Same with this.' He produced a tin plate. 'So keep them safe.'

'I've been at sea before, Mr Turnmill. I know what's what.'

Turnmill pulled out a small packet of tobacco and a clay pipe, then a hunk of bread and a sizeable pat of butter. 'And here's your aqua vitae.' He unhooked a small stoppered flask from his belt, took out the cork and poured a large measure into Boltfoot's cup. 'That'll give you back your sea legs.'

The spirit bit the back of Boltfoot's throat and burnt its way down his gullet. He began to feel a good deal better. He put down his cup and crumbled some tobacco into the pipe.

'When am I to be allowed out of this stinking hold? I am no use to you down here.'

'When we're far enough from land. Captain says he don't want you swimming to shore.'

Boltfoot pointed to his club foot. 'And does it look to you as though I could swim?'

'Not for me to say.' Turnmill lit a thin taper from the lantern's flame. He handed it to Boltfoot, who held it to his pipe and drew deeply on the fragrant smoke.

'Well, Mr Cooper, you know how to smoke and you know how to drink, so maybe you'll survive the voyage.'

'What vessel is this?'

'Three-masted bark. No herring-buss or ketch this, Mr Cooper.'

'A deep-sea bark . . .' His heart fell.

'Aye. None deeper.'

'Where we headed?'

'A long way from here. There's six vessels in all. First we're headed to Brittany for salt, then across the western sea to the Grand Banks. Men say you can drop a pail into the sea and you'll catch a cod. Others say they've seen a cod as big as a man.'

Boltfoot closed his eyes in despair. They would be away months; possibly through the autumn and into winter. He knew all about the Grand Banks, the great shallows off the northern coasts of the New World. The lure of the cod fishing there and the great wealth to be made had drawn many ships from England and the other maritime nations to try their luck. Some had grown rich, but many more had never returned. It was the worst of destinations, especially as there was absolutely no hope of getting off this vessel.

Chapter 26

SHAKESPEARE BADE JANE goodnight and retired to his solar to read and think. After an hour, his eyes heavy, he put down the book and knelt on the floor. He closed his eyes and said a prayer for the lives of both Kat and Boltfoot. Then he picked up the candle and went to his chamber.

As he entered the room he caught his step, and his heart began pounding. A man was sitting on the edge of the bed, his head in his hands, tousled fair hair tied back. He breathed out. It was Kat Whetstone in the dirty jerkin, shirt and hose of a labouring man.

Catching his breath, he held up the candle so that its glow fell across her. 'Kat?'

Slowly, she removed her fingers from her face and met his eyes. 'John.'

'How . . .'

She smiled. 'I lived here once, if you recall. It was simple to get in. You should bolt your front door.'

'I have nothing worth stealing, no treasure.'

'But you have enemies. How can you not have enemies when you work for Walsingham?'

He closed the chamber door. He did not want Jane to be implicated in the harbouring of a wanted felon.

'Thank God you are safe, Kat.' His prayer had been half answered. 'I have been in a frenzy of worry.'

'Do not be concerned on my behalf. When have I not been able to look after myself?'

Never. But this was different. He could see the strain and fear in her eyes.

'John, have you made any progress in your inquiries?'

'I have found out that Will Cane was dying anyway. Joshua Peace discovered that he was riddled with cankers.'

Her face brightened. 'Surely that must help.'

'It gives him a possible motive for lying about you. But it does not clear your name.'

Shakespeare sat down on the edge of the bed at her side. She looked worn and haggard. How was it, then, that she still managed to look so beautiful, even in Osric Redd's old jerkin? Just sitting next to her like this, the old stirrings returned. Absently, he began to brush one of the stray locks from her face, tucking it behind her ear, but then stopped. 'Forgive me . . .'

'You have nothing to forgive.'

'Where are you hiding? Be straight with me.'

'I cannot say. No, I *will not* say.'

'Why did you leave Oswald Redd?'

'I had to. He was seizing upon my misfortune to lock me away.'

'What of his brother?'

'Osric? What has he to do with this?'

'When Redd told me you had disappeared without trace from the farm, I confess I looked at his brother with suspicion.'

'Osric is harmless. I made his meals and we passed no more than two words a day. He talks to his sheep more than ever he would talk with me. Had I stayed, that would have been my life, for ever. Oswald had plans to make a farm wife of me.'

✠ 228 ✠

It was a familiar story. 'Just as I had plans to make an intelligencer's wife of you,' said Shakespeare ruefully.

She had her hands to her head again. For a moment, he thought she was sobbing. Kat Whetstone weep? Was such a thing possible?

'Kat,' Shakespeare spoke gently. 'Can you tell me who would benefit from the death of Nicholas Giltspur? Tell me everything you know about his family and associates. I have been to Giltspur House and I cannot but wonder whether the secret we are seeking abides there.'

She raised her tear-stained face. 'What do you wish to know?'

'Tell me about Arthur and his grandmother. And the steward, Sorbus. What about your maidservant, Abigail? And perhaps you need to tell me more about your late husband. You told me you loved him. But you also said that you would not have married him had he been poor.'

'That is true. I would not have married him, but I would have loved him and shared his bed.'

'What of Severin Tort? You placed a great deal of trust in him.' A sudden thought struck him. 'It is Mr Tort who is now hiding you, is it not?'

She shook her head, refusing to acknowledge the question. 'Nick was a hard-working, God-fearing man,' she continued. 'An honest man, too, and I can think of no one who would have wished him harm – least of all me. But in the days before his death something *was* worrying him. When I asked him what was amiss, he just smiled and said that all would be well. Once he said he was worried because a ship was overdue, another time he said he had a difficult transaction to negotiate. I did not believe either explanation, but what could I say? All I knew was that he wasn't sleeping.'

'And his nephew, Arthur? He seems a charming fellow. That is all I discovered – that and his fondness for tennis.'

'He is a privileged young man who enjoys his wealth. And when he is not at court playing sets with the nobility, you will see him at the gaming houses. He attracts women like jam attracts wasps.'

Another thought struck Shakespeare. 'Did he ever display affection for you? You are more his age than your husband's.'

She leant back across the bed and sighed with exhaustion. 'You know, John, I am not sure. I usually know when I catch a man's eye. There were times when I thought . . . but if so, he never made a move. He was a perfect gentleman. I think he sated his appetites elsewhere.'

'Did you ever have cause to believe that he might resent your husband – either because of you, or for any other reason?'

'I cannot imagine why he would have resented Nick.'

'Then if neither you nor Arthur commissioned his murder, who did? What of Sorbus? Did he bear a grievance against his master? Did he begrudge you your place in the household? He does not seem like a man who would welcome change.'

Kat raised her hands as if in supplication. 'Sorbus can seem severe, I grant you, but no, I am certain he would have done no harm to Nick. He was always loyal.'

'Then what of the Giltspur grandmother? She has always been the power of the house, I believe. Is she ruthless enough to kill her own kin if crossed?'

'Grandame? Nick was the joy of her life. I have not seen her since Nick's death, but I am certain she would have been broken by the murder.'

'She is surviving on spirit of opium.'

'That is nothing new. Nick used to warn her it would kill her, to which she always replied that she had lived quite long enough and desired to die without pain.'

This was going nowhere. Shakespeare pushed on. 'There are

many servants. Perhaps one of them bore a grudge. Tell me about your lady's maid, Abigail.'

'She has no money. How could a woman without money offer a hundred pounds to commission a murder?'

'She is fair enough, if a little plump. Beauty can bring rewards.'

'Abigail could have had no cause. If you must know, I did not like her much but she was already part of the household. In truth, I rather think she had got herself with child, for I noted that her breasts were swelling. I would have had to broach the subject eventually.'

Abigail with child. That might change things. 'Who was the father?' Shakespeare rested back on his elbow and looked at Kat, lying on his bed. Her eyes were still closed.

She shrugged. 'Who knows?'

Another thought was taking form. What if Nick Giltspur was the father-to-be?

'You have gone silent, John.'

'I am thinking.'

'Keep thinking. Think me a way to avoid the scaffold.'

She pushed herself up, then stood.

He watched her as she undressed. He had always loved the slow way she undid her stays and slipped from her clothes, but this was different, for she was removing man's clothing. Her skin was burnished gold in the flickering candlelight. She stood before him, naked. Never had she been ashamed of her body. He recalled the first time he saw her unclothed, in the waters of the Avon, before ever they were lovers. Her shoulders were straight, her breasts firm and unbowed by age or child-bearing. He gazed at her with longing. If only she had never left him, how different would both their lives be now.

Without a word, she pulled back the blankets and slid between the cool linen sheets.

He hesitated. He should not be doing this. She was a widow, her husband barely cold in his grave.

Her slender arm snaked out from beneath the sheets. Her eyes were steady and sure. 'Come, John. This one night, no more. I am so afraid. Alone in bed I feel the rope about my neck and cannot breathe. I need you.'

This one night. The affirmation of life to scorn death. She had been his long before Nicholas Giltspur ever saw her. Their union might not have been blessed in the eyes of God, but he had never felt any guilt for enjoying her body and her love, nor would he now.

He undressed and joined her in the coolness of the bed. Her skin was as warm as summer sunshine. Her fingers on his body drew a long moan from his throat. 'Kat . . .'

'I will go before dawn, John.'

'No, stay here. You will be safe. I will send Jane away for a few days. It will be better for her not to know. She should have no part in this.'

'That will never work. Anyway, your house is watched. You notice things when you are a fugitive. I see watchers in shadows. I can pick danger in a doorway or among a crowd.'

He could not help laughing. 'You should become an intelligencer. Sir Francis Walsingham would love you.'

'I had thought he rather liked me anyway.'

'Yes, indeed he did. And he knows I am trying to find the truth about your husband's murder. He has afforded me some leeway, but he can do nothing to prevent the law taking its course.'

'And so you cannot afford to have me here. Fear not, I will slip past Justice Young's man unseen. But you, too, should be careful, John.'

'How did you get in here unseen?'

She kissed his cheek. 'Men have needs, John. Drinking or

pissing. He went for a pint of ale at the Blue Boy. How could he know that he was watched by me?'

'Perhaps there were two of them.'

'No there was only one. Trust me. Anyway, they would have battered down your door by now if they had seen me.'

'They wouldn't have needed to.' He returned the kiss. 'As you pointed out, my love, it is unbolted . . .'

Chapter 27

K AT LEFT AN hour before dawn, her hair tucked up beneath her plain woollen cap, still refusing to say where she was going.

'How will I contact you if I discover anything?'

'Post a note on the Si Quis Door. Mark it a notice of vacancy for a footman, inquiries to be referred to Lady Cutler.'

Shakespeare nodded. The Si Quis Door – from the Latin *Si Quis*, meaning 'if anyone' – was a door at St Paul's where notices of jobs for would-be servants were posted every day. 'So you will be staying close by? Do you not think it would be wiser to leave London? Your man's guise does not bear close inspection.'

'I must be on hand. This must be solved or I will have no life worth living.'

Shakespeare kissed her farewell. For the first time, he truly believed that she was both desperately afraid – and innocent. He had discovered something else, too: he no longer loved her.

Shakespeare went back to bed for two hours' sleep, then took his time over a leisurely breakfast. If Jane had any suspicion that there had been anyone else in the house overnight, it was not evident in her demeanour or anything she said. She bustled about brightly, bringing her master fried links of sausage and eggs. Her one concern seemed to be Boltfoot.

'Will Mr Cooper be away long, master?'

'Not long, I hope.' There was no point in letting her know that he feared the worst. The poor girl could have had no idea what she was letting herself in for when she agreed to enter this house.

Babington arrived at nine o'clock, ready for his meeting with Sir Francis. He was attended by a richly attired valet and was himself dressed in court finery: a doublet of silver and red with a surprisingly modest ruff, probably worn so as not to risk irritating the Puritan sensibilities of Sir Francis Walsingham.

'We are to meet Mr Robin Poley at Greenwich. Do you know him?'

'I have heard his name. He is a Catholic gentleman, is he not?'

'Indeed, he is, Mr Babington, but he has the ear and friendship of Sir Francis Walsingham and has already spoken to him on your behalf, entreating him to grant you a passport.'

Babington was shocked. 'I had thought *you* would be making the arrangements, Mr Shakespeare.'

'I feared my own intercession would be treated with suspicion. Walsingham is my master, not my friend.'

'But this Mr Poley. Can we trust him?'

'He is devout and honourable. He also has great beauty of face and character and he is as wedded to the true faith as we are, Mr Babington. Though he is not wealthy, he gives whatever he may in the way of grants to seminary priests. Being of modest means, he must always live in the households of great men.'

'His patron is Sir Philip Sidney, I believe.'

'Indeed, but with Sir Philip away at the wars, Poley has been taken into the house of Sir Philip's father-in-law, who you will know to be Sir Francis Walsingham himself. Robin Poley has full use of Mr Secretary's home and has even invited me to mass with him at Barn Elms, under the very nose of his host. I fear I took the coward's way and did not attend.'

Babington was aghast. 'Does Sir Francis *know* him to be a Catholic?'

'He does, and likes him none the less for it. I would go further and say that he has Walsingham's love.'

'How can he bear to live with Walsingham? He is Satan made flesh.'

'You could ask the same of myself or Abingdon or Tilney – or a hundred other men at court. Mr Byrd of the Chapel Royal has the Queen's favour, and yet she knows he cleaves to his Catholic faith. We work among them because how else are we to live? And more to the point, how are we to defeat them? Our time will come soon enough.'

'But Poley—'

'Enough, Mr Babington. If you do not want his help, then do not come with me.' Shakespeare took Babington's hand in both of his. 'Mr Poley is charming, pious and full of wit. But the greatest of his virtues is honesty. Which is why it is my firm belief that it were better for you if *he* rather than I were to broach the subject of your passport with Mr Secretary.' He frowned anxiously. 'I hope I have not gone beyond my brief.'

Babington hesitated, then nodded. 'No. You have spoken well, Mr Shakespeare. I will take Robin Poley as I find him.'

'If you still harbour doubts after meeting him, inquire at the French embassy where he has their full trust. Mr Poley is considered a very prince among the Catholics of this realm. And yet I must repeat that he is not wealthy. So he will ask money of you in return for his services.'

'How much?'

'Whatsoever you can afford. But bear in mind that he will be putting himself at great risk on your behalf.'

'Fifty pounds?'

It seemed Babington had plucked the figure from the air, but Shakespeare imagined he had already given the matter of money thought; something as valuable as a licence to travel was not easily come by in these troubled days and would always cost a great deal.

'I should not speak for him but I think he would consider that fair.'

Babington shook his handsome head. 'Fifty pounds to put my head in the lion's mouth . . .'

'Fifty pounds to seek safer shores and protect your inheritance. Will you send for your wife and child when you are abroad?'

Babington did not answer. 'Let us get to it, Mr Shakespeare. Midsummer is past. Time catches us unawares. Let us go now to Greenwich and meet your Robin Poley.'

The trip downriver to Greenwich Palace was swift and uneventful. On arriving, Shakespeare escorted Babington to the presence chamber.

If Babington was anxious, he disguised it well, for he held his head high and smiled at the numerous courtiers with whom he was acquainted: a wave of the gloved hand here; a nod of the head there.

Walsingham had been as good as his word. Shakespeare spotted Poley instantly.

'Good morrow, Mr Shakespeare.'

'And to you, sir.' He extended his hand to indicate his companion. 'This is Anthony Babington. Shall we step outside, gentlemen? I think it a fine day to stroll in the gardens.'

As they walked from the palace into the southern gardens,

away from the river, Shakespeare observed his two companions with a little inner smile. Babington had fallen in love at first sight. Poley was as perfectly formed as a Roman statue; not tall, but lean and muscular with long fair hair and an aspect of innocence that would have won an abbot to his cause. Shakespeare stood back and watched as Poley drew Babington into an arbour of roses. It made a pretty picture. With fortune on their side, Babington would not notice the thorns until it was too late.

'It will be my great pleasure to help you, Mr Babington,' Poley said. 'I believe I can judge a man at first meeting, and I know that we will be the firmest of friends.'

'Thank you, Mr Poley. My hopes accord with yours.'

'Then let us get straight to business, for we have little time before you are called in to see Mr Secretary. I am so well acquainted with his daughter and wife that I flatter myself I know the innermost workings of his mind. He is a secretive man, but not beyond knowing, as some would have it.'

Shakespeare laughed. 'He is beyond *my* knowing, Mr Poley.'

Poley dismissed Shakespeare with a playful flick of the hand. 'Do not listen to him, Mr Babington. What you must realise is that while Sir Francis scorns the Pope and Catholicism, he does not bear antagonism towards those Catholics whom he sees as loyal to Her Majesty. He does, however, see them as misguided. And so you must be open and honest with him and declare your faith. He will tell you that you are a fool and may try to convert you to his interpretation of the scriptures, but that is all. Merely endure his barbs and all will be well. And then you need a story – a tale to convince him that you are not fleeing England into the embrace of the Jesuits. You need, too, to offer your assistance. Do you understand?'

'I believe so.'

'Then let us rehearse. Come, sit here at my side'

*

Anthony Babington had always looked down on men such as Walsingham. They were dour creatures, mere functionaries, men of poor family. A gentleman of great family did not spend his time dealing with papers and administrative duties unless they related to his own estates. And yet he smiled at him, bowed extravagantly and put out his hand as though he were his dearest and most respected friend.

'Sir Francis, such a pleasure and honour to meet you.'

'Come in, Mr Babington, come into my humble office. The pleasure is all mine. I am sure I have seen your face at court. I know you have attended on Her Majesty, for she has often mentioned you with affection and some disappointment that she does not see more of you.'

'You flatter me, sir.'

'No, indeed not. She has an abiding fondness for young men of dash and character. And she knows your history as grandson to bold Lord Darcy. And how is your aunt, Lady Darcy, whom I know of old?'

'She is well. I take my dinner with her at noon almost every day.'

'Ah yes, now that you have moved from Temple Bar to Hern's Rents, she must be close to you. Does she not have a house close by Lincoln's Inn Fields?'

'She does, sir.'

'Well, I would be honoured if you would convey my very good regards to her. Now then, sir, sit down if you please. I have just poured myself a small cup of sweet Rhenish. Would you care for some?' Without awaiting an answer, the Principal Secretary began to pour the wine into a small silver goblet, a match for his own.

Babington took a seat at the table opposite Walsingham. 'Thank you, Sir Francis.' He put the cup to his lips, then gave a little nod in warm appreciation of the wine's quality.

Smiling serenely, Walsingham looked at him and waited.

At last Babington spoke. He had already decided it would be best to get straight to the matter in hand. 'Has Mr Poley given you some inkling of why I am here?'

'Indeed he has, Mr Babington. He tells me you wish to have licence to travel out of England. And before you say more, let me put your mind at ease; I know that you are of the Roman persuasion. But this is no concern of mine if you are a true Englishman and if your loyalty is to Her Royal Majesty, Elizabeth. This is so, is it not?'

'I am always happy to proclaim my loyalty, my fealty indeed, to the Queen of England, Sir Francis,' Babington replied.

Walsingham was not so easily won. 'The Queen of England being Elizabeth Tudor, Mr Babington? Not, as some would have it, some foreign-born princess.'

'As you say, Sir Francis.'

'No, Mr Babington, as *you* must say it. Say: I am always happy to proclaim my loyalty to the true Queen of England, Elizabeth Tudor, anointed by God.'

Though a dagger stabbed at his heart Babington repeated the words. He had no choice if he was to gain anything but a noose from this meeting.

Walsingham smiled again. 'Good man. Now we know exactly where we stand. Let me reassure you, it is the Pope and his acolytes who are my enemies, not good English Catholics. I have many friends who are Catholic, both in my office and at court. Their religion is no concern of mine, only their loyalty. Why, Robin Poley himself has heard mass at my own house, though he thinks I don't know! A man's faith is his own concern; his loyalty is mine.'

Babington ran a sleeve across his damp brow, then drank the

remainder of his wine in one swallow. He was not sure that he believed a word Walsingham was saying. 'Loyalty means as much to me, Sir Francis. Rest assured you have mine.'

'Good, then you can be sure of my love and assistance, as I am certain that I can be sure of yours. Fear not, Mr Babington, there will be no problem issuing you with a passport, for travel does wonders for a young man's mind. I still recall my own time in France, as ambassador. I believe it showed me the true nature of England's foes and informed the work I now do for my country. When first you are in a foreign land, you see things that others do not see. So, yes, the passport will be there for you. But before I sign it, I must be able to convince Her Majesty of the justness of your suit.'

'I understand.'

'Then tell me, what precisely are your plans, so that I may make out a good case to Her Royal Majesty?'

Babington swallowed hard. He had had the story all worked out, but now he found the words bubbling in his head like water in a kettle. 'I wish to travel through the lands of France and Burgundy.'

'You have travelled there before, have you not?'

How did Walsingham know that? Did he truly know everything that every man and woman in England had ever done? Some said he conjured and knew the innermost thoughts of the lowliest subject in the land. Babington nodded; denial seemed useless.

'What was it, four or five years ago? Within a few months of your marriage, I believe?'

Babington stiffened. This was becoming more uncomfortable by the moment. 'It was something I had been planning before ever I thought to wed Margaret. Indeed, it was our marriage that stayed me longer than I intended.'

'And so you travelled to Rouen and Paris. A man of your

good family must have had introductions to some of the great men of that beautiful land.'

'I was a young man, not yet twenty. And though my mother's father was titled, I was not and so I attracted no attention from the French court.'

'What of the English exiles? The treacherous Morgan – did he not seek you out? Or Beaton, the so-called Archbishop of Glasgow, who styles himself the Queen of Scots' ambassador?'

Babington was silent. He had both met them and been pressed by them to work for Mary. Clearly Walsingham knew all about it. He could not gainsay the Principal Secretary, and so he said nothing, but smiled like a loon.

Walsingham picked up the silver pitcher and refilled Babington's goblet. 'Forgive me, I am discomfiting you. You were young when you went before and, anyway, these things are not important in themselves. Thomas Morgan and James Beaton and Charles Paget seek out all young Englishmen as they travel through France. It means nothing as long as you understand this time that you must report back all such encounters to me, and all that is said to you. No secrets must be kept from me.'

'I understand, Sir Francis. Of course, I will be happy to report every word I hear.'

'Good. I knew you were a fine man, for only the best of men have Her Majesty's love. And so to your plans . . .'

Babington breathed a heavy sigh of relief. Walsingham seemed to have no knowledge of the secret work he had done for Mary on his return to England – the long rides across country carrying letters, escorting priests, providing horses and carriages and money. Work that would have cost him his head had it been uncovered and that he had eventually given up through fear of discovery. He had made a momentous decision: he would eschew such dangerous pursuits. Let others hazard their lives.

But in the early months of this year letters had arrived from Paris via the French embassy in London. Babington had handed them back, unread. He would have nothing to do with such things. And then in May, Father Ballard had arrived from France with persuasive arguments. Catholics were suffering under the yoke of tyranny. No true Catholic could stand aside and do nothing. More than that, he was a man trusted and loved by Mary of Scots and was uniquely placed to further her cause, with many young friends at court and beyond. Babington was flattered. Yes, he had said at last, he would help in whatever way he could.

But that was then. Now, everything had changed. Now it seemed that Ballard's constant companion, Bernard Maude, was a Walsingham spy. The cause was lost – and so he must go into exile, like so many young Catholics of good family.

He sipped the wine and tried to appear relaxed.

'Will you travel to Rome, Mr Babington?'

'It is my intention . . .'

'Then you must go to the English college. Send me details of every young man presently there, for I know some of them will return to England secretly, to sow dissent and treason.'

'I will consider it my duty.' *I will consider it my duty to cut my own throat before ever I do such a thing as betray my fellows.*

'Then I am sure we can do business, Mr Babington, and the passport will be yours. Robin Poley will deliver it to you as soon as the papers are prepared. Now if you will excuse me, I must attend upon Her Majesty.' The dour spymaster rose from his plain chair, gathered his grim features into something akin to a smile, and extended a hand to his guest. 'Good day to you, sir.'

*

'Has he granted you a passport?' Robin Poley had been waiting outside the chamber.

'I believe he has, Mr Poley.'

'But he demanded much in return, yes? You look as though you have run a mile through a rainstorm, Mr Babington! Come, let us find you a towel, and then I would be delighted to escort you back to London where we shall dine together at my expense.'

Babington looked at Poley's soft skin and exquisite features. Perhaps the meeting with Walsingham had not gone so badly; he was still alive, at least, and not imprisoned. Perhaps he had truly gulled Walsingham into believing that he would spy for him. His spirits lifted. He looked around. 'What of Mr Shakespeare?'

'He has business to attend to here at court. Come, let us drink wine together and discuss what is to be done to heal the rotten heart of this state.' Poley lowered his voice. 'I would do all I can to assist you in your endeavours, both at home and abroad.' He put out a slender hand to touch Babington's arm. It was almost a caress, and Babington did nothing to move away. And then he allowed the arm to encircle his shoulders. 'You know, Mr Babington,' Poley said, drawing him away from Walsingham's quarters, 'it would be my greatest joy to come with you to foreign lands, away from these persecutors of the true faith.'

'Then why not come with me?'

'Is it possible you would truly accept me as your companion, sir?'

'I would.'

'Then I must find a way. In the meantime, let us to London, for I know you have had a most trying morning. We must look after you well, Mr Babington, for all our hopes rest on these fine shoulders of yours.'

Chapter 28

WALSINGHAM STROKED HIS coarse dark beard in thought. 'I wonder whether I pushed him too hard. Do you think he might take fright and flee, John?'

Shakespeare shrugged non-committally. 'That all depends on Robin Poley.'

'He is slippery, is he not? I would not trust him.'

'Not to all men's taste, certainly. But those who are drawn to him cannot resist him. Mr Babington's eyes lit like a beacon at the sight of Poley. Am I permitted to know more of his background?'

'Robin? He was born a gentleman but penniless and had to go up to Cambridge as a Clare's sizar, a time he clearly resents, waiting on his betters. He claims kinship to the Blounts by marriage and I know from Tom Phelippes that he once carried letters to the Catholic exiles in Paris on behalf of the damnable Christopher Blount. Blount even offered him money to kill my lord of Leicester. That is how far the Catholics trust him.'

'But not all of them.'

'No. But we only need the one – Mr Babington. And you say he is smitten.'

Shakespeare was silent.

'Once again I see that you are squeamish, John.'

'Perhaps my conscience is too fine. But these men are going

to the scaffold and I struggle with their guilt. I know that Ballard and Savage are assassins and must be put down; I understand that well enough. But for the others, like the vain Babington, sometimes it seems to me that they are happily imbibing a summer cordial of youthful indiscretion, not knowing the poison it contains.'

'They are not children. I grant you they are fools – but not such fools that they are unaware of the line between idle talk and treason. These men crossed that line long ago. Do you not think that I too have a conscience? I promise you this: if Babington balks at the final hurdle, I will allow him to slip away to exile. I will not have innocent blood on my hands.'

Shakespeare nodded. 'Thank you.'

'Remember, John, this is war. On the eve of battle, you may dine with your enemy in his camp. You may drink with him and enjoy his company. But come morning, you must kill him, for if you do not, he will surely kill you.'

Shakespeare knew it to be true. It was, indeed, the nature of war, and this was war. England's enemies had made that plain enough.

'And so, let us proceed. When you see Poley next tell him I want Babington to return to me in three days' time. He is to bring him to me at Barn Elms. Soon after that, I will have Mary's letter delivered to him. His reply – if he writes one – will tell us all we need to know.'

Shakespeare bowed and walked down to the quay to hail a boat for London. Gilbert Gifford should be waiting for him at Seething Lane, and he had a plan to put to him; the exposing of Harry Slide had left a dangerous hole in their surveillance of Ballard. He needed to take matters into his own hands, to push forward the plans of the conspirators.

As he was stepping into his craft, something made Shakespeare turn back and look up. At a leaded window, he saw the face of Sir Robert Huckerbee. Their eyes locked for a second, and then Huckerbee moved away.

One thing puzzled him: if Sir Robert Huckerbee had reported his so-called misuse of Treasury funds to Walsingham, as threatened, why had Sir Francis made no mention of it? And what was it about Huckerbee that enraged him so?

As Shakespeare walked up Seething Lane he saw six or seven men gathered outside his house. They were standing beside a handcart, laughing. One of them spotted him and pointed, then they all looked his way.

He walked on without breaking his stride, but jolted to a halt as he came within fifteen yards of the men, for he saw that their leader was Richard Young, magistrate of London. Hanging loose from the back of the cart was an arm, and it was attached to a body which had all the appearances of being lifeless.

Shakespeare's heart stopped. Boltfoot. They had brought him the dead body of Boltfoot Cooper. For reasons which he did not understand, his hand instinctively went to the hilt of his sword. He breathed deeply and tried to maintain his composure. 'What is this, Mr Young?'

'I have a corpse, dragged not an hour since from the river by the bridge. It was brought to my attention as Justice of the Peace, for it is feared some foul play has been used.'

'Why have you brought it here? Who is it?'

'I believe it is a friend to you and your whore. Take a look, see if you recognise him.'

Shakespeare removed his hand from his sword and walked forward. The body in the cart lay on its front. His first close look told him it was not Boltfoot, but he did know the dead man. From the red of the lank hair and the shape and size and clothing of the body, he was almost certain that it was Oswald

Redd. Shakespeare grasped the hair and pulled back the head to look at the face. Yes, it was Redd. There was no blood, obviously washed away by the waters of the Thames, but a large indentation in the back of the head was clearly visible. He lowered the head to the wooden boards of the cart.

'Why have you brought him here?'

'To see your reaction. You can tell a murderer by his eyes.'

'Really?' Shakespeare inclined his head. 'So you must think he was murdered. What evidence do you have, Mr Young?'

'It is plain to see that he was clubbed across the head. And you are my chief suspect, Shakespeare.'

'Why would I kill Oswald Redd?'

'That is for me to discover. Perhaps a falling-out of felons? Perhaps you fought over the whore's dirty favours. Don't think I am unaware that you two have been conspiring together to conceal the whereabouts of the notorious murderess Katherine Giltspur.'

'You gibber, Young. You know not what you say.'

'I know more than you think. I have been to a farm at Chigwell, not far from London, as have you. And I know what you did there. You took her away into another place of hiding and you burnt her dress. Did you believe a change of clothes would disguise the bitch?'

Shakespeare looked Young straight in the eye and did not attempt to conceal his contempt. 'Do you think it befits a man of supposed magisterial dignity to be wheeling a corpse about the streets of London? Take this body to the Searcher of the Dead at St Paul's. Mr Peace will tell us all we need to know.'

'I have more of a mind to take you to Newgate and hold you there for murder and for harbouring a murderer.'

'Try it. Arrest me if you wish to feel the wrath of Mr Secretary. He will have you stripped of your office by day's end

✠ 248 ✠

if you interfere with me. You are a paltry maggot of a man, Young. Now do as I say – take this corpse to Mr Peace.'

'That sodomite necromancer? He knows nothing.'

Shakespeare grasped Young by the throat. As he did so, the six deputies moved towards him with menace, but did not attempt to drag him off. The words *Mr Secretary* clearly carried more weight than the authority enjoyed by Justice Young. 'Just do as I say, Young, do your duty under the law. Or I pledge there will be consequences for you.' He pushed Young and watched as he gasped for breath and stumbled into a pile of dung. Then Shakespeare turned away and walked through the men.

As he opened his front door Shakespeare glanced back to glimpse a scowl on the face of Justice Richard Young; the scowl of a man with a costly boot coated in steaming horseshit.

Boltfoot was brought up from the hold as the ship reached the wide estuary of the Thames. On deck the stink of fish was greatly reduced by the stiff breeze that billowed the sails above him. He looked to starboard and saw, ahead of him, the squat buildings and smoking chimneys of Gravesend, on the southern shore of the river. The town's quays were full of ships, moored two or three deep, their masts and skeletal rigging singing in the wind. It was a town he knew, a town of chandlers and sail-lofts, taprooms and taverns, whorehouses and gaming rooms. If only he could land there now and catch the long ferry back to London.

His heart sank as the ship cut through the choppy waves and made no attempt to veer towards port, instead carrying on eastward towards the North Sea. His last hope of getting ashore had gone. He looked to larboard and astern and saw the other vessels in the flotilla, all under sail and maintaining good progress with the ebb tide.

'Say farewell to England, Mr Cooper. You won't see her again until Christmas.'

'I'd make it worth your while if you could somehow get me ashore, Mr Turnmill.'

'You know there's no chance of that.'

'At least tell me what ship this is. Who is her captain?'

'You're aboard the *Giltspur Falcon* and the captain is a gentleman out of Hamburg, name of Bootmann. Reinhard Bootmann.'

'Giltspur? Is this a Giltspur ship?' Was it mere coincidence that he should have been pressed into service aboard a Giltspur ship?

'Aye, one of their finest and newest. Mostly they have smacks and ketches for the North Sea, but they have bought into these race-built galleons for the long runs to Iceland and the Grand Banks. She'll be ready to carry cannon if ever called on. And if any ship in the flotilla can get to the Grand Banks and back, the *Falcon* is the one. But they're all fair enough – as is Herr Bootmann. I've sailed with him ten years and he is a fine navigator and taker of fish. You'll have a good share of the catch on the *Giltspur Falcon*.'

'So what will happen now that Mr Giltspur is dead and gone?'

'That's the fear for all of us. His nephew knows nothing of fish nor ships and cares less. Who knows what will become of the fleets?'

'And what do men say about the killing and the guilt or innocence of his widow?'

Turnmill laughed. 'She's as guilty as a bushy-tailed vixen with a fowl in her mouth.'

There had to be a way off this ship. *Had to be.* He tried again. 'I have little money, Mr Turnmill. But I would give it all to you, with the promise of more, if you could but find a way for me to talk with the captain.'

'Herr Bootmann won't let you go. He needs you, for there is no other cooper aboard and only two others in the fleet. Had he not been offered your services, the whole enterprise might well have been delayed.'

Boltfoot dug into his purse and pulled out the coins. 'Here. Take it. Try, I beg of you. This is not just my life. There is more at stake here – much more.'

As he spoke, a man was descending the companionway from the poop.

Turnmill cupped his hand and spoke into Boltfoot's ear. 'That's the ship's master, Maywether. Don't cross him.'

Boltfoot looked up and realised his situation was not improving. He knew Maywether, all right. How in God's name had a dirty, scheming rogue like Godfrey Maywether ever ended up as a ship's master?

Maywether looked at Boltfoot coldly, then turned to Turnmill. 'Mr Turnmill, stop your damned idling. Get this man to work.'

Gilbert Gifford was in the anteroom, smoking a pipe. He smirked as Shakespeare came in, having clearly seen the confrontation between Shakespeare and Justice Young from the front window.

'Mr Gifford.' Shakespeare looked at the pink pigling with a mixture of relief and displeasure. 'I trust I have not kept you waiting too long.'

'An hour, maybe two. I thought to enjoy the company of your young housemaid, but she scuttled away to her chamber.'

'You remember my warning with regard to her.'

'What little faith you have in me!'

'You forget, I know a great deal about your appetites, Mr Gifford. I trust Jane at least served you some refreshment?'

'Fear not. I have wit enough to find your casks. Now then, is it time to deliver the letter?'

'Soon.'

He exhaled loudly to demonstrate his frustration. 'When exactly? I cannot wait in London for ever.'

'When Mr Secretary decides. It is up to him, no one else. In the meantime, I have another task for you.'

Gifford brushed this aside with a wave of his plump little hand. 'Before we discuss other matters, there is the question of the Smith sisters. I went to the Holborn house last night. They were not there.'

Ah yes, the Smith sisters. Shakespeare's uncomfortable session with Sir Robert Huckerbee came to mind. Their favours were not to be dispensed lightly, it seemed. Walsingham's assurance that expense would be no object in this endeavour was clearly founded on quicksand; the constraints of the Treasury were not being helpful. 'You will have to prove your worth to us if you wish to see them again. I need you for a singular purpose.'

'God's faith, Mr Shakespeare, I have proved my worth time and again! No letters would have gone into Chartley without me. The letter now awaiting delivery to Babington would not be in Mr Secretary's hands without my skill. You would not have knowledge of Goodfellow Savage's deadly intentions without me. No man has done – *is* doing – more than me. I have risked life and limb and pushed myself to the edge on England's behalf.'

Shakespeare could not deny it. The whole affair hinged on Gilbert Gifford, from Rheims to Paris and from London to Chartley; none of it would have happened without him. 'Forgive me, I have great admiration for you, as does Mr Secretary. But as for the Smith sisters, their services are to be used sparingly. I swear I will bring them to you again, but I must ask this other service of you.'

Gifford eyed Shakespeare with suspicion. 'What is it?'

'It is Father Ballard, who presently goes by the name of Captain Fortescue. We had him closely watched, but his shadow has been discovered and so Ballard is on the loose. We cannot allow that. Get close to him, Mr Gifford.'

'If he has discovered one shadow, he will be yet more wary than before.'

'He will trust no one above you. You have mutual friends in the seminary at Rheims. Ballard must be acquainted with your cousin Dr William Gifford from the English College. He knows the history of your family.'

'I want more. I want the Smith sisters – and I want more money. A lot of money.'

'I will do what I can for you.'

'And I want a written assurance from Mr Secretary that when this all blows up my head will be safe.'

'No blame will attach to you.'

'I want it written. Preferably in Walsingham's blood.'

Shakespeare realised he was losing Gifford. He leapt forward and clasped Gifford in a bear-like embrace. 'I *will* have the Smith sisters for you, sir, even if I pay them from my own pocket. I pledge this. Go to the Holborn house. They will be there. And you will have more money: a pension from the Treasury.'

'And the assurance?'

'That is for Mr Secretary.' It was the one thing Shakespeare could not promise. Never would Walsingham put into writing the truth about his use of Gilbert Gifford, for if it ever came out, such a document would play straight into the hands of England's enemies.

As Shakespeare released him from his grip, Gifford smiled, but the suspicion in his eyes was not diminished. Trust? Gilbert Gifford had long ago learnt never to trust anyone.

'Now find Ballard. And remember: if you abandon this enterprise now, you will be England's enemy and you will pay a heavy price.'

Gifford was looking out of the window again. He did not turn around. 'Mr Shakespeare, do I detect the spirit of Mr Secretary in your words?'

'Never doubt his ability to find you, wherever you are. He will not forgive you if you leave this endeavour uncompleted.'

'That sounds very much like a threat. Have I ever let you down?'

'You are like smoke in fog, Mr Gifford – and you know it.'

'There are times when we all struggle with our loyalties, Mr Shakespeare – even you.'

'Do not fail me.'

'Your point is noted.' Gifford gestured with his hand for Shakespeare to come to the window. 'It seems your friends have left you their corpse.'

Young and his men had indeed gone, but the cart was still there. The body of Oswald Redd was being poked and prodded by a crowd of children. Shakespeare cursed.

Chapter 29

SORBUS STOOD AT the door of Giltspur House and sighed as though the weight of the world had suddenly descended on his narrow shoulders. 'He is at Greenwich with the court, Mr Shakespeare.'

'I am not here to see Arthur Giltspur. I wish to talk with the maid, Abigail.'

'I cannot admit you to the house without the express permission of my master.'

'Then talk to his grandmother. She is the master in this house, I believe.'

Sorbus moved to close the door, but then appeared to reconsider. 'Come in, Mr Shakespeare. I will speak to Mistress Giltspur. I believe she is awake.'

'Thank you, Mr Sorbus.' He looked at the retreating back of the steward. For the first time, he had not looked down his sharp nose at his guest. Why? Shakespeare was left on a settle in an oak-panelled anteroom. A footman appeared with a tray, bowed low, and poured a small measure of brandy into a fine Venetian glass. Shakespeare sipped at it. He did not have to wait long before Sorbus reappeared.

'Mistress Giltspur would like to talk with you herself. Please come with me.'

*

Joan Giltspur was sitting bolt upright in a high-backed chair, beside the window in her room. Her door was open, but Sorbus knocked at it anyway. The old woman's head turned slowly and a slight nod indicated that they should enter.

'Good day, Mr Shakespeare. Please come in. You may go, Sorbus.'

The steward bowed stiffly and left, closing the door behind him.

'Mistress Giltspur, thank you for receiving me.'

'Indeed, I was rather hoping you would come again. I have been thinking much since last you were here.'

The old woman was dressed in a gown of gold and red which must have been the height of fashion fifty years earlier. He looked down where the sunlight fell on her feet and was surprised to note that they were bare.

Her eyes followed his. 'I can no longer abide shoes, Mr Shakespeare. Tell me, have your inquiries proceeded to any degree?'

'They are by no means complete, but I believe I have made some little progress. I have come here today in the hope of talking to your maid, Abigail.'

'And why would that be?'

'Because I think she is with child and I would very much like to know who the father is.'

She moved forward in her chair. 'Abigail? Who told you this?'

'No one,' he lied. 'It was the look of her, the healthy blossom on her cheeks, the swelling of her breasts and belly. If I am wrong, then I can only apologise.'

'Abigail!' The old woman's voice was surprisingly loud and piercing.

The maid came scurrying in from an adjoining chamber.

'Yes, Mistress Giltspur? Yes, ma'am?' Her eyes swivelled between her mistress and John Shakespeare.

'Is this true?' The old woman pointed a bony finger at the girl's belly.

She hesitated a moment too long and then shook her head. 'Forgive me, ma'am, what are you suggesting?'

'Who is the father? If you do not give me his name, you will be out of this house within the hour. Do you understand?'

'But I am not with child, ma'am.'

'When were your last flowers?'

'Not two weeks since. Please, ma'am, I beg you don't dismiss me.'

'Get out!'

Abigail gasped, then put her hand to her mouth, burst into tears and ran to the door. Loud sobs trailed back into the room.

Shakespeare put his hand up. 'Mistress Giltspur, let me speak to her. I had not meant to bring this upon the young woman. We cannot even be sure my suspicion was correct.'

'Of course it was correct. I must be losing my mind, Mr Shakespeare. I have no notion how I failed to note it before. She must be almost six months gone.'

'Allow me a few words. At least we might discover the name of the father. Perhaps the offer of a reference or a few shillings to tide her over while she seeks another position . . .' Shakespeare looked for some forgiveness in the old widow's eyes, but saw only stone.

'I thank you for bringing me this news, but now I must ask you to go.' Joan Giltspur snorted. 'It will be some grubby serving boy from the kitchen, or a groom from the stables.'

'There is another possibility. What if Nicholas was the father? What if the babe she carries is your grandchild?'

Silence hung in the old woman's chamber. The deep lines in her face showed every one of her eighty-one years. She pulled her lips back from her teeth, which were remarkably white for one of her age. For a moment it seemed she would speak, but no words came.

'It is a possibility, is it not?' Shakespeare broke the silence. 'She is a very pretty young woman. If the child was conceived five or six months ago, then it would have been long before he met Katherine.'

'This is scurrilous talk. How dare you! This family has done more for England than the whole Privy Council combined, and yet you have the temerity to suggest such a thing. Get out.'

'Of course I will go, but think on it. Why not Nicholas? She is a comely young woman and he was an unattached man. She would not have been the first maid to slip into her master's bed of a night . . .'

'And you believe this is something to do with his murder, Mr Shakespeare? Is that it?'

'I don't know. But I must look at all possibilities, and spurned love has led to many murders. But before I can even begin to think such things, I must ascertain the name of the father.'

'Go to her. Tell her she can stay if she is honest with you. She will work in the kitchens. I do not wish to see her, but I wish to know the truth.'

Shakespeare found Abigail in her bedchamber, one of a number of small rooms in the extensive attics. She was sitting on a narrow cot with a thin mattress and meagre bedding. Her head was in her hands and tears streamed from her eyes. He sat down beside her and put a comforting arm around her shoulders. The gloom was pervasive, for there was no window and the only light came through the open hatch.

'Come now, Abigail, dry your eyes. I believe your mistress can be persuaded to relent.' He tried to soften his voice.

The sobs were choking in her throat. Shakespeare had not expected such intensity of emotion. Suddenly his arm around her shoulders felt awkward, a little too intimate. He stood up. Still she did not raise her head from her hands or allow her eyes to meet his.

'How long have you been here at Giltspur House?'

She did not answer, but kept on weeping.

'I know you were lady's maid to Mistress Katherine Giltspur. I can understand how dismayed you must have been at the events of a few days ago. It is all still a mystery, is it not? And that is the reason I am here – to try to solve this terrible puzzle. What I need from you is any information you might have; anything you might not already have mentioned, which is why I want you to tell me the name of your baby's father. Perhaps he might know something. Anything you can tell me, however insignificant it might seem to you, could assist me.'

Her tears continued unabated. How was he to extract information from this woman? And then he seemed to hear a whisper through her sob.

'*Help me.*'

The words were so quiet that at first he was not certain he had heard them.

'What would you have me do?'

'Help me, sir. I have done a bad thing,' she whispered.

'What have you done, Abigail? What bad thing?'

'Please, Mr Shakespeare . . .'

'Is this something to do with Mr Giltspur's death? If so, it were better you speak now. Or are you speaking of the babe that grows in your womb? Is that the bad thing?' He leant forward and took her face in his hands.

Briefly, Abigail's moist red eyes met Shakespeare's, then went back down, demurely, as though she were a virgin at the altar. She slid forward from the bed onto her knees. For a moment, he thought she was about to pray, but instead she clasped Shakespeare's legs like a supplicant. 'Please, sir. Please, help me.'

'Yes, I will help you, but you must be straight and honest with me. Answer my questions truthfully and I will try to assist you. I ask again, what is this bad thing you speak of – do you mean the swelling of your belly? Or is there something else I should know?'

'I will do anything. Anything.'

He tried to remove her arms from about his legs, to make her either stand up or sit back on the bed so that they could converse properly, but she held him tighter and nestled her tear-stained face into his groin, so that he could feel her warm breath through the wool of his hose.

'Abigail, you must move away. This is not seemly.'

Her hands slid up the back of his legs and tried to venture into the gap between his thighs. 'Abigail!' He tried to wrench himself away from her, but she clasped him all the harder. Now her right hand went to the front of his hose and began to stroke him. He grasped her hand to pull it away and was astonished by her strength in resisting him. But he was stronger. With his other hand he gripped her upper left arm and forced her back onto the bed. She let out a strange laugh, half tearful, half insane.

'Abigail, this will not end here. Tell me, the bad thing, what is it? Tell me now.'

She pulled back her shoulders and turned her head sharply to the left to shield her face from him.

For two minutes he stood and looked down at her. But she did not move, except for the occasional shudder, which might have been a residue of her tears or the convulsion of a laugh.

There was nothing more to be said. Without another word, he clambered through the hatchway and down the ladder.

*

He found Sorbus in the hall close to the front door.

'Mr Sorbus, a word.'

'As you will, sir.'

'The maid Abigail, I wish to know more about her. She seems almost deranged.'

'I fear she has not been herself since the recent events, Mr Shakespeare. And now I am led to believe that you think her with child.'

'Where did you hear that?'

'Old Mistress Giltspur, sir. She is most displeased.'

'So you suspected nothing, even when her belly swelled and her breasts grew?'

Sorbus cast his face into an apology. 'I am but a man, sir, and a bachelor. The ways of women are a mystery to me. I do not notice things as others might. Indeed, as *you* might, sir.'

'How long has she been in the house?'

'A year. She was in service to Mr Tort. He had overheard me saying to Mr Nicholas that we needed a new housemaid and he said that he had a good girl who was surplus to requirements. And so we took her on. She did well and was promoted to lady's maid when Mr Nicholas brought his new bride into the house.'

'What is her family name?'

'Colton, sir. But I am afraid I know little more about her. She was so highly recommended by Mr Tort that we did not consider it necessary to look into her family nor seek other references.'

'Did you notice any of the men of the house taking an interest in her?'

'No, sir. No, I did not.'

'Neither servant nor master?'

'No.'

'Is it possible that she conducted a liaison with your late master before his marriage? Might he have been the father?'

'I would say that nothing is impossible under God's heaven, but in this case I would most certainly not believe it. In truth, Mr Shakespeare, I would stake my life on it. Mr Nicholas Giltspur is not the father of her child – and before you ask, neither am I.'

'It seems you cannot stay away from me, John. Another corpse, another visit.'

Joshua Peace was looking down at the body of Oswald Redd, which was laid out on its back, blank eyes seeming to gaze up at the damp ceiling of the crypt beneath St Paul's. The body, brought here by the grooms at Seething Lane, was now naked, the skin dull and clammy. And yet the hair, so red and striking in life, maintained its vibrancy.

'Justice Young had some idea he might have been murdered. He thought to accuse me. Sadly for him, he had no evidence.'

'Well, what do you think?'

Shakespeare held up a sheet of paper. 'I rode here by way of Shoreditch and found this on Mr Redd's worktable.' He handed it to Joshua Peace, who read it quickly, then smiled at his guest.

'That simplifies matters.'

'Does it accord with your findings?'

'Indeed. Of course, it is possible he was clubbed and thrown from the bridge, but I had already decided that he probably took his own life. The bridge's footings protrude well into the water away from the piers, certainly further out than the rail. Any man who jumped at night would not see the footings and would most likely hit one before bouncing into the water. I would guess he hit the back of his head in the fall and that his death was quick and pain-free.'

'Unlike his life.' Shakespeare took back the proffered sheet of paper. They were clearly the words of a tormented man who had given up the struggle.

I pray God forgive me for what I am about to do and for the manifold sins of my wretched life. Whoever finds this, please take word to my brother Osric at Chigwell that I turn over my share of the farm and all properties within and without to his ownership and keeping. Though he may have difficulty understanding, tell him all is well and that I am at peace, and that I am with Mother and that he is to continue looking after the sheep. Also, I would ask that you go to the Paxtons, in the Glebe Farm, to the west, and ask that they look in on Osric from time to time and take his lambs to market when they are ready for slaughter. To this end, I leave the finder a sovereign. Tell Osric that I die in the certain hope that we will meet again, with Mother, in the hereafter. Pray for me.
    Oswald Redd

The writing was scratchy and hurried, with many ink blotches. There was no mention of Kat. Perhaps his love had turned to loathing. She had abandoned him twice; perhaps he could no longer bear to utter her name.

'Why did he kill himself?' Shakespeare asked. 'Out of grief for lost love – or because of the burden of guilt for killing Nick Giltspur and condemning Kat?'

'That really is your line of work more than mine, John. I examine the body, not the mind.'

'But I would value your opinion, as always.'

'Well, for a gage of ale, I would say the first option is the most likely. Unrequited passion has turned many minds. Had he been guilty of murder and was going to his death, I think he might have confessed it in hope of a better hearing at the day of judgement.'

'Worthy of a gage of ale.' Shakespeare turned away from the

✝ 263 ✝

body and lifted the latch on the door. Though he always enjoyed the company of Joshua Peace, he did not like his place of work. The cool dripping of the walls, the stink and stillness of death. As for the death of Oswald Redd and his reasons for taking his own life, perhaps Redd had deliberately avoided confessing to the murder of Nick Giltspur so that the finger of guilt would still be pointed at Kat. Some men's desire for vengeance knew no end. And if that was the case, then it might now be impossible ever to prove her innocence.

Shakespeare rose from his bed. Something the old woman had said was spinning around his head like a child's top. A few simple words that he had not considered of any relevance to his inquiry, and yet they had lodged themselves in his mind. What, precisely had she meant by them?

'*This family has done more for England than the whole Privy Council combined . . .*'

What had the Giltspurs done for England? Caught fish to fill the nation's bellies? Or was there something more, unspoken? He could find no answer in his own head and was not at all sure why it bothered him so. After all, they were a notable family, of wealth and distinction. The large vessels in their fishing fleets would always be ready to arm and join the fray in defence of the realm. Of course the Giltspurs had always helped England.

He sat in his chair, beside the shuttered window, trying to dispel the puzzle from his mind. He thought instead of Abigail Colton and continued to wonder about the father of her child. Why did she worry him so? It was because he was looking for a motive: jealousy, revenge, greed. A scorned lover might be goaded to horrors by any one of those violent emotions.

Every man in the Giltspur household must be under suspicion of being the father, of course: all the servants, the late

Nicholas Giltspur, his nephew Arthur, even Sorbus. No, not Sorbus. Shakespeare doubted he ever looked at women in that way. Arthur Giltspur? Surely Arthur could find all the delightful female company he desired among the merchant classes or the young noblewomen of the royal court. He did not need to bother with maidservants, however pretty. His uncle Nicholas, on the other hand, had been older and less eligible; perhaps in the months before meeting Kat he had found comfort closer to home.

There was another name, too: Severin Tort, attorney-at-law. He had certainly known Abigail Colton, for she had been employed by him. Perhaps matters had become awkward or unpleasant; was that why he wished her to leave his household? Or perhaps Tort had been protecting someone else in his household . . .

In the office at Walsingham's Seething Lane mansion, Frank Mills slid a transcript of the letter across the table. 'There, Mr Shakespeare, read it.' He managed to make each word sound grudging, as though it were not his place to be showing anything to this upstart.

Shakespeare took the decoded letter. It was written in the neat hand of Thomas Phelippes. He knew that the original of the letter – encrypted in letters and symbols – was in the safe hands of Sir Francis Walsingham.

> *Babington*
> *My very good friend, albeit long since you heard from me, no more than I have done from you, against my will, yet would I not you should think, I have in the meanwhile, nor will ever be unmindful of the effectual affection you have shown heretofore to all that concerneth me. I have understood that upon the ceasing of our intelligence there were addressed*

unto you both from France and Scotland some packets for me.
I pray you, if any have come to your hands, and be yet in
place, to deliver them unto the bearer hereof, who will make
them to be safe conveyed to me, and I will pray God for your
preservation.

On June the twenty-fifth at Chartley,
Your assured good friend,
Marie R

'It says nothing,' said Shakespeare. 'She says she is sorry not to
have written earlier and that she would like the letters he has in
his possession. There is no declaration of subversion or conspiracy here. I am not surprised Mr Secretary has not yet had it
delivered to Babington. He must have hoped for a great deal
more.'

Mills grinned as though he understood something that
Shakespeare did not. Hunched and thin, his smiling mouth
looked almost obscene. 'It will do very well, for Mr Secretary
has a plan and he wishes *you* to execute it.'

'Continue, Mr Mills.'

'What is remarkable is that I must brief you in this matter
rather than perform the task myself.'

'Perhaps Mr Secretary does not trust you.' Shakespeare
could not resist the barb.

Mills managed to flounce without leaving his seat. 'And he
should trust you, should he, given that you spend your days chasing across London on a some fool's errand for a murderess?'

'Get to the point, Mills.'

'Very well. The point is this: Mr Gifford will prepare the
way, just like Baptist John. It is a scheme of exquisite cunning.
All Babington's doubts will be washed away. And it all hinges
on the persuasive powers of Mr Gilbert Gifford, whom you are
to instruct most precisely.'

'He is presently working his wiles on Ballard.'

'Then remove him and send him to Babington – for he is the key. He is the one who must write to Mary and elicit an incriminating reply. I shall explain to you, Mr Shakespeare, just as my master at school taught me the rudiments of reading and writing. For that is how simple it is for one with the wit to see . . .'

Chapter 30

I T WAS A perfect summer Sunday. The river was alive with
traffic; families visiting each other, men and women escaping the stink of the city for a day in the meadows of Surrey,
sportsmen with their fowling pieces heading to the woods
upriver for some shooting. None of them would have noted
the tilt-boat carrying Anthony Babington and his companion
Robin Poley.

The two young men reclined at the back of the craft in the
shade of the canopy, so close together that their thighs and
shoulders touched, and yet neither of them sought to shift away
from the other. Each held a cup of wine and, at their side on the
bench, they had half a flagon. Their touching might have been
yet more intimate, but for the watchful eyes of the tilt-boat's
rowers who toiled against the current while their clients took
pleasure in the wine and the breeze blowing off the river.

Babington and Poley had hired the vessel at the Temple
Stairs, having strolled there from Hern's Rents; they had
scarcely been out of each other's company since their meeting
at Greenwich Palace. Now they were on their way to Barn
Elms, a journey that would take them two hours at the present
rate of progress.

'Perhaps they might row harder if we offered them a few
pence more,' Babington said, whispering into Poley's ear.

'Are you in a hurry?'

'Yes, I am in a hurry – and a state of panic, Robin. I fear what Mr Secretary will say to me. I fear what he will *ask* of me. Am I not right to be afraid? Is he not Beelzebub made flesh?'

'Then, dearest Anthony, why rush to meet the devil?'

'Because I wish to get it over and done with.'

'Like the child who hastens to his father for a birching! Anthony, you fear too much. Mr Secretary will have your passport, all signed and sealed.'

'And if he doesn't?'

Poley held up the flagon. 'Come, sup your wine and enjoy the day. Never has the Thames looked so beautiful.'

Walsingham did not have the passport. 'I have not yet been able to secure Her Majesty's approval, Mr Babington. She considers all matters, great and small, with the utmost care. Never was there a more discerning monarch. I will not hide from you that this, at times, can cause some frustration among her ministers and petitioners. I can only apologise to you; the matter is out of my hands.'

Babington somehow managed to prevent his shoulders from slumping and even achieved a discreet smile and modest bow of the head in acknowledgement.

'I do believe, however, that I will be able to bring her around to my way of thinking. What I need from you today is a list of specific tasks you will be prepared to carry out on her behalf while you are in foreign lands. Such a list, I am sure, will tip the scales in your favour.'

'Tasks, Sir Francis? What manner of task would Her Majesty require of me?'

They were seated amid the apparent chaos of Walsingham's office within his country manor at Barn Elms. The room was littered with piles of books, correspondence, maps and writing materials. Despite the summer, it was as chilly as Walsingham's manner. He made no allowance for the warm weather outside, dressed all in black save the modest white ruff at his neck. And he was nowhere near as welcoming as he had been at his first meeting with Babington.

'The tasks we spoke of before – word from the cities you visit, information about the people you meet, both the nobility and the common folk. But most particularly she would like to hear word of those Englishmen who have chosen exile and now plot against her. You know of whom I speak, I am certain: Dr Allen, Mr Persons, Dr Gifford at Rheims, the Jesuits. *All* the Jesuits, for they are betrayers of both God and man. And the snakelike Morgan, corrupt Paget and the Spanish intriguer Mendoza, who is England's sworn enemy. Her Majesty would like your assurance that you will seek out these people, discover their movements and their conspiracies, and send intelligence of the same to us post haste. That is how these infamous beasts will be brought low. Is this well with you, Mr Babington? I am sure you would wish to help us in such wise.'

'I can but promise to do my very best on Her Majesty's behalf.'

Walsingham pushed a blank sheet of paper across to Babington, followed by a quill and inkhorn. 'Then write down the details of your planned route. Whom you hope to meet and where, what letters of introduction you have. Add your mark and I will present the list to Her Majesty so that she will know how dearly you love her and how courageous you will be in defying her enemies.'

'But Sir Francis, my plans are not so well formed. Initially, I had planned to go to Paris. But I know not how long I will be there, nor whom I will be able to meet. I have no letters of introduction.'

Walsingham sighed heavily. His dark, hooded countenance betrayed no good humour. 'This will not do.'

'I beg you, Sir Francis. I will do all that you ask and more – but as yet I am in no position to write down the precise details.'

'What of the traitors in London?'

The question made Babington start. 'Traitors, Mr Secretary?'

'You know who I mean. The Pope's White Sons: the young gallants you run with. The whole court knows of them. Some of them conspire against us. Will you bring me word of *their* scheming?'

'I am sure I know no traitors, Sir Francis. A few men might speak too loudly and a little unwisely when cup-shotten, but they are harmless enough. No, there are no traitors among us.'

'Then if they – and *you* – are harmless, you will not mind providing me with their names and their indiscretions. Yes, Mr Babington?'

'Were I to hear of any indiscretions, I would bring them to your notice immediately, as would be my bounden duty.'

The Principal Secretary was silent, save for his laboured breathing. His eyes were fixed on his young guest, like a circling hawk staring at a fieldmouse a hundred feet below. 'I have an idea,' he said at last. 'A way forward, perhaps. You are a handsome, charming young man, Mr Babington. I am certain I could persuade the Queen to give you an audience where you may explain to her why you desire this passport – and just what you can do for her in return. How does that sound to you?'

Babington was horrified. The last things he wanted were the Queen's beady eyes and sharp, inquiring tongue examining him. 'I – I – I am most flattered that you should think me worthy of such a signal honour.' Even as he spoke, he knew Walsingham must see how flustered he was. How he sweated, how his hands quivered . . .

'Good. I do believe you will be able to speak more freely with Her Majesty than with me, for she has a way of putting men at their ease, and I seem to be discomfiting you. I shall have word brought to you when a time has been arranged.' Walsingham rose from his plain-backed chair and put out his hand.

Babington rose, too. He was being dismissed. Walsingham's hand was as cold as a winter's day.

When Babington had gone, Walsingham clapped his hands twice. 'You may come out of your hidey-hole, John.'

An inner door leading off from the Principal Secretary's office creaked open and John Shakespeare emerged carrying a heavy black book and writing implements.

'Did you hear it all?'

'Yes, Mr Secretary.'

'And you noted it all down?'

'Indeed, I did.'

'What did you think?'

'He must be scared and bewildered. I find it hard to believe he will do what you hope of him.'

'Then this will be a remarkable lesson for you, for I am certain he will do precisely as I hope; and more. Wait and see, John, wait and see. He thinks he has me. Even now he will be congratulating himself that he has triumphed over the Principal Secretary.'

'I am not so certain, Sir Francis. Nor do I see how he can be persuaded to write a letter to the Queen of Scots in the manner you hope. Were I in his place, I would gather together what gold I could muster and pay for passage out of England without a passport – even at the cost of losing my estates and all my treasure.'

'But you are not Anthony Babington. You are a man of wit

and cunning. He is a vain young traitor who aspires to murder Elizabeth and raise up the Scots devil in her place. He thinks he will sit at her right hand. Perhaps he would like to be her Principal Secretary. His vanity and his treachery will most certainly be his downfall. Everything depends on Mr Gifford now. When he goes to him at Hern's Rents tonight, it is important that Robin Poley is not there. Nor will it work if Babington's companions Salisbury or Tichbourne are in attendance. Mr Gifford must have space and time to work on Babington alone. Then you will see the measure of the man. Then you will see what treason he is capable of.'

'If Gifford is to do this, I must offer him sweeteners.'

'Spend whatever you need.'

'Are you not concerned that Sir Robert Huckerbee considers them beyond his budget?'

'I care not a jot what Huckerbee thinks. Take no notice of him. He is a functionary whose life is spent fretting like a fool, but he will pay up as ordered, for I have Lord Burghley's full support.'

'Gifford wants written assurances from you that he will not face charges of any kind.'

'Then assure him that my word is my bond. He needs nothing in writing. Now, John, be seated. Talk with me a while and then take dinner with me. My wife and daughter would be most pleased of your company.'

Talk with me a while. Dine with me. Shakespeare almost laughed aloud. They were words he had never expected to hear from the lips of Sir Francis Walsingham. But he took a seat at the table. The straight-backed chair was probably the least comfortable he had ever sat in.

Walsingham did indeed seem in the mood for conversation. 'How fares your inquiry into the death of Nick Giltspur? Do you still believe his widow to be innocent?'

'I do. Yet my inquiries are not promising. My man Mr Cooper has gone missing while investigating the killer Will Cane, one of Cutting Ball's henchmen. This Mr Ball truly seems beyond the reach of the law.'

Walsingham shrugged. 'Cutting Ball is a gross carbuncle on the face of the realm. But he is not a threat to it, and so my priorities must lie elsewhere.'

Shakespeare raised an eyebrow. Nothing was so small or so large that the Principal Secretary did not take an interest.

'Do not raise your eyebrows at me, John Shakespeare! Of course, I would happily see Mr Ball hanged, but first I would have to find him. Mr Phelippes believes he has never been caught because he gives money to corrupt constables and justices and breaks the bones of those who will not be bribed.'

'Well if he has harmed my man Cooper I shall make it my life's work to do for him myself.'

'Enough of Cutting Ball. If you find him be sure I will have him prosecuted to death. What possible motives have you discovered for the murder of Nick Giltspur? You must have some, I am certain.'

'I have twice been to Giltspur House. So far all I have discovered is that Katherine's lady's maid is pregnant and will not say who the father is.' He shook his head, hesitated, and then ventured a question. 'Sir Francis, what do you know of the Giltspurs? The old matriarch, Mistress Joan, says the family has done more for England than the whole Privy Council combined. What did she mean by that?'

Walsingham did not speak for a few moments, seeming to weigh up how much he should reveal. Eventually he said, 'It is true Nick sometimes lent assistance . . .'

'May I ask how?'

'His ships would call in at the ports of northern Europe, from the Baltic all along the coasts of the Low Countries and

France to Aquitaine and the Iberian Peninsula. He would carry messages – and sometimes men. In both directions.'

'Is that what the old lady meant?'

'Possibly. I can think of nothing else, save the getting of fish.'

'Was there anything in these helpful trips by the Giltspur ships that might have led to him being a target?'

Walsingham shrugged. 'I know not. But we both know this, John: the getting of intelligence is a deadly business.'

Chapter 31

ANTHONY BABINGTON HAD never felt so low. He sat alone in his rooms at Hern's Rents, as the day began to fade, obsessively going over the events of that afternoon.

He had left the audience with Walsingham in a sweat, yet certain that he had convinced the Principal Secretary of his loyalty and willingness to help. But at the mooring where a pair of Walsingham's boatmen waited to convey him back to London, Robin Poley had been less sure.

'I must warn you, Anthony, that I have learnt much since I came here to live in this household. Walsingham will say one thing and mean the opposite. If he says he trusts you, it may well mean he distrusts you.'

The change in Babington's spirits had been as sudden as a thunderstorm out of a blue sky.

'Then do you think I should go now? Flee England with all that entails? Give up my estates and live as a pauper in a monastery?'

'Is that what you want?'

'Perhaps. I would never see my wife or daughter again, nor my aunt. But if you would come with me, Robin, it would be bearable. Tell me true what you believe.'

They were standing beneath the tall elms, a little distance from the river, too far from the house to be seen. Poley had clutched Babington's damp hand in his. 'A monastery? I cannot believe that that is God's calling for you. I think the opposite. I think you should stand and fight for your true mission; the raising up of Mary to her rightful place as Queen of England. I will follow you, Anthony, wherever you lead. I will follow you though we hazard our very lives. But I tell you this: I would rather a thousand times follow you into the glory of battle than to the oblivion of the monk's cloister.'

'Come to London with me now,' Babington had pleaded. 'Stay with me tonight. We will talk until dawn if need be, for I cannot do this alone. I am scared.'

But Poley had been adamant. 'This is the one night I cannot. I must stay here for my mistress, Lady Frances, demands my presence. If I am not here, Walsingham's suspicions will be roused. That is the last thing we need.'

Babington thought of the long kiss that had followed and his heart ached. He would not see Poley until the next day. He considered venturing out to meet Salisbury and Tichbourne, but they both seemed angry with him, jealous of the time he was spending with Robin. Well, he had no time for such things. If they envied Robin, it spoke to their detriment, not his.

He downed another cup of wine and immediately refilled it. Never, he thought, was a man so torn as he was now. Go abroad and live; stay and die? The coward's way, or the lionheart's? The bells chimed nine hours. It was dusk and his shutters were thrown open, letting in the warm night air along with the din of laughter and argument. He paced his parlour, irritated by the sounds of revellers in the street below. Men and women should be abed, for come dawn it would be a day of work.

He stared down into his cup of wine. He had been drinking all afternoon since leaving Barn Elms.

Perhaps he should call on his aunt. She lived only five minutes away and would still be awake. And yet he rather thought he knew what her advice would be: do not betray your faith, do what God asks of you, life is short, eternity is for ever. He knew all this, so why ask her? He did not wish to hear her say it.

There was a knock at the door. He downed his wine and walked across the room.

'Yes?' he demanded.

'Mr Babington, sir?'

It was his young valet, Job.

'There is a man here to see you, master.'

'Who is it?'

'He says his name is Gilbert Gifford.'

Gifford. He had heard of him. Ballard and Savage had spoken of him often enough. Both had known him at the English College in Rheims, where he had reached the level of deacon but failed to stay the course in his studies for the priesthood. They did not, however, speak of him as a failure but as one who had found other ways to serve God. Indeed it was said that he had the ear of the seniors of the Church of Rome and the English exiles and carried secret messages for them.

Babington pulled open the door. Beside Job, another youth stood before him, his chin hairless, his face unlined and pink.

'Who are you?'

'Mr Gilbert Gifford, sir, at your service.'

'Gifford is a man. You are a boy.'

'No, sir, I am Gilbert Gifford. Twenty-five years old. In fact I am probably a little older than you, Mr Babington. Nor are you the first person to remark upon my youthful aspect.'

'Why are you here?'

'I wish to speak to you. I bring messages concerning a friend of mutual acquaintance.'

'Well, you had better come in.' He nodded to his boy. 'You may go, Job. Do not wake me before ten.'

'Yes, master.' The boy bowed low and scurried away.

'Do you drink wine, Mr Gifford? You look as though you should still be suckling at your mother's teat.' Certainly he did not look old enough for the responsibilities laid upon him by their masters.

Gifford ignored the barb. 'A cup of wine would be most welcome.'

Babington looked around for a cup and found a used one on the floor by the settle. With unsteady hands, he poured the wine, spilling half of it onto the rush matting. 'Here,' he said. 'Drink this – and tell me why you are here.'

'It concerns John Savage. I have recently come from Mr Morgan in Paris. He is most concerned that Goodfellow Savage appears to have forsworn a certain vow he made at Rheims. You know of this, I think.'

Despite the effects of the wine, Babington had the sense to proceed with some caution. 'I know Mr Savage. What vow is this?'

Gifford tore the cup of wine from Babington's hand and flung it to the floor. 'Do not play games with me, sir! You well know the vow of which I speak. The vow to kill the usurper.' He spat the sentence through his teeth.

Babington shook at the starkness of the words and the sudden violence of his visitor's action. 'I think you should go, Mr Gifford.'

'Go? I will not go. I have not yet begun.'

'You have no power over me. Go, I say, go.'

Suddenly Gifford's dagger was at his throat. 'I do not have time for this. We both know the truth and we are both on the same side, and of one mind. We are both working for the overthrow of this heretical regime, so let us speak plain.'

Babington backed off from the blade and Gifford replaced it in his belt.

'Now, Mr Babington, we will begin again – and there will be no secrets between us. I know it all from Father Ballard. What is needed is the final plan.'

'May I pour myself another cup of wine?'

Gifford picked up the spilt cup. 'I'll do it. You keep your strength for talking, Mr Babington.'

Babington took a deep draught. 'It is true that Father Ballard approached me to lead his enterprise and that I have sought the support of my friends, whom I know to be of a similar mind. But we have now decided to leave the plan alone, for it has become clear that Ballard was betrayed by a man he trusted.'

'You mean Bernard Maude?'

'You know him?'

'I met him in France. I tried to persuade Ballard not to trust him. Now he wishes that he had listened to me. Men would always do well to heed my words.'

'If only Father Ballard had seen as clearly as you,' Babington said sardonically.

'If you think to mock me, Babington, you have chosen the wrong man. Men tend to rue the day they cross me.'

'Forgive me, Mr Gifford. It was not merely the question of Maude. It was also Goodfellow Savage's vow. Most of those amongst us doubted the legality and morality of what he proposed. I also had grave doubts about the practicality. A man alone could never get to her to carry out the deed; I believe it would need four to six men.'

Gifford's voice softened. 'But surely you have more men: what of Abingdon and Tilney? Also Tichbourne – and Charnock. Was he not a soldier like Savage? Ballard tells me these men all have access to court and are to be trusted with the deed. You must not – *you will not* – abandon the enterprise, sir.'

'The arguments ring around my head like church bells. I have even considered leaving the country.'

'Then I will get straight to the point,' Gifford said. 'I have just come from Paris and I can reveal to you this: the Holy League princes have given their pledge that they will invade England by September. That is less than two months away. Two months to save our souls, Mr Babington. Parma's men-at-arms are prepared, as are the fleets of Spain and France. Their force will be overwhelming and this attack will take place whatever the Catholics of England do, whether they rise up in support of the liberating army or no. And so for you to talk of leaving England when you are most needed is to shirk your responsibility to God. You would lose all honour.'

Shirk responsibility. Lose honour. The very words his aunt would have used, and ones that cut to the heart.

'If we were to proceed,' Babington began tentatively, 'then we would need assurances from the highest authorities that our actions were directly lawful in every part.'

For the first time, Gifford smiled. 'That is easy. I have the written authority of Cardinal Allen that the excommunication wholly justifies the action against the heretic usurper. And this is agreed by all the doctors of Rheims and the divines of Rome. None expresses even the merest shade of doubt. The only authority I have *not* seen is that of the Queen of Scots herself. And this we must have – for she is the heart of the enterprise.' He poured another cup for Babington. 'Have you had word of such authority, Mr Babington?'

Babington sat down on the settle. His legs were becoming wobbly. 'I must tell you in all sadness, Mr Gifford, that I have had no correspondence from her.'

'Have you not then received her recent letter? I know for

certain fact that she has written to you lately and that the letter has come from her by a secret network of supporters.'

'How is this possible?'

'Through the offices of an honest man. A courageous Catholic brewer in the town of Burton has the contract for supplying Chartley with beer and ale. Each week he takes in new kegs – with letters concealed in a waterproof bung. And Mary's replies come out the same way. That is how your letter will come to you.'

'It has been so long that I heard from her, I can scarce believe it.'

'Her silence has not been of her doing. Trust me, you will know the truth when you see it.' Gifford suddenly hammered his fist on the table. 'I have it! Indeed, I do have it, sir. It is the opportunity you have been waiting for.'

Babington, heavy-lidded, looked at his visitor and waited for his revelation.

'You have a cipher, Mr Babington; the one the Scots Queen will use to write to you?'

'Indeed.'

'Good, then we can use it. You must write to Mary, laying forth your plans on her behalf. Your letter must be encrypted, for there are spies everywhere. This must be done without delay, so that you will be ready to hand it direct to the messenger who brings her letter to you.'

'When will that be?'

'It could be at any time. Perhaps tomorrow. We have no time to lose.'

'But what must I say, Mr Gifford? You must help me with this.' All Babington's doubts had been washed away. He was to hear from Mary herself! The blessed Mary, queen of all true Catholic hearts. He was consumed by excitement. 'Shall I fetch paper and quills?'

'Yes, do so. We must give her the glad news that her cousins in France and Spain are to send armies into England on her behalf. Tell her what ports are designated for the landings and reveal the hopes that sixty thousand or more true Englishmen will rise up and join with the armies of France and Spain to bring down the heretics. That is the figure given me by Father Ballard following his trip to the north country. It is said, too, that the invading armies will be of a similar strength.'

'A hundred and twenty thousand men in total then. Surely this heretical regime will crumble to dust before such an onslaught.'

Gifford had his eyes closed, his hands gripped tight together, deep in thought.

'We must have this right. You, Mr Babington, must have it right, for it will be your letter and you have her trust. Phrase it well and she will read every word with hope in her royal heart. You should tell her how pleased you will be to serve her once again and what joy there will be among her subjects both in England and Scotland when you ease her path to freedom and the throne . . .'

'You mean the dispatch of the usurper.'

'The dispatch of the usurper. Yes, indeed. And then, at last, you must humbly entreat her to reply as soon as possible, giving her authority for you to proceed with these plans. For she is not only your sovereign but your captain-general in all things. We must have this authority.'

Babington was up from the settle, striding around the room with renewed vigour. The room was almost dark. He needed to light candles. With Gifford's help, he would draft the letter now, even if it took until dawn. And then he would have to encrypt it; a chore, but one that had to be done.

For a mad moment, he wished to take Gifford in his arms.

No, not Gifford. It was sweet Robin Poley he wanted. If only he were here now, to share this moment.

'But first, Mr Babington,' Gifford said solemnly. 'I think it only meet that we both go down on our knees and pray for God's wisdom . . .'

Chapter 32

'YOU HAD A visitor, master,' Jane said when Shakespeare returned to Seething Lane in the early evening. 'A young lady named Bathsheba Cane with three small children.'

Shakespeare accepted the news without really taking it in. 'Who is she?' He was still thinking about his dinner with Robin Poley and the Walsinghams and wondering whether Gifford had been received into Babington's bosom or thrown out by his heels.

'She said she was the widow of Mr William Cane.'

The name jolted Shakespeare from his distraction. 'Will Cane's widow? God's teeth, Jane, what did the woman want?'

'She wished to speak with you, sir, and she wanted to return Mr Cooper's weapons. His sword and hagbut. I think it was a great struggle for her to carry them all this way.'

Jane nodded towards the settle beneath the window, a mere two yards away. Shakespeare picked up Boltfoot's cutlass and caliver; they were in perfect condition. His heart sank. If Boltfoot's weapons were here, that did not bode well for his health.

'How did she get hold of these?'

'She did not say, sir. She said she had hoped to find Mr Cooper here to return them to him.'

'Did she give any indication as to his whereabouts?'

Jane shook her head nervously. 'I did ask her that, but she merely said that she didn't know. She said that if you came home before Mr Cooper arrived that she would be happy to talk with you, and she told me how you might find her. Should I have asked more? Did I do wrong, master?'

'No, you did well. What manner of woman was she?'

'Of a pleasant disposition, but exceeding worried, I would say. Worried for Mr Cooper. And that, in turn, caused me great concern for his welfare.'

Shakespeare breathed in sharply through his teeth. He, too, was worried for Boltfoot's welfare.

Darkness was falling when Shakespeare found the house. The woman seemed relieved that he had come, but put a finger to her lips and begged him to speak low, for her children were asleep.

'How did you come to be in possession of Mr Cooper's arms, Mistress Cane?'

Bathsheba Cane told him all that had passed between them. 'After he left me, he must have been followed, for Tom Pearson the water-bearer saw him being apprehended by three men, who were accompanied by two women. Mr Cooper was still unarmed and so would have had no way to defend himself.'

'Did Mr Pearson have any idea who the abductors might be?'

She nodded, her face drawn and fearful. 'They were three of Cutting Ball's men. They are well known around here, for they prey on the ships moored at the wharfs.'

'Did he know their names?'

'No, sir.'

'What of the women?'

Bathsheba looked pained. 'It is a life I would wish to put behind me, sir. But from the description, I believe one of them was likely to have been Em, the sister of Cutting Ball. I have met her – indeed she has been here in this parlour with my late husband and Mr Ball himself – and I would be content never to see them again.'

'What do you think they might have done with Mr Cooper?'

'I fear the worst, sir. But before he left, I did talk a great deal with him and there was one matter he believed would be of great import to you . . .' She tailed off uncertainly.

'Please continue.'

'My husband had another woman. You might call her paramour or lover, but I would call her whore and trug. Her name was Abigail and she was a lady's maid in the household of the Giltspur family. He liked to spit her name in my face.'

So his doubts about Abigail were confirmed, but not in the way he had expected. Surely Cane must be the father of her unborn child. Now, at least, there was a certain link between the murderer and Giltspur House.

Shakespeare absorbed the information. What precisely did it mean? Did the connection help Kat's case, or hinder it? 'Mistress, did your husband know this Abigail before she went to work there – or was he already acquainted with someone within the house?'

She shook her head. 'That is not the kind of thing that he would have told me.'

'I have met this Abigail and she is big with child. Do you believe your husband is the father?' He tried to speak gently.

'Who can tell? The woman is a harlot. When next you see her, please spit in her face for me.'

'Did your husband ever talk of the Giltspur family?'

'He trumpeted their great wealth and ease of living and how, by the grace of Mr Ball, he would one day rise to such wealth and stature himself.'

'What of Cutting Ball? Do you know where I might find him?'

She hesitated, then shook her head. 'No.'

'I beg you, mistress. If you know something, tell me. Mr Cooper might yet be alive – it might not be too late to save him.'

She sighed. 'Ask Em Ball. She runs all the whores for her brother in the stews east of the Tower. Mr Cooper met her in the Burning Prow, which is no more than five minutes from here.'

He nodded. 'Boltfoot told me of the place. Can you take me there?'

As they walked through the darkening, dangerous streets, Shakespeare felt an icy chill in his veins. If Boltfoot had been at the mercy of Cutting Ball all this time, then there could be little hope for him. What evil had they wrought upon him before merciful death? The bile rose in Shakespeare's throat. Someone had to pay.

From the outside, the Burning Prow looked like a large alehouse, set into the centre of a woodframe house without windows. The street was largely deserted, for this was Sunday, but a few men were making their furtive way towards it. Shakespeare was painfully aware that he had no plan, nor any strength of arms against Cutting Ball's men. But nor could he simply wait and do nothing. He had to confront Em Ball, whatever the risk.

Inside, the main hall was busy and stank of perfumes from the Orient. A young black man sat on a stool, playing a ballad on the lute. Men drank and sized up the women, of whom there were about ten, deciding which one they wished to buy. The room itself was decorated in shades of red and black, with commonplace tapestries and painted cloths on the walls, depicting scenes of bawdiness: satyrs with pricks like Priapus, fleshy women with no clothing but welcoming smiles, devils with forks chasing bishops into the fire.

'There she is,' Bathsheba said as soon as her eyesight had adjusted to the candlelit interior. She nodded towards a good-looking woman talking with a pair of girls at the left side of the room. 'Don't be fooled by her comely face and manner, Mr Shakespeare. She is pretty like the falcon, but with sharper talons.' And with a squeeze of his arm, she slipped unseen into the crowd.

As Shakespeare approached Em Ball, she turned to him and smiled in welcome. He did not smile back.

'Well, sir, and who might you be?' she said.

'John Shakespeare, master to Mr Boltfoot Cooper.'

If she was surprised, it did not register on her handsome face. 'Then it is my pleasure to welcome you. Indeed, I had been expecting you.' She swept her hand around the room to indicate the scantily clad women. 'Is there one you like? I would offer the very finest to a Walsingham man.' She pointed to the far corner where a young woman with fair hair was seated all alone. 'That is Kristina. She came stowed away aboard a carrack from the Swedish lands. Is she not a faerie princess, all pale and smooth? She knows tricks that even the French have not yet learnt. Take her, she is yours for the night.'

There was a hardness in Em Ball's bright eyes that Shakespeare had not noticed from the other side of the room. This was a woman of ruthless intelligence.

'I want to speak with your brother, Miss Ball.'

'Ah.' She feigned disappointment. 'That will not be possible, I fear. He has gone to the country to recover from a summer sweat. Forget him. Kristina will soothe you, sir. Both soul and body. '

Shakespeare bent his head to her ear and spoke slowly and

clearly. 'Do you wish me to bring this empire of yours crashing down around your ears? Do you wish to be brought to the scaffold for being accessory to murder? Take me to your brother, now. I want to know what he has done with my man Cooper, God damn your filthy, rotten soul.'

Em Ball widened her eyes. 'Why, sir, he has gone to sea! My brother found him a berth aboard a great vessel.' She shook her head and tutted. 'But fret not, he will be back by year's end. Gone fishing to the Grand Banks, I do believe. A long voyage, but a profitable one.'

'You lie. Mr Cooper would not take ship if he had the choice.'

'But I do know for certain sure that he has gone to sea, and I will happily swear it to you. Think of it as a favour to you and the esteemed Mr Secretary. Come, Mr Shakespeare.'

Without waiting for him, she turned and pushed open a door into an inner chamber. He followed her into a functional room with dark panelling, very unlike the bawdy, colourful den beyond.

'Take a seat, Mr Shakespeare. Can I bring you refreshment? I have some fine apple brandy.'

'I want none of your ill-gotten produce. Nor do I want to sit down. I want Boltfoot Cooper – and I want him alive.'

'You have nothing to fear. He will come back from his voyage a wealthier man. My brother would do nothing to harm any man or woman close to Sir Francis Walsingham.'

'This has nothing to do with Walsingham.'

'Oh but it has, Mr Shakespeare. It has everything to do with the Principal Secretary. Why else do you imagine I allow you the services of Beth and Eliza Smith?'

For a moment Shakespeare was speechless.

'Did you not know they were my creatures? Every profession needs a company or guild, even night-workers. And so you may think of me as their warden.'

'Warden? You are a grubby bawd, madam. You trade in flesh and disease.'

She arched an eyebrow. 'And you and your master are among my finest customers.'

'And do you think then that Walsingham would protect you?'

'He protects us all, does he not? England, Queen Bess and all her true subjects are safe thanks to the vigilance of Mr Secretary and the work of good men such as yourself.'

'No.' Shakespeare's voice was cold with fury. 'He would hang you, and all your villainous crew. And I would fashion the noose for him.' Should he cart this woman to gaol? See how she fared under hard questioning with her hands and legs in irons.

She seemed to read his mind. 'Do not even think of it, Mr Shakespeare. There are four strong men out there, each of them armed with blades and pistols. You would not get me past the door.'

It was true. For a moment he considered his options and realised they were exceedingly limited. 'Damn you, madam, I will be back – and with a squadron of men-at-arms, if necessary from the Queen's own guard. *They* are not in your pay.'

She tutted again. 'Oh, Mr Shakespeare, there is so much that you seem not to understand. You rail against me, and yet it was *I* who saved your man. He was set on a path to self-destruction and I rescued him.'

He slammed his fist into the oak-panelled wall. 'Saved him? Rescued him? You abducted him and I know not what else. You say you esteem Walsingham and all who work for him, yet Boltfoot Cooper worked for me and, in so doing, served my master, too.'

'Which is why he is still alive.'

Shakespeare forced himself to calm down. He cursed himself

for his impetuosity. Where was the cold logic Walsingham so prized? He had barged in here with no thought except to rescue Boltfoot and now he had no way of knowing if this woman spoke the truth, although it was an elaborate tale for a lie. Maybe Boltfoot was indeed on some wretched fishing vessel headed for the Grand Banks across thousands of miles of ocean.

'And so if you are done with me, good sir—'

'No.' There was still time to take control of the encounter. 'There is the other matter. The reason Mr Cooper first came to you. What do you know of the death of Nicholas Giltspur? My man had discovered something, had he not? That was why he was made to disappear. So tell me about Giltspur and your foul confederate Will Cane. Tell me what you know about his liaison with the lady's maid Abigail.'

'I think it is time for you to leave, Mr Shakespeare.'

'I want answers.'

'You are swimming in dangerous waters. There are matters here that do not concern you.' She tapped on the door and two men immediately appeared, powerfully built men with bare arms carved with snakes, and weapons at their belts. 'Mr Shakespeare is leaving.'

They stepped forward, but he was already moving. He had no intention of giving them the satisfaction of slinging him out onto the street.

'I will return, madam.'

'Then you will regret it.'

Chapter 33

A s he walked through the dark streets into the city, Shakespeare attempted to connect everything he knew:

Nicholas Giltspur had been killed by Will Cane; his widow Kat had been implicated by Cane, but denied any part in the murder; Kat's lady's maid, Abigail, was mistress to Cane and was now pregnant – probably by him; Cane was a member of the villainous crew run by Cutting Ball and his sister Em; Em was bawd to the Smith sisters, now being used by Shakespeare to keep Gilbert Gifford happy.

So suddenly there was a link, however tenuous, between the murder of Nicholas Giltspur and the margins of the conspiracy surrounding Anthony Babington and the Queen of Scots. But what precisely was the nature of that link? Could there be something of greater moment in the murder of Giltspur than jealousy and avarice?

The old Giltspur widow had said her family had done more for England than the whole Privy Council combined. Walsingham had admitted that the Giltspur ships secretly carried men and messages to the northern ports of Europe.

There were other matters too that could not be ignored: the death of a love-crazed suitor, the curious behaviour of his simpleton brother.

It was all like a tangle of rope. Would he ever unravel its knots?

The lantern at the entrance of Seething Lane cast a welcome glow across the street. The watchman was trying to harry and jostle people to their homes, his mastiff straining at the leash and growling. He hailed Shakespeare with a wave. 'Don't know what's becoming of London, Mr Shakespeare. It's long past curfew but when I kick them up the arse and tell them I'll have them in Bridewell, they laugh me to scorn.'

'Well, I'll be abed soon enough, Joe.' Just as Shakespeare stepped forward to his front door, an explosion split the night air. He recoiled. No, not an explosion – a pistol shot. A spray of splinters had stung his face and he felt certain he had caught the wind of the bullet, but he had not been hit. All around him people were rooted to the spot in shock. A woman was cowering in the gutter, screaming.

'God's faith, Mr Shakespeare! I'm bleeding.' He turned to see the watchman holding up his hand, blood dripping from his thumb. The man's dog wagged its tail and licked the blood where it fell. Shakespeare turned back to scan the crowd and saw the assailant twenty yards away, standing stock-still in the doorway of the house opposite Shakespeare's. He was trying to reload the weapon, pouring powder with steady hands. His head was cowled like a monk's. Shakespeare started towards him, ripping the dagger from his belt. Realising he did not have time to load and fire, the assassin thrust the unloaded weapon into his belt and turned to run.

'That's him!' Shakespeare shouted. 'That man. Take that man.'

He flung himself forward at full sprint, but the shooter had ducked right, down a narrow passage between houses. Shakespeare ran after him, certain he would not be outpaced, ready to launch himself at the man. Ahead of him he could see the dark hood, blown back from his head, and the cloak billowing behind him, like a bat in the dusk. There was something in his movements that seemed familiar, but it was too dark to get a proper look and he could not place him.

In dismay, he realised that he was making no ground on the fleeing man. The pistolier was as fleet as a hound. By now he had reached the end of the alley and disappeared. When Shakespeare finally reached the corner, there was no sign of the man.

Somewhere in the distance, back in Seething Lane, he heard whistles. A hue and cry was being raised. It would be too slow and too late. He was the only chance they had of apprehending the would-be killer. Ahead of him, fifty yards away, he saw a slight movement and began running again. This time he gained ground easily but soon realised he was chasing a husband and wife, walking arm in arm. He rasped an oath. How could he have lost him? He thrust his dagger back into his belt and drew his sword and began a slow, meticulous search of the street in both directions. Surely the man could not have gone far. He, too, must be exhausted. Another member of the watch appeared. 'Are you Shakespeare?'

'Yes.'

'Time to go home, master. There's nothing to be done. We've got a hue and cry up, but the man's long gone.'

'And Joe?'

'Bullet took a chunk out of his thumb and broke his staff in two. The thumb's nothing his wife won't be able to kiss better, but the staff is only fit for firewood. Come, sir, let me accompany you back to Seething Lane.'

Shakespeare gritted his teeth. By now the assassin could be in any one of a hundred streets in this maze of a town.

'Master?'

'Very well, I'll come.'

Jane was most solicitous. She applied strips of linen to the watchman's injured thumb and provided ale for him and the other members of the watch who had gathered in Seething Lane and were discussing the shooting like gossips at the birth of a baby.

'Time to go about your business, gentlemen,' Shakespeare said at last.

'We'll keep a guard in the lane until dawn. I do believe you were his target, Mr Shakespeare.'

Yes, he believed it too. 'Thank you,' he said. 'But a guard won't be necessary. I can look after myself well enough.' But why was he the target? Was this to do with Cutting Ball and the murder of Nick Giltspur – or had the Pope's White Sons decided they didn't trust him after all?

In the morning, Shakespeare was eating a large breakfast when there was a hammering at the door. Jane appeared. 'The door, master. Should I answer it?'

'Indeed, Jane, I doubt whether an assassin would knock before he entered.'

She bowed quickly then hurried off to open the front door. A minute later she was back, just as Shakespeare was finishing his eggs.

'You have a visitor, master, a Mr Sorbus.'

Sorbus here? What could he want? Shakespeare patted his lips with his kerchief. 'Tell him I will be with him shortly.'

'Yes, master.'

In the anteroom, Sorbus looked stiff and uncomfortable. He afforded Shakespeare a perfunctory bow of the head. More a hen's peck than a bow.

'Good day, Mr Sorbus.'

'Mr Shakespeare, sir. Thank you for receiving me.'

'I had always thought it good manners to welcome guests.'

If Sorbus spotted the intended barb, he did not react to it. 'Indeed, sir,' was all he said.

'This is a most unexpected visit. I had no idea you ever left Giltspur House.' *And I am most surprised you should deign to come to the lowly home of a commoner such as me.*

'My mistress sent me, sir. She would like to see you this morning. She says it is a matter of some urgency.'

'Well then I shall try to find time for her. Is that all?'

'Yes, sir.'

'Then you may tell Mistress Giltspur I will do my best to be with her within the hour.'

'Thank you, sir.' He made no move to go.

'That will be all, Mr Sorbus.'

'Before I do, sir, I thought it well to tell you that my mistress is in a tempest of rage.'

'Do you know why?'

'Indeed I do – but I think it best if she tells you herself. And there is one more matter. The maid Abigail Colton has gone.'

'Gone where?'

Sorbus shrugged. 'I know not, but she has taken all her belongings, so I do not expect to see her again.'

'Someone must have seen her go.'

'Oh, indeed, the guards at the door saw her. She cursed them roundly and then spat at their feet.'

Shakespeare was not surprised. She must have known that more questions would be coming her way. 'Tell me, Mr Sorbus. Did you know that she was enamoured of Will Cane, the man who murdered your master?'

The steward recoiled. 'No, sir, I did not know that. Is this true?'

'I believe so, as does Mr Cane's widow.'

'Then I confess I am shocked. No, that is not a strong enough word; I am horrified, sir. And mortified that such a thing should happen under my watch. I had no notion.'

'Had you never seen Cane about Giltspur House?'

He shook his head vigorously. 'No, sir. I would never have allowed such a man within the confines of the house or grounds. The first time ever I saw him was at Fishmongers' Hall, the night he murdered my master. The fiend was red with poor Mr Giltspur's blood. His hands, his face . . .'

Shakespeare looked at the steward closely, trying to spot clues to his honesty. If he was play-acting, he was a master of the art, for his revulsion at the murder seemed all too real. Yet still Shakespeare felt unsure. Sorbus harboured secrets. He would need watching.

The old matriarch of Giltspur House had left her chamber and was waiting for Shakespeare in the hall. She was thin and frail, but she held herself at her full height with her shoulders back. In her hand she held a large bunch of iron keys.

'I am delighted to see you up and about, ma'am.' He bowed low.

'Are you, Mr Shakespeare? I doubt you care a jot for my health. However, for myself, I wish I had been up and about, as you call it, rather sooner. Come with me. And you, Sorbus, bring a lighted candle.'

Shakespeare smiled to himself. Her tongue was as sharp as an adder's and as commanding as a Caesar's.

Without another word, he followed her through the ancient hall, then down a low, arched corridor which, Shakespeare imagined, must have once held the cells of the monks who lived here in another age.

At the far end of the corridor was a strongroom fronted by a heavy door which was reinforced with bands of iron and locked with a variety of bolts and padlocks. Two guards bowed their heads to Joan Giltspur. She ignored them and with her long bony fingers selected a series of keys and undid the locks, then, with more strength than he would have imagined, she pushed open the door.

The room, which was about eight feet by eight, had no windows. Shakespeare imagined the walls would be even stronger than the door; stone-built, probably three or four feet thick on all sides. This was a room for treasure.

'The candle, Sorbus. Light the room, man.'

Sorbus stepped into the small cell and held up his candle. It cast a glow which enabled Shakespeare to see a coffer and two smaller chests.

The old woman pushed past Sorbus, elbowing him as she did so. Without ceremony, she unlocked the bolts on the coffer and pulled open the lid.

'Come, Mr Shakespeare. Come. Take a look.'

Shakespeare advanced further into the room and peered into the coffer. The glint of gold and the sparkle of gemstones flashed their promise. Never in his life had he seen such riches.

'How full would you say this coffer is, Mr Shakespeare?'

'About a quarter full. You have remarkable wealth, ma'am.'

'Do I, indeed? This coffer has been sore depleted, Mr Shakespeare. I have done an audit against the ledgers and the amount here does not accord with what is written. Indeed, great amounts of gold and silver coin are missing. My best estimate is that forty thousand pounds in coin and bullion is gone.'

The sum was scarcely credible. A man could almost buy a county with such riches. Peering into the chest, the glint of gemstones caught Shakespeare's eye. 'What of the diamonds and emeralds?'

'The gems are almost all there. It is the gold and silver that is depleted.'

'And your great diamond, ma'am?'

'What do you know of that?'

'It is famous. Besides, your grandson told me of it.'

'Well, he had no cause to.'

'So you still have it?'

'Mr Shakespeare, will you please keep to the matter in hand. It is the theft of gold and silver that concerns us.'

'Indeed. Had the locks been forced or broken?' he asked.

'No.'

'Then who had access to the keys?'

'I did,' Joan Giltspur said. 'And Nick. They were the only sets of keys. And since his death I have possession of both sets. No one else has ever been allowed in this room.'

'What about your grandson?'

'No, Arthur did not have keys. He has never shown the slightest interest in the fortunes of this family, so there was no need for him to have them. If ever he needed gold, all he had to do was ask Nick or me.'

'You must have the house searched – thoroughly. Every nook of every servant's room, beneath the boards and in the attics. Check the yards and gardens for freshly dug earth. This is an enclosed house so not easy for anyone to leave with such a quantity of treasure.'

'No.'

'No, ma'am?'

'No, I will not have my house searched.'

'Do you not wish to find your gold – and the person responsible?'

'Of course I do. And I have summoned you here because I wish you to discover these things, Mr Shakespeare. Find the culprit and I suspect you will also discover the name of Nick's murderer. For myself, I have only one name in mind: Katherine Whetstone. She must have somehow acquired use of Nick's keys. Perhaps he found out. Perhaps that is why she killed him. Bring her to justice for me and I will reward you well.'

Chapter 34

Babington was putting the final touches to the letter. Gilbert Gifford had gone two hours since and left him with the chore of enciphering the thousand-word missive. Fighting the exhaustion of a night without sleep and a great deal too much wine, he slogged on through the morning, transfiguring his finely wrought words, character by character, into the secret code that would keep it safe.

Sometimes he wondered about this cipher. How secure was it truly? There were twenty-three symbols, each denoting a letter of the alphabet. Only the letters J, V and W were absent. In addition there were thirty-five symbols standing for whole words or, sometimes, whole phrases. To make things yet more complicated for any would-be codebreaker he used four nulls – symbols without meaning – and a separate symbol which signified that the next symbol equated to a double letter.

Surely no man could break such a code. It was hard enough to read or write even with the cipher at his side.

His valet tapped at the door, then entered. He did not look happy.

'What is it, Job? I am mighty busy.'

'A boy, sir. I told him to go away, but he would not. Says he has a letter for you.'

'A letter?'

'I told him to hand it to me, but he said he had to put it in your hand and no one else's.'

'Bring him in; and fetch him ale.'

Job frowned as though he must have misheard his master. 'You wish to see him?'

'Did I not just say so?'

'Yes, sir. But I thought—'

'Sometimes you think too much, Job. Now go and bring him to me.'

'Very well, master.'

Babington turned over the draft letter and the encryption he was working on so that neither the words of the original nor the strange symbols of the secret code should be visible. A few moments later Job reappeared with a boy of about eleven years.

'This is the boy. Are you sure you wish me to fetch ale?'

'I am as certain of it as I am that you will have a birching by day's end. Now go and do as you are told.'

As Job slunk away, Babington looked at the messenger boy. He was clean enough and bright-eyed. A small leather satchel was slung across his shoulder.

'I am told you have a letter for me, boy.'

'Are you Babington?'

'I am indeed.'

'What is your church-given name?'

'Anthony. What is the meaning of such an impertinent question?'

'I need to be sure you are the man I am looking for, which I now am – for I was told you dressed bravely and had a lordly manner. Here, take this.' From his satchel he pulled out a sealed letter and handed it over. Babington received it with trembling hands. Was this truly the work of the blessed Mary Stuart, Queen of Scotland and rightful Queen of England? He kissed the paper, scarce daring to break the seal. So Gilbert Gifford had spoken true; he had hardly dared believe it.

'I was told that I should wait if you required me to, Mr Babington.'

'Yes, please, do wait. I will have a letter for you to take whence you came.'

'Then I shall be pleased to have the ale.'

'What is your name, boy?'

'Call me whatever you like. Boy will do.'

Babington nodded and gestured to the boy to sit at the far end of the room to wait. He had two paragraphs more to transcribe. Not much, perhaps, but it was a painstaking business and would take him the best part of an hour. First, however, he must give himself the pleasure of opening the letter he had received.

Using his dagger, he slit open the seal, then unfolded the paper. It was encoded. He smoothed the paper down on the table and squinted at the symbols, comparing them with his cipher. The tiredness fell away as he worked and the sense appeared before his eyes. The very first words made his heart leap. 'My very good friend . . .' She called him *friend*! He read the words quickly, then again, more slowly, savouring each one, and worked on. And at the end of the letter, the name he most desired to see: *Marie R.*

Once more he pressed the letter to his lips and kissed it.

'Are you done yet, master? You must know that I will require recompense for my time.'

Babington looked across the room at the small boy. Impatience and boredom were evident in his sullen voice. No, he was far from done. But he had a new surge of energy to finish his own letter, one that he was certain would make Mary's spirits soar and give her hope that her long confinement would soon be over.

*

Off Margate Head, Boltfoot was allowed half an hour's respite from his labours for food. He stood on deck and stretched his aching back, smoking a pipe of tobacco and looking out across the choppy grey water to the coast of Kent. It was no more than half a mile away but it might as well have been ten thousand miles for all the use its proximity might be to him. He would never be able to swim such a distance.

'Take a good long look at it, Mr Cooper, you'll not see England again for a few months.'

Boltfoot grunted. He had lost hope some hours ago when they rounded the Nore, the sandbank that marked the end of the Thames and the beginning of the North Sea. Maywether was making things worse, seeming to take great pleasure in his discomfort, working him to exhaustion in the mending of kegs. And with the ship tacking into a freshening gale, it felt as though the voyage would take years not months. He knew all that any man needed to know about long voyages; three years before the mast under the command of Sir Francis Drake had taught him of the privations that inevitably lay ahead: hunger, thirst, foul ale and fouler food, beatings, sickness, scurvy, storms and deaths. Such had been the mariner's lot since man first went to sea.

'I'd make it worth your while to get me ashore, Mr Maywether.'

'Would you now. Would you now.' It wasn't a question, more a statement of mockery.

'How would ten pounds sound to you?'

'And you got ten pounds, have you, Cooper? Show it to me.'

'It'll be there when I get back. I pledge it. You know me of old, Mr Maywether, I'm an honest man.'

'Aye, that you are. But what do you think Herr Bootmann would have to say about it?'

'Same for him. You got another two coopers in the fleet. That'll do – and they could apprentice another.'

'So that's ten pounds for me and ten for Bootmann?'

'Aye.'

'Which means, if I've done my reckoning right, that you got twenty pounds – and you're only offering me ten. And there was me thinking you an honest man.'

'If you could get me to land without Herr Bootmann's cooperation, then the twenty would all be yours.'

Godfrey Maywether laughed. 'You'll have to do a lot better than that, Mr Cooper.'

'And does our time together under Drake mean nothing to you? We travelled the whole world together, you and me. We're copesmates, you and me. Last time I saw you, I was planing staves and you were sewing sails.'

'What's past is past, Cooper. I'm the ship's master now and you're the dirty knave that does what you're told or feels the lash of a whip. So get yourself back to your work – and you'll do a double watch. One wrong move and I'll have you striped at the mainmast for attempting to bribe an officer.'

Shakespeare scratched letters on a square scrap of paper: 'If anyone requires a position as footman, apply to the household of Lady Cutler, Seething Lane'. Soaking in the afternoon sunshine, he rode at a brisk trot along the straight mile to St Paul's, where he nailed the notice to the Si Quis door. Without waiting, he rode back to Leadenhall and the home of Thomas Phelippes.

The excitement of Walsingham's codebreaker could not have been more evident. He and Gilbert Gifford were in the back garden drinking beer with Phelippes's new bride, Mary. A table had been dragged out into the space; on it lay plates of delicacies, which kept being added to by a pair of maids.

'Take a seat, Mr Shakespeare. Drink and eat your fill.'

'I take it something has happened,' Shakespeare said.

'As I said it would, Mr Shakespeare. Mr Gifford and I have organised it all. We had no need of any help from the sly Robin Poley.'

'I share your distaste, Mr Phelippes, but in truth Poley has helped keep Babington from fleeing in panic. We have much to thank him for.'

'If you say so. But I say more fool you. For myself, I would rather trust an envenomed serpent than Robin Poley.' He threw a glance at Gifford and grinned. 'Shall we show him what we have?'

Shakespeare's eyebrows shot up. The slimy and brilliantly devious Phelippes comparing another man to a serpent was indeed a curious turnaround, for no man was more reptilian than he.

'Show him, Tom. I think it will be a wondrous surprise.'

'Here then. All deciphered for you.' He pulled out sheets of paper. 'Mr Anthony Babington's letter to the Queen of Scots, which arrived not two hours since.'

'Then he has written it?'

'Hence the beer and cakes, by way of celebration.'

'Has Mr Secretary seen it yet?'

'I have sent him word. He sent a message back that I should decode it first then bring it.'

'Show me.'

Shakespeare took the deciphered letter. It was covered in blotches of ink and occasional crossings-out, but it was easy to read and understand. He grasped his beer and drank it halfway down in one draught. The letter was a lighted taper at the edge of a trail of black powder.

'Is this all true?'

'All true.'

'Surely these are your words, Mr Gifford – you have merely counterfeited his writing.'

'Not so. They are all Mr Babington's own words – and encoded in his own fair hand. We have him, Mr Shakespeare. We have him as close-tied as a hog at the slaughter. And soon we shall have her.'

The letter began, *Most mighty, most excellent, my dread sovereign Lady and Queen, unto whom I owe all fidelity and obedience.* That alone would be enough to secure a death warrant for treason. But there was much more. The letter spoke of invasion plans, ports of entry, parties of rebels to welcome the invaders ashore, the deliverance of Mary from captivity and, most deadly of all, 'the dispatch of the usurping competitor'.

Shakespeare read the words aghast. So vain, lazy Babington had poison in his heart after all. Walsingham had been right. He even spoke of sending ten gentlemen with a hundred followers to free Mary – and of having six 'noble gentlemen, all my private friends' prepared to kill Elizabeth.

And there was a postscript for Mary's secretary, Gilbert Curl, begging information about Robin Poley.

Shakespeare handed the letter back to Phelippes. 'God in holy heaven, sir. I think we had best take this to Mr Secretary without delay.'

'Then you are impressed, Mr Shakespeare?'

'I confess I had not seen such darkness in Babington.'

'Then let us go now. You, Mr Gifford, will stay here until I return – and keep your pink little fingers away from my bride. All being well, you and I will be required to ride, separately, for Chartley this night.'

Shakespeare rose from the bench. How would the letter be received at Chartley, he wondered. Would Mary take the bait and reply in kind; or would she have the sense to simply throw Babington's letter in the fire?

Chapter 35

'MR SCUDAMORE, YOU will begin to clear the gaols. We must make space for many men.' Sir Francis Walsingham was in businesslike mood. Ebullience could wait until they had the head of Mary Stuart on the block, but no one here in this small room in Greenwich Palace doubted that they were halfway there. All that was needed now was for the Queen of Scots to take the bait; Walsingham was certain she would do so. He had been studying her character these eighteen years and believed he knew her as well as any man.

'Yes, Mr Secretary. How—'

'Those awaiting hanging, dispatch. Send other priests to Wisbech, where they may rot. Free those petty criminals and recusants who are no danger to the commonwealth.' He handed a sheet of paper with names on it to his clerk. Shakespeare saw the macabre heading: *Prisoners to be disposed of.* Walsingham continued his instructions. 'Double the watch on the ports. It is said two Jesuits have arrived: Garnett and Southwell.' He turned to Francis Mills. 'Frank, you will find them and apprehend them.'

The atmosphere at this meeting was very different from that of the gathering when plans were first mooted. Now, at last, the impossible seemed almost probable. And imminent.

Phelippes ran a hand through his lank yellow hair and

continually pushed his small round metal-rimmed glasses up along his slippery nose. It seemed to Shakespeare that he might dance for joy.

'And you, Tom,' Walsingham continued, jutting his beard in the direction of Phelippes. 'Return home to Leadenhall Market with the letter and apprise Mr Gifford of our plans. You are both to ride for Chartley, but separately. Offer him whatever he wants, for I still expect him to slip away from our grasp. Let him know that he is in line for a magnificent pension from the Treasury. Threaten him, too – remind him that my reach is long if he should let us down.'

'And the letter?'

'You will retain possession for the duration of the journey. Only when you are in the county of Stafford will you pass it to him and he will take it direct to the brewer at Burton. He will brook no procrastination from the brewer. It must go in with the next delivery of beer, though he demand twice his usual fee. Threaten him, if need be. Go now.'

Phelippes puffed up his slender chest, bowed, threw sly, triumphant glances at all those present, then slid from the room.

Walsingham turned back to Mills. 'Frank, I wish certain Catholic houses entered and disturbed. The Vaux house, Arundel in the Strand. That old fool Swithun Wells. The Copleys at Gatton. Hunt for priests on the pretext of looking for Southwell and Garnett. Use the services of Mr Topcliffe and Justice Young. Have them raise a standing squadron of pursuivants, fifty strong. I want them seen around London, their escutcheons and weapons visible and bold. But make sure they avoid the immediate families of the Pope's White Sons.'

Shakespeare understood his reasoning. He wished to sow fear and confusion in the ranks of the conspirators. The committed hardliners would react to the provocation of night raids by bringing forward their plans for insurrection and firming their resolve. Those who vacillated or wished no part in the plot would melt away to their country estates and could be forgotten.

'John . . .'

'Mr Secretary?'

'These Pope's White Sons. Do they still trust you?'

'I know not. Someone tried to shoot me last night outside my house.'

'You look well enough.'

'I was saved by the staff of our ward watch.'

'Then be wary. I would rather you stayed alive for the present. Feed Babington little nuggets. Let him believe you to be indiscreet and on his side. Keep company with Savage and the others. Do not be deflected from your purpose. Their conspiracy must not decay on the vine, but nor must it come to fruition. Savage must not get anywhere near Her Majesty. The court moves soon to Richmond where she will walk in the gardens unaccompanied. I will post guards where I may, but she will never be safe there.'

'Can the move not be delayed?'

'Have you no sense of smell, John? It is high summer and this palace has become a stinking jakes. We have already been here far too long. She harangues the Lord Chamberlain every day to bring forward the move, not delay it. We leave by week's end.'

'What of Robin Poley?'

'He has done well, has he not? Two days ago, Anthony Babington had set his heart on a life of quiet contemplation and poverty in a monastery. Now he is raising a hundred men to attack Chartley. This is Robin Poley's influence.'

Perhaps, thought Shakespeare. It had been his own suggestion that brought Poley into the intrigue in the first place. And yet he was inclined to believe that Gilbert Gifford had the greater influence. It was almost as if he had taken the damning letter to Babington fully written and had merely said, 'Make your mark here.' But such a thing would be unthinkable. Would it not?

As he passed through the elegant hall that faced the river, Shakespeare was taken aback to see Arthur Giltspur, his tennis racket slung over his shoulder, deep in conversation. Yet why should he be surprised to see him here? He was a wealthy young man and had friends among the nobility, so of course he would come to court. And from his racket and attire of loose chemise and soft shoes he had clearly been playing a set or two. Perhaps he had finally managed to get his match against the dashing young Earl of Essex. Now that would be a contest to see.

It seemed a good time to talk to him about the gold missing from the family coffers. It was possible he had some ideas, however vague. Perhaps, too, he had heard of the disappearing lady's maid Abigail and her connection to the murderer Will Cane. Shakespeare turned and began to walk in his direction and almost immediately stopped dead in his tracks.

The man Arthur Giltspur was talking with was Sir Robert Huckerbee, who was also dressed in loose-fitting clothes suitable for tennis.

Shakespeare quickly turned away, certain he had not been seen by them. He rounded a corner, leant against a wall and breathed in deeply. His heart was pounding, as though he had stumbled on something shameful. What was he thinking? Why had he avoided them? Why had he not wished them to see him?

He pushed away from the wall, held back his shoulders and strolled once more into the hall. Arthur Giltspur was alone now and walking away. Shakespeare hastened after him and tapped him on the shoulder.

Giltspur turned at the touch and a smile lit up his handsome face. 'Why, Mr Shakespeare, what a pleasure, sir.'

'Good day, Mr Giltspur. I saw you deep in conversation with Sir Robert Huckerbee and did not wish to intrude.'

'Hah! He still believes he can beat me, poor fool. No, I shouldn't speak so, Sir Robert is not a bad tennis player. In truth he taught me the game, but the novice now outstrips the master, which vexes him greatly.' He laughed and clapped a hand around Shakespeare's shoulder. 'Come, sir, let us find a beer, for after my exertions I have a thirst to quench – and you can entertain me.'

Shakespeare was about to decline the offer, but instead he nodded. 'Yes, I will, Mr Giltspur.'

Giltspur raised a hand and a footman hurried over. 'A pitcher of beer and a pair of blackjacks. We'll take it outside by the river.'

The footman bowed low and backed away. 'Cover your nose, Mr Shakespeare and let us find a spot beside the Thames and watch the ships glide by.'

'Mr Giltspur, did you know your grandmother summoned me?'

Giltspur lounged back on his elbows, his lean legs swinging over the edge of wharf. 'Yes, Mr Shakespeare, I did. I am not such a sybarite that the whole world passes me by. Frankly, I am shocked and appalled. Did Katherine really rob us?'

Shakespeare took a deep draught of his beer, which was too warm to be truly refreshing. He looked out across the Thames, which here was turbid and dark. He watched as a bark, heavy-laden and wallowing, drifted upriver on the rising tide, its sails full with the blustery wind. Closer to shore the bloated body of a black-and-white cat rose and fell on the swell, in a tangle of human waste and detritus. 'I don't know, but I would like to find out. Did you also hear about Abigail Colton and Will Cane?'

'Words fail me, sir. Sorbus insists the man never set foot on our land, but I do not know whether to believe him. If such men have been wandering around Giltspur House, then none of us can sleep easy in our beds.'

'You see, what worries me, Mr Giltspur, is how Kat – Katherine – gained access to the strong room and how she was able to remove so much gold and silver unseen. From what I know of Giltspur House, you have many guards. How would she effect such a crime undisturbed? Nor can I understand how she did it without the aid of an accomplice. So much precious metal would be no easy thing for a young woman to drag away. Unfortunately, your grandmother refused to sanction a search of the house, which might have revealed much.'

'And who would do the searching? She would never allow strangers to trample across her property.'

Perhaps, thought Shakespeare, there were too many other secrets concealed within those walls.

'You believe then that she did not work alone?' Giltspur continued. 'You seem to be saying this Will Cane was her partner in the crime of robbery as well as murder.'

'I didn't say that.'

'But the implication . . .'

'Was yours to read. For myself, the whole thing is a maze or puzzle. Cane said he was offered a hundred pounds. From what I know he was quite specific about that. That does not sound like a man taking a share of thousands of pounds. Nor does it explain why he killed your uncle or why he was so quick to implicate his so-called acomplice, Kat.'

'Your point is taken, but the riddle is far from solved. I still find myself wondering whether Cane and Katherine were . . .'

He hesitated, then spoke the word low. 'Lovers. If he was in the lady's maid's chamber, why not the lady's too?'

'Do you believe that, Mr Giltspur? For I do not.'

'Well, as you say, it is indeed a puzzle. Grandame and I would be most grateful if you could solve it. The Giltspurs are a wealthy family, but that will not last long if our gold and silver disappears in such quantities. Did she tell you, too, that the Giltspur Diamond is missing?'

The small hairs on the back of Shakespeare's neck stood up. 'No. She refused to even discuss the jewel.'

Arthur Giltspur all but laughed. 'I think she is ashamed as much as she is distressed at its loss.'

'Ashamed?'

'Such a valuable piece. One hundred carats. It is the size of a small egg. I had always thought she kept it separate from the other treasures. Now I am not so sure. She is extremely secretive about such matters.'

Shakespeare tried to make sense of this news. Why would the old woman call him in to investigate the disappearance of the gold and silver but not mention the Giltspur Diamond?

'I believe Grandame has promised to reward you handsomely if you can bring the culprit to the noose.'

Shakespeare met Giltspur's eyes. 'I think you must know that money is not the reason I have agreed to help with the inquiry, sir.' Shakespeare finished his beer and stood.

'Off so soon, Mr Shakespeare? Perhaps I could teach you some strokes.'

'Your sporting prowess is remarkable. I can imagine you must be an exceedingly fast runner.'

'I suppose I am. Yes, I skip about the tennis court quickly enough. But what a strange thing to say, Mr Shakespeare.'

Shakespeare smiled again and handed his empty blackjack to a passing footman. 'Think nothing of it, Mr Giltspur. My mind sometimes travels in curious directions, that is all. One more thing: did Sir Robert perhaps mention the Smith sisters?'

Giltspur frowned in curious bewilderment. 'Smith sisters? What are they?'

'Whores, Mr Giltspur.'

'Well, well, the Smith sisters, eh? Has Robert been up to some mischief? I shall make a fine jest of it at his expense.'

'Indeed.' Shakespeare nodded his farewell and began to walk away. He could not get the picture of Huckerbee and Giltspur out of his mind. Somehow seeing them here in the different context of court, with thoughts of gold in his head, changed everything.

Shakespeare found Goodfellow Savage in the King's Head, by St Giles in the Fields. He was drinking with Dominic de Warre, at the younger man's expense. De Warre looked at Shakespeare through bleary eyes and offered no word of welcome, merely continued to sup unsteadily.

'We are all to meet at the Three Tuns in Newgate Street,' Savage said when Shakespeare had ordered himself wine. 'Will you come with us, John?'

'I will.'

Dominic de Warre grunted and announced to no one in particular that he needed a piss. With glazed eye and teetering step, he stumbled outside into the night.

'He is as drunk as a seasick dog.'

'Don't blame me, John. He has been boozing all day. He called on me this evening and begged me to go out with him. I only agreed to accompany him so that I might keep an eye on him, for I feared he would be easy meat for footpads.'

'But why do you have anything to do with him? If you need a few shillings, I can help you.' He poured a few coins from his purse into his left hand and held them out to Savage. 'Here, take this.'

'I have no way of repaying you, nor any prospect of ever being able to do so.'

'It would please me, Goodfellow. Take it.'

Savage hesitated, then nodded. 'Thank you, John. You are a good friend.' He looked at the coins and counted them out. Two pounds and an angel. 'This is too much.'

'No, it is not, and nor am I a good friend. I wish to God that you had never entrusted your secrets to me. If you want to repay me the loan, keep young Dominic de Warre away from Babington. *We* all know the dangers, but to him it is a fine game. He should be at his studies, not talking sedition.'

'Then let us convey him back to Barnard's Inn and put him to bed. He will sleep like a babe while we head for the Three Tuns. I am told that Anthony has tidings of great moment to impart to us.'

De Warre came back into the taproom and stood in front of Shakespeare, his face so close that Shakespeare could smell his beer-drenched breath.

'You are Walsingham's man. You work for the tyrant.'

Shakespeare stood back and threw a look at Savage. 'I think it is time to go.'

'Mr Shakespeare is one of us, Dominic.' Savage's voice was quiet. 'You would do well to listen to him.'

'You look a good man, Mr Shakespeare. Are you a good man, or are you a tool of the tyranny? Do you stretch men on the rack and press women to death for the crime of being a Catholic?'

'You are drunk, Mr de Warre.'

'And so I speak false because I have taken beer?'

'This is a public place. Walsingham's spies are everywhere.'

'One day, Mr Shakespeare, men and women will worship

free in this land. All will be as one. And none shall have their bellies ripped open to spill their bowels for their faith. Would you say that were a good world to hope for?'

Shakespeare did not reply.

'I drink to the Pope and the death of tyrants.' De Warre said the words without lowering his voice. Though his speech was slurred, the words were all too easily heard. Two men drinking nearby turned and looked upon him as though he were mad.

Savage was behind de Warre. He had his upper arms in an iron grip and was pulling the young man towards the door.

'All tyrants,' Dominic bellowed. 'Topcliffe, Torquemada, Protestant and Catholic. I curse the torturers—'

But before he could say any more, he was out in the street and Shakespeare was wrapping a kerchief about his mouth to shut him up.

They left a subdued de Warre at his lodgings in Barnard's. He stood unsteadily, glaring through half-closed eyes. 'I am coming with you, Goodfellow,' he said.

'No, Dominic, you are cup-shotten. Bed is the place for you. I think you will need a seven-night to sleep it off.'

The youth stood in the doorway to his small chamber, gazing blankly at Shakespeare and Savage as they took their leave.

'He is confused,' Savage said after the door was closed.

'Is he, Goodfellow?' It seemed to Shakespeare that Dominic de Warre had spoken much sense for one so young and intoxicated. He, too, loathed the torturers, be they Catholic or Protestant. He despised Richard Topcliffe, chief torturer and persecutor of priests, and he was certain he would have felt the same way about Tomás de Torquemada, the founding Grand Inquisitor and the cause of so much death and misery in Spain and beyond.

✝ 317 ✝

Perhaps there was more to Dominic de Warre than met the eye. His idealistic fervour reminded Shakespeare of himself at that same age, though a great deal less restrained.

They walked slowly westwards in the direction of Newgate Street. Gusts of wind blew dust and debris into the air. Shakespeare felt uneasy; high winds were harbingers of change and they unsettled him. As they came to Holborn Bridge, a band of horsemen came towards them at a hard trot. Savage and Shakespeare both saw what they were: pursuivants, all dressed in black leather quilted doublets. There was no room for pedestrians on the bridge while the horses were coming, but instead of making way, Savage deliberately placed himself in the centre of the bridge, as though a man alone could bar the way of a dozen steeds. Shakespeare tried to drag him away, but Savage shook him off.

The horses came to a halt. Shakespeare noted with revulsion that four people – two women, a girl and a boy of about twelve, all bound by the wrists – were being dragged behind the rear horses. They were probably being taken to the Fleet prison or Bridewell. Their crime? Most likely the sin of having a priest in the house or being in possession of forbidden Catholic books.

Shakespeare whispered urgently in his companion's ear. 'Don't do this, Goodfellow. Don't draw attention to yourself.'

'They are the devil's riders. I'll take them on. One at a time or all at once.'

'You will be of no use to anyone if you are trampled underfoot. We can do nothing here. Come, Goodfellow, our feasting awaits us. Let us hear what Mr Babington has to say.'

'First these.'

The lead rider walked his horse forward. He was a man in his sixties with no cap, his white hair hung about his ears. Shakespeare recognised him instantly as Richard Topcliffe, and shuddered with loathing. Their paths had crossed before, and no good had come of it.

The rider looked down with disdain at the two men blocking his men's way. 'What is this? Do you wish us to beat you from our path?' He raised his crop and was about to crack Savage about the head when he noticed Shakespeare and his hand faltered.

'Satan's turd, it is Shakespeare . . .'

'We are going about our business, Topcliffe. My friend has had a drink or two. I will move him from your path.' He wrenched at Savage's arm and growled, 'Come away, Goodfellow. I know this man. He will kill you if you cross him.'

Savage did not seem at all perturbed. He narrowed his eyes as though to imprint a portrait of the infamous pursuivant into his brain. 'So *you* are Topcliffe,' he said, not moving an inch. 'The man who torments women and children. And I see you are such a brave man that you have friends to help you.' He raised his fists like a pugilist. 'Dismount and try me man-to-man. If you dare.'

Topcliffe glared at Savage with such seething hatred that Shakespeare feared he would draw his sword and cut him to death there and then, but something held him back. He raised his hand to signal his men to move forward, then leant low in the saddle and spat words into Shakespeare's ear. 'Take this man in hand, Shakespeare for if I see him again, I swear I will do for him.'

He shook the reins and urged his horse forward, brushing past Savage and knocking him away. The other pursuivants followed, finding a path through the two men. And then they were past. Topcliffe kicked on into a trot, and the others followed suit, making their captives stumble and run just to keep up. They disappeared into a cloud of dust.

'The devil damn you, John. Do you not know about that man? Did you not see those poor women and children he held? I wanted to kill him.'

'I know him better than you, Goodfellow, and I despise him as much. But there were a dozen of them. You would have died – and your vow to God would have died with you.'

Savage would never know it, but Shakespeare was certain that the only thing that had saved his life was his own presence there. Walsingham's command that the Pope's White Sons were to be allowed to go unmolested must have been forcefully made. Even Topcliffe had noted it.

'Perhaps it would have been better that way,' Savage said. 'If I had but killed Topcliffe, my own death would have at least served some purpose. Death has never held terrors for me, John. It would have been an end to all my troubles.'

Shakespeare gripped his friend by the arm. 'You have said enough.' In the pit of his stomach, he felt sick with apprehension. Darkness was enveloping his world. A great deal of blood would spill forth before the light of hope returned.

Chapter 36

S ALISBURY AND ABINGDON were at the door to the upper
room at the tavern in Newgate. They looked at Shakespeare
and Savage with cold eyes. 'Come in,' Salisbury said, pulling
Savage by the sleeve and dragging him through into the noisy
interior.

Shakespeare attempted to follow him but Salisbury held up
the flat of his hand against his chest. 'Not you.'

'Mr Salisbury, what is this?' Through the door he could see
a crowd of perhaps twenty young men. Robin Poley was there,
laughing at some jest made by Babington and touching his arm
with affection. Ballard was there, too, dressed in all his soldierly
finery, in the guise of Captain Fortescue. Tichbourne, Tilney,
Dunn, Gage, Charnock, Edward Windsor, Travers and others
that Shakespeare could not put a name to. And then he spotted
Dominic de Warre. How had he found his way here? He must
have run along side alleys. He should be in bed asleep.

'You are not wanted,' Salisbury told Shakespeare, his face as
hard as his words.

He tried to catch sight of Savage in the throng, but he had
already disappeared into the crowd of young men. Had he seen
him being barred?

Through the throng, Shakespeare caught Poley's eye. He
smiled and seemed to wink. Shakespeare did not return the

wink, but concentrated on Salisbury. 'May I at least know why I am to be excluded?'

'Mr Babington has taken advice. He thinks it safer for everyone – you included – that you take your supper elsewhere. He would not wish for an accident to befall you.'

'Advice from whom?'

Salisbury ran a hand through the wild tangle of his hair. 'Why, his new friend, Robin Poley. It seems he has some doubts about you. As do I, Mr Shakespeare. As do I, which I have said all along.'

'May I at least speak to Mr Babington?'

'No.'

Shakespeare half expected to find Kat waiting for him when he returned to Seething Lane, but she was not there, nor was there any word from her. Perhaps she had not yet seen the notice on the Si Quis door. Perhaps she had seen sense and had returned to the north of England. Or maybe there was a simpler explanation: the note had fallen from its hook and flown away on the wind.

He thought of their last night together. Her slender body between his cool sheets. The love had indeed gone, he knew that for certain; but the pleasure had been undiminished.

'Good evening, master.'

'Good evening, Jane.'

'A messenger came and said that Mr Tort would be calling on you in the morning, at ten o'clock.'

'Thank you.'

'Will that be all, sir – or can I bring you some pigeon pie?'

He had almost forgotten; his ejection from Babington's feast meant he had not eaten. 'Indeed, Jane, that would suit me well.'

But what of Babington's decision to exclude him? Had he

put a foot wrong somewhere, said a word out of place? Or had it all been Robin Poley's doing? Laughter welled up in Shakespeare as suddenly he understood. Poley had cast doubts on Shakespeare to boost his own credibility. Poley was a sly one. Well, perhaps there was nothing lost by his absence. Poley would bring word of the feast to Walsingham. And Shakespeare already knew Babington's momentous news: he had received a letter from the Queen of Scots and had sent one back. Now was the time for all those who loved her to rally to the cause.

Boltfoot was locked in the hold, curled up asleep on a coil of rope, like a cat. Something touched him and he was instantly awake, imagining the pointy teeth of a rat gnawing at his face.

'Hush, Mr Cooper, it is only I, Maywether.'

Boltfoot sat upright.

Godfrey Maywether had a lantern which lit his straggle-bearded face. 'No sudden movements, there is a dagger in my hand.' He held up the blade so that it caught the light.

Above them, a high wind blew through the rigging of the eighty-ton ship. They were rocking, not pitching, moored at the port of Sandwich in the south-east corner of Kent, safe from the gales that might otherwise have driven them onto the Goodwin Sands, the great ship-eater; only God knew how many thousands of mariners and vessels had been sucked to their death there. Here in safe harbour, though, there was another danger for the crew – the danger that Boltfoot might try to escape; that was why he had been locked in the hold once more.

'No let-up in the gale?'

'We're here a day, that's for sure, maybe more. Here, drink this.' He put a cup of ale to Boltfoot's lips and he drank thirstily.

'The offer stands, Mr Maywether. I could improve on it.'

'I want a hundred and fifty pounds. Not a penny less.'

So Maywether was as much a rogue as Boltfoot had always believed him. He sucked air through his teeth. 'That's a lot of money.'

'It's up to you, Cooper. A hundred and fifty, mariner's solemn pledge, or you stay here in this hold and spend the next five or six months sawing staves and packing fish into salt.'

What would Mr Shakespeare say? Would he even be able to find such money? He was not poor, but nor was he a rich man. There would be time enough to raise the money, however, for Maywether would not be back in London before Christmas.

He nodded. 'Very well. I will have the money when you return. Mariner's solemn pledge.'

'No. I'm coming with you. We'll travel together and you'll give me the money in London. Then I'll be off to Lincolnshire, for I'll be done for if I stay anywhere near the Thames.'

It was a huge sum of money, yet somehow he had to get to his master the information that he had learnt from Bathsheba Cane: that Kat's maid was the lover of the murderer Will Cane. More than that, new and important intelligence touching on the Giltspur family given him casually by Maywether in their last conversation, intelligence that might be at the very heart of the murder and all the mysteries surrounding it. He sighed heavily, then nodded his acceptance of the deal. 'Hundred and fifty in London,' he said.

'Mariner's solemn pledge.'

'I swear it. Perhaps you're not such a swine after all, Mr Maywether.' In truth nothing had changed about the man; he was simply doing what he had always done – looking out for himself. 'So, what will you do with this new-found fortune?'

'I'll get myself a chandlery in Grimsby. You can come with me. I'll set you up with a cooperage. We'll be the wealthiest men in town soon enough.'

'When do we go?'

'Now. Captain Bootmann's drunk, limp-pricked and snoring in a whore's loft. And the rest of the crew are in much the same state. Pissed as bilge rats. They won't notice we're gone until dawn, and we'll have walked twenty miles by then. Breakfast in Canterbury. That'll suit me. A nice little pilgrimage. You coming, Cooper?'

Did he trust Maywether? He had no choice. 'Aye.'

Maywether thrust his dagger back into his belt and held out his hand. Boltfoot took it and the deal was sealed. He'd have to find the money now, even if he had to sell his soul to do so.

Severin Tort arrived promptly. Shakespeare was in his solar, working on a bundle of correspondence that had been couriered to him from Mr Secretary's offices. When Jane announced the arrival, he asked her to send him up.

He shuffled away the papers and stood to welcome his guest. The men shook hands, then Shakespeare invited him to sit on the settle beneath a shelf of books.

'I am glad to see you, Mr Tort. I wanted to ask you about Abigail Colton, the maidservant you recommended to the Giltspurs.'

'Ah, yes.'

'What do you know of her?'

'Absolutely nothing. She worked for us but was surplus to requirements. That is all.'

'She is with child – and I believe the father is probably the murderer Will Cane.' Shakespeare looked into Tort's eyes for a reaction.

Tort looked puzzled, then laughed nervously. 'Well, that is of course alarming, but in truth I can barely even recall the young woman's face.'

Did he believe the lawyer? He wasn't at all sure. 'Well, let us move on. How may I help you, Mr Tort?' Shakespeare took the straight-backed chair at his desk.

'May we speak privately?'

'There is no one else in the house save my maidservant. Speak freely, Mr Tort.'

'That is not what I meant. What I wish is to speak to you as my friend, rather than a Queen's man.' The attorney looked ill at ease. He seemed to have shrunk in his neat black suit since last they met. His hair, so distinguished with its silver sheen, now seemed flat and white, like a winter sky. 'I have a favour to beg of you, Mr Shakespeare. A very great favour.'

'Then speak and I will listen, as a friend. I can promise no more.'

'It is a matter of the utmost delicacy, touching on my step-son Dominic de Warre.' He clutched at his throat, smoothing down his ruff as though it would choke him.

'You are distressed, Mr Tort. Would you care for aught to drink?'

'No. No, I will be well soon enough. You must excuse me.'

'Please continue. You mentioned Dominic.'

'He came into my household with my late beloved wife. As she lay dying, I vowed that I would always do all in my power to protect him and to ensure that he prospered. He is a good boy of great wit, but sometimes he thinks too much. He was but twelve years of age when his mother died and I have struggled to be a good and worthy father to him. I fear I have failed.'

'What is this to me, Mr Tort?'

'I am not a fool. I know what is going on. My stepson runs with these Pope's White Sons. That is what everyone calls them, is it not? Divers young men who do services for the Bishop of Rome against this realm.'

'Is that so? I know nothing of such things. What are these Pope's White Sons?'

Tort threw him a look that said *you do not fool me with your denials.* 'Come, Mr Shakespeare, let us speak like honest men. The whole of London knows who they are and what they are about. Insurrection ... freeing the Scots Queen. And the whole world knows where it will end: on the scaffold. I cannot allow that to happen to Dominic. He is but a boy. He knows not what he does.'

Shakespeare gave a small laugh and spread his palms as if he were totally bemused. 'If I could help, I would, but I know nothing of such matters. Who are these desperate men? Where do I find them? I am certain Mr Secretary should be told of them.'

Sharp irritation flashed across Tort's equable features. 'You know them as well as any man, Mr Shakespeare. Indeed you do, sir. Indeed you do. You work for Walsingham. These Pope's White Sons, as men call them, they are all going to die. You know this to be true.' He rose from the settle and began pacing the room.

'No, sir. I know nothing of the sort.' He could not admit to any knowledge of such things to this man. He could not admit that he, too, feared for Dominic. Never reveal your knowledge, never reveal the game to any man. He watched the pacing Tort with sadness. Shakespeare tried to ease the tension. 'What of you, Mr Tort? You are a Catholic, are you not? These years have been hard for you. I am sure that Dominic is merely enjoying London life with a group of like-minded friends. It is the way with young men. As a Catholic, is it not possible that you are seeing conspiracy and danger where no such things exist?'

The lawyer's eyes widened and his shoulders stiffened. He stopped and glared at his host. 'What are you saying, sir? Do you tell me Catholics are not persecuted in this realm? Do you tell me that no one has been torn apart on the scaffold for the crime of being a priest?'

Shakespeare did not answer, for he could not deny it. And yet he knew, too, that not all priests had benign intent. He knew that the exiles Father Persons and Cardinal Allen would back an invasion of their own country by the Catholic powers of Paris, Rome and Madrid.

Tort seemed to read his mind. 'And before you ask me the bloody question – would I support the Pope if he were to lead an army of invasion – the answer is no. I may be a Catholic, but I am loyal to my sovereign lady Elizabeth, Queen of England, and I would rather be sliced open by a Tyburn butcher's knife than have any foreign power invade this realm. I would take up weapons against the Pope himself rather than any Spanish or French man-at-arms walk along Cheapside. So please, I beg you, listen to me: Dominic de Warre is a sensitive youth, an innocent and foolish boy. He is on the path to perdition. They all are. Everyone knows it. You know it, Mr Shakespeare. And so I entreat you: save him.'

Shakespeare very slowly and very deliberately shook his head. 'I can do nothing for you or for Dominic because I know nothing of these things. You are his stepfather; if you do not like the company he keeps, then forbid him to meet these people you talk of. This is your fatherly duty, not mine. Now if that is all, I have much work.' He stood and began to move towards the door to show his visitor out.

Tort grabbed hold of his sleeve. 'No, I will not be dismissed so easily. Help me, Mr Shakespeare, and I will help you.'

'Mr Tort, I understand that you are in anguish over your boy, and I sympathise, but there is nothing I can do for you and nothing I need from you. In truth, I do not know why you wish to help him, for from what you say he seems to be singularly lacking in any sense of filial duty to you. To speak plain, he seems to have no time for you, sir.'

'He resents me for living when his father and mother are

both dead. He has never known that I love him as much as any father ever loved his son. I see his mother in his eyes and I love him all the more. If only . . .'

'If only what?'

'If only he would love me as I love him.'

The lawyer closed his eyes. His teeth were now clenched tight and his lips were no more than a line, a gash in his face, as though he had words to spit out but his heart would not let him; as though his mouth would never open to utter words again.

Shakespeare lifted the latch and held open the door. 'Well, sir, I think we are done here. We share a bond of care for Kat Whetstone, but that is all. If you will forgive me, I have work to do.'

Tort made no move to exit. He opened his mouth like a fish, but no words came out, only a sigh.

'If you have something else to say, then speak, I entreat you, for the morning moves on apace.'

'If I give you this, you must help me.'

'Give me what? I told you, there is nothing I need from you. And nothing I can give you, for I have no knowledge of this conspiracy you claim to have uncovered.'

'Then I must tell you what I know, but in doing so, I place my trust in the honour and decency that I hope to find in your heart. Help Dominic, I beg you. And if you ever make use of the information I impart, you can never say that it came from me.'

Once again, Shakespeare declined to speak, merely waited for Tort.

'Very well.' Tort nodded. 'I am about to tell you a great secret. It is a matter of import that touches on the very govern-ance of this land – and involves both the Giltspurs and the felon known as Cutting Ball.'

Chapter 37

SHAKESPEARE LISTENED IN silence, astonished and yet believing. The tale Severin Tort told him was simple enough and credible, but agonising to listen to, for it seemed to eat at the very cornerstones of the England he believed he knew and loved.

'Almost all of my practice as an attorney-at-law has been in the service of Nicholas Giltspur,' Tort said. 'Over a long period of years – since I was a young man – I have been entrusted with intimate knowledge of much that is private touching the family's affairs. It is this position of trust that I am about to betray to you, though it cuts my conscience sore to do so.'

'Continue, Mr Tort. What is this secret?'

'What do you know of the criminal practices of Cutting Ball, sir?'

'He extorts money from the merchants. Some say he demands one part in a hundred of every cargo landed in the wharfs of London, and that those who refuse to pay have their ships burnt or their merchandise destroyed. I know, too, that he and his sister run bawdy houses and take a portion of the whores' earnings. I am sure they are guilty of many other crimes, including violence against the person. Even murder.'

Tort nodded. 'You are correct in almost every detail. How,

though, does such a man continue to prosper when you might expect him to be swinging from the Tyburn tree? How does he walk free when every other highwayman, cutpurse and footpad is rounded up and dispatched?'

'It is a question I have asked myself, sir.'

'Well, I can satisfy your curiosity. He is not arraigned, nor ever will be, because he is protected by powerful men.'

Shakespeare did not like the way this was going, but he needed to hear it out. 'Please continue.'

'I will explain. Yes, Ball takes one part in a hundred of every cargo landed from Katharine's Dock to the bridge and beyond. Sometimes more. But he keeps only a small part of it, paying out nine parts in ten of his own portion to the Treasury of England. It is, if you like, an unofficial tax on the merchants by the Lord Treasurer, Lord Burghley.'

'Is this true?'

Tort nodded, his face drawn. 'Yes, it is true, though it pains me to say so.'

'And this sum is over and above the common levies that all traders must pay at the Custom House?'

'Over and above.'

'Burghley is involved in this?'

'Faithful, trustworthy, God-fearing, white-bearded Burghley himself. Elizabeth's most loyal minister and England's truest friend.' Tort smiled. 'Treating with the commonest of common criminals.'

'God's blood but that must be a vast amount of money.'

'Much needed, I believe, for the Commons subsidies go nowhere near the amounts required to protect the realm. A great deal of these unofficial earnings are passed on to Mr Secretary to pay for his covert dealings. I doubt not but that your own wages come from this source.'

Shakespeare was reeling, but he wanted the whole story.

'How does this involve the Giltspurs? Do you mean that they, too, have faced such extortion?'

'No. They were excluded, because they had a much more important part to play in the enterprise. They were the linchpin that kept the wheel turning.'

Shakespeare was beginning to understand. Tort continued.

'The Treasury could never be seen to be taking such illgotten gains. If the merchants learnt that the money extorted from them was, in effect, a tax, there would be uproar. They have often complained to the Privy Council of the activities of Cutting Ball and his crew and they become infuriated when nothing is ever done to stop the man. The excuse by Burghley is always lack of resources, empty coffers and not enough men. And then when pressured he makes promises that he will find a way to deal with the felon . . . promises that are never kept.'

'Yet the merchants of London are powerful men.'

'Indeed they are, and they must be kept sweet. Burghley, Walsingham and Her Majesty know that they need them. In truth they cannot do without them, for they provide the wealth of England. That is why the link from Mr Ball to Lord Burghley could never be made public.'

'And so they needed a facilitator . . .'

Tort nodded. 'That was Nick Giltspur. The money went from Cutting Ball to Nick and from Nick to Burghley. And before you judge him, I would say only this: Nick did not profit from the deal; he did it for England.'

'But you, Mr Tort, you must have felt compromised. Was there no sense of shame, no guilt?'

He hesitated before replying, then shrugged. 'If we are honest with ourselves, surely all taxation is money demanded with menaces. Were the tithe-gatherers of old any better than Cutting Ball and Nick Giltspur.' They were not questions, but statements, for he truly believed the words he spoke. 'If you did not pay your tithes, the punishment was severe.'

'But you did not just *know* of this matter. You played a part, too, did you not? For Nick Giltspur would not have confided in you unless he had a purpose – and that purpose was that he needed your help.'

'I was always Nick's confidential adviser. He knew that he could turn to me and talk in complete confidence. Were he alive today, I would not be telling you this, for I never betrayed his trust.'

'Tell me the truth then. I am thinking he asked you to assist him in some way? Is this not the case?'

Tort paced some more, and then stopped. 'I oversaw the accounts, which were always complex. There had to be two sets of books. The trick was to keep one clean and the other secret. Nick was a busy man; he needed someone he could trust when the workload was too great. This was not something that could be entrusted to a ledger clerk.'

'A remarkable state of affairs.'

'Remarkable, indeed, Mr Shakespeare. And you will understand why you can never repeat what I have told you.'

'Who, then, had access to the dirty ledger?'

'Nick kept the books under lock and key. They were never allowed out of Giltspur House and so that is where I would work, when called upon to do so.'

'What of his mother? What of Arthur?'

'No. Not then. However, since Nick's death, I do not know what has happened. There has been no call for me at the house.'

But this was not the whole story. A man was dead and a vast amount of gold and silver was missing. The link with Cutting Ball was proved; so there had to be some connection between the murder and robbery and the work that Nick Giltspur did for the Treasury.

'Are you suggesting that Nick Giltspur fell out with Cutting Ball – and that Ball ordered the murder?'

'I have no idea. It is a possibility – and for you to find out. But I know that something was worrying Nick in the days before he died.'

'And the missing gold. Have you heard of that?'

'Yes, indeed I have. Word travels in London.'

'You know Giltspur House as well as anyone, Mr Tort. Who could have broken into the strongroom and removed it?'

'No one.'

'No one?'

'Don't you understand? The robber or robbers didn't need to enter the strongroom. The missing gold and silver was never there. I believe it had already been stolen. The answer lies in the black books.'

As he rode towards Giltspur House, Shakespeare tried to make sense of all that Severin Tort had told him. Before taking his leave, the lawyer had begged once again for help in saving the life of his stepson. Shakespeare had, at last, clutched the man's hands. 'If there is anything that can be done, I will do it.'

But some things were still unclear: how had Nicholas Giltspur and Burghley made their unholy contract with Cutting Ball in the first place? More importantly, what – if anything – did this all have to do with the murder?

Tort's revelation had opened the shutters on an unwholesome world of government deceit and official criminality, but it did not give a firm answer to the fundamental question: who killed Nick Giltspur and why? From what Tort was saying, someone must have got at the books, massaging the amounts received and passed on. But if the books had never left Giltspur House, that meant it had to be someone within the household: Nick Giltspur himself, his ancient mother or his nephew

Arthur. Unless it was one of the servants – or someone who had illicitly gained access to the house. Will Cane for instance?

Or the obvious one: Kat herself.

Shakespeare very much wished to talk with her again. He also very much desired to interrogate the sportsman Arthur Giltspur; fleet of foot and supremely competitive.

One thing that had become abundantly clear was the meaning of the words used by old Joan Giltspur: *This family has done more for England than the whole Privy Council combined . . .*

Not just the conveying of men and messages in and out of the ports of Spain and France, but keeping the Treasury coffers full of extorted gold.

The sentries at Giltspur House looked at the would-be visitor as though he were an insect, then smirked at each other. 'Ah yes, you are Mr Shakespeare,' the chief of the two said. 'I recall your face. How may I help you?'

'I wish to see Mr Arthur Giltspur.'

'He's not here.'

'Then his grandmother, Mrs Giltspur.'

'I am told she does not wish to be disturbed.'

'Who told you that?'

'One of the maids. Does it matter?'

'Then I will speak with Sorbus.'

'Sorbus? Sorbus?' he turned to his fellow guard. 'Do we know a Sorbus, Hubert?'

'Wasn't he that steward fellow, the one that got himself arrested this morning for harbouring a known felon?' The second sentry grinned. 'If that's the man you want, Mr Shakespeare, sir, you'll most likely find him just around the corner at the Counter in Wood Street. I do believe that's where Justice Young took him.'

'Sorbus arrested? What is the charge?'

'Ask him yourself.'

Shakespeare moved forward. The sentries crossed their swords to bar his way.

'You will pay a heavy price for your insolence.'

'Not as heavy as you will pay if you try to move an inch further forward.'

The Counter in Wood Street was less than five minutes' walk from the splendours of Aldermanbury and Giltspur House, but it might have been a world away, for it was a mean place, usually set aside for debtors and criminals awaiting trial. The keeper allowed Shakespeare into the gaol in exchange for six-pence. 'Strange thing, Mr Shakespeare,' he said as they walked through the dark bowels of the prison, 'this man Abraham Sorbus is the only prisoner I got. Mr Topcliffe came around this morning and cleared out the rest. Two went to the scaffold and I know not what he did with the others.'

Shakespeare knew all too well why the gaols were being evacuated but said nothing. At the door to the cell where Sorbus was being held, he turned to the keeper. 'Leave us now.' The turnkey bowed and left, clutching his coin. Shakespeare gazed at Sorbus. He looked a sorry sight.

He was sitting disconsolate on the floor, his small legs in rusty irons, his normally immaculate clothes torn and coated in dirt and dust. His hair was awry and his face bruised. A drop of blood had trickled from his nostril and was now dried to a crust. He had either been dragged here or had been beaten and knocked to the ground. He was such a slender fellow, thought Shakespeare, that he could easily have been carried here like a child, under a strong man's arm. And yet somehow, despite being brought so low, he still contrived to look stiff and aloof.

'Mr Sorbus, I am sorry to find you here.'

At the prisoner's side was a leathern blackjack and an empty platter. 'Indeed, Mr Shakespeare, so am I. I am told these fetters will lose their rust and gain a bright sheen if I am here long enough, which they doubt.'

'I see you have ale, at least. And food.'

'Aye, the keeper was happy to provide it for a penny. He'll bring me more, too, if I pay him.'

'What is the charge against you?'

'Harbouring a known felon, Mistress Katherine Giltspur.'

'And is there any truth in this allegation?'

'I do not think it wise for me to answer such questions under the present circumstances.' He raised a finger and ran it across his throat. 'My prospects for long life do not appear too healthy. I am not sure that speaking to you will improve my chances.'

'Has she, too, been arrested?'

He shrugged, then surreptitiously shook his head.

'I have just come from Giltspur House. I must tell you I was shocked more than I can say to hear of your arrest. The sentries would not allow me entry.'

'Well, clearly my arrest must confirm Mistress Katherine's guilt. That is what they will now be saying. That is what the old widow, Mistress Joan, will say. She will be spitting blood and pins.'

'You know, Sorbus, I had always imagined you felt disdain for Kat, as though she were not good enough for your master or, indeed, for you.'

'Folk are wont to make assumptions, usually false.'

Shakespeare went down on his haunches so that he might speak more quietly. 'I beg you, if you know where she is, tell me.'

'I know nothing.'

'If you are innocent, Sorbus, I may be your only chance of life. Yours and Kat's . . .'

The prisoner laughed bitterly. '*You*, save *me*? Mr Shakespeare, you are the reason I am here in these shackles. Just ask him.' He nodded towards the cell door.

Shakespeare turned. Richard Young was standing there, hands on hips and legs akimbo. Shakespeare rose to his feet, annoyed that he had not heard the justice's approach.

'Well, you're here now, Shakespeare. That'll save me the chore of picking you up.'

'Why have you brought his man here, Young?'

'For harbouring a most notorious murderess and keeping her from the righteous clutches of the law, a felony for which he will hang by the neck until dead. Probably on the same scaffold as you and the bitch herself, God willing.'

'You are talking of Katherine Giltspur. Where is she?'

'I know where she was – Mr Sorbus's little hiding place in Pissing Alley. We will have her soon enough.'

'Pissing Alley? What house is that?'

Young jutted his chin at Sorbus. 'His. And he had her there.'

'What evidence is there?'

'We have evidence. The evidence of the Si Quis door and a note left for her which this man took. He was followed to Pissing Alley. She wasn't there, but there was a comb with strands of fair hair. That's evidence enough for the court – that and the Si Quis note. And so he will pay the penalty.'

'A friend of mine is seeking a position as a footman,' Sorbus said quietly. 'He cannot read, so I went there to see if I could find him a suitable position.'

'A mere coincidence then, Mr Sorbus,' Young sneered. 'Tell that to the court of law. That will save your neck by and by.'

'What court of law?' Shakespeare demanded. 'You do not have the woman, so you cannot have a charge; thus you have nothing.'

'God damn you, Shakespeare, we have all we need. Did you think we would not follow you and discover your tricks? We will find her and then you will *all* hang. You may think yourself protected now, but you will see the truth soon enough.' His hand went to his dagger.

Shakespeare's hand instinctively went to the hilt of his sword, but he did not draw it for he saw that Young was not about to enter the fray. Instead, Shakespeare addressed Sorbus. 'Do not despair, sir. There is error here. I know you to be wholly innocent and will do all in my power to prove it.'

Then he pushed past the weakling frame of Richard Young and strode out into the warm summer air.

Chapter 38

SHAKESPEARE HAD NEVER seen Sir Francis Walsingham in such a high state of anticipation. Though no word had come down from Staffordshire, he had convinced himself that Babington's letter must have already made its way into Chartley Hall and, even now, be in the eager, shaking palms of the Queen of Scots.

'Her Royal Majesty awaits news with ill-concealed elation. The ambassador of France was with us this morning, and I feared for a while that she would reveal all to him. "Monsieur Châteauneuf," she said, her eye twinkling like the Venus star, "you have much secret intelligence with the Queen of Scotland. But believe me, I know *everything* that is done in my kingdom". The Baron de Châteauneuf looked full of suspicion at this.'

'Will he act on it?'

'He can do little now. It is too late for the French to intervene. The only thing they could do is warn the Pope's White Sons, but all the ports are now closed. To leave the country, they will have to go by secret means. That will not be easy. One or two might escape – but we can live without them, so long as we have Babington, Ballard and Savage.' Walsingham rubbed his hands. 'And that is in your hands, is it not, John? Yours and Poley's.'

'You will probably know by now that I was not admitted to their feast last night.'

'I heard. But it will not prevent you from observing them. You are still intimate with Savage, are you not?'

'Perhaps. I will seek him out this day, but the fact that I was barred from their company will not have helped his own anxieties.'

'What's done is done. I believe Babington at last realises how high the stakes are and has begun to take precautions. Excluding you was perhaps the first sensible thing the man has done. Poley told me in great detail how Babington revealed the contents of his letter to all present, and the mixed reactions he received. The news was certainly not met with universal rejoicing.'

'That does not surprise me.'

'There was a measure of panic. Both Salisbury and Tichbourne seemed on the verge of storming out and riding for their home counties. It was only Robin's clever assurances that calmed their anxieties. Doubtless some will try to go in the next few days. In the meantime, I must prepare for the move. The court goes to Richmond in the morning. You must hasten to Savage's side.' He nodded to Shakespeare that it was time for him to depart.

Shakespeare did not move. 'Before I go, Sir Francis . . .'

'I am busy, John. The council meets in ten minutes. There are arrangements to be made, correspondence to be read and written.'

'Forgive me, it is the matter of the murder of Nicholas Giltspur.'

'What now? I do not have time for this.'

'I need a warrant to go into Giltspur House, and a squadron of guards to enforce it.'

If Walsingham thought his man was jesting, he did not

laugh, merely stared at him with disbelief. 'What insanity is this? Have you gone moon-mad, John?'

'I am certain the truth about Giltspur's death lies within the walls of that house. There are secrets there, and I need to conduct a search.'

This time Walsingham did laugh. 'Forget it, John. It will not happen.'

'Believe me, Mr Secretary, I do not enjoy coming to you with this matter. I would go to Judge Fleetwood, but I need more than he could provide. I need a royal guard, untainted, for this involves matters of a sensitive nature. I believe you know what I mean, sir.'

'Do I?' Suddenly suspicious.

'Would you have me speak it?'

'Yes. If you have something to tell me, then say it. I may delve into men's souls but I cannot read the contents of their minds.'

Shakespeare had been considering this on the boat journey downriver to Greenwich Palace; could he afford to let Walsingham know that he was now privy to this great secret? Now it was being unavoidably prised out of him, for he had already said too much.

'Speak, John.'

'It is something I should not know, something I was reluctant to believe – and yet now I do believe it to be true.'

'You are circling the subject. Time presses.'

'Money, Sir Francis – the money that comes from the felon Cutting Ball to the Treasury of England. It passes through the hands of the Giltspurs.'

'Who told you this gibberish, this half-boiled kettle of lies?'

'It is true, is it not?'

'Who spake it?'

Shakespeare shook his head. 'I discovered this for myself. You pay me for my ability to seek out such secrets. My method is mine to know, but not to say. But I *can* tell you this: a great sum has disappeared from the Giltspur coffers. I am not yet certain why, but I believe this to be the reason for Nicholas Giltspur's death.'

'You surpass yourself. Am I to believe you are saying that my lord Burghley conspired with Cutting Ball to murder Nick Giltspur? Next you will be writing comedies for the playhouse stage.'

'Mr Secretary, that is not what I am saying. But nonetheless, I am certain the truth lies inside the heavily guarded fortress that is Giltspur House. And so if you wish to know who killed Nick Giltspur – a true friend of England – then I must crave your assistance.'

He wanted to ask about Sir Robert Huckerbee and his links with the Giltspurs, yet this seemed neither the time nor the place. He had clearly pushed his master as far as he would go this day.

Walsingham said nothing for a few moments. His long features were drained of the jubilation that had greeted Shakespeare on his arrival. His eyes moved from his intelligencer's face to the open window through which the sound of birdsong intruded, then back to Shakespeare. 'What I crave from you is your mind to be fixed to the purpose in hand: keep tight with the plotters who would kill our Queen and supplant her with another. I fear you are straying into dangerous waters.'

'Again, it is what you pay me for.'

'Be careful. Clever answers will not always save you. As to Giltspur House, it is not going away, so you have time. I must take advice, John. This matter you speak of concerns others. Come to me at Richmond and I will give you my answer.'

*

The walking was slow and becoming slower. At first, Boltfoot had kept up a reasonably steady pace, but his club foot made the going tough.

'Shall we take a horse or two, Mr Cooper?' Maywether suggested as they passed a fenced field with half a dozen of mares grazing, just west of Faversham.

'I have no wish to be hanged, Mr Maywether.'

'At this rate, we won't be in London by Christmas. It would have been quicker to go by way of the Grand Banks.'

'Go on ahead if you wish.'

'And you are certain you have nothing of value to sell, whereby we might buy or hire a mount?'

'You have seen the contents of my purse. Not enough to buy a horse's leg.'

'That's England. The poor get poorer and the rich get richer. Tell me, do you like the cockfight, Mr Cooper?'

'I'll eat a fine capon; don't need to see him get ripped apart.'

'But the cockfight's the place you'll find rich and poor together, the nobleman and the peasant – but never the honest burgher. I went to a fine cockfight at the Isle of Dogs not a month ago. And Arthur Giltspur was there.'

'Arthur Giltspur?' Boltfoot was taken aback.

'Indeed he was. Biggest night of the year it were, bigger than anything at the Smithfield cockpit. Five hundred or more of us, I reckon. Cost half-a-crown to get in if you wanted a pitch anywhere near the pit. Shiploads of beer and sotweed, scores of trulls and every outlaw within fifty miles of London Town. They were all there for the main event, A proud ten-fight battlecock against an eight-cock - England's finest roosters, so they said. Oh, the thrill of it, the smell and the excitement. And Giltspur was there all right, weighed down with a bag of gold to stake on the ten-cock. Five thousand pounds he laid out on his feathered darling that night. Five thousand pounds on a bird!'

'What happened, Mr Maywether?'

'What do you think happened? As soon as I heard the bet had been laid I knew to stake my sovereign on the eight-cock. Do you think the layers were going to pay out on a stake of five thousand pounds? Course they weren't. They fixed it so the eighter won. The ten-cock's spurs were blunted and loosened and he was fed grain to slow him down. Never stood a chance. Cut to pieces. Blood, flesh and feathers spread like straw across the pit.'

'So Arthur Giltspur . . .'

'Lost five thousand pounds in the blink of a chicken's eye.'

Boltfoot listened grimly. The story was revealing. An ox-dray, unladen, drew to a halt at their side a little way along the dusty highway.

Boltfoot and Maywether approached the carter, an old man with thin grey hair and a long beard.

'Good day to you, gentlemen,' the carter said.

'Are we on the right path to London town?'

'You're on the right path to Tenham, where I'm going. Do you want to hop aboard? I can drop you at Hinkley's Mill.'

'How far's Tenham?'

'Two miles.'

Boltfoot and Maywether looked at each other and nodded. An ox-drawn wagon would be scarce faster than their own feet, but it would give them a little respite from the endless miles of walking.

'Trusty and well-beloved . . .'

So began the letter from Mary Queen of Scots to Anthony Babington. It was a deciphered copy of the original encrypted version. Thomas Phelippes, the codebreaker, had drawn a little gallows on the cover.

Walsingham ran his elegant finger along the lines, picking out the passages he wished to read aloud to those present.

'Trusty and well-beloved . . . you must first examine deeply: what forces, as well on foot as on horse, you may raise amongst you all, and what captains you shall appoint for them in every shire . . .' He looked up from the paper. 'That alone must cost the devil her neck, gentlemen. It is proof of hostile intent. Listen carefully as I read on, for you will see that she presumes not merely to accept their plan of insurgency, but to tell them how it would best be organised. She raises herself up as their captain-general.'

So the letter Walsingham sought had indeed come. And with such little delay. How, Shakespeare wondered, had the Scots Queen been so foolish as to commit such words to paper, even in cipher?

Walsingham resumed reading. She demanded details of invasion plans, of munitions, troop numbers, and then came to the heart of the matter: 'By what means do the six gentlemen deliberate to proceed?'

He allowed a smile to pass his brooding features. 'The assassination. You see, she even asks – with no trace of shame or horror – how her cousin is to be killed.' He stabbed the paper again. 'She then demands that the assassins be accompanied by four men to ride with the news of its success to Chartley so that her own freedom may be effected before retaliation can be made. And here . . .' He wagged his finger at the four men listening – Shakespeare, Scudamore, Gifford and Mills – 'And here, gentlemen, she even designs her own escape by one of three means. The first, to sweep her to safety with a force of fifty men while she is out walking. The second, to start a fire in the barns and outbuildings at Chartley so that the guards will run to douse it, leaving her alone to be sprung away. The third, to send in a force hidden in wagons in the early morning like some Trojan horse, to overpower the sentries.'

Shakespeare was watching Gilbert Gifford. The pink pigling's eyes were fixed on the gallows that Phelippes had drawn so triumphantly on the letter.

'Her Majesty,' Walsingham concluded, 'has seen this letter and is deeply shocked. She had always known this Scots cousin to be ungrateful and scheming, but never had she expected to see written in her own words the devilish designs that she intends on her throne and life. She now fears there are courtiers about her willing to carry out this assassination and so has asked Mr Phelippes to add a postscript to the Scots Queen's letter asking the names of the would-be murderers, which he is now engaged upon. The letter will be ready by noon tomorrow, at which time you, Mr Gifford, will take it personally to Babington.'

Gifford nodded, but said nothing.

Walsingham turned to the others and continued his instructions. 'Her Majesty also demands that our name be kept from the warrants of arrest when at last they are issued, and so you will use the name of the High Admiral, Howard of Effingham, in all such matters. And remember, there is but one plot, the plot of Babington and the Queen of Scots to destroy this realm. There must be no confusion about this.' He folded the paper.

One plot. Would the world believe that? There were clearly two plots here: one by Babington and Mary to usurp Elizabeth, the other by Walsingham and his men to have Mary's head. They were like two briar stems, intertwined and sharp with thorns. But that was not for John Shakespeare to say. Let others deduce what they may.

'Well, gentlemen, I think we have succeeded,' Walsingham concluded. 'All that we now await is a reply to the postscript, with the names of the assassins. And then we round them up and allow the courts and the headsmen to deal with the rest. God speed your efforts. You have done well.'

And so saying, he swept from the room, with Scudamore in his wake, leaving Shakespeare no time to beg for a decision on a warrant to enter Giltspur House.

'I think a night with the Smith sisters is called for, Mr Gilbert, to celebrate your remarkable success in bringing this episode to a satisfactory conclusion.'

'Thank you, Mr Shakespeare. My loins cry out for their tender ministrations.'

'Then I shall see you at the Holborn house at seven o'clock.'

Shakespeare gripped Gifford's pink hand and noted that it was sweating. It occurred to him that it would be well to stay with the man.

'I have had another thought, Mr Gifford. Come to Westminster with me. We will seek out the sisters together.'

'You led me to believe that such a thing was impossible.'

'Times change.'

'You think me most wondrous gullible! I know you, Shakespeare – and I know Mr Secretary. No, no, I will not come with you. Let us stay with the system we have used thus far. It has worked well, has it not? I will prepare myself for the delight of their company. You go to them alone, and I will see you at the Holborn house at seven.'

Shakespeare was still clutching the sweaty pink hand, as though by holding it he would keep Gilbert Gifford from fleeing. Of a sudden, he let it go and it flopped like a falling bird. 'Until later, Mr Gifford.'

'Indeed. Farewell, sir.'

Shakespeare knew that he had lost him and there was nothing he could do. The gallows on the letter had sealed his decision. Yes, he could use one of Mr Mills's hired men to follow him, but what was the point? If Gifford had to be stopped from fleeing forcibly then he would not cooperate anyway. Nor did Shakespeare altogether blame the man. He had done good service, but he was afraid. He knew that the culmination of this enterprise was going to be a storm of blood, and that no one could tell who would be washed away in the cataract.

Chapter 39

ANTHONY BABINGTON WAS at The Garden, the London home of his good friend Robin Poley, just by Bishopsgate. They had dined at the Castle tavern, by the Royal Exchange, with Ballard and others. There had been arguments; none of them was clear what to do, what step to take next.

The letter from Mary had been delivered to Babington at his Hern's Rents lodgings by a blue-coated serving man. When questioned as to who he was and who had sent him, he made no reply. He merely bowed his head and departed.

What were they to do about the letter? The first thing after it was deciphered and read was to burn it. The flames had leapt and they seemed to see their hopes fade and die in its black smoke. Now what? How were they to proceed? How do you set a date for an assassination?

The Queen of Scots had asked for the names of the assassins. It was a strange, worrying request.

Babington had conveyed the contents of her letter to Ballard, Savage and the others. He had hoped for a decision from Ballard; he, after all, was the priest, the prime mover in their great endeavour. But Ballard had merely suggested that he say a mass and that they seek divine guidance.

And so the men at the Castle all looked to Babington for leadership. In its absence, the arguments raged: to kill the

Queen or abduct her? To support the foreign invaders or to resist? None could agree on anything.

Dominic de Warre was most vocal and fervent. He raged against the tyranny and demanded they all lay their lives on the line to do for 'the wicked few who bring our land to pain and ruin'.

Babington had tried to bring order to the motley band. He said it was quite clear what was required – and what was promised. The case for the killing of Elizabeth was made; the greatest doctors in the Church had agreed to its legality. And now, most important of all, Mary had given her seal of approval. She was their true Queen; they must obey her. As for the planned invasion by France and Spain, he could understand why some men had doubts, yet without such assistance their uprising was doomed.

Now here he was at Robin Poley's beautiful house. The Garden. It was well named; the walled garden was large and rich with the scents of thyme and lavender. Apricots and apples made their slow journey towards ripeness. Bees and butterflies sucked the nectar from the flowers.

Here, for a while at least, he could find peace and comfort.

Babington would be happy to stay here for ever with this man, his boon friend. He was more of a companion than Margaret, his wife of six years, had ever been or could ever be. If only sweet Robin had been a woman, how happy they would have been.

The blue-coated serving man had come again last night. Here, to Robin Poley's home, without explanation of how he knew where Babington might be.

'I am instructed to ask whether you have a reply, Mr Babington?'

'Who has sent you?'

'Those are my instructions, sir.' He had bowed.

Babington had hesitated. This was certainly the same man who had brought the letter from Mary. It must follow that he was equipped to deliver a letter to her.

'I . . . I have not finished writing my reply.'

'Shall I return in the morning?'

'No . . . yes. Yes, I have something for you.' He *had* written a reply. Not finished, perhaps, but the salient points were there. 'But I must date and sign it.'

'Very good, sir. Then I shall wait.'

Babington had left the bluecoat at the door and disappeared into the house. Poley had looked at him questioningly, but he said nothing. He took the incomplete letter from its hiding place and scrawled the date upon it. *London this third of August 1586.*

The letter told of Maude's treachery while in the company of Ballard, it spoke of the grave danger the conspirators now faced, but then it mellowed into soft, reassuring words that all would, indeed, be well, for God was on their side.

We have vowed and we will perform or die. There, it was said. He had made a vow, just as Goodfellow Savage had made a vow. Vows that could not be undone.

Did he believe any of these words? He folded the paper and sealed it, then returned to the front door. The bluecoat stood, impassive, and took the proffered letter. Without another word, he bowed again and departed into the night.

It was morning now. A glorious summer's morning; soon the August winds would come. How fleeting brief were these golden days.

He reclined in Poley's feather bed. Robin had already thrown open the shutters so that sunlight spread across the linen sheets.

Perhaps he and Robin could still leave the country. Slip aboard a fisher's boat for a sovereign or two. They would be able to take little money, but they could seek out a monastery and live out their days together in the chapel and the gardens. This place of Robin's had the feel of a monastery garden. Through the bedchamber window, he imbibed its scents and heard the song of the thrush and the blackbird. And then another sound – footsteps on the path, followed by voices, ones that he knew: John Ballard talking with Robin Poley.

Babington stayed in bed. He had no wish to talk with Ballard. No one called him Captain Fortescue any more. What was the point when all the Pope's White Sons knew him as a priest, not a soldier? As for talking with him, there had been too much of that already. *Endless* talking!

There was yet another sound: the clattering of arms and the shouting of men. Babington froze with horror, then slid beneath the bedclothes like a child hiding from its nurse, knowing that he would be found. So this was it; this was how it happened. The pursuivants had come for him. He tried to lie still and silent, his head hidden, but his heart pounded like a hunted stag's and he knew it must give him away.

There was bellowing, a shout from Ballard, then the stamping of feet, moving away from the house.

He waited beneath the bedclothes for two minutes, five minutes, all the time expecting the sound of breaking furniture and stoved-in panelling. That was how these pursuivants worked. They broke apart property as well as lives in their hunt for priests and forbidden books.

The door opened and he could not suppress a groan.

'Ballard is taken!' It was Robin Poley.

Babington pushed back the bedding and looked at his friend with wide, questioning eyes.

'Pursuivants?'

'Sent by warrant of the Lord High Admiral. They have taken Ballard at the point of a sword.'

'And they are gone, you say?'

'Gone.'

'What about you? Why did they not take you, Robin?'

'I hid behind the privy and watched them. There were six of them. I could do nothing to help him.'

'We are no longer safe.'

Poley smiled. 'That is not so. This was not Mr Secretary's work. I am sure he still means to deal honourably with you and afford you your pass into foreign lands. The pursuivants called Father Ballard *priest*. I think he was taken for that alone, not for his part in your enterprise, Anthony. We are both still safe.'

'Thanks be to God,' Babington said, but without conviction.

'I will go to Richmond this day and crave an audience with Mr Secretary. It may be he still desires you to go to France. It may be that I can persuade him to have Father Ballard set free.'

Babington sprang from the bed with the energy of a newborn lamb, as though the languor of the past moments had been sloughed off like a good night's sleep. 'Enough of talk. Enough of Walsingham and his false promises. They are attacking us, Robin, and so we have but one course of action left to us. We must attack them back.'

He strapped on his sword belt, embraced his friend and kissed him. He knew what he had to do. It was all clear now. There was no time to lose. 'Go, then, Robin,' he said. 'Go to court. See what can be done for Father Ballard, though I fear the worst for him.'

'Farewell, Anthony.'

Babington gave Poley one last kiss and set off walking down the path, then broke into a run with his boy Job trailing in his wake. First he must find Chidiock Tichbourne and Tom Salisbury. They, surely, were the truest of friends and the most dependable of men. They must set off for Chartley without delay to find some way of securing Mary's freedom.

Chidiock was not at his lodgings, so he tried Mane's barber shop where they often met. Mane shook his head. 'I heard he was kicked by a horse and was carried to St Bartholomew's for a splint. He would have done better to come here, for I can set a bone as well as any man.'

Babington groaned with frustration and set off at a loping run westwards. He was about to go into Bart's when he spotted Tichbourne sitting against a wall of the hospital, smoking a pipe. His left leg was stretched out before him

'Chidiock, what has happened to you?'

'Maggot of a horse kicked my shin.'

'Is it broken?'

'No, but I can scarce hobble, let alone walk.'

'Can you ride?'

'No distance.'

'Chidiock, this is bad. I had wanted you to ride for Chartley with Tom Salisbury. We must act now or be for ever damned. Father Ballard has been taken. He will talk under torture – and then they will come for us all. We must either fight or flee.'

Tichbourne drew a lungful of smoke from his pipe, then blew it out. 'Well, I can do neither. I am just trying to drag myself home, yard by yard.'

Babington stared at his friend in disbelief. Then he knelt down at his side and tried to push his hands under his arms. 'I will carry you.'

'Leave me. I will only serve to slow you down.'

'I cannot leave a friend.'

'Go, Anthony. With God's grace, I will be well in time. Lame but limping, perhaps.'

Babington nodded. Yes, Chidiock was right.

'Have you been to Hern's Rents this morning, Anthony?'

'No.'

'Then do not go there. It is watched. Before my injury, I was on my way to you when I saw two men in the shadows and walked on.'

So nowhere was safe. They knew of Poley's house, for they had taken Ballard there. Babington clasped Tichbourne's beloved face in his hands and kissed his forehead. They had been on so many journeys and adventures together, across France and England. And now it was all going to end in horror. '*Dominus vobiscum*, dearest Chidiock.'

'God go with you, too, Anthony.'

Babington's aunt, Lady Darcy, pushed her maidservant out of the way and tugged her nephew into the hall of her sumptuous house. 'Come in, dear Anthony, come in.'

He kissed her peremptorily, then gazed about the dark pan-elled room with hunted eyes. With his hand he waved the maidservant away and she scurried from the room.

'What is it?' his aunt demanded when they were alone.

'We are discovered. I no longer know what to do. Perhaps if I were to stay here . . .'

'You sound most agitated. Calm yourself. Tell me all that has happened.'

He sighed, then slumped onto a settle by the window. 'Yes, I will tell you.'

His aunt listened in silence. She was a woman of fifty years with greying hair and the sharp, defiant air of certain women of the gentry and nobility who looked with undisguised scorn on any who thought to embrace England's new faith. 'You must steel yourself, Anthony,' she said at last.

'But what should I do?'

'You must do what you have planned all along. You must play your part in deposing this usurper queen and her devilish acolytes and pseudo-bishops – and you must raise Queen Mary to her proper place.'

'But—'

'Only then will you restore this family to its heights among the greatest in the land. Did your great-grandfather not attend on Henry the Eighth at the Field of the Cloth of Gold? He had Darcy courage. Now you must show *your* mettle.'

'But, Aunt, you know what became of him. Lopped at Tower Hill.'

'In defence of his faith. So must you defend the faith, though it cost you your life. Do not shirk.'

Babington was no longer listening. He had known all along what she would say. Great-grandfather had been executed for his part in the Pilgrimage of Grace – the northern rebellion against King Henry's assault on the Roman religion – and so the same was expected of him. It was the Darcy way. And, through his mother, Babington was a Darcy by another name.

'I know not who to trust.'

'Trust in God. Trust in your great-grandfather.'

Old Lord Darcy, whose head was planted on a pike at the southern end of London Bridge. He might have been a saint for all the talk of him since the day Babington was born. The first words he remembered from the age of three or four were his mother's refrain: *You are a Darcy, Anthony. You must not allow Great-grandfather's death to have been in vain.*

They were the words that had brought him to this pass. There were times he would have liked to have wielded the axe himself, so sick was he of the family's beatification of a man he had never even met.

His aunt was still talking. Her tongue so sharp and precise she could slice bacon with it.

'Send your man to court with his pistol and you go to Chartley. If there were but two of you, it could be done.'

'Savage? I am sure I can trust Goodfellow not to betray us – but will he do the deed? And what of Gifford? What manner of man is he? He was at Rheims, ordained deacon. Surely he must be true. John Shakespeare? No, I do not trust him. Too close to Walsingham. Poley was right; they should never have had anything to do with a man like that. Oh, but Shakespeare had seemed useful at the time, bringing tidbits of information from the very office of the devil. And what of sweet Robin himself? Some say he is sly, but I must trust him for he has my love. What of Ballard?'

'Anthony, you are babbling. I know none of these names.'

'Ballard. Why did he ever come to me with this plot? Why did I ever listen, for now I am damned; and I have damned my beloved friends. Without Ballard I would have lived my life in quiet comfort. Then there was Ballard's friend Maude. Yet another traitor to our cause. Aunt, I believe there is no man I can trust. This was always Walsingham's plot, not ours. He owned us and used us for his foul purpose. To what ends? Oh sweet Mary of Scots, I fear I know what ends . . .'

His aunt slapped his face. Hard. 'Are you a man, Anthony? Be a man.'

Babington held his face where her palm had stung him. He looked into his aunt's cold eyes. She had more courage than he could ever have. But it was not she who would be laid out on the scaffold to have her belly sliced open and her heart torn out.

'I will go now, Aunt. I should not have come.'

As Babington left Lady Darcy's house and walked eastwards past Ely Place, he did not note the two men following him on horseback, at a slow walk.

'He knows not what he does, Mr Shakespeare.'

'He sees danger at every turn, and yet he does not see for want of looking, Mr Scudamore.'

'He is a traitor, yet a man could almost feel sorry for him.'

'Indeed. And yet we have both seen the words he wrote. He would kill Her Majesty, smooth the way for England's enemies to invade and put a foreign princess upon the throne. These are not the words of an innocent.'

Babington, for all his languor, had lethal ambition and ruthless arrogance.

Chapter 40

HOW MANY DO *we have?* Babington was back at Poley's home, though there was no sign of Poley yet. Why had he not returned from court? Even with the long river journey to Richmond he should surely be here.

How many do we have? Babington was scraping names on a sheet of paper, placing forth all those who might be counted on: Tom Salisbury, Chidiock Tichbourne (if his leg were to heal), Goodfellow Savage, Robert Barnwell, Henry Dunn, Edward Windsor, Edward Abingdon, John Travers, John Charnock, Dominic de Warre, Charles Tilney, Edward Jones, Gilbert Gifford, Robin Poley, Robert Gage, Sir Thomas Gerard, Jerome Bellamy, Katherine Bellamy. No, not Mistress Bellamy. This was no work for women.

All had been at the meetings in his rooms and at the tavern feasts. All had heard at least part of the plans. All had agreed that the Queen of Scotland must be set free, but few had spoken of assassination. Indeed, he knew that even Tom Salisbury had great reservations about such a course of action.

He cursed. There were simply not enough committed men. Where was Gifford? Where was Poley and why had he not come home from Richmond? Chidiock was wounded. Edward Windsor was gone to the country. During their meetings, it had seemed there were so many like-minded men willing to lay down their lives for the Holy Father. But now, looking at this scrap of paper, the total seemed paltry.

There was a soft knocking at the door. Babington tensed, then relaxed. Pursuivants did not tap at doors. They hammered them down with battering logs and announced their arrival with shouts and stamping and the clatter of arms.

'Come in. Whoever you are, come in.'

There were two of them. Goodfellow Savage and young Dominic de Warre.

'Thank God. I feared . . .'

'Anthony, we have just heard about Father Ballard.'

'Oh, Goodfellow, Dominic, this is a bad day. Robin has gone to court to find a way to have him released. And yet he has been gone a long time. Perhaps he, too, has been taken.'

'We must act now.' It was de Warre who spoke. 'If we do not take the initiative, we will all die – and for nothing. At least let us bring down the tyrants first.'

'He is right,' Savage said.

'Then we are all agreed.' Babington handed a flagon of brandy to his two visitors. 'Be seated, take the warming spirit, let us discuss our plan.'

'It must be now,' Savage said. 'I will go to Richmond and find her. I am told by our Irish friend, Barnwell, how easily she might be surprised there – that she walks alone and unguarded in the gardens. I will do it though I die in the doing.'

'Will Barnwell join you in the enterprise?'

'He is with his master, the Earl of Kildare. I do not know if we will find him in time.'

'I will go with you,' de Warre said.

Savage gazed at him without expression. 'What use will you be?'

The slender young man shrugged. 'Whatever you wish. You are my captain, so I will do what I am told. I will fire the bullet if you desire, or hold the horses in preparation for your escape. Command me and I will obey.'

'He has courage, Goodfellow. You may need assistance.'

'Very well. Come with me. But first I need weapons; and I need court attire.' He held wide his arms to indicate his poor costume, a tattered remnant of a black suit of clothes begged from a lawyer at the inns of court. 'I will never be allowed near the Queen in this.'

'Is that truly all the apparel you own?'

'I am destitute, Anthony.' All the money from Shakespeare had gone in settling debts.

Babington drank his brandy. 'Stand up, sir.'

Savage stood from the settle and raised himself to his full height. Babington shook his head in despair. 'Clearly, you will fit no clothes of mine.' He wrenched a gold ring from his finger and found a purse, emptying the few gold and silver coins into his palm. 'This is all I have. Take it. Go to Tredger's in Cheapside. He will have something, I am certain. If he demands more than I have given you, charge it to me. What weapons do you need?'

'Two wheel-lock pistols. As small and as finely wrought as possible, for I must needs hide them within a bag or sleeve. They must be of the highest quality, for I will have to be sure that both will fire. If it is to be done, the end must be certain.'

'And do you know where to acquire these dags?'

'Yes, indeed. But the gunsmith will charge a great deal.'

'Then use all the money and my ring to pay for them. Charge the whole of the apparel to my account, though it cost you fifty pounds. It matters not, for if God grants us success, then we will be repaid a thousandfold, both in this world and the next.' He had a sudden thought. 'What of John Charnock? What of Edward Abingdon and Roarer Tilney? Will they join you? It was always supposed to be six, but five will surely suffice. Edward and Charles are members of the Queen's Guard – they must have access to her person.'

Savage looked doubtful.

'Goodfellow?'

'Abingdon and Tilney do not have the mettle for it. If John Charnock can be found, I think he would strike the blow with me, for he is a soldier. Can we find him?'

'He keeps company by St Paul's.'

'I will go,' de Warre said.

'No,' Babington said. 'I will find him. Do you have horses?'

Savage grinned. 'Dominic has a fine mount and I have an old gelding. Long of tooth but he has served me well. In truth he is all my wealth. When he is gone to the knackers, I will have nothing left in the world.'

'Take one of mine for Charnock. If I find him I will send him to you at St Paul's. If he is there, ride with him to Richmond. If not, then do not wait. Go alone. Dispatch her.'

Shakespeare and Scudamore watched Goodfellow Savage and Dominic de Warre depart from The Garden. They now had another horse. That must mean they were expecting a third man to join them or they needed a sumpter to carry equipment.

Within the past hour, word had reached Shakespeare by messenger that it was finally considered that there was no hope Babington would reply to the forged postscript to Mary's letter demanding the names of the would-be assassins. It was almost time to proceed with the arrests.

'I will follow Savage and de Warre,' Scudamore said. 'They know you well. I think there is less chance of them spotting me.'

'No. I will follow them. You stay here with Babington. I think you know what must be done.'

'You are well armed? Savage is dangerous.'

'Well enough.' He felt the weight of a heavy petronel slung along his horse's flank.

Without another word, Shakespeare wheeled his mount and kicked it into a slow walk, following his quarries at a suitable distance as they rode back into the city.

So it was really happening. Savage had steeled himself to carry out his vow. Shakespeare watched Goodfellow and de Warre with increasing dismay as they visited various shops in Cheapside and bartered for fine clothes and weapons. Two small wheel-lock pistols. Shakespeare saw them both, for Savage had them in his hands as he emerged from the shop, before looking around with suspicious, squinting eyes and concealing the weapons beneath his cape.

And then they mounted up and rode for St Paul's, leading the third horse on a long rein. Whoever they were hoping to see was not there. They waited no more than ten minutes before they rode back eastwards, turning south towards London Bridge. He felt certain of their destination; they intended to go south of the river, then take the highway west towards Richmond Castle and a deadly appointment.

Anthony Babington was more scared than he had ever been. The vision of the scaffold and the rope and the knife were too real in his mind. If he closed his eyes, he knew the rope would twist about his neck and the knife would begin its horrible work. He was gasping for air and breathing in blood.

He forced himself to find something to eat. There was bread and cold beef, both of which were so old and dry he could not swallow them. Instead he subsisted on brandy and ale. He was alone in the house for he had already sent Job away, telling him to return to his parents in Surrey and to stay there until he was sent for.

Job was a Catholic boy who might have been happy to join the Pope's White Sons. For his own safety, however, he had never been taken into Babington's confidence. And yet he must have harboured suspicions. Indeed, he must have overheard certain conversations, as must other servants in the employment of Babington's friends.

This was not work for such lowly men. This was work for courtiers and gentlemen. Men born to lead and rule.

There was a tapping at the door. Was Robin back at last? He threw open the door and his heart sank. It was not Poley but one of Mr Secretary's men.

The man bowed. 'John Scudamore, sir.'

'I recognise you, Mr Scudamore. Why are you here?'

'I had hoped to find you, sir.'

'Why here? This is not my home.'

Scudamore did not answer the question. 'I have been sent by Mr Secretary. He fears you might be under a misapprehension concerning the priest Ballard. I have brought a letter from him.'

'What of Mr Poley? Has he been arrested, too? Was it he who told you I was here?'

'I know nothing of Mr Poley,' Scudamore lied. Indeed, he knew all too well that Poley himself had been put in the Tower; Mr Secretary simply did not trust him enough to be at liberty at this most crucial of times. 'As for Ballard, Mr Secretary wishes to make it clear that the man's arrest was none of his doing, that it was effected by Justice Young on a warrant from the Lord High Admiral. Mr Secretary has thus asked me to stay with you, so that you will not be molested by Mr Young. My master is certain that you and he can still trade intelligence to your mutual advantage if you are still of a mind to travel into foreign lands, and if you have information concerning certain men in London.'

Babington smiled through tired eyes. Was there still time to escape to a monastery in the Low Countries or France? Did he believe this man? Not for a moment, but what was he to do, short of killing him? And that might not be so easy; Mr Scudamore, for all his good manners and pleasant smile, was a brutishly powerful fellow, strong-armed and squat, an unquestioning servant and clerk to Walsingham.

It occurred to Babington that he was in a trap and that he must make a move. He was sweating like a frying onion, though the morning was cool. This man Scudamore was not here to save him from Justice Young, but to keep him close-watched. Babington was nothing but a magpie in a cage, kept out in the open to draw others of the flock in to their doom.

'Come, Mr Scudamore, have you eaten? Let us repair to the tavern where I shall buy you the finest links and eggs with plenty of buttered bread and ale.'

'Thank you, Mr Babington. Yes, that seems a fine idea.'

'Then allow me a few minutes to write a letter.' In his heart, he knew he would never return to this house of Robin Poley's. What he did not know was Robin's own heart. It was a matter of unutterable sadness, for he was beginning to suspect the worst.

Shakespeare followed the two riders, lagging behind them at a distance of about a hundred yards. Occasionally, Goodfellow Savage looked around but did not seem to note his pursuer. Suddenly, it occurred to Shakespeare that Savage's eyesight might be a little feeble. Was that, perhaps, the reason he had given up soldiering? Was that the reason he bent so close to the paper while at his law studies?

The highway out of Southwark heading south-west was busy as far as Lambeth, so they had no reason to pick him out from the throng, but then the traffic of horses and wagons grew sparser and he had to take care to remain out of view. His intention was to move in on them on a remote stretch of the path where no innocent passers-by would be injured if it came to gunfire. It was important, too, that they should be going in the direction of Richmond so that he could testify as to their intended destination.

They were close to the Thames, a mile or two before Barn Elms, on the long arc of the river before it angled to the north. In the far distance, an ox-dray lumbered slowly into the haze. This was the moment; there would be none better.

Shakespeare unstrapped the petronel from his horse's flank and loaded it with black powder and a single bullet. He drew a wheel-lock pistol from his belt and loaded that, too, then tucked it back. With the petronel resting across his right thigh, he kicked his horse into a trot.

Savage and de Warre did not turn and spot him until the very last moment, by which time it was too late for them. He had the butt of the petronel against his chest and was pointing it straight at Dominic de Warre's body.

'Rein in, Goodfellow. Do nothing foolish. A movement of my finger will blow Mr de Warre to his death.'

Savage smiled. If he was surprised, he did not show it. They might have been old friends meeting by chance on the highway. 'John Shakespeare. I am pleased it is you. I see you have a fine Spanish petronel. I saw some like it when I served in the Low Countries with Parma. They are reliable and accurate, but inclined to go off. So I beg you, point it at me rather than my friend. If it please you, end my sorrows here and now, for I am sure you will save me much pain.'

'I have not come to kill you, but to prevent you murdering the Queen.'

'She is a tyrant!' The words were shouted by Dominic de

Warre. 'You cannot kill both of us, Shakespeare. One will survive and do for her.' He was reaching for a pistol.

'Tell him to stay his hand, Goodfellow. I have no wish to kill a boy.'

Savage nodded to de Warre. 'Hand him the pistol, Dominic.'

'No! I am man enough to kill – and die if necessary.'

Savage reached over and, without ceremony, wrenched the pistol from de Warre's hand as he pulled it from his belt. He turned it around in his hand so that he was clasping the muzzle, and proffered the handle to Shakespeare. 'It is not even loaded, John. My young friend is a little too eager for martyrdom.'

Shakespeare took the weapon. 'Wheel your horses. I am taking you back to London.'

'I say again, shoot me here. It will be a kindness, for you know what is stored up for me. You would do as much for a dog.'

'I cannot shoot you. In the name of the Father – both of Catholic and Protestant alike – I swear I do not want this. I would let you go, if you would only let me. I would even give your horse a slap, point it southwards and send it galloping for the coast so that you could take boat to France. I would do this with a glad heart if only you would pledge to me that you will desist from your wicked design.'

'Wicked design?' Savage emitted a despairing sigh. 'The greatest doctors of the Church have told me that her death would be God's work. I cannot make such a pledge to you, John. A vow to God cannot be undone by a pledge to man.'

'Then I have one more offer for you.'

'Name it.'

Shakespeare jabbed the petronel in the direction of de Warre. 'I will allow *him* to go free. But you must come with me, Goodfellow. Come without dissent or fight. Ride with me unbound. Do this and the boy goes free. He is no Pope's

White Son. We both know it. He fights injustice, nothing more. And I confess that in many ways I am as one with him.'

Savage turned to the boy. 'Dominic?'

'Where you go, I go.'

'No, if you love me you will stay alive. You say you are obedient, in which case do as I say.'

'Go to your home in the country,' Shakespeare said. 'Far from London – and do not stir from there for a year.'

'They will find me.'

'Will they, John?'

Shakespeare was not at all certain how this would work. Other men had seen Dominic with the Pope's White Sons. Yet somehow he would have to be protected, even if he had to go down on his knees and kiss Mr Secretary's feet in supplication. He nodded. 'I give you my word. If Dominic turns now and rides north, he will be safe. This is my vow to you, Goodfellow.'

'Is this well with you, Mr de Warre?'

'No.'

'And if I say you *must* do it?'

'I entreat you not to say it.'

'I say it: you *must* go.'

'You are a cruel master, Goodfellow Savage.'

'Kiss me farewell.'

'It cuts me to the heart to leave you.'

'It would cut me deeper if you were to stay.'

De Warre looked longingly at Savage, like a puppy turned out from the warmth of the kitchen on a bitter winter's day. At last he leant across and embraced Savage. 'You are a man among men, Goodfellow. I will pray for you and remember you always.'

'This is my journey, not yours.' He pulled at his reins to create distance between his horse and de Warre's.

Shakespeare handed the boy his unloaded pistol. 'Take this

– and go. And when next you see your stepfather, take him in your arms. For he loves you as though you were his flesh and blood. One day you will know how much.'

Shakespeare and Savage watched as the boy rode off into the distance, northwards, away from Richmond and London.

'Thank you. You are a fine friend, John.' He patted his horse's neck. 'Here. It would please me if you were to have my horse. I bequeath it to you.'

'Do you have no kin?'

'None.'

'You should have stayed a soldier, Goodfellow.' Shakespeare tilted his chin towards Savage's garish and ill-fitting court clothes of blue and yellow. 'I am certain steel armour suits you better than satin.'

'This? It was acquired in great haste.'

'Come, let us ride.'

As he spoke, they both turned and saw a rising mantle of dust along the highway to the east. A large band of riders was coming their way, at speed. And at their head was Richard Topcliffe, his white hair billowing in the wind.

Chapter 41

THE PURSUIVANTS CAME to a juddering halt on the highway. There were twenty men, all attired in black leather jerkins, complete with the Queen's escutcheon, just as Walsingham had ordered. Their horses were flecked with foaming sweat, their faces coated with dust.

Topcliffe drew his sword, rested it across his lap and urged his horse forward until its head was beside the head of Shakespeare's mount, their breaths mingling. He gazed first at Savage, then at Shakespeare.

'Hand over your weapons or die here like dogs.' He wiped his sleeve across his besmirched face, turning his head sharply.

'I do not need you, Topcliffe. This man is arrested and is now under my charge. I have his pistols already.'

Topcliffe raised his arm as a signal to the men behind him. They all drew their own weapons, swords and pistols. 'Your weapons, Shakespeare.'

'What is this?'

'Your weapons. All of them. I will not ask again.'

Shakespeare suddenly understood. 'This is madness. You will not get away with it.'

Topcliffe laughed with scorn. 'When you are pacing your cell, waiting to die a traitor's death, I will be safely abed, sleeping as sound as a newborn, knowing that I have done my duty by God and Her Majesty.' He raised his hand again and the pursuivants began to move forward, waiting for the hand to drop as a signal to fire their pistols.

Shakespeare realised all too clearly that Topcliffe would do it. He could kill both men here and now and he would get away with it. To survive, Shakespeare could neither fight these men, nor defy them. He threw the petronel and the pistols to the ground, and then the swords.

'There, grovel for them.'

Topcliffe gestured to five of his men, who immediately dismounted. One of them began gathering up the array of firearms and blades while the others wrenched both Shakespeare and Savage from their saddles and forced them to their knees, with their hands on their heads.

'Where's the other one, Shakespeare?'

'What are you talking about?'

'Savage was with another – a young one. You followed them. Did you think you were not watched? Did you think we would not discover your foul plan to murder the Queen?'

'There was no one. Savage alone had the plan and I captured him. He is *my* prisoner.'

'Bind them across their horses,' Topcliffe ordered, then waved two men forward. 'Tom, Jacob, you carry on along the highway towards Richmond. Go at speed. If the young one is there, arrest him or kill him. I care not which. It is these two I most want for questioning.' He pointed his sword at Shakespeare and Savage. 'Let us see how they enjoy my entertainment in the Tower. I am sure we shall have them dancing like bears for our pleasure.'

'Mr Secretary will not let you get away with this.' Even as he said the words, his hands were being tied with thin cord that bit into his wrists, as were Savage's.

'And how, pray, will he know of it?'

'God damn your stinking hide to hell, Topcliffe.'

Topcliffe laughed again, then leant from the saddle so that his mouth was close to Shakespeare and his fetid breath assailed his nostrils. 'I have fine news for you. Your murdering whore is in custody, awaiting the hangman in short order.'

Shakespeare's blood ran cold. He tried to get up, but was instantly tripped and his captors set to work binding his feet.

'Indeed, I am led to believe she gave herself up. Walked all alone to Richard Young's house and turned herself over to his mercy. But that will not save her; no soft womanly entreaties or feigned remorse will save her neck.'

'And if she is innocent?'

'Innocent? She is as guilty as you, and you will both die. You are an accessory to murder and a traitor. The company you keep is all the evidence needed. Indeed, the judge may have to invent a new form of execution to reflect the depravity of your crimes.' Topcliffe had his silver-tipped blackthorn stick strapped to the horse's flank. He pulled it out and jabbed at the silent figure of Goodfellow Savage. 'Your friend is very quiet, Shakespeare. He won't be so quiet when I burn him with irons.'

Anthony Babington scraped his knife across the trencher, pushing his food to the side. He had eaten almost nothing. John Scudamore, meanwhile was eating with great relish. He cut an enormous chunk of pork, wrapped it in a hunk of buttered bread, then dunked it into the middle of a fried duck's egg, so that the yolk burst forth like a golden sun and covered the bread. He forced the whole into his mouth and chewed with enthusiasm.

'This is fine fare,' he tried to say, then took a sup of ale to wash the mouthful down. 'I say this is fine fare, Mr Babington.'

'I have no appetite.'

'So I see. Perhaps you would allow me to finish your food for you.' He was sitting opposite Babington in a small booth and pulled the trencher towards him and piled the food on top of his own. 'It would be a crime to waste such fare, for it will only go as fodder for pigs or dogs if I do not eat it.'

The tavern was almost empty. This was a working day. Scudamore tucked into Babington's meal, looking at him occasionally with what he clearly intended as a reassuring smile, but saying little.

The reassuring smiles did nothing for Babington, who was as tense as a line with a trout on the hook. He was horribly aware that *he* was the catch. He leant back. His sword-belt and cape were slung casually over the back of his chair.

The terror was worse here, in this mundane place in the company of this pleasant, ravenous man. The visions of blood were more real now; he saw his own blood washing into the earth but also that of his friends – Tom Salisbury, Chidiock Tichbourne and the rest.

What had he done? Oh dear God, what had he done to them? Neither man had been a willing accomplice when first he mooted Ballard's deadly schemes. Tom would never have become involved in such things without his insistent urgings. And now poor Tom was to die, as were they all.

And yet, surely there must still be hope of escape.

The tavern door opened and Scudamore looked up and nodded. Babington turned. He thought he recognised the newcomer from court, but he was not sure. He was tall and bent and dressed in the sober attire of one of Walsingham's men. Without a word or other acknowledgement of Babington's presence he walked up to Scudamore and handed him a sealed note.

'Thank you, Mr Mills.'

'My pleasure, Mr Scudamore.'

'Will you have some ale with us?'

'Indeed not, I must be away. Good day to you.' He departed without another word.

Babington watched as Scudamore took his dagger and sliced open the seal on the note. Trying not to make himself obvious, he strained to read the words upside down. He had to stifle a gasp. There was his own name. And another word: *arrest*. Scudamore had been ordered to arrest him.

Babington stood up. 'This was my idea, Mr Scudamore, so I shall pay the shot.'

Scudamore merely grunted. He was reading the note.

Without touching either his sword or cape, which he left slung across the back of his chair, Babington strolled towards the counter to pay the reckoning. He asked the sum, then handed over a half-crown. He noted that his hands were shaking. 'Keep the small coins, Master landlord.'

'Thank you, sir.'

Babington glanced back at Scudamore. He was still engrossed in the note. As silently as possible he opened the door, stepped outside, and began to run, harder and faster than he had ever run before.

The journey to the Tower was long and exhausting. Strapped face down over the barrel of his horse, the pressure of the constant movement of the animal along the bumpy highway continually knocked the breath from Shakespeare's lungs.

He was desperately fearful for Kat. If she was now in custody, he knew there would be little delay before her trial and execution. Somehow he needed to find the proof of her innocence at great speed. And he could not do that incarcerated in a cell. Even a day's delay could prove fatal to her.

As he was being unstrapped from the horse, he looked up at

the bleak, impregnable walls of the Tower and its mass of turrets. This *notorious and doleful place*, the young Princess Elizabeth had called it when she was brought here one wet and miserable day thirty-three years earlier on the orders of her sister Queen Mary.

Notorious and doleful. Though the day was warm, Shakespeare shivered with foreboding.

He and Savage stood side by side at the gate as they prepared to be received into the custody of the Tower warders. Shakespeare tried to protest, but the chief warder merely said, 'Save it for your examination.' He turned to Topcliffe, who was still mounted. 'I am uncertain how to proceed, Mr Topcliffe. We have orders that Savage is to be taken to Ely Place for his interrogation. They are being sent to many different gaols and great houses in the first instance.' He indicated Shakespeare. 'I have no orders regarding this prisoner.'

'This is a most notorious conspirator and spy, sent by the Antichrist. You will find accommodation for him here before the Council decides how to proceed with him. As for Savage, you will depute a well-armed squadron to remove him to Ely Place, if that is what is required. I will be back soon enough.' Wheeling his horse, he pushed the animal into a walk and turned back towards the heart of the city.

The chief warder knew better than to gainsay Topcliffe. He ordered a detachment of men to escort Savage to Ely Place, the home of Sir Christopher Hatton, then he handed Shakespeare into the care of one of his men and he was marched towards the south-east corner of the Tower.

'This will be your home until the trial, Mr Shakespeare,' the warder said as they halted outside one of the turrets, topped by battlements. 'The Salt Tower. You will be brought ale and some supper before dark and in the morning there will be bread. If you require a bed, then that will be for your friends to provide. Otherwise you will have a scattering of straw on which to recline.'

Shakespeare wished he could have said a proper farewell to Goodfellow Savage, his beloved enemy. He would like to have embraced him, or at least promised to say a prayer, but he knew that any such gesture would be used against them both by Topcliffe.

'Up the stairs, Mr Shakespeare.'

'Can you get word to Sir Francis Walsingham for me?'

'No, sir, I cannot. The instructions from Mr Topcliffe are clear and specific, and accord with the Lieutenant's wishes.'

'I will give you gold.'

'And I will report to the chief warder and Mr Topcliffe that you have attempted to bribe me. I know from experience that that will not sit well with either of them.'

'How then am I to ask my friends for furnishings?'

'That, sir, is not for me to say. I am merely obeying Mr Topcliffe's command.'

'At least talk to the Lieutenant of the Tower. Tell him I am here and that I am an officer in the employment of Walsingham. I am a Queen's man.'

'Indeed, Sir Owen Hopton will already know that you are here. He is expecting the arrival of many others and I don't doubt there will be protests and complaints from all of you.'

Shakespeare's eyes grew accustomed to the gloom. The only light he had in the small room came through arrow slits. The only thing he had to occupy him was trying to decipher the marks in the stone where former prisoners had carved their names or prayers. Many men and, perhaps, women must have spent their last night on earth in this little cell. Their ghosts were all around him, filling the space.

The Salt Tower warder came back soon before dark and

threw down a little straw as promised, then put down a black-jack of ale, along with a platter containing bread and half a pound of cheese. 'You are fortunate to be here rather than the city gaols, for here you will have dinner and supper at the Queen's expense.' He was a man of good humour and he bade Shakespeare goodnight, then left, locking and bolting the door.

Shakespeare drank half the ale and retained the rest, then arranged the straw as best he could as a bed. When darkness came it was all-enveloping, like the darkness falling over England. There was no candle, nor any glimmer of moonlight. He had nothing to do but sleep. But sleep refused to come, and so he was left with his thoughts: the grisly fate awaiting Goodfellow Savage and the other conspirators; the fate of poor Kat and Boltfoot. Never had Shakespeare felt so utterly desolate and despairing. He had failed everyone. At last sleep came, but it was fitful and brought no peace.

He was awoken by the drawing of bolts and the rattling of keys. The door was thrown open. Richard Topcliffe stood in the doorway, his cold face and white hair lit by the guttering light of a torch. He had four men behind him, all bearing torches and swords.

'Get up, Shakespeare. There is something I wish you to witness.'

Shakespeare had to go where he was led, along the lantern-lit passages and well-guarded ginnels of the Tower until at last he came to the Lieutenant's lodgings. He knew the place. It was pleasantly appointed and his hopes leapt at the prospect that the Lieutenant might be about to release him. But the man wasn't there and, instead, he was forced through a concealed doorway into a short subterranean passageway.

They stopped. 'You know where we are now, Shakespeare?' Topcliffe's thin lips were moist with unwholesome pleasure and excitement. 'Directly beneath the White Tower. I am sure you have heard of this chamber.'

The entrance was dark, but as they stepped inside the light of the torches and the addition of light from a cresset of red-hot coals illuminated the immense vaulted chamber. He thought he knew the Tower well enough, for he had been here before to examine prisoners in their cells. But he had never been to these vaults. He knew instantly, however, that this place was the rack room.

As his eyes grew accustomed to the red and black gloom, the sight that greeted him was a scene from the darkest and vilest corners of hell.

The evidence of torture was all around him – instruments of pain were scattered carelessly about. The foulest refinements of torment known to man. Even the Inquisition could boast nothing worse.

To the left stood the rack, its ropes and pulleys vacant and unused. To the right were the manacles, gauntlets of iron that could hold a man suspended from the ceiling for hours on end. Then there were the red-hot irons in the fire that might brand a man, burn his parts into impotence or, when necessary, cauterise wounds. On a table lay a range of fine-honed knives for cutting.

The true obscenity that confronted him was a melding of naked flesh and black iron, in direct line of vision, not ten feet from him. At first he could not comprehend exactly what he was witnessing. A man was on his knees, his body folded like a cat at prayer. Two circular bars of iron enclosed him, meeting above his straining back, holding him down in a most unnatural position, crushing his spine and causing untold pain. How could a man even breathe when pressed so?

Shakespeare gritted his teeth in shock and fury. 'This is a crime against God and man.'

'You talk of crimes against God and man. Have you met Mr Ballard, priest and conspirator, otherwise known as Captain Fortescue? I am sure you know him well, Shakespeare. And I am sure you must know what crimes he had planned – the murder of the Queen and the destruction of England at the hands of the Pope and his blood-soaked demons.'

'You are the devil, Topcliffe. Have you no shame?'

'Say good day to Ballard. He knows *you* well enough. He calls you conspirator and assassin. He has heard you say the Queen must die and the Queen of Scotland must take her place. He is very talkative. Indeed, I would have to cut out his tongue to stop his mouth, so eager is he to tell me everything he knows.'

'What is this wicked engine? I welcome the taking of Ballard as much as you, but I would not treat the lowest of earth's creatures in this way.'

'Have you never seen the Scavenger's Daughter? It is remarkable effective in eliciting information. But not all survive it . . .'

'You will pay for this, Topcliffe. You know well that torture is the last resort and is not permitted without a warrant from the Privy Council.'

Topcliffe held aloft a paper. 'I have it here. Read it yourself. It is clear enough. Ballard is to be examined by all means to reveal everything he knows about the Pope's White Sons and their designs. And he knows a great deal. How much will *you* tell, Shakespeare? The rack or the Scavenger's Daughter – which shall we choose?'

Shakespeare took the warrant. *You shall by virtue hereof cause the prisoner John Ballard to be taken to the Tower and there be put to the rack, manacles or Skevington's Irons and such other torture as is used in that place.* It was genuine, complete with the signatures of three Privy Councillors, Leicester, Burghley and

Hatton, but not Walsingham. Was Mr Secretary still distancing himself from these events? He dropped the warrant to the ground at Topcliffe's feet.

Topcliffe picked it up with a light laugh. 'I expect the warrant for you to be put to the rack shortly. And then the remainder of your friends, when we have discovered them all. Babington and some others are presently cowering in the woods north of Tyburn. There is no way out for the paths are all guarded. The mastiffs will have them soon enough. Others have been taken in the west and messengers have gone forth with names and descriptions into Wales and the north. Your conspiracy is done for and you will all die.'

Shakespeare did not bother to argue. He began to turn away. Topcliffe was well aware that he was a Walsingham man and that he had been working as a spy – but that did not mean he was safe. The worst thing was that every hour he spent imprisoned here was an hour closer to the death of Kat Whetstone for a murder she had not committed.

Topcliffe grasped his shoulder and tried to make him turn back. 'Feast your eyes on the priest. That is what happens to traitors.'

The stench of fear and ordure was in Shakespeare's nostrils. It occurred to him that to be constricted into immobility in such agony must be a hundred times worse than the pillory. He did all in his power to avert his gaze; he could no longer bear to look upon the priest. Topcliffe would not have it. He held his dagger point to Shakespeare's throat and with the other hand pushed his face so that he had to look. Shakespeare closed his eyes. If he died here at the tip of Topcliffe's blade, so be it.

'Smell him, Shakespeare. Smell the fear and the shit. You told me once that torture is worthless because men will say anything when examined in such circumstances. But look on this man. Look on him. He refused to talk, but now he will beg to tell me everything he knows: the name of every papist traitor in England. Nobles, gentry and common men – he will give me names by the dozen. Men and women at court and in the shires. He knows them all and he knows the priests' hidey-holes. Now tell me that torture does not work!'

Chapter 42

Boltfoot Cooper limped to the front door of the house in Seething Lane. It was early morning, not long after dawn, and they had just arrived in London, having walked the last leg through a series of villages along the Kent road overnight. He and Maywether had avoided the obvious route via Deptford and the south bank of the river because they both had their own reasons for wishing not to be seen by other mariners. Too many men would be willing to sell them to Cutting Ball for a few pennies.

As Boltfoot lifted the latch, he was confronted by Jane Cawston. Her eyes widened and the blood seemed to drain from her skin. Her hand went to her mouth.

'Jane . . .'

'Oh, Mr Cooper, sir, you are alive.'

'Do you think so? You may change your mind when you see my blisters.'

'We thought you were dead, sir. You are truly alive, God be blessed.'

God and a little bit of the same cunning that kept me quick when so many others were dying of hunger and disease on Drake's great voyage. 'Yes, God be blessed. And mistress, you will be pleased to call me Boltfoot, for I am no sir, neither to you nor any person living or dead. Now allow me in for I have a mighty hunger and a thirst to match it – and I must talk with Mr Shakespeare without delay.'

'He is not home, sir. I have not seen him in a day and a half.'

'Well, where is he?'

'He went with a man called Scudamore. I believe him to be a gentleman in the employ of the Principal Secretary. They went on horseback and I think they were engaged upon important business of the state. In truth, I am sure of it, but that is all I know.'

'And there has been no word?'

'None. It seems much danger lurks in this household. I never knew such things in all my born days. My family home was always a place of peace and tranquillity.'

'Even with a dozen or so sisters? I cannot believe such a house ever knew peace.' Boltfoot tried to lighten her mood, for he could see she was sore tried. 'And I have another matter to mention.' He moved to one side and an equally worn and tattered man stepped forward. 'I have brought this man with me. He is a seafarer named Mr Maywether and he is to be our guest. I would ask you to make him up the truckle bed in my chamber and find food for us both. We have both been walking all night and I owe him a great debt.'

The man grinned. 'Aye, that he does, mistress. And he can start paying it by giving me the featherbed – while he has the truckle.'

After they had eaten a large breakfast and washed away most of the grime of the long walk, Jane came to the table with her arms outstretched. Boltfoot's caliver and cutlass were laid across them. His tired eyes lit up. 'Where did you find them?'

'A young lady named Bathsheba Cane brought them. She seemed to know all about you.'

'Aye, well, I'll have to thank her, won't I.'

'Indeed, I got the sense she wouldn't mind a visit from you when you have the time.'

Boltfoot grunted and looked away. He didn't need no housemaid telling him what he should and shouldn't do. Without a word, he pulled Maywether up from his chair before he fell asleep in his potage and they both trudged off towards the bedchamber. The prospect of a real mattress and a real bed could not be put off any longer.

Within ten minutes, Jane could hear them both snoring as she cleared away their platters and went about her chores, but then she heard another sound, a light rapping at the front door.

The sound worried her. What was it about this house that every knock at the door made her jump? She smoothed down her linen apron and pulled open the door. The man she knew as Mr Tort stood before her. He did not seem threatening, but he was looking about him like an alarmed rabbit which, in turn, frightened her.

'I am afraid Mr Shakespeare is not here, sir.'

'I know, but he has a man, does he not – a Mr Cooper. Is he here?'

'May I ask why you want him, sir? He is presently indisposed.'

'There is no time for questions. Lives depend on bringing Mr Cooper to me without delay. And that includes your master's life.'

Jane did not move or say anything. She was trying to make sense of the man's words.

'Please, allow me in, mistress, for I fear the house may be watched.'

Jane held open the door yet wider. 'Yes, come in, sir. Forgive me. I will fetch Mr Cooper to you straightway.'

*

Severin Tort was not a man of courage. He had no desire for martyrdom, merely wishing to practise his faith in private and his business as a lawyer in peace. At times recently, he had felt the noose tightening about his neck; such matters as the secrets he held for the Giltspur family, the assistance he had given to the fugitive Katherine Whetstone, could not help a man sleep well at night.

But the greatest danger of all in these days was his Catholicism and his stepson's association with Babington and the rest. That brought them both a great deal too close to the scaffold.

This last night had been the worst. Dominic had come to him in the early evening with the dread news. Shakespeare had arrested Savage but had spared Dominic. The young man had ridden away, but some instinct had made him stop and look back; he had watched from a distance as both Savage and Shakespeare had been taken captive by a band of pursuivants and then carried away strapped across the backs of their horses. Dominic had followed them, unseen, and had watched as John Shakespeare was delivered to the Tower.

What was to be done? His first action was to send Dominic away, telling him that he must do exactly as John Shakespeare had ordered: go to his country estates and remain there a year at least. But what of Shakespeare? He, Tort, could do nothing for him without facing arrest himself. His Catholicism was too well known. It had always been winked at, but it would not remain his own affair long if he attempted to go against Justice Young or Richard Topcliffe. He could not afford to make enemies of such men if he and Dominic wished to stay alive.

Boltfoot was pulling up his hose and trying to adjust his worn and grubby shirt as he limped to the door. He looked at Tort through angry eyes. 'What?' he said.

'Mr Cooper, your master is being held in the Tower. I have no way of helping him.' He said the words blankly, hoping this simple man might understand plain English. He tried to gauge a reaction, gazing at the exhausted face of Shakespeare's man-servant without much hope. What could this poor, lame creature hope to achieve if he, one of the great lawyers of the age, could do nothing?

'The Tower of London? Why is he there?'

'I think he has been taken in error. Beyond that I know not and have no way of finding out without compromising myself, but we must find a way to remove him.'

'How do you know he is there?'

'I cannot say.'

Cooper scratched his head. He was bleary-eyed. Did he understand, Tort wondered, what was being said to him?

'Well the only man who can get him out is Walsingham,' Boltfoot said. 'You should go to him. He will more likely listen to you than me, master. You are an attorney-at-law, are you not?'

Tort shook his head vigorously. 'I would do so, but believe me I cannot. I beg you to trust me, Mr Cooper – there is no one else I can turn to.'

'Trust you, Mr Tort? I do not know you.'

'But you know Katherine Whetstone, I think. Did your master not tell you that I, too, am a friend of hers? It was I who sought his assistance.'

Boltfoot nodded. 'Yes, I do know that.'

'Then I entreat you, do not question me further – but trust me. You must find a way to have your master freed. Katherine Whetstone is now on trial for her life and by day's end will be condemned. I can do nothing more for her. The only slender hope she has is your master.'

Chapter 43

CHURCH BELLS PEALED out across the city. As the news spread, they would ring across villages in the shires. In the gloom of evening, Shakespeare shook hands with the chief warder of the Tower and thanked him for his hospitality.

'I take it you know what the bells signify, Mr Shakespeare?'

'The plot is broken.'

'Aye, they are making arrests hour by hour. I know not how many.'

'There will be many.' Shakespeare gritted his teeth. There would be a great many. He wondered which of the conspirators had been taken so far. And which would escape. Topcliffe had boasted that Babington and others were in the woods north of Tyburn. Had they been captured yet? If not, they would be soon enough; their names were all known and their fates were sealed. The thought gave him no pleasure. The deaths of hapless, foolish young gentlemen should not be the cause of bell-ringing. Even the likely execution of the serpent-like Queen of Scots should not be an occasion for joy; but sadness that it had had to end this way.

Boltfoot walked the horses forward. Shakespeare nodded to him, then allowed the warder to help him into the saddle.

'Where are they, Boltfoot?'

'Newgate, master. Condemned to death by Judge Fleetwood. They will die at dawn.'

'Then let us ride.' He shook the reins and dug his heels into the horse's flanks, urging it into a canter, the bells tolling in his ears like the chimes at the gates of hell.

On every street and corner, townsfolk were gathering and bonfires were lit. The people were drinking and dancing and crying eternal life to England and Elizabeth and death to all papists, Jesuits and traitors. But especially death to the Queen of Scotland. Let demons and devils prod her obscenely with their forks for all eternity. Let her burn for ever.

Shakespeare felt a chill in the air. Summer had fled and even the bonfires could provide no warmth.

At Newgate, they had to wait ten minutes before the keeper came from his supper at the tavern. It was the moment for Shakespeare to hear the full story of what had happened to Boltfoot and how he had managed to walk to freedom from the port of Sandwich in the east of Kent. What mattered most was the vital information about the Giltspur family that Boltfoot had learnt in his conversations with Maywether. Suddenly he understood the motive behind the murder of Nicholas Giltspur.

He thanked Boltfoot. 'We will find the money for Mr Maywether somehow. Fear not.'

'I felt I had no choice but to agree to his terms, master.'

'You did well. And tell me, Boltfoot, did Mr Secretary hesitate before ordering my release from the Tower?'

'A moment or two, perhaps. No more.'

'And did he wish me well?'

'In truth, sir, I cannot recall. But he did tell me to demand of you what had become of Gilbert Gifford.'

Shakespeare smiled to himself. Walsingham would hesitate while he pondered the consequences before freeing his own mother from a gin trap. Well, so be it. Shakespeare would have expected it no other way. As for the pink pigling, Shakespeare had no doubts: Gifford had fled the country at the first sight of Mr Phelippes's ill-advised drawing of a gallows on the letter out of Chartley. The intelligencer-priest, the holy spy, whose double dealing was about to do for Mary Stuart and Anthony Babington, knew all too well how innocence and guilt could become confused at the sharp end of such an endeavour. He had fled to save his skin.

The keeper appeared. As he nodded to his guests some unspecified insect fell from his knotted hair. He picked a piece of food from his beard, put it to his nose, decided against eating it and flicked it to the ground. 'Seems you just can't keep away, Mr Shakespeare. Perhaps you'd like a cell of your own. Take up residence here.'

'I believe you have two prisoners awaiting death.'

'Indeed I do, master, and you're in time to talk to them. They have a few more hours until they are carted to Thames Street.'

'Is that where they are to be hanged?'

'Aye, next the clock, the scene of the crime. I am told the carpenters' work is done. The scaffold is ready. They will die where their victim fell.'

'Take me to them.'

'They're kept separate being of differing sexes. Which do you want first?'

'The woman.'

'Very well. Follow me.' He put his hand up to Boltfoot. 'The cripple stays here with his strange weapons.'

Kat was not shackled. She was in a cell alone and was sitting at a small table with a quill, ink and a blank sheet of paper. She looked up as the door opened and her eyes met Shakespeare's.

'So you have come to say farewell, John. I prayed you would. I have been trying to write you a letter, but no words appear.'

He smiled at her. Never had he seen her so forlorn. Her blue eyes shone in the light of a single candle but they retained little of their vitality, as though she already thought of herself as dead. 'No. I have not come to say farewell but to try to find a way to save you.'

'You were not at Justice Hall, for if you had been you could not possibly believe in my innocence.'

'What happened? Why did you hand yourself in?'

'Won't you at least kiss me?'

He took her face in his hands. Her fair cheeks were cold to the touch. He kissed her and she buried her face in his neck. He stroked her hair.

'Your lips,' she murmured. 'The touch of your tender, familiar lips. They are like life in this place of death. Did you know that I am to hang at dawn?'

'Yes, I knew it.' The words scarce escaped the back of his throat. The mere thought of that soft, slender neck being tightened by rough hemp was an abomination.

'Does the whole world know it then?'

'The streets will be thronged, I fear.' He sighed. 'Why, Kat, why did you come out of hiding? You could have got away. We would have found you a way to safety.'

'I had to try to save Abraham Sorbus. He had done so much for me, keeping me safe. I had to testify on his behalf, but they would not listen.'

'And now you are both condemned.'

'I no longer care, not for myself leastwise. The pain will last a few minutes and then nothing.'

'You must care. You are innocent.'

'Am I? The people do not believe so. They are already

rejoicing. The bells peal and the smell of woodsmoke fills the air. They are already dancing for joy. How they will sing and laugh when they see the unnatural hag, the demon murderess, twisting in the air.'

'The bells and bonfires are not for you. Conspirators have been caught – traitors against the crown. That is why they drink away the night.'

She pulled away from him. 'And yet they will throng the streets for me, too, you say. That girl . . .'

'What happened? I have heard nothing of the court proceedings.'

'Abigail Colton happened. Justice Young brought her forth, though I know not where he found her. He told the court she had been in hiding, fearful for her life, as if I might kill her. She testified against us with lies. She said she had caught us naked in my chamber. Me and Sorbus! No man or woman could believe such a thing of a soul like Sorbus.'

No. Indeed, they could not, thought Shakespeare.

'She described it all in such detail. Our naked flesh, his prancing prick, our moans of pleasure and delight, our tongues and hands – and then the threats against her when we saw her. And none of it true, not a word. Then she said that she had seen me talking with Will Cane, which again was a lie. And so, with Cane's dying confession already before the court, I had no defence.'

'Had you been hiding with Sorbus?'

'He has a small house in Pissing Alley. It is no more than two rooms and a back yard, but he found a way to buy it so that one day he might retire from his employment at Giltspur House. He dreamt of seeing out his days in solitude and peace. No one else knew of the house, so I was safe there. He was a friend to me, but I did for him with my mad notion of using the Si Quis door to communicate with you. It led the pursuivants to him.'

She laughed. 'I would never have believed them possessed of such wit.'

'How did you escape?'

'I had gone to the market. When I returned, I saw that the house was surrounded by pursuivants, and so I walked on. Since then I have lived from day to day, squatting in tenements.'

'Let us move on to other matters, for time is short. Tell me, Kat, what do you know of Arthur Giltspur? Was there ever anything between you?'

She shook her head. 'No. Nothing. Never. Why do you ask this now?'

'Because he killed your husband.'

Kat recoiled. 'No, not Arthur. He loved Nicholas.'

'You know that for certain, do you?'

'Yes, I know him well. He was always pleasant of nature. He could charm the birds from the air.'

'There is another side to him, a merciless, ruthless side.'

'What reason could he have had for murder?'

'Money. It is always money or love, is it not? Did you not know that he liked to gamble?'

'As do many men.'

'Arthur Giltspur gambled vast sums. He threw away his birthright. He was ruined.'

'But he was so rich.'

'He has another life – one which he kept secret from Nick and his noble friends at court. He consorts with outlaws, tricksters and whores, and stakes great quantities of gold. It slipped through his fingers like flour through a sieve.'

'He could not have squandered it *all*, John.

Shakespeare smiled grimly and shook his head. 'He is a man of immense hungers, only one of which is his love of winning at tennis. He gambles at cards and dice, anything. A man named Maywether saw him lose five thousand pounds on a single cockfight. He takes his dangerous pleasures in the dens and bawdy houses east of London, and he always loses. He loses because he does not understand, or does not care, that the games are always stacked against him. He cannot win because when the stakes are high – and they are *very* high when he is involved – he is always dealt a losing hand.'

'I cannot believe it.'

'Each man has a weakness.' A truth he knew instinctively but one that had constantly been reinforced by Sir Francis Walsingham, the relentless spymaster. *Find the weakness, John, then play it.*

'But why kill Nick?'

'There is something else you need to know.' He lowered his voice, certain that the keeper was listening at the door. 'I cannot explain this to you in full, but suffice it to say that the Giltspurs have long been involved in transferring moneys to the Treasury. To cover up his losses, Arthur began skimming gold from these transfers of funds and made forged entries in the black books to conceal his deeds. I believe your husband found out – and confronted his nephew, threatening to cut off his access to the family's riches. That was when Arthur decided to resort to murder. His plan was to silence Nick, inherit the remainder of the estate – and blame you. That is the truth about your charming and pleasant Arthur Giltspur.'

'John, stop, I cannot bear this.'

'But I am certain of it. All I need now is the evidence to prove it.'

'You are torturing me.'

'Torturing you? I would never harm you.'

'Do you not understand? You are giving me hope when I had resigned myself to death. How now am I to get through this night? Every minute of waiting, not knowing whether you will return will be like an eternity in purgatory, not knowing whether I am to be damned or saved . . .'

Abraham Sorbus's last night on earth was a great deal less comfortable than Kat's. He was in Limbo, the lowest pit in Newgate where men facing death spent their final hours in airless squalor.

Shakespeare put a blackjack of ale to the prisoner's parched lips.

Sorbus drank deeply, then gasped. 'Thank you, sir.'

His visitor nodded, trying not to gag at the stench of ordure that assailed him in this filthy place. 'I wish there had been some trust between us sooner, Mr Sorbus. Had you allowed me into Giltspur House when I desired I might have got to the truth long since.'

'I did not know you then. I was trying to protect Katherine. That is why I kept you away.'

'So it was you who helped her flee to safety in the first place?'

'Indeed, I was with poor Mr Nicholas when he was murdered and I heard the accusation against Katherine from the lying mouth of Will Cane. I hastened home to get her away for I knew she would never have a fair trial once she had been accused like that.'

As has since been proved, thought Shakespeare. 'What made you believe she was innocent? Did you have no doubts?'

'I love her like a sister. We became friends the very moment that Mr Nicholas brought her home. I would say we were soulmates, though not in any physical sense. It was the best thing that had happened to Giltspur House in years. She brought life and happiness to the house – and to me. I had been with Mr Nicholas since I was a boy and never knew such contentment. The same was true for my master. I knew by instinct that she was right for him. She loved him, you know. She truly loved him.'

'If you were her friend, as you say, why did she first go to Oswald Redd after the murder?'

'We felt he would be safe for we knew he was still besotted by her. The danger with my poor dwelling was the possibility that someone in Giltspur House might have noted our close-ness and followed me there. Eventually, of course, we made the decision that she should go there after all, for Mr Redd was becoming more captor than saviour.'

Shakespeare drew a powerful breath and proceeded to tell Sorbus all that he knew about Arthur Giltspur and the murder. The condemned man seemed neither disbelieving nor sur-prised. 'I confess I have always had doubts about Mr Arthur. His sybaritic ways offended me. He was a great deal too pleased by fleshly pursuits.'

'Expound, Mr Sorbus. But briefly.'

'Sometimes when he went out he had a habit of dressing in working man's attire: rough hose and hide jerkin. When I asked him about it, he merely laughed and said he liked to study the common sort at close hand. A sciencer's project, he called it.'

'What did you think?'

'I thought he was going whoring among the stews of Southwark. Such practices are common among the sons of the wealthy. They swoon and kiss the hands of gentle-born maid-ens, then go to the whorehouses and sate their lust on the trugs. Courtly clothes merely make them a mark for cutpurses, so they affect labourers' attire – as if that fooled anyone. Likewise gaming. Foolish young men are wont to fritter great fortunes on the turn of a card or the speed of a nag. But Mr Shakespeare, what is to be done? Are Mistress Giltspur and I truly to die in the morning?'

'I pray not. But you must help me. I need to get into Giltspur House. I need to find the black books.'

'That will not be easy.'

'But possible?'

He tried to smile, although the expression seemed more like a rictus of death.

'Well, Mr Sorbus?'

'Yes, I believe there is a way. However I must tell you about the guards. They are not what they seem.'

Chapter 44

S HAKESPEARE AND BOLTFOOT reined in at the beginning of a rough path through the woods. In the distance they could see the faint glow of lantern lights. Above them, the sparkle of stars in a cool, clear sky.

'Is this the place?'

'I believe so, master, though I could not swear to it.'

'It accords with Mr Sorbus's directions, but he only came here the once.'

'We have nothing to lose by finding out.'

Except our lives. 'I can go alone, Boltfoot. You do not need to come with me. He will bear a grudge against you for jumping ship.'

Boltfoot grunted but said nothing. Nor did he make any move to abandon his master.

'Very well. Kick on.'

They rode a hundred yards along the path, but before they came into the clearing four men appeared from the trees, each bearing a petronel.

'Halt,' one said.

Shakespeare and Boltfoot stopped, then held their hands aloft to show themselves to be no threat. 'We mean no harm,' Shakespeare said. 'I come to talk with Mr Ball, for I have a matter of great import to tell him.'

'I know that one.' Another of the men thrust his bearded chin towards Boltfoot. 'He's been here before. We gave him a beating.'

'As I said, we come as friends.'

The man laughed. 'Friends? You don't look like no friends of Mr Ball!'

'Take us to him. Let him decide.'

'As you will, but it's your throats he'll cut. Dismount and follow me.'

'Our horses . . .'

'We'll look after the horses. Fine-looking animals. Might just keep them for ourselves when you're bathing in blood.'

The area around the barn was lit by a hundred lanterns and torches. Wild music drifted out from the great doorway into the night air. Inside, they could see that the cavernous space was filled with light and people. There was laughter and movement, raucous cries of delight and violent, intemperate dancing.

The stench of sweat, beer and tobacco smoke hung in the air like the brimstone fumes of some debauched netherworld.

Shakespeare, held between half a dozen heavily armed guards, looked at Boltfoot in astonishment. His assistant had described this place as it had been in daytime; he had not expected to find it like this. It had the glitter and life of a great hall of the nobility, but there the comparison ended. There was no elegance, no grandeur. The women had the abandon of whores, their flesh exposed to the elements without shame. Many of the men were stripped to the waist, their muscles and scars rippling to the rhythm of the minstrels. No soulful ballads here; this music came from the earth and had the tenor of battle and sex. Who were all these people?

The lead man appeared at the barn doorway, his petronel

pointing down loosely. 'Well, masters, fortune may yet be with you. He is in a fine humour this night and will talk with you.'

'Are you afraid, John Shakespeare?'

They were sitting at a table in a room adjoining the great hall, away from the riotous carousing. Shakespeare had been given to understand that a wedding was being celebrated. It was a little quieter here, but the menace was palpable. This was Cutting Ball's private apartment. More than that, it was the place where he dispensed terror. Shakespeare could sense it in the air; unspeakable things had happened here.

Two men stood behind Cutting Ball. Their bare arms were crossed, bulging snake-scarred muscles that clearly served as their escutcheon or livery, depicting membership of their master's outlaw band.

And yet the strength of their arms and bulging chests seemed as nothing compared to the ox-like power and wolfish barbarity that emanated from the figure of Cutting Ball. He lounged back on a plain-backed chair as though he owned the world and all in it, as though a command to kill would arouse no more emotion in those eyes than an order for another cup of ale. He had clearly been whirling and throwing himself about like the rest of his crew, for his face was dripping in perspiration. He ran a hand through the greying edges of his long hair and, as he did so, the shining snake carved into his sweat-slick arm seemed to writhe like a living python.

'I have heard your reputation, Mr Ball. I also know that you have no desire to enrage Mr Secretary, to which end I have left letters to be delivered to him informing him that I am coming here. These will be delivered should I disappear or should any harm befall me. If I judge correctly, you would not wish to provoke Sir Francis Walsingham.'

'You presume much, Shakespeare. Well, I will hear what you have to say.'

'I want access to Giltspur House.'

'Do you? And what has that to do with me?'

'The chief of guards is your man.' For all he knew, every one of the guards belonged to Cutting Ball. Sorbus had not been certain on this. Shakespeare could not help wondering whether the strongroom holding the Giltspur fortune also held much of Cutting Ball's own ill-gotten gains. But that was not something to refer to here and now.

'Where did you hear this?'

'From the lips of Abraham Sorbus, who now awaits the hangman.'

'Ah yes, Sorbus. I recall the day he came here with a message from his master. Never have I seen such fear in a man's eyes. Well, he is ripe for the noose for he is a sodomite and the woman is a whore. They will be no loss to the world.'

'We are none of us guilt-free,' Shakespeare said, looking Ball directly in the eye. 'But they are innocent of the crime for which they will hang. I must get into the house to discover proof, for I know the name of the true killer: Arthur Giltspur. If I am correct, then he has stolen not just from his own family's coffers but yours, too.'

Ball was silent for a few moments, then he flicked his fingers as a signal to the men behind him. 'Go,' he said. The men bowed to their master and hurried from the room. When the door had been closed, he jutted his forked beard at Shakespeare. 'Continue.'

'He has been skimming vast sums from the money you pay to the Treasury and then tampering with the entries in the black book. Nick Giltspur discovered what was happening and, for his pains, was silenced by his own nephew.'

'What is your evidence?'

'Arthur Giltspur had the motive – he had squandered his great fortune gambling. He had the means – for he must have become acquainted with Will Cane through Cane's association with Abigail Colton, a lady's maid in Giltspur House. And then, when he feared I was beginning to get too close to the truth, he tried to shoot me dead.'

'And you are certain of this?'

'I am staking my life on it by being here.'

Ball took his bollock-dagger from his belt and spun it in his fingers. The blade glittered in the candleglow. He twisted it and turned it, his eyes on it as though he would find answers there. 'Arthur Giltspur, you say. He is a libertine, I grant you.'

'You know him then.'

'I know that he has lost a great deal at the tables. This is true enough. But I had never thought he had the balls to kill. And even if he did the deed, that does not make Sorbus or the woman innocent. Perhaps they were all in it. Perhaps Arthur had his prick up the widow's skirts.'

'I need to find out the truth. I can only do so with your assistance, Mr Ball.'

'If someone has been stealing from me, I deal with it myself.'

'No. I must do it. Otherwise Kat and Sorbus will die. I must find the evidence this night.'

'I care nothing for them. They are fartleberries on my arse. Let them hang.' He began to rise, the discussion over.

'One more moment, if you would, Mr Ball. Let me just say this: the man who ordered the deaths of Kat Giltspur and Abraham Sorbus has also expressed a powerful desire to hang you. So, you see, you do have something in common with the condemned.'

'You mean Recorder Fleetwood. I have heard as much.'

'He tells me he wants you in his courtroom so that he may sentence you to death. It is his life's work.'

'Perhaps I will do for him first.'

'Before then, however, it would be good to thwart him in this case . . . for both our sakes.'

'Indeed, I would see Fleetwood discomfited. No, I would see him *rot*.'

'To help me now would sore vex him.'

Ball tapped the point of the bollock-dagger on the oak table, delineating an image of a noose. 'Very well,' he said. 'I will send my man Wicklow with you. Go into Giltspur House. Find this evidence if it exists. But be very careful; the strong-room is to remain untouched. And after this night, there will be no more cooperation between us, Shakespeare. As for the matter of the crippled cooper . . .' He pointed the dagger at Boltfoot. 'As for this beetle, he has deserted his post aboard the *Falcon*. I saved him once because of your connection to Mr Secretary. Take him with you now, but think on this: I am not inclined to save his skin again.'

Chapter 45

S HAKESPEARE HAD NO idea of the time, only that it was
somewhere between midnight and dawn. No, that was not
entirely true; he had heard the watchman calling the third
hour. He had a *precise* knowledge of the time but could not
bear to admit it to himself, for there was simply not enough of
it. Not enough to do what needed to be done at Giltspur
House, not enough to find a way of securing a stay of
execution.

The ride here had been hectic and perilous along the dark
paths east of London. They had driven their horses hard. Now
they strode to the door of the fortress-like house, where the
guards took one look at Shakespeare's two companions –
Boltfoot and a small, weaselly man named Wicklow – and
stood back, fear in their eyes. It was Wicklow that engendered
the terror. Shakespeare guessed that he was a senior lieutenant
of Cutting Ball and was a great deal more deadly than he
looked. He had been sent not merely to smooth Shakespeare's
passage but to protect Ball's interests and to report back to his
master.

'Mr Shakespeare and Mr Cooper are to be admitted and
have free range of the house, save only the strongroom.'
Wicklow's orders from Cutting Ball had been concise and now
he delivered them with equal sureness.

The guards bowed low and stood aside.

'And you, Mr Wicklow?'

'I will accompany you so that the indoor guards do not bar your way. You have an hour, no more. Those are my instructions.'

He nodded. An hour would be more than enough. If they had found nothing in that time, then Kat and Sorbus were certain to die.

Their boots rang out on the ancient stone floors. Otherwise, the house was silent. At every corner, guards slid from the shadows, weapons at the ready, only to salute and shrink back at the sight of Wicklow.

They went to the old woman's chamber. She was of venerable age, but Shakespeare would waken her nonetheless. He pushed open the door. The room was in darkness so he took a lantern from the wall outside and walked into the familiar room. He held the lantern over the bed.

She seemed so small and insignificant in her sleep. Was this the woman whose wealth had once been almost as great as the Queen of England's, the woman whose beauty had stirred Great Henry? Neither the lantern light nor their footsteps woke her. Shakespeare touched her shoulder. It was cold to the touch. He put the back of his hand to her face: the coldness of death. He felt for a pulse in her neck and found none.

'She's gone, Boltfoot.'

Shakespeare saw two vials on the pillow beside her. They were empty. Beside the bed, her small silver goblet was upended. Perhaps she had finally decided she could no longer bear to outlive those who mattered to her. She had been killed by the very spirit of opium that she believed preserved her; he cursed beneath his breath. There would be no information or evidence from Mistress Joan Giltspur, the grandame of the family and its great corporation of fishing fleets.

How long had she been gone, he wondered? Hours? Days? With her son Nicholas murdered, there was no one left in this house to care whether she was alive or dead.

Shakespeare and Boltfoot searched the room. They delved in coffers, beneath the bed, on shelves and in drawers. It was Boltfoot who spotted the small distinguishing line of the floorboards in the corner furthest from the window. It was a trapdoor set in the floor, but without any handle or grip to raise it. He thrust his dagger blade between the edge of the trap and the rest of the boards. The two-foot-square hatch sprang open. Shakespeare held the lantern above the hole, which was lined in scarlet satin. Two heavy books bound in black leather lay there.

'So she had control of the books.' But they would, of course, have been easily accessible to another when she was in her opium stupors.

Shakespeare pulled them out and flicked through the pages. The books were dense with small script. Masses of figures and words, much of it abbreviated and, possibly, coded. His heart sank. It would take an expert many days to sort out the truth secreted between the covers of these volumes.

They moved on, with Wicklow in close attendance. In the darkness and quietness of the early hours, the house seemed like an anteroom for the shades of death, inhabited by the ghosts of a once-great family, now fallen. From the top of a long wooden staircase, they heard sounds behind a closed door. Shakespeare stopped and looked at Boltfoot. 'That must be Arthur Giltspur's bedchamber. It seems he is both here and awake.' He spoke in a low voice.

'And judging by the voices, master, he is not alone.'

'Mr Wicklow?'

'I will wait down here. This is yours to deal with.'

Shakespeare and Boltfoot began to climb, on their toes,

✢ 406 ✢

trying to remain silent. They were halfway up when the door burst open. Arthur Giltspur stood at the top of the stairs, lit from behind by the flickering glow of two dozen candles.

He was naked, brandishing two wheel-lock pistols, one clasped in each hand.

Boltfoot already had his caliver in his arms, primed. Without a second thought, he raised it and levelled it at Giltspur.

The peace of the night was broken by an explosion, then a second. Smoke engulfed the stairway. As it cleared, they saw that Giltspur was no longer there. He had retreated back into his room. Below them, at the bottom of the stairs, Wicklow was sitting on the floor clutching his chest. Blood was pouring through his fingers.

Shakespeare stepped down to go to the man but Boltfoot took his shoulder. 'Leave him, master. The guards will help him.'

He nodded. 'Did *you* get off a shot?'

'No. They were both his. He'll be reloading.'

'Take him alive. He is worthless dead.'

'I've seen that man before, Mr Shakespeare. He staked a thousand pounds on the throw of a dice that might have killed me.'

Shakespeare had his sword out, the blade honed and lethal. He was moving up the staircase, not knowing what he would meet. Did Giltspur have other pistols loaded? Boltfoot had his own gun square into his shoulder.

Giltspur's chamber door was closed. The air was thick with the stench of burnt blackpowder.

Shakespeare's eyes met Boltfoot's. The first man through the door would be an easy target. He signalled with his hand and Boltfoot backed off, taking a kneeling position, his weapon trained towards the door. Heart beating like the sails of a mill in a gale, Shakespeare lifted the latch and pushed. The door was unlocked and swung open inwards. He flung himself flat back against the jamb, scanning the chamber. He could not see Giltspur. But there were two others there, women, unclothed – and he recognised them instantly.

The Smith sisters were lying nonchalantly across the great tester bed, gazing at Shakespeare as though he were some curiosity that had made an entrance at the Circus Maximus for the delight of a Caesar. One was on her front, resting her chin on her elbows, gazing at him with interest but no fear. The other sprawled on her back across the pillows, her breasts pointing to the ceiling like ripe plums.

'It seems you alarmed our friend,' Beth said in her light, tinkling voice. 'He left clutching his hose and shirt.'

Shakespeare glanced at them, then removed his gaze. He wanted Giltspur. Something caught his eye: a hole in the wainscotting. Two panels had been removed, revealing the opening to a hide or tunnel.

'Stay here, Boltfoot. I'll follow him.'

'He's gone, Mr Shakespeare. Forget him,' the elder of the Smith sisters said, the one lounging back against the pillows. 'Come join us on the bed, for we delight in making men's pistols go bang. Do we not, Beth?'

'Where, oh where, is our little pink pigling?'

Shakespeare strode across to the hole in the wall, his sword in one hand, lantern in the other. He held it into the darkness. A tunnel ran downwards like a chute; he could not tell how far it went. Was it a self-contained priesthole or an escape route? There was nothing for it but to go onwards.

'If you must go, take the caliver, Mr Shakespeare,' Boltfoot said.

'No. I need him alive.' He tilted his head towards the Smith sisters. 'Don't let these two get away, Boltfoot.' Crouching down, he swung himself into the hole feet first and began to slide, like a boy going downhill on a tray on snow. He gathered speed, then stopped as suddenly as he started. He reckoned he had slid down at least thirty feet, which meant he must have descended beyond and below the ground floor. He was underground in some sort of cellar. The air was dank and dusty. He held the lantern aloft and saw that it was a small circular chamber, no more than eight feet in diameter.

Three tunnels led away from the chamber. He muttered an oath. Which way had Giltspur gone in this warren? He held the lantern down to the dusty ground, looking for scuff marks to identify the route taken. But there were marks all around and none was more notable than the others.

All he could do was take one tunnel and see where it led. Crouching down, for the passageway was no more than five feet high, he stepped in and loped along. No time for caution. The tunnel forked after fifteen yards. He took the left way, ran for twenty-five yards more, then reached a bricked-up dead end.

He turned and ran back, taking the other fork. Again it reached a dead end. He had wasted valuable seconds. Panicking now, for time was desperate, he tried another tunnel, which was longer and curved to the right. At the end he spotted a pinpoint of light. He ran faster and finally came to a small door, which had been left ajar.

Shakespeare stepped outside into the night air and tried to gain his bearings. He was in a garden. Ahead of him was a wall with branches splayed across it, all bearing fruit. Beyond the wall he heard a familiar sound – horses whinnying. He had found the back of the stable block. Of course, where else would a fugitive head?

Rounding the wall, he found that he was correct. Two rows of stalls stood on either side of a flagstoned yard. A groom was just closing one of the stable doors.

'Where is he?'

The groom turned with a hand to his chest, as though he had had one shock too many this night. His eyes went to Shakespeare's sword.

'Master?' The groom backed away.

'Mr Giltspur. Where is he?'

'You have just missed him, sir. Rode away not two minutes since.'

'Where? Which direction?'

'Couldn't say, master. Could have gone north or south, east or west. I've no way of knowing. Not my place to inquire.'

Shakespeare stalked past the groom to the gates which led out onto the street. The gate was locked. 'Open this!'

The groom scurried after him with a ring of keys and unlocked the gate. Shakespeare stepped out and looked both ways. There was nothing, no clue as to where he had gone. He threw down the lantern and grasped the groom by the throat. 'You must have seen which way he went – north or south?' The groom was not a big man but nor was he weak. He wrenched himself free and rubbed his throat.

'Well?'

'Master, I know not – and even if I did I would not tell you, for my loyalty lies with Mr Giltspur.'

'How do I return to the house from here?'

'There is a back way.' He tilted his chin towards the garden from which Shakespeare had just come.

'Show me.'

Wicklow was unconscious. An old serving woman was applying bandages and herbs to his wound. A physician had been sent for. There was nothing Shakespeare could do to help, besides which he had other matters to deal with.

Not for the first time in recent days, he felt utter

helplessness. With the flight of Arthur Giltspur all hope had gone. Given time, he might be able to make a case that his shooting of Wicklow was the act of a man with a great deal to hide, but he didn't have time. He might, too, unravel the secrets of the black books which he now clutched. Dawn was approaching. To halt an execution would require nothing less than a confession of guilt by the true murderer or, at the very least, some material evidence, of which there was none.

He returned to Giltspur's bedchamber. The Smith sisters were dressing with nonchalance. They displayed no fear of Boltfoot and his caliver, nor any interest in him, but smiled lewdly at Shakespeare.

'How much do you know?' He was having none of their wiles.

Eliza feigned a puzzled expression. 'We know our trade, Mr Shakespeare, that is all. And we have been plying it.'

'About the murder, the missing money, God damn you.'

'And we know the price of good French brandy,' Beth said.

'Where is he? Where has Giltspur gone?'

'We have no notion. We are night-workers, Mr Shakespeare. We do what is required of us and more and we take our money. We neither ask questions nor wish to know any man's business. If you want to know more, ask his friend.'

'What friend?'

'Why, your paymaster, sir.'

'You mean Walsingham?'

'No, indeed not. We like Mr Secretary. He is an *honest* villain. It is the other one we dislike. To the world, he has the air of a noble but in private he has the evil-smelling ways of a shit-shovelling gong farmer.'

'What other one? Explain. I beg you, help me with this. Lives are at stake.'

'Huckerbee, of course. He is the man to ask. They are as close as fish salted in a barrel.'

Sir Robert Huckerbee. The paymaster, the man who dispensed gold on behalf of Burghley. He collected it, too. Of course. He was the conduit for Cutting Ball's ship tax. Burghley would always keep his own hands clean in such a matter.

That would have placed immense power into the hands of the unpleasant Huckerbee. Enough power for him and Arthur Giltspur to skim money together. Yes, he was in this with Giltspur. So, where was Huckerbee? Perhaps that was where Giltspur had ridden.

The chances were that Huckerbee was at court. He could never be far from his master, Burghley. But the court was now at Richmond in Surrey, a distance of some eleven or twelve miles. If Shakespeare left now . . .

No, it was impossible. He would still have to get powerful evidence and lay it before a senior judge or Privy Councillor and then return to London before the hangman did his dread work. There was nowhere near enough time for that. No man could ride or row that far and be back by dawn.

'This is no help to me,' he muttered angrily.

'We are doing our very best, Mr Shakespeare, but you seem unwilling or unable to listen,' Eliza said.

'Sir Robert Huckerbee is *here*,' her sister said. 'In this house.'

Chapter 46

SHAKESPEARE PUSHED OPEN the door. The chamber was in darkness, but the smoke of snuffed candles hung in the air like a poor man's incense.

He held the lantern aloft and looked around. A large four-poster bed dominated the room and its curtains were drawn. The soft breathing of sleep came from within. Shakespeare gestured to Boltfoot to relight the candles, of which there were ten or more spread around the chamber on table, sill and coffers.

When the chamber was fully lit, he pulled back the bed curtains. A woman lay there alone, beneath the covers, seemingly asleep. She wore no nightcap and her long hair was splayed across the pillows. He could not see her face, for she was on her side, facing away from him. Yet there was something familiar about her.

He touched her shoulder. 'Wake up.'

She groaned groggily and pulled the blankets up to cover herself more. But Shakespeare had already worked out where he had seen her before and knew from the hastily extinguished candles that her sleep was but play-acting.

'Get up, Abigail.'

She moaned again, but Shakespeare ripped back the blankets and sheets. Her body was naked, her pregnant belly swollen. She grasped at the bedclothes to cover herself and Shakespeare did not try to stop her. She huddled back against the head of the bed, her eyes aflame, staring at him with loathing.

'I have come for Huckerbee.'

'He's not here. He went when the shooting started.'

'No, he's here.'

Boltfoot was already searching the room. He opened a coffer and poked around inside amongst the linen, then he looked under the bed but there was nothing save a truckle there. At last he came to a closed cabinet. He looked back at the woman in the bed and saw from her eyes that he had found his quarry. He aimed his caliver at the door and stood back.

'Come out, Sir Robert, you have been discovered.'

For a few moments nothing happened but then the door began to open. The elegant figure of Sir Robert Huckerbee stood there, half clothed, wearing no shirt but only breeches. He had his back to the panelling at the rear of the cabinet. He was a wretched sight.

'With your hands up, step out slowly. No sudden movements. Mr Cooper is a very good shot.'

Huckerbee raised his hands above his head and stepped down from his meagre hiding place. He began to protest in his courtly, languid tones. 'I don't know what any of this is about, Shakespeare. We heard shooting. I hid to protect myself. May I put my hands down now? Your man is frightening me.'

'See if he is armed, Boltfoot.'

Boltfoot moved forward, the caliver still pointing at Huckerbee. With one hand, he patted the man's breeches, then looked at his master and shook his head. 'Nothing.'

'Good. Now you may lower your arms, Sir Robert.'

'You realise of course that this will all be reported to Lord

Burghley and Mr Secretary. Do you really think you can treat me this way? Your career is over, Shakespeare.'

'Speak when spoken to if you hope to live. I know what you and Arthur Giltspur have been doing so do not insult me by denying it. Now, you will write everything you know about the involvement of Arthur Giltspur and this woman in the murder of Mr Nicholas Giltspur, and the reasons for it. You will then come with me to Recorder Fleetwood's house.'

'I will do nothing of the sort.'

Shakespeare found himself laughing, though there was little enough to amuse him with the minutes vanishing like sand through his fingers. 'Or, Sir Robert, I will take you from here to the presence of Mr Cutting Ball and you can face *his* brand of justice, for he does not like to be robbed. You may think you were skimming Treasury money, but I doubt Cutting Ball will see it that way. Nor will he like to hear that his man Wicklow has been shot and may die. The choice is yours – Fleetwood's justice or Ball's.'

Fleetwood's house lay a little west of Aldermanbury at the junction of Foster Lane and Noble Street. The sun was not up but the sky was lightening across the rooftops to the east of town and the early risers were already going about their business, trudging to work, setting up market stalls, preparing for the day ahead. Many others were making their way east – and Shakespeare realised with a shudder that they were seeking a prime spot at a double hanging.

William Fleetwood, Serjeant-at-Law and Recorder of London, was still in a deep sleep when his four visitors arrived. With age, he found it ever harder to shift his grey head from his soft feather bed in the morning and today was no different.

As they waited at the door, Shakespeare could not take his eyes off the sky. It seemed that any moment dawn would break upon them and it would all be over. He knew the way things worked at Newgate; Kat and Sorbus would have eaten their final meal if they had the stomach for it, and would now be bound, standing in the courtyard ready to mount the cart that would haul them to the scaffold.

Here, at the door to the house, Sir Robert Huckerbee, gagged and with hands bound behind his back, stood beside him. Then came Abigail Colton, also bound and gagged. Behind them was Boltfoot, his caliver covering them in case they tried to run.

The maidservant returned to the front door. 'Forgive me, master, we are having difficulty rousing Mr Fleetwood this morning.'

'We're coming in.' He nodded to Boltfoot. 'Take them to the parlour and remove their gags but not their bindings. I will go to Fleetwood.'

He pushed past the flustered maidservant who tried in vain to bar his way into the hall. 'Where is his chamber?'

'Please, master, Mr Fleetwood will brook no disturbance. I will lose my position if I allow you—'

Shakespeare was already moving away. He could hear snoring. *Thunderous snoring. Like a hog in a storm.* Without hesitation he ascended the wooden stairway and pushed open the chamber door. Fleetwood was lying on his back, his head and the top half of his face swathed in a linen nightcap. His mouth was open and his body rose and roared with a great drawing-in of breath. Shakespeare clapped his hands, then leant across the bed and shook the judge by both his shoulders. 'Wake up, sir, wake up. I must talk with you.'

Fleetwood sat upright, scrabbling with his hand to remove the nightcap from his eyes. His mouth, which had closed, fell open again. 'Mr Shakespeare.'

'Your honour, Mr Fleetwood, I beg your forgiveness for this

intrusion, but I crave a most urgent favour of you: an immediate stay of execution for Katherine Giltspur and Abraham Sorbus. They are due to die within minutes.'

The old judge shook his head so violently that his nightcap fell off. 'Impossible. They are guilty. The maid's evidence was conclusive.'

Shakespeare pulled a sheet of paper from his doublet. 'I can prove otherwise. I entreat you, sir, read this: there is no time to lose.'

'Find my spectacles. Where are they? I cannot read a word without them.'

'I have them here, master.' The maidservant had followed Shakespeare to the chamber and now held out the round-framed glasses to Fleetwood. 'They are cleaned and polished, sir.'

Fleetwood pushed the spectacles onto his nose, then flattened the paper and moved his nose to within four inches of it. His head moved from side to side quickly as he scanned the words.

I Robert Huckerbee, knight, do hereby testify that I have information pertaining to the murder of Nicholas Giltspur, gentleman, lately killed by stabbing in Thames Street. It is my certain knowledge that the crime was committed by one Wm Cane at the behest of Arthur Giltspur, gentleman, and that no blame can be attached to the deceased's widow, Katherine Giltspur, nor his steward, Mr Abraham Sorbus. The aforesaid written this day with my right hand, my left upon the Holy Bible.

It was dated and signed. The hand was scratchy and unsteady and there were several blottings.

'Where is Huckerbee now?'

'In your parlour.'

Fleetwood rose from his bed, assisted by Shakespeare with a hand beneath his elbow. 'My quill and ink,' he barked at the maidservant. 'Quickly, girl, quickly. Have them ready in the parlour. And my seal and wax.' He turned to Shakespeare. 'First, I will talk with Sir Robert. Take me to him.'

'Remove his bindings, Mr Shakespeare. And Mistress Colton's. This is most irregular.' He sighed. You make a sorry sight, Sir Robert.'

'Indeed, your honour, but it is none of my doing. I beg you take no notice of that paper in your hand. It was written under duress, at the point of this brute's gun.' He thrust out his chin at Boltfoot and creased his mouth as though indicating something putrid and pleasant.

Neither Shakespeare nor Boltfoot made any move to remove the prisoners' bindings.

'With your hand on the Holy Book?' Fleetwood peered above his spectacles at Huckerbee.

'No, sir, I would not write lies with my hand on the Bible. I wrote that because I was ordered to and would have had my head blown off had I not. This man Shakespeare and his assistant are felons. They should be removed to Newgate forthwith.'

Shakespeare clenched his hands into fists. 'You have seen the paper, Mr Fleetwood. I entreat you – on bended knee if you wish – to sign the stay of execution. If later you have doubts, then it can all be argued before you in your court of law and you can reverse your decision. But for the present, two innocent lives are at stake. If you do not sign the stay now, then your decision is irrevocable.'

Huckerbee gave the judge an unctuous smile. 'Mr Fleetwood, you and I are men of standing. Surely you would not take the word of this common felon above mine. He is the lowest of the low in the service of Mr Secretary.'

Fleetwood did not reply. Instead he turned his gaze to Abigail Colton. 'And you, mistress, what do you have to say?'

'They are liars.' Her countenance, which Shakespeare had once thought comely, was set hard and hostile. She turned her head to one side, refusing to meet the judge's eyes.

'You were most convincing in the courtroom, Mistress Colton.'

'Because I was telling the truth.'

'Did she tell you that she is the paramour of this man Huckerbee, who is himself engaged in a criminal enterprise with Arthur Giltspur – the man who will inherit his family's fortunes now that his uncle is dead and the widow is to hang?' The words ran from Shakespeare's mouth like quicksilver; there was no time for subtle dealing. 'Tell me, Abigail, did your other lover, William Cane, know that you were bedding this man?'

She jerked her face towards him, hatred in her blazing eyes. 'Will Cane? I cared not a jot for him . . .' She stopped, realising she had already said too much. Simply admitting the thing she had denied in court, that she knew Cane, was enough.

Without another word, Fleetwood sat down at the table, his ears deaf to the protestations of Huckerbee and the sobs and howls of Abigail, and scrawled out two notes – one addressed to the keeper of Newgate, the other to the officer in charge of the execution. He then sealed them and handed them to Shakespeare.

'Thank you, Mr Fleetwood.'

'Go. And I will keep these two here under my servants' watchful eyes. God speed, Mr Shakespeare. I fear the sun is up.'

The crowd was dense. They had come out in their thousands, relishing the prospect of the hanging of the dirty, murderous

Giltspur witch and her sordid partner in lust and crime. They had heard she was beautiful and they wanted to see her face. How could a face be both beautiful and evil? Was that the likeness of a succubus?

The execution was to be a grand affair. It would all be the most delightful appetiser for the greater spectacle that was to come: the godly butchery of the plotters who planned to kill the Queen and throw open the ports of England to Spanish men-at-arms.

Shakespeare and Boltfoot had remarkable difficulty driving their horses through the thronged streets. Every street for a quarter-mile was blocked by the press of people and the stalls selling ale and cake, the jugglers, the broadsheet sellers, the cutpurses and minstrels.

He urged his horse on, ruthlessly pushing aside men and women. In his urgency and frustration he lashed at shoulders and backs with his crop. Some men tried to pull him from the saddle, but Boltfoot, just behind his master, held them at bay with the muzzle of his caliver.

Being on horseback, they could see above the heads of the throng. In the distance the crossbar of the scaffold was visible. It was so close, yet still out of reach. From a hundred yards away, they heard a loud gasp from the front rows of the enormous crowd.

Shakespeare's horse was bucking and jinking. It was going to kick someone to death if he carried on. He slid from the saddle and handed the reins to Boltfoot.

'I'll go ahead on foot. Tether them, then follow.'

Though he was tall, he could no longer see above the mass of people. Everyone wanted a better look and they all surged forward. Using elbows and hands he propelled himself through gap after gap. Each gasp of the crowd, each shout sounded like a death knell.

'You, get back.' A thickset man whom he had jostled grabbed his arm and punched the side of his face with venom. Shakespeare took the blow and wrenched his arm free and thrust into a breach between two old women, moving ever onwards, a yard at a time, towards the platform of death.

The two black-hooded figures, both slender and of a size, twisted and turned in the early morning air. Their arms were bound behind their backs, their legs bound at the ankle. The hemp ropes suspending them creaked against the rough wood of the gallows. Was the wind moving them? Were they struggling? Were they alive or dead?

Shakespeare leapt up onto the scaffold. Justice Young stood in his way, his sword drawn and held two-handed, ready to deliver a thrust into the belly or throat of any man who tried to get past. Shakespeare threw the hastily written document at him. 'There's a stay!' Then he brushed him aside as if swatting a fly.

His sword was already drawn. Two guards pounced forward with their halberds to bar his way, but he was too quick. With a mighty slash, he hacked at the rope above the first figure's head. But the cut did not sever the hemp. The fibres were frayed but held the body still. He hacked again. And again. Arms tried to grapple him, but with the strength of a madman he fought them off, drew his dagger and sawed through the remaining fibres. As the figure fell, he tried to break its fall, but stumbled. He watched helpless as the knees cracked into the wood of the scaffold, then the body tumbled forward. No sound came from the lifeless form. He tore at the tight noose, to loosen it. He did not have time to see whether there was any sign of life.

Justice Young was holding his arms. Shakespeare tried to tear himself free. 'God damn you, Young, read the order staying this execution. Help me . . .'

Before he could say more, the butt of a petronel smacked into his chest like a smithy's hammer on the anvil and he was thrown backwards, falling awkwardly against the sharp edge of the scaffold, and then crashing down into the street, head first. Into oblivion.

A buzzard circled high above the verdant countryside. Wafted on the warm air, it rose to ever-increasing heights, its sharp eyes questing for prey on the greensward below. It was looking for mice and shrews and small birds. Had it had but eyes to see, it would have spotted prey of a different nature.

But the raptor had no interest in the carriage of the Queen of Scots that trundled from her prison at Chartley on a three-mile journey towards the deer park of Sir Edward Aston at Tixall.

Like the mouse or shrew, Mary was unaware of the encircling forces that sought her death. She was in holiday mood. Her keeper, Sir Amyas Paulet, had allowed her this rare excursion to join the hunt. She was, too, in remarkably good health, the pain in her legs all but gone and her stoutness reduced by increasing amounts of exercise.

She gazed from the carriage window. In the distance she could see a new building which she was sure must be Tixall Hall, but one of her secretaries put her right. 'It is the new gatehouse, Your Majesty. Note the turrets and cupolas.'

A gatehouse as big as a palace. Her spirits rose. After months of confinement at Chartley, she was at last to enjoy the glittering life to which she was born, even if only for a day. Then she looked to the side. At the edge of the woods, she saw a band of horsemen. At first she thought it must be the Tixall hunt. But they were not attired for the hunt; they were men-at-arms.

She drew a sharp breath and her whole body tensed. Was it true? Was this was the troop of young men come to free her, the one promised by loyal Mr Babington? She tried to count their strength. There were many of them – surely enough to outgun her guards. It was really happening.

There had been so many disappointments in the eighteen years of her captivity, but now at last she could dare believe she was truly to be brought to freedom. More than that; the throne of England was now within her grasp . . . God willing. She put her hands together and intoned a prayer.

The carriage stopped. The horsemen were approaching – fifty strong, in military attire, the horses caparisoned. All were armed with pistols and calivers. She searched for Babington's handsome face; it was not there. Mary Stuart's heart pounded, like the mouse the moment it feels the hawk's talons on its back. The colour drained from her already pallid face.

She opened the carriage door and stepped out. Nearby, just out of earshot, she saw that the captain of the troop of men was conversing with her keeper, the Puritan Sir Amyas Paulet. She began to walk towards them. The captain slid from his horse, bowed low to the Queen of Scots.

'My lady,' he began. Not the *Your Majesty* that her own people would use as a mark of respect. 'My lady, a plot has been uncovered to kill the Queen. I am under orders to take you into custody and await instructions.'

'A conspiracy, Captain? What has this to do with me?'

'I simply obey. You will come with me now.'

Whether she was overcome by a slight fainting fit or whether it was an act of defiance was unclear, but she instantly collapsed to the ground and sat on the grass. 'I will die here. Shoot me if you will.' And then she put her hands together and began to pray.

Did they look like farmworkers? Could five young men, gently born and reared, truly transform themselves into peasants with a change of clothes, rough cutting of hair and the application of walnut juice and dirt to weather their faces?

Anthony Babington had his doubts, but he had no other notion of what to do. His companions – John Charnock, Robert Gage, the Irishman Robert Barnwell and Henry Dunn – looked to him for leadership and so this was his decision. Somehow they would make their way out of this wood, find horses and go their separate ways to the coast where they would try to secure passage to France.

After days without food or shelter, they were in a hayloft beneath the roof of a barn on the estate of the moated manor of Uxendon Hall, home of the Bellamy family. They would find assistance there, for none in England was more true to the old faith than the Bellamys. Henry Dunn had already gone to sound out the family. Babington was certain he would return soon with food and the promise of horses.

He heard a sound outside and signalled with his hand for silence. Peering down to the gaping doorway of the barn, he sighed with relief. It was Henry, and he had two of the Bellamys with him, Bartholomew and Jerome, both of them good Catholics and occasional members of the Pope's White Sons. They were carrying a basket, covered with white linen; so there would be food and ale.

Hope had been in short supply these past few days, sleeping in the bracken, listening for sounds and then hurriedly moving on when they heard the barking of dogs as the searchers mounted their hue and cry. But there was hope now. God and this godly family would save them.

No one was better than Jonas Shoe at watching and waiting. He had been in the woods near Uxendon Hall for five days, observing the comings and goings of the household. And now it had paid off. He allowed himself a smile. A young man poorly disguised as a farmworker, with neither the strength of arm nor the gait of a labourer, had appeared at the back door to the old manor house. Now, an hour later, he had emerged and this time he had two of the young men of the house with him.

It was the easiest thing in the world to follow them, for it did not even seem to occur to them that they were being watched. So here they were at last, walking into the barn. Shoe moved closer and listened. Yes, there were other voices there. With the newcomers, he was certain there were at least six. He had found his quarry. All that remained now was to fetch the pursuivants.

Shoe slipped away into the woods and headed for the eastern highway.

Chapter 47

THE DARK, BROODING face of Sir Francis Walsingham peered closely into Shakespeare's eyes. 'Are you well again, John?'

'Well enough, Sir Francis.'

'Your wounds are healed?'

'I fear it will be some little time before my ribs are fully knitted together. Three of them were broken, as was my collarbone. I keep my chest braced with tight bandages, like a child in swaddling bands.'

'And your head?'

'The fall rendered me unconscious for a minute or two, but there seems to be no further complication, God be thanked.' The physician had said he was fortunate to be alive, that the skull had broken behind the temple when he bounced off the sharp edge of the scaffold onto the hard ground. The blow would have killed many another man. But that was not to be dwelt on; not here, not now. He had already spent too many days and nights recuperating.

'Good.' Walsingham limped away from the object of his concerned inquiries and sat in a straight-backed chair at the end of the table. 'And it is most gracious of you to make the journey here, for I am ailed by another damnable furuncle, and the gout never leaves me. Which is why I cannot travel to London.'

'The trip upriver was a pleasant change from my own sickbed.' Shakespeare smiled at the Principal Secretary, not believing for a moment that he was prevented from travelling to London by a common boil and his new-discovered gout; this was a political absence. He did not wish to be anywhere near the courts of law lest his own part in the Babington affair be suspected.

'You will doubtless have heard of the arrest of Babington and others,' the Principal Secretary continued, as though reading his intelligencer's mind.

He nodded. Yes, he had heard the story of Babington's arrest from Mills who called on him as soon the news came. 'It was my man Shoe as found them,' Mills had said with an unpleasant laugh, his pride all too evident. 'A poacher of men, my Mr Shoe. They had walnut juice on their faces to look like ploughmen!'

Shakespeare had heard, too, of the arrest of the Queen of Scots, though no one seemed clear what would become of her.

And then came the trials of the Pope's White Sons. The verdicts were a foregone conclusion and their executions were imminent. The streets were once again filled with Londoners rejoicing, lighting their bonfires, burning their effigies, drinking themselves insensible.

He put the thought aside. The prospect of all the blood and pain that had already been suffered in the torture chamber and the yet more gruesome spectacle to come seemed mercifully distant in the quiet of Walsingham's dim office at Barn Elms. It had been good to leave London; the celebrations in the streets were hard to endure. The river journey had been a pleasant contrast, reclining in the back of a tilt-boat enjoying the late summer sun and the warm breeze.

A serving man entered and placed a tray with two silver

goblets and a flask of French brandy at his master's side, then bowed quickly and departed.

'The events at Thames Street are a great sadness,' Walsingham said, his sincerity evident. 'It is tragical that they could not both be saved.'

Shakespeare said nothing. He did not know what to say. The word *tragical* hardly did justice to the terrible outcome of that grim morning when Kat and Sorbus swung from the gibbet.

'I do believe the angels weep each time an innocent dies, especially in such circumstances,' Walsingham continued.

'Perhaps the punishment is at fault,' Shakespeare said. 'If a penalty cannot be undone when a verdict is reversed . . .'

Walsingham shook his head slowly. 'I hear you well, John, but I cannot agree with you. What is the alternative to hanging? A sentence of life imprisonment? I do believe God would rage at such cruel treatment. Would you wish to sit in a cage for years without end? I would not treat a mad dog so. Death is quick. And if an error has been made, we can at least comfort ourselves with the certainty that the soul will fly straight to God's bosom.'

Shakespeare wished he were convinced, but there was no more to say on the subject. What was done was done and the penalty for murder would never change. For the present, he was more concerned about the fate of Huckerbee and Abigail, and mentioned their names to Walsingham. 'My man Boltfoot Cooper tells me they have both been freed. How can this be so?'

'Ah, yes, Sir Robert Huckerbee. A corrupt and rotten man. He has been relieved of all his duties in the office of my lord Burghley and will retire to his country estate. He will also pay the crown ten thousand pounds in gold, in lieu of sums which he is believed to have embezzled.'

'And no punishment other than that? He may lay the blame for Nick Giltspur's death at the door of his confederate Arthur Giltspur, but I am not convinced. I believe they plotted the murder together, and Abigail found a killer for them. Cane was besotted by her and she made him believe the child was his . . .'

'Perhaps it is, John.'

'Yes, perhaps. I am told she still won't say. Maybe she doesn't know.'

'Anyway, there is no proof of murder against them. The black books reveal a crime – but not who committed it. For all we can tell, poor Nick Giltspur embezzled the money and adjusted the entries himself. We have nothing that would satisfy a jury.'

'But there *is* proof that Huckerbee stole from the monies he was supposed to convey to the Treasury. His own written confession. A repayment of ten thousand pounds? He may have taken twice that sum, or more.'

Walsingham handed Shakespeare his goblet of brandy. 'John, drink. Your soul is sore troubled by these events.'

'Brandy will not ease it!'

'Nor will it harm you. I beg you, try to understand. If I have chosen you right, then one day *you* will wield power in this land – and there will be times when you will have to put a peg to your nose and sup with the devil. The arrangement between Lord Burghley and Nick Giltspur could never be admitted openly. If Huckerbee was arraigned, he would reveal everything to judge, jury and the wider world. And then what? Imagine the reaction in the guilds; if the merchants discovered that Burghley had dealings with a man such as Ball and was levying such a tax on them, there would be uproar. I dread to think of the consequences.'

'And so you buy his silence. He walks free while others die.'

Sudden anger flashed across Walsingham's brow but then, instead of the expected storm breaking, he controlled his rage. 'Yes, he walks free. It is as galling for me as it is for you. But I would just say this on his behalf. The whole scheme with Giltspur and Ball was always Huckerbee's idea and was administered by him. Her Majesty keeps me woefully short of monies. Without the funds channelled to me, I would have been unable to do the secret work I do. I would never have been able to bring Mary Stuart to justice.'

So it was mere political expediency. Shakespeare laughed; Walsingham and Burghley proving yet again that they had learnt their statecraft at the knee of Niccolò Machiavelli. Morality had no part to play in such considerations. Whatever means were needed to defend England would be employed: deceit, torture, theft, supping with devils like Cutting Ball. Anything. And perhaps they were right. The alternative – Spain's heel of iron, sword of steel and Inquisition of fire – had to be fought with any means at England's disposal, however dirty.

'What is to happen to the woman, Abigail Colton?'

'Would you see a mother-to-be hanged?'

'No. Let her stew with Huckerbee. I pity the child, whoever its father may be.'

'And before you inquire, I can tell you that there is no sign of Arthur Giltspur. It seems likely that he has fled abroad. Nor is he the only one gone to foreign parts. I have had word from Henbird in Paris that Gilbert Gifford has turned up.'

'Ah, the little pink pigling has made good his escape. I thought it would be so.'

'Little pink pigling?'

'It is a private jest, Mr Secretary.'

'It is apt. But what made you think he would go to France?

Does he not know that Her Majesty values him highly? Why, she means to grant him a pension of one hundred pounds for his services.'

'I saw his eyes when he spotted Mr Phelippes's gallows drawn on the letter out of Chartley.'

Walsingham threw Shakespeare an apologetic smile. 'Tom should not have done that. But there were few mistakes. Even the exposure of Harry Slide did not break us. You know he is back in London, demanding money? He claims for every inn between here and Edinburgh.'

'He did dangerous work. As did Robin Poley. I truly believe Babington fell in love with him.'

Shakespeare finished his brandy. *Anthony Babington.* A vain fool who had brought fourteen young men to their doom. Shakespeare could no longer shut out the knowledge of what would happen on the morrow. He wanted to get away from this room for he could not share in Walsingham's rejoicing. He felt sick; he could smell the blood in nostrils. In the morning, the first seven men would die in the most horrible way imaginable. And the day after that, seven more. A hard price to pay for snaring the Queen of Scots.

He rose from the chair. 'Sir Francis, I fear I am not yet well. If it please you, I will return to London.'

'As you will, John. I shall have my best rowers take you.'

Shakespeare bowed to his master.

'And John, thank you.'

Shakespeare could not suppress a shudder as he stepped through the gate into the Tower. This time he was a free man, but he knew that his mind would never free itself of the dark and fiery vault beneath the White Tower where the living body of Father Ballard, a man of flesh and blood, had been fixed in iron, crouched in agony, enclosed in the Scavenger's Daughter.

A man in a machine made with no purpose other than pain. Such black dreams did not disappear with the dawning day.

John Savage was praying in his cell. He had a makeshift cross clasped in his hands and was muttering, *In manus tuas, Domine, commendo spiritum meum.* Commending his spirit to God, his last hope of salvation.

Shakespeare stood in the doorway and allowed him to complete his supplications. Finally Savage said *Amen*, crossed himself and turned towards Shakespeare. He peered closely as though struggling to see who his visitor might be.

'Forgive me, Goodfellow, I intrude.'

'Ah, John Shakespeare. You are more welcome than any man. We are friends, are we not? I will die your friend.'

'You honour me, Goodfellow.'

'And you have my horse, I trust?'

'I have indeed retrieved it. I thank you for it. A good beast.'

'Take it in repayment of the two pounds and an angel you gave me.'

'I told you, that was a gift.'

'Then so is the horse.'

'But the horse is not why I am here. I came because I had to say farewell, though you would be within your rights to club me to the ground.'

'You are a fine man, though wrong-headed.'

'I did what I had to do, Goodfellow.'

Savage climbed to his feet. He still looked more the soldier than the scholar. 'And I would have done the same to you, so I cannot hold your actions against you. We were two soldiers on opposing sides of the field. Kill or be killed. In all my life I never expected quarter nor gave it.'

Shakespeare's injuries had, at least, given him an excuse not to appear in court and testify against Savage; not that his testimony was needed, for Savage had confessed all, as had the other conspirators. 'I take no pleasure in winning this battle.'

Savage smiled. 'My death is nothing. In truth I welcome it, for my eyesight fails me by the day. I pray that God will restore my vision so that I might see the Lamb in all His glory.'

A pair of spectacles would have done that, thought Shakespeare, but he did not say it. 'Be honest with me, Goodfellow. With your eyesight, you would never have spotted the Queen, let alone have had the aim to shoot her.'

'God would have guided me, had He wanted it. It seems He did not . . .'

'You still have a few hours. Can I have anything brought to you?' He held up a small flagon. 'Perhaps some aqua vitae.'

'I crave no food but I will drink with you. It may ease my passing. Will you be at St Giles Fields in the morning?'

'Do you want me there?'

'No.' He shook his head firmly. 'Remember me as a man, not meat. And grant me one boon if it is in your power: do not allow any of your pseudo-ministers near me – either here or at the scaffold. Their babbling offends me more than the rack or butcher's knife.'

'I will do what I can.'

'And now, the aqua vitae, if you will . . . let us see if we can get roaring drunk together one last time.'

Chapter 48

THE MUD-COVERED BOYS poked their fingers into the eye sockets, made faces of disgust and laughed. One of them caught Shakespeare's gaze, stuck out his tongue, then graced him with a toothless grin. 'Here, mister, want to know what happened to their bollocks and glazers? Give us a penny and I'll tell you.'

Shakespeare ignored the boys, who were eight or nine years old. Joshua Peace stepped forward to examine the two bodies, which were naked and bound back to back against a tall fence-pole that had been hammered deep into the mud at the water's edge.

'Come on, mister. Only a penny. Nothing to a gent like you. They've both had their balls and their glazers cut away. You must want to know what happened to them.' They giggled, then one of the boys threw a fistful of the dark clay mud at the other one and got the same returned to him.

Peace, meanwhile, was examining the dead face of Sir Robert Huckerbee.

'As you will, mister, a halfpenny.' The taller of the two boys took a breather from his mudfight, determined to make some profit from the corpses. 'Tell you what, I'll give you what I know, then you, being a gent, will give me the money. So here goes: their bollocks were shoved down each other's throats and their glazers were poked up each other's arses.'

Peace turned away from his examination. 'How do you know?' he asked.

'Because the men as put them here told us. And they told us to stay with them.'

'When was this?'

'Last night, an hour before high tide. We was told to watch until the water covered their heads and drowned them, and so we did. Gave us these for our trouble.' The boys both drew bollock-daggers from their belts. 'Said we could join their crew when we're growed.'

'Why did you not fetch help?'

'Help? What help? Can't sew back glazers and bollocks, mister.'

'They might have been saved nonetheless.'

'Saved? Why would they want to be saved without eyes or balls? Can't see, can't swive. What's left?'

Peace turned away from the boys. 'Are you certain of their identities, John?'

'Yes. This one's Huckerbee. The other is Arthur Giltspur.' He gazed on their disfigured torsos and faces. So alike; conspirators in death, as in life.

'I fear I have disturbed your day bringing you here, but I needed someone with legal authority. The coroner, sheriff, justice – all are gone to St Giles in the Fields.'

Shakespeare managed a smile. 'It is nothing. To tell you the truth, Joshua, I would rather be here looking upon this obscenity than at St Giles. If I am the one man in London not there, then I am glad of my absence.' Seven men were to die this day: Savage, Babington, Ballard, Barnwell, Dunn, Salisbury, Tichbourne.

Seven more would follow tomorrow: Abingdon, Tilney, Bellamy, Charnock, Jones, Gage, Travers. Some had been prime movers, some had played little part in the plot. The penalty was the same for all.

Walsingham had confided in Shakespeare that the Queen had ordered that some extra torment should be added to the punishment 'for more terror' so as to deter other would-be assassins and plotters.

For more terror. As if the prospect of hanging, drawing and quartering were not terror enough for any man. Yet Shakespeare knew exactly what those three cruel words meant. They meant that the men would be cut down almost immediately from the noose so that they were still alive and fully conscious for the godly butchery. The execution would be deliberately prolonged.

First the prick and balls would be sliced off, then held before the victim's eyes and tossed into the cauldron. Next the belly would be opened and the bowels drawn forth. Again, these would be shown to the condemned man before being dispatched to the pot. Finally the ripping out of the heart and merciful death. And in the aftermath, the quartering and decapitation, the head held up to the cheering crowd, the proper end of a traitor.

For more terror.

Which was worse, the punishment meted out by a criminal to two men who had stolen from him or the punishment ordered by the state for those deemed traitors?

Shakespeare took one last look at the corpses of Huckerbee and Giltspur. 'I will leave this matter to you, Joshua. I will send Boltfoot to assist you in removing the bodies. Deal with them as you wish. The sheriff may have other thoughts, but I doubt he will wish to take the matter further.' He was turning away when one of the mudlarks thrust his hand in his face, holding his new bollock-dagger menacingly with the other hand. 'Come on, mister, a penny – or we'll pelt you with sludge.'

Shakespeare pulled a penny from his purse and spun it in the air so that it fell to the muddy ground near the boys' feet. They fell to fighting over it. Then the smaller one stood up, bit the coin, held it in the air to goad his friend, and began to run.

'Come on, I'll race you to Giles Fields!'

'Hey, half that's mine.'

'Only if you get it off me. But I'll buy you a beer. Come on – I want a place by the scaffold!'

The streets from the Tower to St Giles in the Fields were thronged. If you couldn't get a place near the scaffold, the next best thing was a position along the route watching the first seven Babington plotters being drawn to their death. They wanted to see the priest Ballard, said to be a Jesuit with a heart as black as his robe; they wanted to see the proud young gentle-man Anthony Babington brought low by overweening ambition and arrogance; they wanted to see John Savage, the soldier who had sworn to kill the Queen.

Shakespeare threaded his way through the crowd back to Seething Lane and called for Boltfoot. Jane came scurrying from the kitchen.

'Where is Boltfoot, Jane?'

'He has gone out, master.'

Shakespeare frowned. 'The executions?' Surely Boltfoot did not wish to join the bloodthirsty throng at St Giles in the Fields.

She shook her head with vigour. 'No, master. Not that.'

'Where then?'

'I believe . . . sir, must I say?'

'Jane, you cannot keep secrets from me. I need Boltfoot – and I need him now.'

'Oh, master, I believe he has gone east of London again.'

Shakespeare rolled his eyes to the heavens. 'In God's name, why?'

Jane hesitated, then said, 'I am not certain.'

'Jane?'

'Then I must say it. He has gone to see Mistress Cane.'

Bathsheba Cane? The widow of the murderer? At first, Shakespeare was dumbfounded. 'What? Why would he do that?' Yet even as he asked the question he realised how foolish it must sound. There was only one reason Boltfoot would go there.

'I believe he wished to thank her for returning his weapons.'

'Indeed? His weapons . . .' Shakespeare shook his head slowly. 'And you believe that, do you, Jane?'

She flushed, as though caught out in something shameful. 'It did occur to me there might be another reason for his visit, sir.'

'Well done, Jane.' He noticed the distress in her eyes. 'Forgive me, Jane – I did not wish to make jest at your expense.'

She performed a little curtsy. 'It is nothing, master.'

'I had better find one of the stablehands to help me.'

'They have gone to Giles Fields.'

'And Mr Maywether?'

'Gone this morning, not an hour since, up to the east coast, his purse bulging, as he insisted on telling me. He bade me wish you a farewell and thanks.'

Shakespeare cursed inwardly. He drank a cup of ale then went to the stableyard. A small handcart was standing on the flagstones close to the stalls. It would just about carry two bodies but, with his damaged ribs, he was not sure that he was strong enough to push it. Well, it seemed he had no option but to try. Without ado, he lifted up the long handles and began trundling south and west towards the bridge, close to where the bodies had been staked out. The wheels ran true and he found the going easy enough.

As he approached the crowds on Tower Street he realised

that the procession was under way. His heart told him to turn away, walk home until the cavalcade of death had passed. But something within him kept him moving forward. Using the handcart to part the onlookers, he pushed himself to the front of the line, right at the edge of the dusty road. A grey mare was approaching, dragging an osier hurdle, which was bumping along the ground. Shakespeare saw instantly that the man on the hurdle was Anthony Babington.

His fine-cut hair, the pride of Mane's of Bishopsgate, was tangled and thick with dirt as it trailed along the road. His eyes were wide open, staring up at the blue sky as though he would somehow take the image with him to the life eternal.

'God go with you.' The words came from Shakespeare's mouth unbidden. Babington's head, juddering from its proximity to the roadway, turned slightly and his upside-down eyes met Shakespeare's. He must have known him, but recognition did not register. And then the procession moved on.

Shakespeare had seen perdition in the eyes. They were no longer the eyes of a human being, but of a wild animal caught in a trap from which there was no escape and only one end.

He would never forget those eyes.

Boltfoot tapped lightly at the door. From within he heard footsteps. He took a deep breath and tried to fix a smile to his face.

The door opened. Boltfoot started to say, 'Mistre—' but immediately stopped, for a man stood in front of him. Not just any man, but the water-bearer Tom Pearson.

'Mr Pearson.'

'Ah, Mr Cooper. It is a fine thing to see you alive and well.'

'I – I wanted to see . . . is Mistress Cane at home?'

'Indeed she is and I am certain she would be pleased to receive you. Come in, sir.'

This was not what Boltfoot had expected, nor what he had hoped for. As he recalled, he owed a debt to the timid little water-bearer for passing on his cutlass and caliver to Mistress Cane and for telling her how he had been taken by Cutting Ball's men. 'I believe I must thank you, Mr Pearson.'

Pearson smiled. 'You must think nothing of it. We are all God's creatures and therefore we are as one under heaven.'

'Mr Cooper!' Bathsheba Cane had appeared behind Pearson with one of her three small children attached to her skirts. She was rubbing flour dust from her hands.

He nodded awkwardly. 'Mistress Cane.'

'It is a wondrous thing to see you well and restored to your home. There was word put about that you had been pressed into service.'

'That is so. I came to thank you, and Mr Pearson here. My cutlass and caliver . . .'

'We were pleased to help. And has Mr Pearson told you our news? We are to be wed.'

The words hit like a blow to the heart. Bathsheba to wed the water-bearer? for a moment, Boltfoot did not know what to say. Feeling foolish, he summoned up an insincere smile and finally some words came. 'Allow me to compliment you.'

Bathsheba clutched Boltfoot's hands. 'Mr Cooper? Are you well? You seem a little pale.'

'I am well.'

'Come, let me pour you some beer.'

He gently removed his gnarled seaman's hands from her light and feminine fingers. 'No,' he said abruptly. 'No, thank you. I have done all I came for. Just my thanks.' He nodded. 'Good day to you both. I wish you all happpiness.' He turned away, for he could not bear to see the joy on their faces, nor have them see the disappointment on his.

*

'Have you heard aught from your boy, Mr Tort?' Shakespeare's voice was quiet; even in the confines of Severin Tort's home there was always the risk of a servant-spy overhearing what was said.

'Indeed. And I do believe he is beginning to feel himself fortunate to have avoided the fate of the plotters. He is resigned to staying in the country. God willing, the experience will have made a man of him.'

'It may be for the best. I have myself been berated by Justice Young, who demands word of him.'

'As have I, Mr Shakespeare.'

'I told him plain that Dominic was never a conspirator, that I had seen him eat and drink with men he considered friends, but he was never taken into their confidence. He was but a roaring boy, like many other innocents associated – foolishly perhaps – with the Pope's White Sons. It is important he remembers that line, for it is misprision of treason not to reveal such a plot once known.'

'He understands that.'

Shakespeare looked around Tort's parlour. From somewhere in the fine house, he heard a rustling. 'And where, pray, is Kat?'

'She has something to show you, Mr Shakespeare. It seems she is to go to court next week. Her Majesty has sent word that she wishes to meet the heiress to the Giltspur fortunes.'

'Indeed?' So the ambitious Mistress Katherine Whetstone, innkeeper's daughter, was achieving her heart's desire. To dally and converse with nobles and royals. Doubtless her story would keep the court entertained for weeks.

'Do I detect a note of disapproval, Mr Shakespeare?'

'No, sir. It is none of my concern. The prize is yours, Mr Tort.' But did he disapprove? He had believed she was eschewing wealth and luxury, that Giltspur House would become an almshouse for distressed mariners, widows and orphans, all funded by the remaining gold and silver in the strongroom. It would be named the Abraham Sorbus Home, in his memory.

Ambition had died on the gibbet, she had told him. Now, it seemed, she was to become just another glittering butterfly, fluttering around the court of Queen Elizabeth. Was that the life she wanted? How long would Severin Tort, attorney-at-law, survive as the man in her life if Kat's beauty were to be spotted by the likes of Leicester or Ralegh? They were men not given to allowing a comely woman's skirts to remain unlifted.

Even without such distractions, would a wild spirit like Kat really be able to abide life with this man Tort, with his damnable precision and painstaking orderliness?

Shakespeare sipped at his crystal goblet of sweetened Gascon wine. Perhaps he was doing her an injustice. Perhaps she and Tort might yet make a match.

'I do believe I hear her coming, Mr Shakespeare. Prepare yourself for the grand entrance.'

Her gown was French satin. The body was russet-coloured, flourished with silver bows and silk golden suns. The whole was lined with orange taffeta and the russet hanging sleeves were slashed with white taffeta. She looked every inch the court lady.

When Shakespeare had first set eyes on her early one grey morning in Yorkshire four years earlier, her hair had been tousled and her attire – a plain linen smock – unkempt and lived-in. Yet he had thought her the most beautiful creature he had ever seen. Now, in this finery, she was still exquisite and yet she had lost something. He could not tell her so, but he preferred her as she was before.

'My lady,' he said with an extravagant bow.

'You are mocking me, John. Will I pass muster before Her Majesty?'

'You are perfect, Kat.'

'It is not too much? I know she does not like to be outshone.'

'No, it is not too much. It is a fine gown that will, I believe, draw admiring glances but not envy, which is as you would wish, I am sure.' His eyes went to her throat and suddenly he felt a chill. The unmistakeable bruising of the hemp rope had been covered up by a necklet with a large gemstone at its centre.

Her eyes followed his, questioningly. 'Do you like it? It is the Giltspur Diamond. Grandame gave it to me on the day I married Nicholas.'

Shakespeare could not conceal his bewilderment. The stone was larger than any diamond he had ever seen, but that was not the issue here. If Grandame had indeed given the jewel to her daughter-in-law, why had she told Arthur that it was missing? Her wit might have been fading when under the influence of the laudanum, but had seemed sharp enough at other times. And Arthur seemed to have no idea what had become of it; there had been much at fault with him, but why dissemble over a matter such as this? And why would the family keep such a generous gift secret?

'I had thought it her most treasured possession . . .'

'Which, I suppose, is why she made a gift of it to me. Is it then too much, John? Is that what you are saying? Will it not be well received?'

No, it was not what he was saying. He could not say what he was thinking. A cloud passed and the light of the sun suddenly lit up the room, catching the dazzling brilliance of the stone so that he had to turn his eyes away from its glare. He felt a deep sadness sucking him down. Whatever the truth was, he no longer wished to know it. Oswald Redd, dead, Nicholas Giltspur, dead, Abraham Sorbus, dead. Like one of Drake's galleons, she left a trail of wreckage in her wake. He no longer wished to be part of her detritus.

He shook his head. Kat lose her ambition? A lioness might as well lose its taste for meat. 'You must decide about the diamond. I cannot say.'

Her eyes narrowed, sensing his disapproval, and he suddenly regretted his censorious reaction. Whatever the truth about the diamond, it was not the full story. She had almost sacrificed her life in an attempt to save her friend Sorbus. The human heart was a strange thing; did God Himself understand His creation? He moved forward under the benign gaze of Severin Tort and embraced the woman he had once loved. He kissed her. Farewell.

Acknowledgements

Heartfelt thanks to my wife Naomi and the rest of the family for their much-needed love and support. Likewise, huge gratitude to everyone who has encouraged me in my endeavours, particularly my agent Teresa Chris and editor Kate Parkin, both of them brilliantly professional.

Two books have been especially helpful in writing this novel: *The Babington Plot* by Alan Gordon Smith; and *Queen Mary and The Babington Plot*, compiled and edited from the original documents by John Hungerford Pollen, SJ.

Historical Notes

The Babington Plotters Who Died

On 13, 14 and 15 September 1586, fourteen men were convicted of High Treason at a commission of Oyer and Terminer in Westminster. Seven were executed on 20 September, with added cruelty 'for more terror'. The remaining seven were executed the next day, being allowed the mercy of dying by hanging before being butchered.

The First Seven Executed

Anthony Babington: aged twenty-four, he was witty, handsome and wealthy, having inherited the family estates at Dethick Manor in Derbyshire when he was ten. He was the great-grandson of Lord Darcy who perished for his Catholic faith in the Pilgrimage of Grace during the reign of Henry VIII. Babington was educated at home, being brought up to believe that no one of breeding could be anything but Catholic. At eighteen he married Margaret Draycot, daughter of his guardian, Philip Draycot of Paynsley, Staffs. They had a daughter but within a year of marriage he went on a tour of France, where he met Chidiock Tichbourne and was visited by Thomas Morgan, the Paris agent of Mary Queen of Scots.

Returning to England, he entered Lincoln's Inn, and began doing secret work for Mary and the Catholic underground. Realising the danger he was in, he ceased this work and planned to emigrate with his friend Thomas Salisbury. But in 1586, the priest John Ballard sought him out and persuaded him to lead a conspiracy to replace Elizabeth with Mary. Babington was flattered and, being a dominant personality, easily drew his young gentleman friends into the plot.

He was enthusiastic when interested but indolent when it came to drudgery. With the other conspirators he heard mass regularly at a house in Fetter Lane. They were known generally among Catholics at home and abroad as '*The Pope's White Sons, for divers pieces of services which they do for Rome against this realm*'. At his trial, he blamed Ballard for all he had done.

John Ballard: aged in his thirties, he was born near Ely. After graduating from Cambridge with an MA he was ordained priest at Chalons, France, in 1581. He was sent to England, where he adopted various aliases, including Captain Fortescue or Foscue. Described as tall, dark-eyed and dark-bearded, he dressed extravagantly in a gold-laced cape, satin doublet and a hat with silver buttons. He became a well-known figure in London's taverns, famous for his generosity, and always addressed as 'Captain'. Something of a fantasist, he boasted to the Spanish ambassador in France that he could raise an army of 60,000 in England, and he boasted to the conspirators that the Spanish were planning a 60,000-strong invasion – neither of which was true at that time. He told his fellow conspirator Tilney: 'We shall have a new world shortly.' On capture, he was so badly tortured that he had to be carried into court. When Babington blamed him for his downfall, Ballard replied: 'I wish the shedding of my blood might be the saving of your life.'

John Savage: Ballard called him 'the Instrument' – by which he meant the instrument for eliminating Elizabeth.

A large and charming young man in his mid-twenties, he had no money. His only possession was his horse. Everyone spoke well of him. Gilbert Gifford, the Walsingham spy, said Savage was 'one of the best companions' and a 'very good scholar'. His friend John Charnock, who was with him both in the Spanish army and at Barnard's Inn, said: 'He was an excellent soldier, a man skilful in languages and learned besides.' Having served with the Spanish forces in the Low Countries, he went to Rheims to study for the priesthood, which he did not see through. Instead, egged on by two priests and by Gilbert Gifford, he vowed to kill Queen Elizabeth, having originally refused to do so. He then returned to England to study law at Barnard's Inn, seemingly reluctant to carry out his mission to kill. When captured, he immediately confessed his part in the plot.

Chidiock Tichbourne: aged twenty-eight. he was born in Southampton, the son of devout Catholics. Chidiock was interrogated in 1583 about some 'popish relics' that he had brought back from abroad, where he had gone without leave; and in June 1586 accusations about 'popish practices' were laid against his family. He was close to Babington and they often met in a barber's shop by Bishopsgate, where they and other conspirators had their portrait painted. At the end, when Babington found Chidiock in Smithfield, he had a mysteriously injured leg and was 'almost too lame to hobble'. In court, he confessed he knew of the treasons and concealed them, but denied active plotting. 'That I knew of these treasons and concealed them I must confess I am guilty.' As he awaited execution he wrote a sad, despairing poem, which can be found in many anthologies of English verse (see page 453).

Robert Barnwell: he belonged to a prominent Dublin family and used to attend Elizabeth's court in the retinue of the Earl of Kildare. He was apparently well known to the Queen. One of Walsingham's agents left a brief physical description of him as tall and rugged, comely, white-faced, flaxen-bearded, freckled, and disfigured with smallpox. At trial he said he never supported plans to assassinate the Queen. 'I never intended harm to Her Majesty's person, but I confess I knew thereof.' He also confessed that he saw Elizabeth at Richmond and later reported to Babington 'how easily she might be surprised'.

Edward Abingdon: aged thirty-three, he was a member of the Queen's Guard and was the eldest son of John Abingdon of Hindlip, Worcestershire, Under-Treasurer to Queen Elizabeth. Edward was educated at Exeter College, Oxford, and took his BA in 1574. In court it was said he was aware of Savage's conspiracy by spring 1586, having met him at Barnard's where his brother was studying law. Having been found guilty, Abingdon said: 'That brainless youth Babington, whose proud stomach and ambitious mind incensed him to commit most abominable treasons, hath been the cause to shed the blood of others guiltless of his actions.' He at first denied any knowledge of Ballard but on being confronted with him admitted he had met him some years ago at Chertsey and again four years later when Ballard came to his lodging at Charing Cross. He told the court he would rather be drawn to Tyburn by the heels than countenance an invasion by Spain.

Charles Tilney: born 23 September 1561, in Suffolk, he was cousin to courtier Edmund Tilney, Master of the Revels. Charles became a gentleman pensioner at court (a member of the Queen's Guard) and later converted to Catholicism. He was aware of Savage's conspiracy by March 1586. He confessed that at the Three Tuns tavern in Newgate Market, Babington had suggested to him and Abingdon a proposal to 'remove' Lord Burghley and Sir Francis Walsingham. He also confessed to receiving the priest Ballard at his chambers in Westminster. On being told that Babington named him as one of six men delegated to kill the Queen, he scoffed: 'Babington told him so! That proves that Babington forsooth will be a statesman, when God knows he is a man of no gravity.' He vehemently denied the charges against him and said he only met Babington on three occasions.

The Second Seven Executed

Thomas Salisbury: aged about twenty-five, he came from an important landed family of Lleweni Hall, Denbighshire. In 1578 Thomas became the head of the household and ward of the Earl of Leicester. He went to Trinity College, Oxford, in 1580, where he seems to have moved in Catholic circles. He and Babington were said to have been 'bedfellows for a quarter of a year or more' near Temple Bar, just outside London. This could simply mean that they shared lodgings. Salisbury was a powerful influence on Edward Jones. At trial he said he had always protested he would not kill Elizabeth 'for a kingdom'. But he admitted plotting to free Mary, inciting rebellion and supporting plans for a Spanish invasion. He begged the Queen's merciful pardon but did not receive it.

Robert Gage: he came from Haling, Surrey (now part of Croydon), and was a cousin of the Jesuit martyr Robert Southwell. He was converted to Catholicism by John Ballard and was confessed by him at a house in Holborn before Christmas 1585. In the fateful year 1586, he rode with Ballard to the north, as his manservant. On arrest, he was charged with knowing Ballard as a priest and being reconciled by him. Gage was one of those who fled into the woods with Babington. In court, when asked why, he said, 'For the company' – and refused to say more.

Edward Jones: from Plas Cadwgan, Denbighshire, he was the son of another Edward, Master of the Wardrobe to Queen Elizabeth, and a former sheriff of Denbighshire. The father was a protégé of the Earl of Leicester, to whom he recommended his son. Edward junior turned to Catholicism under the influence of Thomas Salisbury, who involved him in the plot. He and Travers were deputed to spark a rebellion in north Wales, but they were reluctant to do so. In fact, Jones did his best to remove his friend Salisbury from Babington's influence. Jones aided Salisbury's abortive escape by lending him his horse and his servant's cloak. At his house in Denbighsire he said to Travers: 'Salisbury has brought us all to destruction.' At trial he explained his awful dilemma: he said he had the alternatives of betraying his friend Salisbury, whom he loved as himself, or of breaking his allegiance to his sovereign. He chose friendship – and paid a terrible price.

John Travers: he came from Prescott, Lancashire, a hotbed of Catholic resistance, and served in the Spanish army with Savage and Charnock. When the plot was discovered, he fled to Jones's house in Denbighshire. They had both been introduced to the enterprise by Salisbury. He denied having any treasonable conversation with Babington. He is said to have commented that 'Savage's sudden bravery would bewray all their matters [leave them all open to harm]'.

John Charnock: one of the six who had agreed to assassinate Elizabeth, he also came from Lancashire (like Travers). He admitted that Ballard had acquainted him with the treasonous plans. Along with Savage, he had been a soldier in the Spanish army and considered him a good friend. They met again at Barnard's Inn where they both studied law. Charnock had promised to do anything to assist Mary Queen of Scots.

Henry Dunn: he was a Londoner and a clerk of the First Fruits Office; he was probably a relative of John Donne, the poet. He was approached by his acquaintance Babington in June 1586, having been recommended by Ballard, who had already confided the invasion plot to him. When Babington sounded him out on the assassination idea, Dunn would have none of it. However, at trial, he confessed he was involved in the conspiracy for his religion and conscience's sake – and prayed God they would be successful. *'Fiat voluntas dei'* – May God's will be done.

Jerome Bellamy: he was the son of a devout Catholic family who lived in a moated hall at Uxendon, north-west of London. When Babington (whom he already knew) arrived at the house hungry and hunted, Jerome and his brother Bartholomew helped the fugitives with shelter and food. Jerome was later tried and executed but Bartholomew never made it to court, having died in prison – either on the rack or (the official version) having committed suicide. In the ensuing years, the family was destroyed, largely by the actions of the priesthunter and torturer Richard Topcliffe.

The poem of Chidiock Tichbourne, said to have been written on the eve of his execution

My prime of youth is but a frost of cares.
My feast of joy is but a dish of pain.

My crop of corn is but a field of tares,*
And all my good is but vain hope of gain.
The day is gone and yet I saw no sun.
And now I live, and now my life is done.

The spring is past, and yet it has not sprung.
The fruit is dead, and yet the leaves are green.
My youth is gone, and yet I am but young.
I saw the world and yet I was not seen.
My thread is cut, and yet it is not spun.
And now I live, and now my life is done.

I sought my death and found it in my womb.
I looked for life and saw it was a shade.
I trod the earth and knew it was my tomb.
And now I die, and now I am but made.
The glass is full, and now the glass is run.
And now I live, and now my life is done.

*weeds

What Became of Gilbert Gifford

The youthful Gilbert Gifford – who was twenty-six at the time
of the events in this book but looked like a teenage boy – was
the key to bringing down Mary Queen of Scots and the
Babington plotters. His actions earned the eternal gratitude of
Sir Francis Walsingham and Queen Elizabeth and they awarded
him a pension. So why, when the arrest of the conspirators was
imminent, did he flee to France?

It is possible that he realised there could be a terrible fall-out
from the discovery of the plot – that the innocent might well
suffer along with the guilty to protect the reputations of great

men. Certainly that other Walsingham spy Robert Poley found himself incarcerated for a year despite his work shadowing Babington.

But it may be that, for all his protestations, Walsingham *wanted* Gifford to return to France, where he could easily insinuate himself back into the world of the Catholic seminaries and continue his spying.

He had all the attributes of a spy. He spoke fluent French and enjoyed going by a variety of aliases. He was known variously as Colderin, Number Four, Pietro, Cornelys, The Secret Party or simply GG. He had escaped from England pretending to be a servant to Monsieur Dujardin of the French embassy.

His first act on arriving in Paris was to go to the Spanish ambassador, Bernardino de Mendoza, and ask him to send a letter to the Babington plotters urging them to proceed with the assassination of Elizabeth. Mendoza agreed to this and sent two letters, one in Italian and one in Latin.

It is likely that Gifford assumed the letters would be intercepted by Walsingham's searchers, thus strengthening the case against Mary and the conspirators. But the letters never reached England, having been retrieved by Mary's agent in Paris, Thomas Morgan.

This was not the end of Gifford's double-dealing activities, however. He returned to Rheims and was ordained a priest but a year later he was caught in a brothel, having his way with a whore.

He was imprisoned – the charge itself is not clear, although it might relate to his part in destroying Mary Queen of Scots – and yet even from his cell he managed to send reports of the movements of various priests back to his masters in England. He died in gaol three years later.

Babington's Last Letter

On the morning of the day he fled in August 1586, Anthony Babington wrote an elegant and anguished letter to Robert 'Robin' Poley, the Walsingham spy he had believed to be his friend and who was now missing. I contend that this letter reveals a great deal more about their relationship than is generally acknowledged.

This is what Babington wrote:

ROBIN,

Sollicitae non possunt curae mutare aranei stamina fusi [nor care nor cunning ever mends of spider's threads the broken ends]. I am ready to endure whatever shall be inflicted. *Et facere et pati Romanorum est* [to do and to suffer is the virtue of a Roman]. What my course has been towards Mr Secretary you can witness, what my love towards you, yourself can best tell. Proceedings at my lodgings have been very strange. I am the same I always pretended. I pray God you be, and ever so remain towards me. Take heed to your own part, lest of these my misfortunes you bear the blame. *Est exilium inter malos vivere* [to live among the wicked is as bad as exile].

Farewell, sweet Robin, if as I take thee, true to me. If not, adieu, *omnium bipedum nequissimus* [of all two-footed things the most wicked].

Return me your answer for my satisfaction, and my diamond, and what else you will. The furnace is prepared wherein our faith must be tried. Farewell until we meet, which God knows when.

Thine, how far thou knowest,
ANTHONY BABINGTON

In fact, Poley was by then in gaol. His master, Sir Francis Walsingham (in whose household he lived), clearly wanted him out of the way so that the world would not know he had infiltrated the Babington conspiracy with his spies. A year later, long after the execution of the Babington plotters, Poley was freed to continue his secret work. Among other things, he was employed as a special envoy to Denmark in 1588 and in the 1590s he was used as a spy in Flanders. Along the way, he is believed to have poisoned the Archbishop of Armagh. He also spent more time in gaol for 'using lewd words against Walsingham' – and then seduced the gaoler's wife! And in 1593 he was to be found in a small room in Deptford with the dead body of the playwright Christopher Marlowe, who had been stabbed in the eye.

There can be no doubt that Poley, a Cambridge graduate of gentry stock – but born poor – was a dangerous and duplicitous man. He claimed to be a Catholic, but some Catholics found him obsequious and never trusted him. Even Walsingham and his top agents had their doubts. Francis Mills called him 'a notable knave' and Thomas Phelippes was jealous of his closeness to Walsingham.

So what exactly was Poley's relationship with Babington? I suggest they almost certainly had a homosexual love affair. The whole tenor of the letter speaks of an intimacy a great deal deeper than mere friendship. And the final line – *Thine, how far thou knowest* – confirms it for me. Homosexuality was illegal in the sixteenth century, the love that dared not speak its name.

Babington is saying, 'You know how much I love you, but I cannot write the words'. And he so wanted to trust him. Yet the truth was he had, indeed, been betrayed by the very person he loved most dearly. Poley was the two-legged beast: *omnium bipedum nequissimus.*